To Amy ⋮

MW00649114

Kepler's Cowboys

Kepler's Cowboys

Edited by
Steve B. Howell &
David Lee Summers

Hadrosaur Productions, Mesilla Park, NM

Kepler's Cowboys
Hadrosaur Productions
First Edition, first printing, continuous printing on demand
First date of publication: March 2017
Editors: Steve B. Howell and David Lee Summers
Cover Art: Laura Givens

ISBN: 1-885093-82-9

Hadrosaur Productions
P.O. Box 2194
Mesilla Park, NM 88047-2194
www.hadrosaur.com

Kepler's Cowboys compilation copyright ©2017 Hadrosaur Productions
Cover art copyright ©2016 Laura Givens

"Step Right Up" ©2017 Louise Webster
"Pele's Gift" ©2017 Gene Mederos
"Over the Ridge" ©2017 Terrie Leigh Relf
"Chasing May" ©2017 Anthony R. Cardno
"Aperture Shudder" ©2017 Jesse Bosh
"Voyage to the Water World" ©2017 Livia Finucci
"The Silent Giants" ©2017 Simon Bleaken
"Calamari Rodeo" ©2017 David Lee Summers
"Tears for Terra" ©2017 J.A. Campbell & Rebecca McFarland Kyle
"Kismet Kate" ©2017 Neal Wilgus
"Carbon Copies" ©2017 David L. Drake
"Assembler" ©2017 Doug Williams
"Twin Suns of the Mushroom Kingdom" ©2017 Jaleta Clegg
"Point of View" ©2017 Lauren McBride
"A Very Public Hanging" ©2017 L.J. Bonham
"The Outlaw from Aran" ©2017 Vaughn Wright
"The Misery of Gold" ©2017 Steve B. Howell
"Backstabbers and Sidewinders" ©2017 Patrick Thomas
"Forsaken by the God-Star" ©2017 Gary W. Davis

All rights reserved. No part of this book may be reproduced in any form or by any means without the express written consent of the Publisher, excepting brief quotes used in reviews. For permission to reproduce any part or the whole of this book, contact the publisher.

"Hadrosaur Productions" and Hadrosaur Productions Logo are trademarks of Hadrsoaur Productions.

This is a work of fiction. Names, characters, places, and incidents are products of the author's imagination or are used fictitiously.

Table of Contents

1   Introduction by David Lee Summers & Steve B. Howell

5   Step Right Up by Louise Webster

7   Pele's Gift by Gene Mederos

29   Over the Ridge by Terrie Leigh Relf

52   Chasing May by Anthony R. Cardno

68   Aperture Shudder by Jesse Bosh

84   Voyage to the Water World by Livia Finucci

87   The Silent Giants by Simon Bleaken

103   Calamari Rodeo by David Lee Summers

116   Tears for Terra by J.A. Campbell & Rebecca McFarland Kyle

133   Kismet Kate by Neal Wilgus

135   Carbon Copies by David L. Drake

163   Assembler by Doug Williams

179   Twin Suns of the Mushroom Kingdom by Jaleta Clegg

198   Point of View by Lauren McBride

199   A Very Public Hanging by L.J. Bonham

214 The Outlaw from Aran by Vaughn Wright

232 The Misery of Gold by Steve B. Howell

244 Backstabbers and Sidewinders by Patrick Thomas

264 Forsaken by the God-Star by Gary W. Davis

266 About the Contributors

Kepler's Cowboys

Introduction
David Lee Summers and Steve B. Howell

Howdy, pardners!

Welcome to *Kepler's Cowboys!* You might be asking what a "Kepler Cowboy" is. "Kepler" refers to a space telescope that has been used for two separate missions to find planets around other stars. It's named for the astronomer who figured out how planetary orbits work. The word "cowboy" first appeared in the English language two centuries ago and was probably a literal translation of the Spanish word "vaquero". While the word literally means a boy who herds cows, it soon came to be associated with resourceful people who would do what it took to not only survive, but prosper, as they explored new frontiers in the Americas. Just as cowboys didn't always herd cows, they weren't always boys. There were plenty of vaqueras in the old west as well!

This anthology explores those tough men and women who will venture out into space in the same spirit as those men and women who tamed the Wild West a century and a half ago. As editors, we looked for stories that gave us the same feeling of adventure as we got from such classics as *Star Trek*, *Firefly*, and *Cowboy Bebop*. *Kepler's Cowboys* looks at the wide variety of exoplanets discovered by NASA's Kepler Space Telescope. The stories imagine the brave men and women who will either explore those worlds or will come from them to explore our own.

Like our previous anthology, *A Kepler's Dozen*, each tale has a connection to one or more alien worlds such as those discovered by the NASA Kepler Space Telescope during the original Kepler or current K2 missions.

This anthology was something of an experiment on a few levels. First off, we allowed the authors a lot of leeway to develop their worlds as they saw fit. While this may seem to let them deviate from true exoplanets, it does not. The Kepler Space Telescope has discovered so many planets that we realized that the reader can find a Kepler or K2 exoplanet to match any of the planets the authors have written about. However,

1

we did check each contribution for accuracy to remain true to the science. Another hallmark of this anthology is that we didn't have "reserved spots" for featured authors. We cast our net wide and chose the best stories for this volume. It's fun to discover the unexpected ways people explored this theme in their contributions. For example, several of the submissions feature very literal cowboys in space, who practically wear spurs and big hats while others feature the intrepid, yet resourceful, explorers familiar from many space adventures. A few of the stories and poems even found ways to stretch the definition of "cowboy" into exciting, new places.

The NASA Kepler and K2 missions have discovered a passel of planets that orbit stars other than our sun. These planets, called exoplanets, are found to be similar in size to some of the planets in our solar system as well as being very different indeed; presenting types of planets we know nothing about. Some are even small rocky worlds like the Earth and this type of planet seems to be fairly common.

Kepler observed one location in our Milky Way Galaxy for four years finding many thousand exoplanets. Most of these exoplanets orbit stars that are far away from the Earth—3000-6000 light years away. K2 began observations in 2014 and has discovered over 200 exoplanets so far in the ecliptic or Zodiac region of the sky. This mission is considered the "Wild West" of space missions by the astronomical community, and as such quite appropriate for this treatise. Many K2 exoplanets orbit bright stars (many visible by eye from the Earth) and systems that are relatively near-by, less than a few hundred light years.

Nearly every conceivable type and size of exoplanet has been discovered, from as small as Mars to larger than Jupiter. Multiple-planet solar systems are not uncommon and, in fact, exoplanets are so common that they are likely to orbit almost every star that exists including stars much hotter and larger then our Sun to those that are only half as hot and as small at the planet Jupiter. Truly a selectory of frontier worlds to imagine and write about.

Since the time of *A Kepler's Dozen*, exoplanet scientists have learned much about the alien worlds they have discovered. Planets can approximately be categorized into four major groups. These groups are related to the size (diameter) of the planet and all four types are featured throughout our stories.

- **Gas Giant exoplanets:** These are large worlds with no solid surface containing mostly hydrogen and helium and likely to have cloud bands and storms (such as the great red spot of Jupiter), strong magnetic fields, atmospheric lightning and aurora. Similar to our planets Jupiter and Saturn, they probably are orbited by many moons, some nearly as large as the Earth and likely to be rock and ice worlds.

- **Ice Giant exoplanets:** These planets are like Neptune. They are about 4 times the diameter of Earth and contain gaseous atmospheres consisting mainly of frozen methane and ammonia. Clouds and weather in their atmospheres are common and probably they have fairly large moons as well

- **Water Worlds:** This type of planet does not exist in our solar system. They are smaller than Neptune but 50% to 2 times larger than the Earth. As such, they may be covered with deep, expansive oceans with little to no dry land. Gravity on their surface would be stronger than Earth, but tolerable, and they could contain an atmosphere similar to that on Earth. This size of exoplanet is very common and may be able to support life like that on the Earth.

- **Rocky exoplanets:** The Earth is a rocky planet; small, solid land surface, oceans, and an atmosphere containing clouds and weather. Rocky planets range in size from about 1.6 times the diameter of the Earth to planets as small as Mercury. Taking a personal and biased perspective, we believe that life such as humans can evolve and exist on this type of planet.

So, saddle up and join this outfit as we travel out to several worlds discovered by the Kepler telescope and imagine how people might survive and prosper. You'll even meet a few cowboys *from* Kepler and K2 planets who visit Earth.

Happy Trails!
Dave and Steve

Step Right Up
Louise Webster

Come one, Come all,
To the Greatest Show
In the entire
Universe!

Meet the Humanauts
Bold enough
To conquest Kepler-186f
First!

See Aliens,
Once fierce enemies,
Now Comrades who share
Space Vessels.

Those silver ships,
 Whose speed and flash,
Will make you gasp
"Incredible!"

Step up and see
The Aerial plants,
From 490
Light years away.

Exotic flora,
Rainbow spiked,
To brighten up
Your day!

Hear scientists,
With Pioneer Hearts,
Tell tales
Of settling Space.

Building up a
Habitat,
To shelter the
Human Race.

Pele's Gift
Gene Mederos

The professor emerged from the wasteland looking like an old prospector of the ancient West, a wide-brimmed hat shielding his head from the desert sun and a many-pocketed vest bursting with precious samples, leading his *camule* by the nose. Although the gene-modded beast of burden was more tractable than either of its ancestors, only the constant tugging on the ring piercing its sensitive nose could force it to walk into the teeth of the glass-laden wind, dust-sized crystalline shards glittering in the light of the blazing sun. Dr. Shay Loren sympathized with the beastie. True, its barding was made of the same durable mesh as his wind-suit, and its eyes were covered by unscratchable glassteel goggles like his own, yet he was sure the creature couldn't shake the feeling that windborne silicate flechettes were cutting their way into its heart. He certainly couldn't.

Just ahead of them a lone giant outcropping of crystal loomed out of the sand, relieving the unrelenting flatness of the glittering desert. The pastel hued facets cast a colorful mosaic shadow on the sands below it. Like all the others of its kind, it most closely resembled a great, rough-hewn human head. But no human hand had been involved in its creation; it was a naturally occurring geologic phenomenon, created in the heat and pressure of the planet's mantle and then thrust up through the desert floor towards the sky during the turbulent height of the planet's volcanic age. That age was now centuries past, by human reckoning, but it was only an instant ago in geologic time. The planet was still volcanically active though, which is why the initial survey team had named it for Pele, the Hawaiian goddess of fire and volcanoes.

Shay knew the scientists on the survey team had been tempted to name the giant crystal heads *moai*, after the carved heads on Easter Island back on Earth. But the people of Rapa Nui who had carved those stones were a distinct culture from the people of Hawaii, so to be true to the mythos they

7

named them menehunes. It was also a joke, of the kind only an academic could appreciate—like calling the biggest of Robin Hood's Merry Men 'Little John'—for the mythical menehunes of Hawaii were a diminutive race.

This particular menehune, the closest to human habitation and the first to be studied, Shay had named Ha'alulu. Ha'alulu means "to tremble" in Hawaiian.

Shay noted that the camule stopped resisting his pull and actually surged forward when it saw the menehune. It had enough gene-modded intelligence to know that home, and the end of its trek, was just over the horizon. Now, it was all he could do to rein the beast in while he lingered to regard his old friend. He had just spent a week in the company of hundreds of such heads never before seen by living human eyes, but Ha'alulu was a particular beauty.

One never forgot one's first.

Like all its kind, the menehune hummed, an alien threnody he theorized was created by an interaction of the ever-present seismic vibrations of the planet's crust and the aerodynamics of the wind. It was a phenomenon unique to crystals on this world and quite possibly the most intriguing aspect of his study of the giant "heads". A snort from the camule broke his reverie so he climbed up the bags of gear secured to the creature's sides and settled into the high saddle atop its hump. No sooner had he released the reins, giving the now eager mount its head, than it took off at a gallop into the wind.

Hilo Station was a small human outpost built around the requisite mineral spring 'oasis' on the edge of the wasteland. Humans had predominantly settled the smaller island continent of Haumea, named for the Hawaiian mother-goddess, instead of the pangean supercontinent they had named after the creation god Kāne, because of the life-giving springs that dotted the smaller island. There were very few springs to be found in the dry and sere interior of the continent however, so it was dubbed the wasteland.

He left the *camule* in a cooled stable stocked with food and water and crossed the unpaved street to the Hilo Trading Post, which also happened to be the outpost's saloon, general store and post office, and went on in for a drink of something a mite stronger than water. He was the only customer of course, only mad dogs and Englishmen ventured out under the midday sun. The outpost, and the saloon, came alive after sunset. He took a seat at the end of the bar and ordered bourbon, neat. Well, they all agreed to call it bourbon, but it was actually a flavored variation of the local mahina-shine, made from the hardy rock-clinging lichen that thrived around the springs. Mahina was the Hawaiian word for moon.

Olaf the barkeep, and of course, post- and stable-master, placed a liter bottle and a clean glass before him on the counter. The label on the bottle depicted a long-haired Polynesian beauty with a crown of stars. This particular batch of bourbon had been named Hina's Crown, for the brighter of Pele's two moons. The other dimmer moon, Lona, was also named for a Hawaiian moon goddess. Her name graced several bottles of a less-than-clear vodka on the shelf.

"Wot you got fer me dis time perfesser?" Olaf asked.

Shay drew his goniometer from his upper left vest pocket and laid it on the counter, then rummaged the bottom of the pocket and extracted two eight-centimeter long crystals, one a light amber in color and the other one a deep violet.

"Here you are Olaf, your pick of two fringe crystals growing from the base of the biggest menehune I've ever seen. It dominated its section of the valley."

"Wot de devil is dat thing?" Olaf asked, ignoring the crystals and pointing at the instrument. Shay realized that to Olaf the goniometer probably looked like a flat sickle with spider legs.

"That's a goniometer. You know how proximity to the crystals disrupts most electro-magnetic based technology?" Shay had a theory the sonic vibrations the crystals emitted acted as a kind of EM pulse. "Well, since I can't use the X-ray Crystallographer to measure and chart the crystal's structure, I use this." Shay placed a crystal in the crook where the protractor was joined to the slide rulers and showed him how he could rotate the device to measure any side or facet of the stone. "So it tells me that this crystal and its twin here are slightly larger than the last one I gave you and so should clear my tab and then some."

"I'll dun take yer word for it. Lemme 'av de poiple one den."

Shay put the amber crystal and his goniometer back in his pocket and poured himself another shot.

"I dun forwarded you a couple of messages you received from duh station. Didja get'm?"

Shay tossed back another shot of moon goddess bourbon and shook his head 'no'.

"Not yet," he added once his vocal chords recovered from the scorching, "I forgot to turn my pocketcom back on." Out deep in a valley full of menehunes, pocketcoms were dead weight, but it was a habit ingrained into every human being to carry theirs with them at all times. He got up to fish the small instrument out of his back pocket. "It's not like anybody on this planet actually needs me for anything."

"Dey were from station-com."

"Really? What would the space station want with me?"

As he switched the pocketcom on the saloon suddenly grew dark.

"What the hay-el?" Olaf drawled. No one knew where Olaf had gotten his accent, but it was common for him to make one syllable words into multiple syllable words when he got the least bit excited. "An eclipse, you think?"

Shay shook his head. "Goddesses or no, Pele's moons are too small to cast a shadow on the surface."

Shay went to the door to peer out at the sky. "Too early in the season for storm clouds..." he said as he stepped outside and looked up.

"Ho-o-ly" He said then, in a fair imitation of Olaf's multi-syllabic speech.

⣿

"So what is so fricking terrible about a fruit salad?"

Phen joins the rest of the team in laughing at Captain Crandel's joke.

Esprit De Corps.

Engineered-Life-Form Trooper Phen has learned the hard way that fitting in cuts down on the harassment and abuse someone like him can expect from "born" humans.

Looking 'down' from the space station orbiting the planet Pele into the largest canyon system any of them had ever seen, the three hundred and fifty kilometer circle of verdant green,

deep reds, pastel blues, amber and purple colored growth surrounded by glittering golden desert sands don't look to Phen
like anything as prosaic as a salad. To his eyes it looks like an
emerging seedling, struggling towards the sun.

"To begin with, it's not vegetation; it just bloody looks
like it from up here. It's a new form of silicate growth satellite
surveillance spotted ten days ago, and it wasn't there during
the last sweep three months ago."

The accent marks the florid ProGen project manager as
an Englishman. Even though the British Isles are now nothing
more than a chain of mountain tops poking up out of the North
Sea, you still encounter Englishmen among the upper ranks of
EarthCorp. He looks too young to be a project manager for a
whole planet but Phen notes the fine lines around the eyes,
the thin lips and other tells that the man has had Rejuv. He
sports the small square mustache and comb-over riddled with
metallic extensions favored by the corporate elite. His suit is in
transition from navy blue to camel as hundreds of tiny gene-gi-
neered silk worm spiders crawl across the fabric, devouring
the blue thread and spinning out the brown. His appearance
is in stark contrast to the nine special-forces troopers standing
around him in the observation port with their crew-cuts, their
clean-shaven faces and their matte-black carbon-fiber armored
suits.

"A GenTech nano-bomb?" The chief asks. The tall sec-
ond-in-command is the unit's science officer. She's the only one
who bothered to read the science stuff in the mission briefing
the company sent them.

"Indeed. Accidental detonation, supposedly. I can't imagine Dr. Sorenson meant to re-sequence her genome in such a
violent manner." The man manages to convey the impression
that he is extremely bored with this minor inconvenience. "It's
possible she was shielded or outside the original blast radius,
which wouldn't have been no more than a klick or two wide,
or so GenTech reported in their last communiqué. They don't
have anyone in this sector so you can imagine the lag as communications have to be carried ship to ship."

He waves a hand and a holographic display appears in
the air before them. They see a time-lapse simulation of the

silicon jungle's growth from its conjectured one klick initial radius to its current canyon-filling size.

"And it's still growing. It's spreading under a rock-hard canopy of crystalline domes that is impenetrable to scans due to the bloody crystal's disruption of EM radiation." Data then scrolls across the heads-up display, Phen recognizes it as a genetic assay. "The first team we sent in accomplished the first of its objectives, it packed a sample of the crystalline structure into a high orbital drone immediately upon landing and sent it back to us. They couldn't find a trace of Dr. Sorenson however. As you can see, the nanites rewrote the code on some sand lice and lichen and spliced it into a sort of silicate proto-code, perhaps obtained from menehune crystals. At least that's the theory."

Phen thinks the project manager knows very well that no one in the unit save possibly for the chief can understand the intricately complex chart. He finds he has to look away as the thought strikes him that the data on display can just as easily be used to describe him as it does a gene-ripped sand louse and a spot of lichen.

"Are you saying the crystals down there are alive?" Captain Crandel asks.

It is then that Phen notes a new arrival has joined them in the observation bay.

▦

The EarthCorp airship was certainly big enough to blot out the sun over the saloon, Shay reflected, as he watched its shadow follow them across the ocean to Kāne. Many of the small, still-forming islands they sailed over were completely covered by it. The airship was the only one of its kind on the planet. It not only carried all the shipping between the continents, it also carried tourists from the spaceport on the Eastern coast of Kāne on luxury cruises around the world.

Ordinarily, if Shay needed to visit the mainland, he travelled in steerage like the rest of the locals, but since EarthCorp had requested his assistance they had put him up in style. That's how Shay found himself sitting back in a fully adjustable recliner in the First Class observation lounge sipping honest-to-God bourbon—from Earth—while enjoying a bird's eye view of the most impressive feature of the mainland below.

The Kanaloa Rift, half again as long as the Valles Marineris on Mars and ten times as wide as the Grand Canyon back on old Earth, gaped like an open maw across the Southern Hemisphere of the planet. It was such a vast system, most of the branching canyons carved out by innumerable lava flows, that it was still mostly unexplored. Its small and widely scattered population of menehunes had all been cataloged, however, which is why Shay had chosen to break new ground on Haumea.

A young ship's steward appeared at his shoulder, her platinum blonde hair and shiny insignia reflected in his glass.

"Your shuttle has landed on the hangar deck, Doctor Loren. You are requested to board as soon as possible."

"Of course. But I still don't understand why I'm being lifted to the space station only to then be returned to the surface to examine this thing which is causing all the ruckus."

"Officially, you are attending a briefing with the military team that is charged with your safety."

"And un-officially, admin wants to keep it a secret until they know what it is, and if it's valuable, so they're keeping this tub full of tourists as far away from that section of the Rift as they can."

His clever deduction earned him a half smile from the young officer, who was obviously more than just a steward.

The small and sleek craft waiting for him on the hangar deck was obviously no shuttle craft. No sooner had he been strapped into the seat behind the pilot's chair, the only seat in the craft, than it leapt into space. In what appeared to Shay as no time at all, it was braking to dock at the station. No sooner had Shay undone his straps than the hatch was pulled open and a stevedore wearing a flight pack took him by the hand and flew him, weightless, through an airlock and into a waiting cargo lift. As the lift ascended, or descended depending on your point of view Shay mused, weight returned to his body and his feet rejoined the floor—or was it the ceiling?—of the lift.

The doors whisked open on a heated and well lit corridor and another smiling steward, this one an older male, was waiting to greet him and escort him to the observation bay where, he was informed, the planet's project manager and a team of EarthGov special forces were waiting.

As the observation bay doors whisked open, Shay could hear a gruff and commanding voice. "Are you saying the crystals down there are alive?"

❖

"The possibility of silicon based life has long been theorized because it has many chemical properties similar to carbon," the man, obviously a civilian scientist, says. "They're both tetravalent for example, meaning that individual carbon and silicon atoms make four bonds with other elements in forming chemical compounds. And it's interesting to note that the double-helical structure of DNA was deduced from crystallographic data. But there are some significant drawbacks to silicon as a basis of life."

Phen notes immediately that the man is un-modded, showing none of the tells of having undergone Rejuv and allowing gray hair to grow at his temples and a little extra weight to gather around his midsection. He deduces that scientists on Pele aren't paid enough to enjoy the benefits of life-extending genetic therapies.

"But the possibility of silicon-based life is what Dr. Sorenson has been researching for most of her life," the scientist says. Phen sees the project manager make eye contact with the new arrival.

"So very glad you could join us, Dr. Shay, and thank you for that brief yet ever so interesting and germane lecture. We'll postpone the introductions until after the mission briefing if you don't mind." To Phen's ears, the Englishman is trying not to sound annoyed.

Crandel finds the momentary silence a good time to interject. "So you need a team of EarthGov special forces to find a scientist lost in a living crystal fruit salad."

Phen knows he's not supposed to laugh when the captain repeats a joke, so he simply smiles broadly with the rest of the team and watches the project manager wince, the sort of reaction the captain was going for. Although the team is technically under the project manager's orders, Crandel has now subtly set the Englishman apart from them and outside the chain of command. Phen has to admit that the man is a very capable Detachment Commander.

"We are grateful to the SecGen of Earth for allowing your team to help us since providentially you were only a few light years away." Phen and the rest of the troopers know that Pro-Gen has made sizable donations above and beyond what its parent company EarthCorp already makes to key EarthGov senators facing reelection.

"As I may have mentioned earlier, the first team wasn't very successful at finding Dr, Sorenson. And those men and women were corporate marines, the very best that money can buy."

"Mercenaries you mean. This team however, is composed of nothing but patriots." The captain lifts his head proudly and the team follows suit. "Hell, I'd even rather have an ELF trooper at my side than a real-born merc. We'll get that scientist out."

The project manager spares Phen the briefest possible glance and visibly struggles for a second to retain his composure. Phen cannot help but note the irony that while the little man has engineered life-forms crawling across his body defecating him a new suit, it is the one shaped like a human being that triggers his revulsion.

"We certainly hope so," is all he says.

***

Shay watched the female officer, Chief Duran, wrap up the briefing with a final admonishment. "And finally, we will remain sealed into our suits, we have no idea what's wafting around in the air down there."

The unit was gathered at the far end of the fancy conference room, leaving a distinct gap between them and the scientists who were busily briefing Shay. The other two scientists, from the University of New Honolulu, seemed rather intimidated by the troopers, but Shay was very glad to have them along on the mission. The unknown was almost invariably dangerous and well armed men and women with the disposition to use those arms in heroic rescue efforts were always welcome in his book.

Captain Crandel inhaled mightily on his cigar and exhaled a great big puff of smoke. Tobacco had made a comeback

since some kid genius a few years back illegally gene-ripped all
the harmful stuff out of the plant while heightening the buzz.

"That's right boys and girls," the captain added as a final
note. "We want to avoid doing any damage to our lungs."

Everyone laughed, including the scientists. Casual conversation ensued and the young female officer made her way
over to Shay.

"You are obviously the geologist assigned to the mission," she said, extending her hand. "I am Chief Warrant Officer Duran, you can call me Chief. I'll be your liaison with the
team."

Shay stood and took her hand for an official and perfunc-
tory shake.

"Dr. Shay Loren at your service."

"Excellent. I was hoping you could give me an idea of what
we can expect on the surface, geologically speaking of course.
This is our first mission on a volcanically active hell-planet."

"As volcanic planets go, this one is quite tame—its major
geological upheavals mostly a thing of the past. I mean, most
of the geological features on Earth were caused by volcanism.
On this world, the majority of the volcanoes are still active,
yes, but it's no hell-planet. Aside from the relatively young
and still-forming seamount island chains and archipelagos that
dominate the oceans, a fair bit is downright stable and habitable. That's why it was named for Pele, a nature goddess, instead of Satan, or Surtur."

The chief smiled. "I'm in the military, so naturally I've a
passing acquaintance with the devil, and seen my share of hell,
but who is Suture?"

"Surtur. Ancient Norse god, evil, wreathed in flames."

"Ah, interesting."

Shay wasn't sure whether she meant that or not.

"The military does not train specialists in geology, or mythology, but you are also the leading expert on these *menehune*
crystals, correct?"

"Yes, mineralogy is a subject of geology. Mythology is just
a hobby." Shay was pleased to note she actually smiled at that
before continuing.

"According to the report, no signal has been able to penetrate the canopy, no scan or spectroscope can see inside, and even shielded probes stop transmitting before they reach the surface. Some property of the crystals interferes with EM radiation. Will the public address units in our helmets function?"

"They should, mostly. There may be static or background noise though."

"We'll be making the drop at 1600. Do you require assistance getting into the armor?"

Shay could not imagine for even a second that she was actually flirting with him, so he answered as soberly as he could. "I wear a similar suit when I poke around active volcanoes. I should be fine." But he had to smile. "And there's always the holo-manual."

Shay arrived at the drop bay at 1545 hours, although geologists generally took a long view of time, he hated being late. He found the Chief standing next to the hatch of a squat hunk of metal which looked like an inverted pyramid with ridiculously small thrusters.

"I'm a geologist, not an engineer, but that doesn't look like a landing craft."

"Oh, it is. It's designed for *hard* landings."

"I beg your pardon."

"The first team entered from the periphery, we're dropping right on ground zero, smashing through the canopy."

"Smashing?"

"Don't worry; we'll walk away from this landing in one piece."

"You've done this before?"

"Only in sims, but I'm looking forward to it. It should be a hell of a ride."

They made the drop right on schedule. At first it was a controlled descent, Shay could feel the effort of the thrusters fighting the planet's gravitational pull. He could see on the altimeter being fed to his helmet's Heads-up Display exactly how fast they were dropping. Suddenly, at just under a klick from the surface, the thrusters cut out. Shay reflexively tightened his grip on the inertial straps holding him suspended in place as his stomach started to rise. He was less chagrined when he saw the troopers had done the same.

And then the altimeter began flashing red and the plummeting craft's nav-comp began blaring out a warning: COLLISION IMMINENT

The altimeter had become a red blur when his straps suddenly sprang taut. Foam sprayed out from the inner hull of the craft, engulfing all on board and a beat later he felt his stomach drop back into place with a discernible thud. That was his only indication that they had struck the ground. Landing didn't feel like the appropriate term.

▦

The last thing Phen sees before the crash foam covers his visor is the look of terror on Dr. Loren's face. He can and does feel compassion for the scientist, but he cannot completely empathize. His genes allow him an instinct for self-preservation, so he can survive to be of use to the rest of the team, but he cannot feel abject fear or paralyzing terror. His body does not produce those hormones. Immediately after the landing there is a whir of exhaust fans as the foam disintegrates into its nanite components and is sucked back into its tank. The scientist looks around to assure himself that they are all in one piece. Phen is pleased the man has regained his composure.

As one, the troopers unclip the straps and drop to the floor of the lander. Morelli, the biggest and strongest member of the team, helps the doctor out of his straps and lowers him gently to the floor. She keeps a grip on his shoulder as her suit grapples on to his. The captain orders the onboard comp to open the top hatch and then vaults up and out. Morelli waits for the rest of the team to exit and then activates the servos in her suit's legs, effortlessly carrying Dr. Loren with her. Phen, as per protocol, exits last.

The lander has left a jagged hole where it crashed through the crystal dome some thirty meters above them. The space around the lander is relatively clear of the multi-hued crystal formations that arch and spiral out of the desert floor to support the domes above them. The sunlight shining through the crystals paints everyone and everything in a rainbow of pastel colors. As he joins the rest of the team gathered around the captain, his suit mic picks up the chief's amplified voice.

"As discussed, we will be using the PA system built into

the helmets, so pay attention and keep your mics hot."

"A freaking hell-hole," an amped voice says.

Phen expected no less a reaction from Sikorski, the unit's com-tech and cyber specialist. His suit speakers are maxed out and the chief gives him a thumb down gesture. Phen wonders if he will actually lower the volume. Sikorski calls the rest of the unit, except for the chief and Captain Crandel, 'gene-tards' and 'tube-wipes'. Everyone calls him an A-hole. Except for Phen of course, Phen has to call him 'Sir'.

As Captain Crandel divides the team into pairs to search for Dr. Sorenson, Sikorski gives the chief a half-assed salute and approaches the nearest column to regard his reflection. Disregarding orders to the contrary he raises his visor and makes a face.

"Sikorski!" Crandel barks. "Lower your visor!"

Sikoski turns toward the captain, but doesn't comply. "This crystal is hot," he says, his voice made excruciatingly loud by the amps. Phen isn't surprised he hasn't lowered the volume on his speakers.

"Hot?" Dr. Loren sounds dubious. "Menehune crystals are chemically inert. They shouldn't be generating heat."

"Well, I can feel the heat on my face," Sikorski responds curtly, turning back toward the crystal column. "We wouldn't have known that if I hadn't lifted my visor, since our sensors won't function in this blasted..."

The crystal pane in front of Sikorski's face begins to emit a high pitch whine which grates across Phen's nerves as his suit mic feeds the noise directly into his earphones. He sees the pane begin to vibrate.

"What the..." Sikorsky begins to say, still at full volume, when the crystal suddenly shatters in his face.

Sikorski's amplified scream echoes off the crystals and causes an excruciating whine of feedback in everyone's earphones. He topples backward, clutching his face.

Jensen is on him in a flash, pulling his body away from the gasses and molten bits of magma still spewing from the shattered section of the column. The unit's medic dials a setting on the back of his suit's medi-glove and plugs the applicator in the palm to the medication port on Sikorski's suit collar.

The anesthetic takes effect immediately, allowing the medic to remove the man's hands from his face. The tech-trooper's face is an unrecognizable ruin of sizzling flesh and blue flames that flow like molten wax. The scientist is the only one to gasp aloud, but Phen knows the rest of the team is equally affected.

Phen can see the optics in Jensen's suit visor spinning furiously, magnifying and sharpening the focus on whatever the medic needs to see. "These are acid burns as well as thermic burns."

"Brimstone," Dr. Loren says, "sulfuric acid."

"Brimstone, you say," the chief remarks. "Not a hell-planet, you say."

Jensen unclips an applicator from his belt and sprays nanite foam on Sikorski's burns. "This will begin to neutralize the acid. His helmet has been damaged, I can't get a read on the extent of his injuries internally, but there is no doubt he's gone into shock. If we can't restore suit integrity and get him into stasis we'll lose him."

Phen feels his psych programming take over. He quickly releases the catches on his helmet and takes it off. He rushes over to hand it to the medic.

"What are you doing ELF...?" Crandel asks over his mic.

"I don't need an integral suit, Commander. My body was engineered to cope with all potential causes of injury. My skin is resistant to hydrolysis and other chemical reactions caused by acid or radiation. I also have twice as many pores as the rest of you and a lower core temperature so I am not affected by the desert heat."

Phen can see the captain's expression through his faceplate. Crandel is chewing on his lower lip and glaring. Phen has seen the commander do this every time he has had to make a difficult tactical decision.

"He's expendable," Crandel snarls into his mic, "and you're not. At least not until we find the scientist and determine whether she needs blood or one of your organs."

"Understood," Phen responds, "I assure you I will not jeopardize the mission...:"

"Blast it," Jensen says, cursing under his breath. He had swapped helmets without waiting for the captain's OK and the readouts show it had been a futile effort. Jensen takes the helmet off Sikorski and hands it back to Phen. "Put it back on ELF," Jensen orders as he stands up from the body. "He's dead."

As Jensen records the fallen trooper's time of death into his medical log, Crandel orders the teams to head out. Phen watches as he and Dr. Loren head off due east.

The chief studies the column where Sikorski got hit from a safe distance and waits for him to put his helmet back on and join her. As he approaches, she points out the gasses spewing out and a number of thin rivulets of molten rock running down the tree bark.

"Lava?" Phen queries.

"It's not melting the crystal. Dr. Loren was right about them, they don't generate heat. But they can withstand and contain magma and acid."

"Who'd design a defense system like this?"

"GenTech is a defense contractor, R&D stuff. But Sorenson is supposedly a pacifist, an idealist when it comes to the inherent goodness of humanity. At least that's what it says in the dossier EarthGov gave us. If so, then I don't think Sikorski was attacked. This structure is not intended as a weapon."

Phen considers for a moment, the lambent fire of the molten rock reflecting in the chief's faceplate, turning the visor the ruddy color of fire and blood.

"Regardless of its purpose," he says, "Sikorski was right. This place is a hell-hole."

███

For well over an hour, Shay stayed silent. Captain Crandel barely said a word, other than mutter imprecations under his breath and none of it directed at him. Perhaps he had never lost a soldier so early into a deployment, or at least not without an enemy to retaliate against. He guessed the captain no longer thought he was traipsing through a fruit salad bowl.

"At the risk of stating the obvious, it's going to take a long while for just four teams to search a little over ninety-six thousand square kilometers without sensors."

"Several lifetimes I'd guess," the captain answered complacently, "even if we weren't using a tried and true search grid pattern and my team wasn't so well trained. Fortunately, we signed up for only a week's deployment. The wee English pop-injay was correct, Dr. Sorenson would most likely have been as close as possible to the point of detonation, one or two klicks at the most, given the EM interference of the crystals on this plan-et. Assuming she wasn't suffering some sort of mental break-down and was committing suicide in a particularly unique way. But mental illness and suicides being so rare these days, I'll lay odds she was within two klicks of the blast. Perhaps five square kilometers at most."

Shay was ashamed of himself for being so surprised that a man who had risen to the rank of a Detachment Commander would be highly intelligent. And more than a little abashed at the obvious insult he had just paid the captain. He hoped the man was truly not as offended as he sounded.

"Look, Captain Crandel, I apologize…"

"No need, Dr. Loren. You bought our act, the one we al-ways use with corporate execs. That an intelligent man like you would fall for it is a compliment to our skill at dissembling. It's EarthGov military standard operating procedure. The corpora-tions are much wealthier and better equipped than EarthGov and outnumber us a hundred to one. Only by allowing them to grossly underestimate our capabilities can we hope to oppose them should they turn on humanity."

Shay had had no idea that EarthGov and its military was on its guard against the corporations. One was led to assume that the corporations 'owned' the government. In any event, Shay mused, the search was brought up short less than an hour later by a distant siren that caused all the crystals around them to hum ominously, although none, Shay was relieved to see, started to vibrate.

Crandel oriented on the source of the sound. "Sounds like someone has found something," he said, smiling through his visor.

They followed the sound for several klicks, moving rough-ly northwest through the crystal cathedral, as Shay now liked to think of it. They soon entered an area where the columns and formations began to cluster closer together. They arrived at the source of the siren at what appeared to be the entrance to a tall corridor, and found four of the troopers waiting for them.

Crandel gave a curt hand gesture to the one whose suit was blaring and it cut out. When he got close enough to see through the faceplates Shay recognized Martinez as the one who had activated the siren, and Saleem, Morelli, and the medic, Jensen as well.

"Martinez, report," the captain commanded.

The female trooper stepped forward. "Sir, as Parsons and I finished the first leg of our search grid, we noticed the columns had begun to cluster closer together. We thought it could possibly be a defense perimeter so we continued deeper among the columns. Soon the structure closed in, forming this corridor, and thirty meters in we encountered a solid wall of crystal. I decided I would remove a suit glove and extend my hand to see if I could feel any heat. I didn't, so we blasted an opening."

Martinez paused as two more armored suits entered the area, obviously Chief Duran and the Engineered Life-Form trooper.

"Continue your report, Martinez," the captain ordered.

"Beyond the wall we entered a large chamber, approximately fifty to sixty meters in diameter under a high dome and found a standard class-four shelter and provisions. At the far end of the chamber we found a shielded remote console station. No sign of the scientist. Parsons stayed behind in case we missed a passage and she returned to the chamber and I came out here to signal the team."

"Lead the way then, Martinez."

The team moved down the corridor and into the chamber beyond. Shay stopped to examine the edges of the wall that the troopers had blasted to pieces. He couldn't be sure of what he was seeing at first.

"Duran!" He heard Crandel bark over the speakers.

"On it sir," she responded. Shay didn't pay much attention after that; he assumed the chief was organizing the team to go over Dr. Sorenson's computer and equipment and to search the chamber for another way in or out.

◼

Phen begins his perimeter sweep on the side of the chamber opposite Salim, and Morelli takes the section of crystal wall at the apex between them. All three have removed a glove and are feeling for warm spots. He leaves dye markers on the crystal panes wherever he feels heat.

Morelli has been moving in his direction during her sweep and eventually intercepts him. "I don't know about you," she says, her speakers turned down low, "but I was expecting to find the scientist somewhere in the immediate vicinity of our landing site. You know, the center of the labyrinth and all that..."

"I don't think I know that story," Phen replies.

"There was a bull-like monster at the center. Probably one of my ancestors."

Phen allows himself to smile. Morelli is the one trooper who treats Phen like he's almost a human being. Perhaps it's because she too was created for a specific purpose.

Built like a tank and incredibly strong, she isn't an engineered life-form like Phen, who was conceived in a test tube and grown in a vat. Melinda Morelli was selectively bred for specific traits, but the breeding pair who were her parents conceived her the old fashioned way. She was then carried to term by a human surrogate—her mother's genes being too precious to lie fallow during a pregnancy—and born like any other human baby. Being conceived by male/female interaction instead of jiggling sperm and ova together in a jar is the difference between being considered a human being and being no more than a tool made to look like a man.

Before they can talk further however, Phen sees that Dr. Loren is leading the entire team in their direction.

"I wasn't sure at first," the scientist was saying over his speakers, but the crystals lining the first aperture are definitely regenerating, which means Dr. Sorenson could have headed in any direction and the crystals would have sealed the passage behind her."

"The remote console is on that end of the chamber, closest to the epicenter, and we didn't find anything there." Dr. Loren pauses to withdraw a strange-looking instrument from his suit's hip compartment. "And if this over-arching structure conforms to the structure of the individual crystals..."

The scientist rotates the protuberances on the device and points along one of the vectors. "Then according to the goniometer, there may have been an opening there," he says, pointing to a section of chamber wall a short distance from Phen and Morelli's position. There are no dye marks.

The captain himself blasts the wall apart and leads the team down the corridor beyond. At its end, they enter an even larger chamber. It glows with a ruddy light that mutes the pastel hues of the crystals. Phen raises his visor for a moment and feels the heat of the walls on his face. In the center is a giant crystal structure resembling a human head.

"That is the largest menehune I have ever seen," Dr. Loren says.

"Why thank you Shay," a female voice says, "I grew it myself."

The troopers look around for the missing scientist but the voice fills the room, coming from no definite source.

"Tabitha? Is that you?" Dr. Loren asks the room.

"Here Shay, let me make this easier for you."

Any doubts as to the source of the room's warmth are dispelled as golden streams of magma become discernible behind the crystal walls. Streaks of golden light illumine the room and everyone in it. And then the light begins to coalesce in front of the menehune. A pillar of gold no higher than its chin resolves itself into the image of a woman. Although transparent and shimmering, Phen can make out the features of a middle-aged woman, garbed in a standard worksuit.

"A hologram?"

The image nods. "The crystals do not just interfere with EM radiation, they can also manipulate it."

"Where exactly are you Tabitha?"

"My physical body, and the concomitant genetic material, is distributed throughout the network. But the node that contains those processes we call consciousness is stored in the matrix behind me."

"In the menehune?" Dr. Loren asks.

And, "Network?" Chief Duran asks.

The image smiles, "Oh, I am sure you all have questions. And I certainly am not going anywhere. There are a multitude of chambers like this throughout the network, and it was quite an enjoyable game keeping them hidden from that first team.

In time, I will speak with you all, with any who wish to interface with the network."

The image stepped forward, as if it were walking on the glittering sand that was the chamber's floor until she stood before Dr. Loren.

"Now come, let me see your face, Shay. I've shown you mine."

"Doctor Loren..." Captain Crandel starts to caution.

"It's all right, Captain," Dr. Loren says as he removes his helmet. "I'm tired of wearing this thing." And then he smiles at the image. Crandel, however, scowls.

"A question I need answered before we continue, Dr. Sorenson. Did you do this to yourself, and, if so, was it intentional or an accident?"

The image moves toward the captain.

"I am sorry for the loss of your comrade, Captain Crandel, I can assure you that was an accident. As for your question, yes, I did this to myself, intentionally."

She smiles at Crandel's answering frown.

"I wasn't at the center of the blast, but a sample of my DNA was, and I was pretty sure the means I had devised to "upload" myself into the network would succeed."

"And how was that done? Exactly?" Chief Duran asks.

"We'll talk later my dear, right now I am eager to begin the next part of this process."

"And what part is that?"

"Sexual reproduction for the continuance of this new species I've created, part human and part silicate life."

"Excuse me?" Crandel asks.

"I beg your pardon," Dr. Loren says.

"I can't tell if you're blushing Shay, not in this light. You're not a biologist but you're a scientist all the same. Something as natural and fundamental as reproduction shouldn't bother you, or these fine warriors."

Phen is surprised when the image turns toward him. "I didn't allow the corporate marines to find anything because they were of no use to me. I knew that when they failed, Earth-Corp, or whatever shell company they wished to employ, would obtain a detachment of Special Forces troopers from

EarthGov. These detachments always have an Engineered Life-Form in their complement."

"And what use is Phen to you?" Crandel asks.

"His rewritable genetic code…" Dr. Loren says aloud.

"Exactly. I've built a womb and provided a synthesis of human DNA and modified silicon bonded molecules to create a unique ovum. Now I just need a sperm cell to begin the process of life."

And then the image winks out.

Immediately, Captain Crandel, Chief Duran and Dr. Loren begin a heated debate over the ethics and ramifications of what Sorenson's hologram has proposed. Phen isn't the least bit bothered that he is excluded from the conversation. While they talk, the room begins to grow cooler. The magma behind the walls was flowing elsewhere.

"Would you like to father a new species?" the voice of Dr. Sorenson says in his earphones. "You can respond without alerting the others, I am transmitting directly to your suit's com system."

"It is not for me to choose," Phen replied, "and I am bound by my loyalty oath and conditioning to tell the captain you are speaking to me."

"I will not prevent you from doing so, but hear me out a moment will you? What I need to tell you will enable you to fulfill your oath and your programming."

"Continue." Phen instructs. He has been trained to recognize the value of obtaining information, even if he has to temporarily go against his programming to do so.

"The captain is duty-bound to report what has transpired here. EarthCorp may then decide to evacuate the planet and irradiate the surface to make sure no new life form arises here. But it is more probable that EarthCorp will exploit this situation, send down an engineered life form loyal to them who would create new allies for the corporation."

"Agreed," Phen says, "that course of action is most probable."

"Then it is in the best interests of Earth Gov, indeed of all humanity, that a being bred to be loyal to the government and human beings should become the progenitor of this new species."

It doesn't take Phen long to arrive at the same conclusion.

▦

"So then we noticed the ELF was gone. We figured Phen must have walked right out of the room through a holographic wall. It was no use searching for him, it was like the crystals just swallowed him up."

Olaf shook his head at the tale and then poured Shay another drink. After a moment he poured himself a drink too. After a long draught, Shay continued, "So now Earth Gov has taken eminent domain of Pele and has established an embassy of sorts to communicate with Dr. Sorenson and this new sentient species of menehunes."

Olaf drains his glass and Shay sighs into his hands.

"In a way, the planet now has a god. But is it a Pele, or a Surtur?"

Both men reached for the bottle.

Over The Ridge
Terrie Leigh Relf

Doug Baxter rebraided his thick blond hair, let it fall down his back. Something caught his eye, sparkling in the morning light. He bent down to pick it up, turned to his friend and boss, Padrick "Paddy" O'Neill. "If I didn't know better, I'd think these rocks were multiplying. Strange, isn't it?"

He handed the black porous rock to Paddy, who held it between gloved palms, rolled it back and forth a bit, hoping to catch a glimpse of its internal fire. It looked volcanic to him, but as far as they'd been able to determine, there weren't any active volcanoes in the vicinity. Then again, they hadn't engaged in many extended expeditions given their primary focus: to establish the infrastructure for their new community.

Once they'd been on Kepler-452b for a few months, they'd started a pool to come up with a new name for the planet and their burgeoning community. The winner would receive some as-yet-to-be-determined prize. Probably coffee. The real stuff. Thus far, none of the names felt right, and most were lame attempts, like New Earth and Scrub Hollow.

"If you don't want the rock, I'll give it to Ole. He's got quite the collection by now. Any word from Tori? She's usually up and about by now." Paddy tucked the rock into his daypack. His dark eyes crinkled at the edges as he peered at the prefab-modular units comprising their little corner of the universe of one hundred and growing.

"She'll be along. I saw her in the supply room before I left. You know how OCD she gets." Doug looked out at the ridge, scratched his head. "One of these days, we've got to climb that thing or figure out a way around it."

Paddy pursed his lips at Doug's comment about Tori. He was right, though, and that was one of many reasons they'd broken up. Again. He scanned the rocky terrain, his eyes lifting to the seemingly impenetrable ridge. Overall, the imagery from the *Hemming*, the Orbital Space Station where they'd all been living for most of the previous year, was clear, hence their current location, but there was definitely something clouding the feed from over the ridge.

"I'll leave it to you to figure out. Meanwhile, Tori and I need to go over the grid plan for the new modular units. We think just below that rise there—" he waved a hand in the general direction. "We want to keep the community tight for now. Eventually, we'll expand further out."

Doug nodded, bent down to pick up another rock, cast it aside. "It's been leveled for the most part. We hauled and sorted most of the surrounding rock, too. I'll use some to create walkways, outline the area. It will be nice."

"A lot nicer than *The Hulk*," Paddy replied, his nickname for the *Hemming*. "That's for sure. Besides, that's one of many reasons everyone loves you, Doug. Always full of ideas for others to make happen."

They both chuckled at what had become common knowledge in the close-knit community. Doug definitely worked slower than most. "It's the gravity," he argued, and had a point. Despite Doug's wiry frame, Paddy couldn't imagine him scaling that ridge any time soon. Since it went on for miles in both directions, it was more likely they'd have to huff it to find an access point.

The area wasn't exactly desolate, as mossy plants grew by the banks of the creek running along the north side of the compound. The entire community imagined the area becoming lush and inviting, complete with some of the banyan-like trees for shade. Attempts at transplanting the trees hadn't been successful, so the horticulturists and hydroponics teams had been experimenting with growing them from seed. There was another tree that resembled bamboo, and it was just as hardy—especially for building furniture and other construction projects.

"When're the new modular pods arriving from the *Hemming*?"

"The *Cygnus* should be here later today. We need to get this project underway. Shouldn't take more than a few hours." Paddy shoved a hand in his back pocket to retrieve a computing pad.

"How many on the next shuttle transport?" Doug toed another one of the orb-like rocks, noticed the glint, picked it up.

"About twenty or so. More scientists. A few all-around-handy types, too. They'll be following in a few days."

Doug grinned. "It will be nice to have some help around here." He glanced toward an adjoining scrub field with a slight frown. "Hope there's a new vet on-board. We lost the last litter of pups along with their mother."

"Pups?"

"Pups is pups, even when they're not like any cattle on Old Earth."

"That's a shame. I really do like that stinky cheese Ole makes."

"You and me both, Doug."

They both pivoted at the cacophonous roar of an approaching scooter.

"There's Tori now. Wonder why she's in such a hurry."

The scooter came to an abrupt stop, scattering dust and rock. She clambered over the side with green eyes blazing.

"The ship," she began, her breath erratic, "the *Cygnus*..."

They took a step toward her, but she waved them off.

"...has disappeared from sat feed."

"It's probably just a glitch," Paddy offered.

She shook her head, tugged a bottle of water out of her belt, took a swig. "We checked. One minute she's there clear as night and the next, just gone."

"Are you sure it was even the *Cygnus*? You might have been tracking some space junk or a downed satellite."

She shook her head. "Not likely. Checked with the *Hemming*. The good news is there's no debris, so—"

Paddy sniffed, looked out toward the left pasture where Ole's "doggies" were milling around, making that odd lowing sound that sometimes gave him the willies. "Maybe there's an electrical storm brewing? Even they seem antsier than usual."

Tori glanced over at the sheep-cows, sniffed at the pronounced stench. "I don't think so. Besides, a storm might mess with our equipment, but not the *Hemming's*." She attempted to make eye contact with Paddy, but he continued to stare off in the distance.

Doug snorted. "Maybe some giant space squid swooped down, gobbled up the *Cygnus*..." He took a step back when

Tori shot him a dirty look. "Sorry. I know this is serious." He squinted as a ray of early morning sun came over the rise, pulled his goggles down.

"You might have something there." She kicked at a rock, then another, watched it fly off and bounce a few times. "Space bandits with superior tech."

Even though he was worried, Paddy wanted to maintain a positive attitude. "I'm going with the glitch theory. The *Cygnus* will turn up."

"And where are we going to put the new arrivals? Do you think they're still coming? It's not like we can ask all those geeks to bunk up together, can we?"

"Tori, let's try the station again? Maybe the *Cygnus* has reappeared."

"See you later then," Doug waved. "I'll lay out the grid line."

"Thank you," Paddy replied, climbing onto his scooter, waiting for Tori to get seated on hers before taking off.

Doug observed them ride off, wondered if the obvious tension between them meant they'd broken up again, if it was the *Cygnus* disappearing—or both. *None of my business*, he reminded himself, but since there were so few couples, Paddy and Tori's relationship definitely stood out.

Pulling out instruments and markers, Doug went to work delineating the compound's new section. Occasionally, he would glance toward the supposedly unmaneuverable ridge looming above him. It definitely reminded him of a wall. While clearly made of rock, there was something metallic about it. There had to be a passageway *through* it somewhere.

Or perhaps a door, he chuckled, then grew serious, hoping the crew aboard the *Cygnus* would turn up, if not the ship.

▓

Initially, the *Hemming's* systems analysts felt confident the *Cygnus* could—and would—be located. Level heads prevailed while searching for glitches. One of the analysts theorized that the *Cygnus's* auto-system had redirected it to land in a different quadrant—perhaps over the ridge. Surface scans hadn't shown any sign of the cargo ship or crew yet, so Paddy and Tori sent teams out to investigate. After several days, they hadn't come up with any sightings of the ship or its four-man crew.

Paddy put in a call to Augustus "Auggie" Deerstalker, the *Hemming's* interim leader.

"Are you still sending the scientists down? Should we prepare for the shuttle's arrival?"

Auggie picked up his mug of coffee, drank a few sips. "Let's give it a few more days. Orbital imagery still hasn't picked up anything, which is strange, but that doesn't mean it won't."

"I'll let my crew know. That's wise," Paddy responded, looking at his old friend through the COM unit. It was clear the man had been up for days, and his usually relaxed, friendly face was haggard.

▓

A few days later, Auggie contacted Paddy. "The advisory board reached a consensus." He paused, rubbed at blurry eyes. "Since all the scheduled personnel but one agreed to take the risk, we're sending the shuttle. They're anxious to get started."

Paddy wanted to say he hoped they wouldn't regret the decision, but refrained. "That's good to hear. What's that old saying about lightning?"

Auggie grimaced. "As Anna would say, 'given half a chance, lightning will strike the same place over and over again,' but you know how she is."

Paddy just nodded, hoping it wasn't true.

The shuttle arrived without incident, and there was a collective sigh of relief. With the new arrivals, their little community now boasted around one-hundred-and-fifty. The people currently planetside were predominantly the advance construction team, and the *Hemming* had hundreds more awaiting placement, some more eager than others to leave the known confines of the orbital city, which housed well over a thousand people, a third, children.

Once the community was established on Kepler-452b, the *Hemming* would maintain a working crew along with the individuals who wouldn't do well groundside or actually preferred life in the orbital city. There would be rotating furloughs as well. Since there were now at least a dozen OSSs in the Kepler-452 and neighboring systems, once the communities were established, there would be opportunities to relocate, share resources, and expertise.

There had already been some talk about one of the other OSSs making off with the *Cygnus*. Auggie had intimated as much during a brief conversation with Paddy, but they were holding off on making contact. "Let's not jump to conclusions," Auggie said.

Fortunately, with a little maneuvering, comfortable housing had been created for the new arrivals. Tori had discovered several modular units set aside for training and guest quarters. They were set for supplies, as in addition to the scientists' gear and personal items, they'd also brought additional stores.

###

Over the next few weeks, the mystery of the missing *Cygnus* continued. Nevertheless, Paddy and Auggie continued to discuss the next shipment of pods.

"We're behind schedule, sir."

"Tell me something I don't know." Auggie's broad face remained serious through the COM screen.

"I heard there's going to be a ceremony for the missing personnel."

"Anna is planning something for tomorrow. Wish you could be aboard. You knew everyone, right?"

"Yes, sir." Paddy's thoughts turned to his friends who were missing and believed dead.

"And stop with the 'sir.' You know how it irritates me." He frowned, seemed to consider saying something else, refrained. "Unless the board tells me otherwise, it appears the *Draco* will be there in a day or two with the next shipment of pods and additional supplies."

Paddy nodded, his thoughts drifting. "That's good to know. I'll get Tori and Doug in the loop."

They signed off, and Paddy just sat still for a few minutes, tears welling up in his eyes. He had so hoped their friends would turn up.

###

A few days later, Paddy received notice that the *Draco* was en route. He joined Tori in the COM center awaiting a more definite ETA when it happened.

The *Draco* was there one moment, then disappeared

from view.

For a prolonged moment, the only sound in the room was the hum of the air circulation and filtration system. Tori broke the tense silence with a forced exhale. Livid, she yelled, "Someone is stealing our ships!"

"Then they must know what's on them," Doug interjected. "It's the most likely scenario since the passenger shuttle arrived safely, so..."

Paddy stared at the visual display, rewound the feed, replayed. "Who was flying that bird? McCormick, right?"

"Yes, and Stanfield. Marty."

Paddy stared at the screen, shaking his head. "How many people did we lose this time?"

Tori looked up, thought for a moment. "Eight or nine, I think. It was a double shipment, a few more construction crew." She paced around the room, kicked one of the stools, toppling it over.

"Calm the Fuck down," Paddy began, swiveling his stool to face her, "I know you're pissed—hell, we're all pissed—but you need to calm the Fuck down. It's not productive. Take five."

Tori stormed out of the COM room, slamming the door behind her.

Doug glanced over at Paddy. "If whoever it is just wants the ships..."

Paddy rested a hand on his friend's shoulder. "Maybe they'll return our people. Let's hope."

\#

With two cargo ships and their respective crew now missing, the *Hemming* was on high alert. After a grueling meeting, Auggie and the advisory board decided to contact the other OSSs in the system.

While initially sympathetic, complete with offering condolences, when pressed again, they denied the accusations. Quite vehemently.

"We have our own manufacturing capabilities, materials, pods under construction. Why would we take yours? We'd ask if we were in a bind."

Not everyone believed them, and further investigation would require time and resources, which they didn't want to expend traveling to the sector's other OSSs.

In private, Paddy and Auggie discussed, then dismissed, the possibility of a fringe group. Aliens? Although there were creatures planetside, they were far from humanoid. For that matter, they'd yet to encounter a humanoid species on any of the Kepler planets.

They were in agreement, however, that this didn't signify they were alone in the quadrant.

Meanwhile, extra security details were posted within, as well as outside, the compound's perimeter. The *Hemming* sent out regular patrol ships as well.

If the thieves had the tech to steal cargo vessels without warning, then they probably had other assets, including the ability to tractor up existing structures. Then again, if they had that kind of tech, wouldn't they have done it already? Perhaps they didn't want to cause any harm, but were in desperate straits?

Then why not just ask for help? A naive thought, Paddy mused, then stood up abruptly, realizing that they, too, might be in dire straits soon. Until they were self-sustaining, housing pods aside, they depended on the food stores and other shipments from the *Hemming*.

"Uh, Paddy?" Tori called out, swiveling away from the monitor.

Preoccupied with scheduling the security detail for the next week, Paddy didn't hear her at first.

"Padrick! You'll want to see this..."

"Hunh?" Paddy turned slightly toward Tori, eyes still glued to his project.

"We've got company."

Paddy extricated himself from the stool. Leaning over Tori's shoulder, he recognized the signature.

"Looks like a shuttle pod from the station, but it's not on the schedule."

He pursed his lips. "Any contact?"

"Negative. It's in range, so perhaps we should hail it first. Be polite and all?"

Paddy threw back his head and laughed, something he hadn't done in weeks since their crew and ships had gone missing. "Go ahead. Perhaps we'll invite them in for tea and biscuits. Keep watching. I'm going to contact The Hulk."

"Will do." Although *The Hulk* was Paddy's pet name for the orbital station, Tori knew he really referred to all six-foot-five and 250 lbs. of their interim leader, Auggie Deerstalker. Living on the station hadn't depleted the man's agility—or stamina —one iota. She often wondered how he would fare on the ground here, and would probably put them all to shame.

Then there was Auggie's wife, the fierce Anna Deerstalker; barely 4'10", she could wrestle her husband to the ground with a glance. Anna was formidable, and it was really her decision as head of the advisory board, not to send the *Lyra* with the third and final shipment.

During a recent communiqué with them, Anna had declared, "We can't risk losing any more of our people—or the habitats and supplies, either. But I have a plan." Apparently, that was her way of announcing she was headed planetside.

"Requesting permission to land," Anna Deerstalker's pilot and personal assistant, Andrade Tellos, announced, pausing after enunciating each syllable. It drove Tori crazy when she did that, but then again, the woman didn't talk much or they'd be there all day waiting for her to finish a thought.

Paddy left the COM room, walked outside to the end of the compound bordering the landing zone. He watched as Andrade made a seamless vertical descent, shielding his eyes from the inevitable spray of dust, sand, and pebbles.

They greeted each other matter-of-factly, and Anna herself led the way into the compound's main meeting area. Paddy was the first to admit, at least to himself, that it was hard to keep up with the woman.

Entering the small conference room, Anna inhaled deeply. "It appears you've still got your manners out in this wasteland."

"Only where you're concerned." He grinned.

"Good answer," she said, pouring a cup of coffee, handing it to her host, the second to Andrade, and the third for herself.

She took a tentative sip, smacked her thin lips with delight. "The good stuff. Not that survivalist shit they pass off as coffee on the station."

"I would say only the best for you, but…"

"Stop while you're ahead. Now," she sat down on a stool, leaning her elbows on the oblong conference table. "What do you think of my plan?"

Paddy sat down across from her. "It just might work. I like the idea of a little bait-and-switch. Besides the ship, what's the bait? Old rusty tools and drilling equipment? Whoever it is might sense a trap with no life signs, though. I'm assuming they're sophisticated enough to detect them. We need someone aboard. I'm volunteering."

Anna shook her head. "Negative. We need you here. We can't afford to lose you."

"Nice of you to say, but seriously, we don't know that they're actually hostile." Paddy reached for the coffee pot, poured another cup of his personal stash. He hoped they'd be able to grow coffee on this planet. Until then, he was glad he bartered for several thousand pounds of the coveted substance along with a few bean roasters.

Anna studied Paddy for a moment. "Some might argue that stealing is a form of attack. If they're so benign," her eyes bored into his, "then why haven't they returned our people? If they have the tech to take our ships, they should have the tech to return our people."

"That makes sense, but we have no clue who—or what—they are. Where their home base is—if anywhere." Paddy took another sip of coffee, set down his cup, wishing there was a window in the room. Just bare walls and more bare walls. He let out an exasperated sigh. "It might still be some natural phenomenon. Something aboard the ship interacting with—"

"I've heard those arguments, and we have people working on it. You're crazy enough to do it," she allowed a smirk to emerge on her still youthful face. "Let me think about it." She took another sip of coffee, set the cup on the table, closed her eyes.

They were all aware of Anna's "thinking about it" practice. Was she just closing her eyes to limit environmental distractions, or was she really contacting some sort of spirit guides as the rumor went? No one knew for sure, and it was one of those off-limits topics with her. Still, it seemed to work, as when her eyes fluttered open, she uttered an emphatic, "Yes."

"Good. Now we have to figure out how I'll communicate with you all once I'm aboard."

"I just hope they're not hostile," was all Andrade said, thankfully, after listening to the rest of the plan.

⸬

After shuttling back to the orbital station with Anna and Andrade, Paddy felt immediately nostalgic about his time aboard *The Hulk*. He'd been planetside for nearly a year now, and had only made a few shuttle trips to the station.

Over the next few days, repairs were made on the *Tigron*, a decommissioned cargo ship. Paddy watched the final touches being completed along with Wolfgang Becker, a young man who had been pestering Anna to go planetside for months. Even though he was anxious to leave, Paddy knew it was risky. The success of the Kepler colonies depended on creating viable communities, which meant permanent structures—and ensuring the colonists' safety to the best of their combined abilities.

There were several questions knocking around Paddy's skull. What else did they possess that might be of value to the thieves—and if they weren't peaceful, or even semi-peaceful humanoids, what did this mean to their continued survival on Kepler-452b? Would they have to join up with one of the other colonies? Was their chance for a better life, a more peaceful life, even possible?

⸬

The night before departure, Paddy stood on the observation deck, looking out at the star clusters. He wanted to be alert for what might occur tomorrow, but felt restless. After twenty minutes or so, he headed back to his temporary quarters and slept like a rock in a storm.

In the morning, he and Wolfgang boarded the *Tigron*. They completed one more systems check before departing for the surface. Despite his incessant pestering to be included, Wolfgang was shaky, his thin face dripping sweat, brown curly hair clinging to his cheeks.

"It's not too late to back out," Paddy offered, hoping he sounded supportive.

"No, no. I'll be fine. Just a bit anxious, as you can well

imagine. There's still a distinct possibility that we'll land unharmed, that our *friends* don't want what we have aboard. Then it's back to square one."

"Well, here we go..." Paddy announced as the cargo bay door slid open and the *Tigron's* systems came online. The ship glided out of the hold, and Paddy could practically feel Anna's eyes boring into the back of his head. He knew she and The Hulk would be glued to the monitors for the duration. *This had to work...*

There were trackers strategically placed in several interior hull compartments and a few containers of old machine parts. Both Wolfgang and Paddy wore subdermal trackers under their left arms that doubled as life-sign monitors.

Eyes glued alternately to the scanners and the view outside the cabin, there were no signs of any other vessels in the vicinity. If all went well, it would take them less than an hour to reach the surface.

Wolfgang continued to sweat, occasionally mopping at his face with a flannel cloth kept tucked in a jacket pocket.

"We'll be on the surface in T-minus..."

And then his jaw dropped as the stars rearranged to form a circular patch of darkness. There was a flash of indigo, followed by midnight blue, then emerald green.

"This is it. Hold onto your seat!"

The *Tigron* entered the strange maw and emerged into a bright, blue-gray sky.

"Where are we?" Wolfgang's large gray eyes widened, a combination of relief and surprise tugging at his face.

Paddy looked through the port window, then eyeballed the scanners. "Looks like we're already landing, but it's not our strip."

"But we were only about ten minutes out! Is there something up with the guidance system?"

Paddy grunted, checked and double-checked his instruments. "Wasn't preprogrammed, if that's what you're asking. Everything looks okay."

The cargo ship landed with a slight thud. In front of them was a lush area of plants and trees. To the right, a waterfall coursed down massive rock slabs and into a large pond, and to the left, a ridge that bore a strange resemblance to the one by their settlement.

"So," Paddy began, "Looks like we may have landed over the ridge."

Wolfgang responded with a puzzled expression. "We couldn't possibly be on Kepler-452b already."

"It certainly appears so. Our system's down—or shut off by our *friends*." Paddy attempted to raise Anna and Auggie, then Tori, to no avail. "I say we sit tight for a few, then suit up. If this is the other side of the ridge Doug is so fixated on…"

"Doug?"

"My buddy, Doug. You'll find him amusing. One of his obsessions is this ridge by our compound. He's curious about what's on the other side. It's difficult to scale and usually interferes with our ground sensors."

Wolfgang paused to look out at the waterfall, mesmerized. "If this really is Kepler-452b and not a hallucination."

Paddy unstrapped his restraints, reached into his provisions' pack for a bottle of water. Wolfgang continued to hold onto his restraints, made a furtive glance out the port window. "I think I just saw something move."

Paddy climbed out of his seat, looked in the direction Wolfgang pointed. "Don't see anything, but that doesn't mean something's not out there."

Wolfgang shuddered, returned to mopping his face.

"This your first time planetside?"

Wolfgang nodded, guzzled his water.

"You'll be fine. Come on, let's go. Maybe it's just a weird guidance glitch after all, and we'll find our missing crew and ships. Bring your gear just in case."

"But what about that tunnel?"

Paddy shrugged, grabbed his gear, relieved there was a manual override for the exits. They clambered out of the *Tigron*, their boots hitting dirt and gravel. Wolfgang checked the oxygen levels, nodded. "These match what I have on record for Kepler-452b."

"I'm keeping my helmet on for the moment. You should do the same."

Wolfgang completed a few more readings. "Temp is good,

too. About 62 degrees."

"Let's head that way," Paddy pointed to a small rise dotted with the grass-like plant the shaggy cow-sheep liked to eat.

"I'm not used to hiking about like you are, especially with this heavy gravity, but would really appreciate some fresh air."

"You and Doug will definitely get along. Let's see what's over the rise. Safety first, man."

It took them about an hour to reach the rise. They paused from time-to-time to scan the area, occasionally glancing behind them. The *Tigron* continued to rest where she landed, thus far unmolested. The incline wasn't as steep as it first appeared from the distance, and only took them a few minutes to scale. There was a long, but smooth, slope ahead, but no sign of their people, no sign of the *Cygnus* or the *Draco,* no sign of any other visitors, alien or otherwise.

"Now *that* is strange." Paddy released the catch on his helmet, slung it over his arm. Wolfgang followed suit, taking several deep breaths of air, an uncharacteristic smile on his face.

Paddy stomped a boot on the ground. It appeared to be packed earth. As he made his way down, there were more patches of stiff grass and a well-delineated trail.

"Hello! Anyone there?" Paddy called out, and Wolfgang grabbed his arm, stopped him from proceeding.

"Are you sure we should broadcast our presence. Maybe we should wait for a few, see if anyone approaches from behind the rocks."

Paddy cocked his head, listened. "If there's someone here, they saw us land. Besides, I don't hear anything other than that waterfall. I'm for taking a look around, but we stay together, got it?" He rested a hand on Wolfgang's shoulder, affected an uncharacteristic stern expression.

"Got it, sir."

There were quite a few boulders strewn about, some formed in clusters as if intentionally arranged.

"Can we sit for a few? This gravity is getting to me." Wolfgang eyed one of the flatter boulders, perched on the edge. "If this is the other side of your ridge, how many days would it take to hike back to your place?"

Paddy reached into his pack for a bottle of water, drank

most of it. "If we are on Kepler-452b, which is an obvious conclusion, and that is our ridge, not sure. We don't have climbing equipment, either, so I don't know how, or if, we can, scale it."

Wolfgang stared pensively at the ground.

"Still glad you volunteered?"

He bent down, picked up a rock. "Look at this."

Paddy turned to look. "Those weird rocks. Strange aren't they? We have them all over the place. I usually give them to Ole. You'll meet him soon, too."

"You always so positive?" Wolfgang asked, then retrieved several more of the rocks, stuffed them in his gear bag. "What does Ole do with them?"

"Just collects them, I think."

"Well, there might be a clue here. Maybe there's a property in the rocks that blocks your scanners."

"Could be, as they're all over the place. One of our new science residents believes it's the ridge blocking our signals. They pulled together a team to work on it. Might be hematite, which would make sense given the volcanoes."

Wolfgang gasped. "Volcanoes? I was told there weren't any active around your compound. Still, these rocks definitely call for further investigation. You'll have to introduce me to this Ole. Maybe we can work together on a project or something. I still haven't decided on a specialty."

Paddy chuckled, said, "Ole's our cheese maker and chef. Not much of a head for science."

Wolfgang frowned. "Cooking is definitely a science. I fancy myself a decent chef. You do know there's chemistry involved—"

"Got it. Let's head back to the ship, see if it's back online. Figure out our next step."

"It can't hurt to do a bit more exploring, can it? Why can't we just take the *Tigron* over that ridge?" Wolfgang paused, his eyes tracking the immense sheath of rock that towered above them.

"It's offline, remember?" Paddy did his best to hide his mounting irritation at the younger man. "Besides, we did try to scale the ridge. Each and every time, the shuttles' systems began to fail. Didn't want to push our luck. We've been planning to take the scooters further out, but mostly, we've been focusing on getting the community up and running. If the *Tigron* does come online again, we may want to just get airborne, scope out the area, avoid the ridge entirely."

Wolfgang pushed off the rock, wobbled a bit until he stood erect. "Did you hear something?"

"Just the wind rolling those pebbles and rocks."

"I just had a thought, Padrick."

"Paddy, please."

"Okay, Paddy, what if we traveled back in time?"

Paddy threw his head back and laughed. "Seriously? You believe that's possible? Like those old Earth SF shows and books?"

"I'll· have you know that those shows and books you appear to disdain inspired generations to travel and colonize space. It's one of the reasons I signed on. While I'm not a quantum physicist, we definitely passed through some kind of portal that not only accelerated our travel time, but apparently took us off-course."

Paddy leaned against one of the pods. "So, you do have a brain. That's good to know. I forget what the specs are, but that ridge may be a few miles wide and extends for miles. Furthermore, *Hemming's* orbital shots have detected crevasses. We don't have the proper gear. We're probably just a few miles off course."

Wolfgang seemed to perk up. "True. Perhaps the ridge has some sort of tractor system?"

"You may have something there, Wolfgang. What if it's an alien-made structure?"

"Makes sense. Please can we check it out before going back to the *Tigron*."

"Splendid," Paddy said, pushing off the boulder's surface. He uncapped his water, checked the level, and only took a few small sips.

"We should probably check to see if that water is potable, too." Wolfgang pointed toward the waterfall-fed stream.

"You read my mind."

"Now who's being ludicrous?" Wolfgang dared a slight smirk.

"I never said—"

"I know you didn't, but the implication was there."

"Sorry. I really am open for suggestions. Here we thought we were going to be abducted by space bandits and now we're planetside and have another problem to solve."

"Then let's check the water and head toward that ridge."

The water met quality controls and was delicious with a slight aftertaste that neither could quite place. They filled their thermoses along with the empties, headed toward the ridge.

Wolfgang took one of the stones out of his bag and worried it in his hand. It felt warm through his gloves, soothing, just like the worry stone he'd accidently left in his quarters.

"Ouch!" he yelled, dropping the stone.

"What happened?"

"It shocked me."

"Static electricity. The way you were rubbing at it, I'm not surprised."

Wolfgang toed it with a boot. "Look! It's glowing!"

"I've never known them to do that. Just a glint now and again when they catch the light. I never got shocked."

"Did you ever handle them much?" He glanced toward the ridge. "Or maybe it's a proximity thing."

Paddy cocked his head to stare at the odd structure looming a few paces ahead. "You know, the more I think about it, and seeing it up close, this ridge can't be completely natural. Let's put our gloves on, see what happens." Paddy pulled his gloves out of his pack, tugged them on. "Let me have one of those rocks."

His hands now gloved, Wolfgang touched the glowing rock. When he didn't receive another jolt, he picked it up between his thumb and forefinger, then reached into his pack for another one, handed it to Paddy.

They each held one of the orb-shaped stones in their palms as they neared the ridge. The rocks' glow increased slightly, fluctuated, and then began to pulse. They stood there for several minutes, curious, expectant.

"Strange and stranger," Paddy whistled. He reached out a hand to lean against the ridge, then pushed off when he felt movement.

There was an odd hiss, and an opening appeared. It took a moment for the door to register in their minds, and when it did, they turned toward each other; with a nod, they took a few deep breaths, stepped across the threshold into a gloomy interior.

A narrow corridor stretched to the left and right, lit with a pale green glow that rose from the smooth floor. They turned around a few times, looked up to discover that the ceiling was about four meters high. "This is amazing," Wolfgang said, his voice further amplified within the space.

"Well, we solved one mystery. It's definitely man-made—or alien-made." He looked down at the orb in his hand, which had ceased glowing. "It seems these rocks aren't exactly rocks. We should probably keep them out. They must be some kind of key."

"Which way should we go?" Wolfgang faced Paddy, his cheeks flushed. "And did you notice the gravity has lessened? Even the air is more breathable." He raised and lowered his arms, pivoted.

"Artificial environment. Clearly." Paddy turned toward the open entryway, lifted his palm, and the door hissed closed.

"Why'd you do that? How will we get out?"

"It's clear these stones activate openings, or at least that one. I seriously doubt, given the size of this place, that it's the only entrance or exit. Let's turn that way." Paddy took the lead, and Wolfgang followed close behind.

They turned left, the floor's green glow extending well ahead. The corridor was several meters wide, the walls blank as far as they could tell. Paddy trailed his right hand along the wall as he walked, occasionally pausing to see if there were any maps or other indicators of where they were. No raised symbols. No signs. Nothing else recognizable as such.

Wolfgang paused for a moment, peered closer at a slight indentation in the otherwise smooth wall. "Hey Paddy, did you notice these grooves? They extend floor to ceiling. Maybe they lead to other rooms."

Paddy took a closer look. "Makes sense. We came in on that side, so if they show where the exits are, we'll probably end up back where we started. This corridor may run the length of the ridge, which is definitely wider than this. Let's check for those grooves on the other side."

Paddy stepped toward the right side of the corridor, raised his palm. Nothing. He searched for grooves, finally found one, reached out his other hand, pressed it against the wall. Another entryway hissed open.

The opening led into another corridor illuminated by the same pale green glow. When they stepped across this threshold, however, they discovered a somewhat spherical room. Taking a step forward, the opening hissed closed behind them.

Eyes wide, Wolfgang approached a bank of equipment that resembled monitors, a dark screen overhead.

Paddy remained silent as he noticed various items, some riddled with alien symbols. "I don't think we should touch anything. Who knows what we might activate."

"Looks like a computer or monitoring device to me."

"Appearances can be deceiving, Wolgang."

"Yeah, but look at this—" He pointed to a palm-sized device that throbbed with green light. "Well, at least we know they like the color green—or perhaps we're just perceiving it as green. Maybe it's in sleep mode?"

"And I repeat: Don't. Touch. Any. Thing."

"Got it," Wolfgang forced out.

The screen came to life above them, revealing multiple views of their compound.

"What the—" Paddy took a step back to watch the activity on the screen.

"Well, it appears whoever's been watching you is also on their way here now."

Paddy jerked toward the direction Wolfgang pointed, heard heavy footsteps. They both watched the wall expectantly.

Three humanoid aliens stepped into the room, their expressions appearing pleasant and devoid of anger or surprise. Somewhat shorter than Paddy and Wolfgang, the aliens made up with girth what they lacked in height. They were quite pale, with wide hairless faces boasting high cheekbones and dark almond eyes. If they had hair, it was probably short and hidden beneath the odd-shaped caps resting on their heads. Dressed in dark-blue clothing that resembled uniforms, Paddy wondered if these individuals were actually aliens or the descendants of the first seed ships that left old Earth.

After a brief pause, one of the aliens offered an amused smile as it glanced at Paddy and Wolfgang's hands, fingers clenched around the rocks. "We see you have finally figured out how to use the orbs."

"You speak English!" Wolfgang exclaimed.

Another one of the aliens nodded, his expression amused.

Paddy swallowed, his throat dry. "We already know you've been watching us," he said, jutting his chin toward the monitor, "but why did you bring us here? Take our people? Our ships?"

The third alien stepped forward. "You also brought yourselves here," then nodded to the first alien to speak.

"I believe some introductions are in order. My name is Fahalit-Asah. This," he gestured to the individual standing next to him, "Malatah." He then pointed to the other alien standing behind them and off to the side, "Nualat. It is, as you originally thought, our command center, and yes, we have been observing the activity in this quadrant. Your people are safe, as are your ships and cargo. We brought you here to—" He turned to Malatah, who interjected, "Outline your predicament."

"Predicament?" Paddy's brows furrowed.

"Yes, predicament. You see, there is an active volcano in the vicinity of your settlement. We are attempting to assist you with relocating."

"But Fahalit-Asah," the name tangling his tongue, and he wondered if the *Asah* was a title. "Why didn't you just contact us? We've been in geosynchronous orbit for over a year. Planetside for—"

"Please do not be angry at our little test. A point of curiosity on our part, and no, to answer your unvoiced questioned, we are not the descendants of your seed ships.

"Please know that we would have interceded earlier if danger were imminent. Since we sent the stones out, several of your people have collected them as if they were mere baubles, I think that's your word for them, but no one has determined how to use them until now."

Paddy pursed his lips, nodded. "Please accept my

apologies. We've been concerned about our people, and yes, our ships as well." He looked from one to another, decided Fahalit-Asah was in charge. "So, with all due respect, where are our people?"

"They are doing well," Fahalit-Asah replied, stepping forward, "and we will take you to them in a moment. We have already been discussing how to relocate your settlement here, and have come up with an effective plan. We understand that your—" He turned to Malatah, who said, "I believe the word you are looking for is *leader*."

"Yes, we realize we need to confer with your *leader*, Deerstalker, as we would like to create positive relations."

"If what you say is true, he will be more than happy to confer with you. In person, most likely."

"That can be arranged. Yes. That will be arranged," Nualat said.

"Isn't this place also in danger from the eruption?" Wolfgang asked.

Fahalit-Asah clasped long, thin fingers to his chest. "We have been safe here for generations. Now, if you will come with us..."

"Auggie isn't going to believe this," Wolfgang muttered under his breath.

Back at the compound, Tori paced back-and-forth in the COM center, clenching and unclenching her fists. She shifted from being pissed off with Paddy, then Anna and Auggie, then back to Paddy. It had been nearly a day since the *Tigron* had disappeared from scanners, so all they—all *she*—could do was wait. Doug looked sick to his stomach, and was probably nursing a hangover. She'd probably had one shot too many the night before as well. Besides, Paddy's disappearance reminded her of how she clearly wasn't over him; that, however, was the least of her worries, as Anna was threatening to return to the surface.

Another hour went by, and then another and another as they waited for a communiqué from Anna or Auggie. Given the *Hemming*'s silence, she could only hope they were in contact with the *Tigron* or were monitoring signals from the tracking devices. Not knowing their status was the worst. It had been a risky—no, a stupid—plan; they should have sent an unmanned cargo ship.

A few more hours went by before Doug called out. "I've got something! Look at this—" He swiveled his chair over so she could see the screen.

"What? Is that the local scanner?"

He shrugged. "Exactly. It's the first signal I've received." He jabbed at the screen. "It looks like three ships are lining up to descend. The south end landing strip."

Tori leaned over, followed Doug's finger as it traced what clearly appeared to be approaching craft. "We need to get out there!"

"I'm coming, too. Grab a few from the security team," he said, briefly taking his eyes off the monitor.

Tori half-walked, half-ran down the hall to the supply center where several men stood guard. "The inventory can wait," she screamed at them. "We have approaching craft."

Without hesitation, the entire guard detail followed her out the exits and into the night. "We're going to the south end of the ridge," she announced, "bring the all-terrain scooters."

⸬

As they neared the landing strip, Tori could see the *Cygnus*, *Draco*, and *Tigron* had already set down. No one was standing by the ships, so she hoped everyone was still aboard.

One of the security teams cautiously approached the *Cygnus*. No one aboard. The same with the *Draco* and the *Tigron*. Where was the crew?

"Check the cargo bays," Tori barked into the COM.

They were all empty.

Tori shook her head. "We're staying put for a few. Let's hope our people are following."

Scrunching up his eyes, Doug looked toward the ridge, then back at the ships. A glint caught his eye, and he returned his gaze to the ridge where an opening shimmered. "What the—Paddy!"

Tori whisked around, then froze in place. There, emerging from an opening in the ridge was a large group of people, Paddy in the lead. Taking up the rear, were three individuals who were definitely not from the *Hemming*.

Paddy was smiling and waving as they approached, and Tori fought the urge to run into his arms. "I brought some company with me," he said with a grin.

Doug whistled, slapped his thigh. "That you did, Paddy. That you did."

After introductions were made, Paddy said, "We need to get Auggie and Anna down here ASAP. Our new friends here are going to help us relocate."

"Relocate? Why?" Tori scrunched up her face, glanced over at the aliens standing quietly by Paddy.

"There's a volcano getting ready to blow. We have a month, tops."

"So all this—" she gestured toward the ships and then the missing crew.

"Was to get our attention."

"Anna will go ballistic..." Tori cringed, trying not to picture the scene.

"Not when she hears everything our friends propose. Besides, we'll break out the good coffee."

Chasing May
Anthony R. Cardno

Guilt strobes Milne's mind in time with the shuttle's warning lights. Alarm claxons hammer his eardrums hard enough he thinks his ears are bleeding.

If his teammates die in this crash, it will be his fault. If the shuttle makes it through re-entry but slams down into their tiny, struggling colony, it will be his own grand-standing that kills his neighbors, his husband, his daughter.

The cabin is bathed in the red light of warning, flaring from deep red to pink and back. The waves of color roil Milne's stomach, already upset from bouncing around the zero-gravity of the cabin. The lack of any other colors adds to his disorientation. He chokes back a bitter rising gorge; his crewmates don't need to add free-floating vomit to their list of distractions.

His seat is much harder to get to than it should be, even with the beating the shuttle is taking. The ceiling and wall handholds he's using to pull himself across the cabin should be closer together. Reaching the next one takes a length of arm he didn't think he possessed, but then the handhold is in his grip and he's that much closer to his seat. But not close enough—he needs to be strapped in before they crash.

Or does he? Dying from being slammed against a bulkhead as they skip across the atmosphere. That would serve him right, wouldn't it?

He risks a glance at the pilots, strapped into the forward seats, facing away from him. In the haze of red, he can make out fingers grazing across consoles, trying to plot a landing vector that will put them down outside the colony. They're not moving fast enough, those fingers. And there don't seem to be enough of them to do what needs to be done. But he can't focus to say for sure.

And he should be able to focus. The warning lights should not be screwing up his vision as bad as they are.

He's in his own seat without knowing how he got there. The shoulder and waist straps dig into him through the extra-

52

vehicular suit he's still wearing. Padding fails to protect him from grating edges; bruises and welts stretch and discolor his skin.

The outlines of his crewmates stutter before him in the flashing lights; the sudden silence of the alarms registers as a different pressure in his ears. The temperature rises as infallible heat shields fail.

The ceiling and walls crumple towards him. He can't move, can't evade. Claustrophobia hunches him into his seat, tightens his chest and throws weight across his eyes.

His pain and fear keen out of him as they plummet towards the planet's surface.

▦

He woke with a scream he only half managed to stifle. Two years since the shuttle crash, two years since Zimmerman died and Milne and Wu survived, Milne's injuries more debilitating than Wu's. Two years of nightmares, some more graphic and divorced from reality than others. They'd decreased in frequency; Milne's subconscious had improved at limiting the outward signs. Most nights, his husband Alek and daughter Renee don't know he's had one unless he tells them.

Occasionally a scream still eked its way out. Tonight, Alek and Renee were nowhere nearby to be disturbed or to soothe him. His family was at home in the colony; Milne and his new survey team a week's drive to the south, the first survey mission to head in this direction.

Milne sat up in his bedroll, looking around to see if he'd disturbed anyone. Each night on this mission, he'd set himself up to sleep as far away from the rest of the team as protocol and safety would allow, just in case he woke up screaming.

Okoreke, the geologist, was the nearest sleeping team member. He snored away, but he was a heavy sleeper. Beyond Okoreke, Milne could see Collinson, the botanist. The gentle rise and fall of her bedroll implied she was still asleep as well. He turned to check on May, the hydrologist. She moved in her bedroll but didn't say anything. So neither did he.

Instead, he looked off in the other direction. Barker, the team's driver and communications specialist, walked their perimeter, his turn on late-night duty. The likelihood was that nothing out here would bother them. Twelve years on the planet, and not a single encounter with another sentient race nor anything in the way of apex predators. Nothing in the kid's posture indicated he'd heard Milne scream. His attention as he walked seemed focused on the same thing that drew Milne's gaze: the lone mesa jutting up from the otherwise flat plains that surround them.

They'd been making their way towards it since first noticing it as a bump on their horizon a few days earlier; Milne estimated another day's drive would get them to it. He laid back, closed his eyes, and settled into a sleep with no further disturbances.

▦

"Thanks for ruining a good night's sleep, Milne."

It was May's turn to ladle out breakfast rations, and Milne's portion got slopped into his plate with extra carelessness. He started to apologize for the disturbance, but she continued to talk right over him. "I mean, hell, it's not like sleeping out here on the ground isn't difficult enough. Why not add screams in the night from your team leader to the mix?"

"Is this the first nightmare you've had since we set out?" Collinson asked, looking up from the tablet she was checking reports on. She lived near Milne and Alek in the colony. She knew how much his night terrors had decreased over the past year.

"Yeah," Milne answered, settling in across from her at the table. "I guess it was bound to happen, but I'm really sorry if it bothered any of you."

"Didn't bother me," Okoreke chimed in.

"An earthquake wouldn't bother you," Collinson teased.

"Are you sure you screamed out loud?" Barker joined them at the table. "I was walking the perimeter, and I didn't hear a thing."

"I had a nightmare, for sure. If May says I woke her up, I must have made at least a little noise."

"A team leader who should still be on disability leave, and his sidekick with hearing problems," May muttered. "We're in great shape. Who the hell thought those assignments up?"

"May, you're being exceedingly unkind," Okoreke interjected. "You know Milne was cleared by medical to lead this mission."

"What I know," May shot back, "Is that the Colony Council caved to pressure from the other qualified military staff's families to add more team leaders into the rotation, and ordered Commander Foley to put Milne back on active duty despite her concerns. So she put him in charge of a mission the Council couldn't care less about."

"Commander Foley has been trying to send a survey mission south since the missions started." Milne didn't have to defend Foley. May was correct that he'd only been returned to active duty because people like his husband and Wu had already led three survey teams apiece in the past two years. "She's said from the beginning that threats could just as easily come from the other side of these plains as from the other side of the mountains. It was the Council that decided to send all the previous missions north."

"Missions that never would have been necessary if you hadn't lost the only satellite linking us to Earth!"

That was the verbal slap Milne had been waiting for.

"We waited ten years, May," Barker jumped in. He'd been a young teenager when their colony ship, the ESS *Poitevin*, had crashed on the planet designated Kepler-1638b, but which they'd come to call Orpheus. "Earth wasn't coming for us whether we maintained contact or not! These missions should have been started a decade earlier!"

"Barker, stand down." Milne was still the mission leader and ranking military official; it was time to remind them of that. May was only saying what he was trying not to think. His insecurity about his recovery warred every day with his need to be useful again, to be on a mission again. "May, I know you're bitter because you wanted another mountain survey, where you might discover our river's source. I know you're unhappy I approved a course change away from the river after we caught sight of the mesa. Regardless of how you feel about the fruitlessness of this mission, we still have a job to do out here, and we're going to do it to the best of our ability. That includes reporting back on anything strange, like this mesa. If you're still unhappy, feel free to add your complaints in writing to the morning report."

"Don't think I won't." Her voice was tight, suppressed anger radiating from her.

"I'll apologize again for disturbing your sleep, and I've already included my nightmare in the official report log. Believe me, I'm as concerned about my PTSD affecting the mission as anyone else. Including my immediate superior."

"You act like the only one who has survived a crash and saw people die around you, Milne. We all survived the *Poitevin's* crash. We've all had trauma. Some of us actually lost loved ones that day, not just co-workers. If you can't handle the residual trauma just because you were part of a second crash, maybe you should retire, raise your adopted daughter, and let your husband do the hard work."

She snatched up her breakfast tray and stalked away.

"She was out of line." Barker stared down at his plate, pushing his food around with a fork.

"No. Better that she got that out of her system. She lost her husband when the *Poitevin* crashed here. I was lucky that I didn't lose Alek. I can't imagine it's been easy for her all this time."

"I lost my mother." Barker shook his head. "My dad misses her every day. But he doesn't blame the folks who didn't lose a spouse. Your daughter lost both of her birth parents."

"But Renee was only two when the *Poitevin* crashed. She barely remembers them. That's different."

"Everyone's story is different. That doesn't give any of us the right to take it out on you. And if you, Wu, and Zimmerman hadn't gone up to at least try to correct the satellite, we'd have lost contact with Earth anyway. And May would probably be holding that against you instead."

"The kid's got a point," Okoreke laughed. "That's one bitter lady. Don't let her get to you. We're doing what we were sent out to do."

"Of course you'd say that," Collinson teased the geologist again. "That mesa is likely to be a geological treasure-trove, unlike anything we've found in the north mountains."

Milne let himself enjoy the light banter Okoreke and Collinson were engaging in while they finished eating. Then it was time to pack up camp and continue toward the mesa that had so captivated their attention the past several days.

The next night, Milne woke from a sound sleep to a sense that something wasn't right.

He could tell from the position of the stars above him that he hadn't overslept; it was still somewhere in the middle of May's watch. He lay on his back staring up, wondering if Alek was awake. His husband had a habit of waking for no reason in the middle of the night and stepping out to stargaze for a few minutes before returning to sleep. But Alek was at home in a comfortable bed and Milne was in a bedroll on hard ground.

He shifted to find a comfortable spot, closing his eyes again. The rhythmic pulsing of the night light around him was enough to lull him back towards sleep.

Rhythmic pulsing?

Milne forced his eyes further open, fought the calming influence of whatever was going on around him. That's what had woken him: the extra light around them, dim and blue and coursing over them in waves. And the air temperature. Distinctly colder than the night previous.

He sat up, listening for sounds of movement from the rest of the team. He heard Okoreke's snore, recognizable and steady. He looked left and right. Barker was still in his bedroll near the vehicle; Collinson was in her bedroll just beyond Okoreke.

May was missing.

Milne fought down the combination of anger and anxiety that rose up his spine. May could be doing a circuit of the perimeter of their small camp, walking to keep herself awake. He forced his breathing to remain regular and focused, listening for the sound of footsteps on the rough scrub of the plain around them.

He heard nothing.

The undulating light continued, but carried no sound of its own. He should have been able to pick out the hydrologist's footsteps if she were walking anywhere nearby.

Definitely something wrong. He unzipped his roll and belly-crawled over to Barker. It took a moment for the young man to wake up. The look of confusion on Barker's face sharpened to attention when Milne held one finger up in front of his own pursed lips. When Barker nodded understanding, Milne leaned down so his mouth was near the younger man's ear.

"May's missing. I'm going to investigate; you wake the others once I'm out of sight, but stay low and stay near the vehicle. And get warmer gear on." Without waiting for agreement, Milne crawled away.

They'd arrived at the mesa's base with just enough daylight left to do a reasonably-paced circuit on foot, and decided to leave actual study and sample collections for the morning.

The waves of light seemed to be coming from only one direction relative to their campsite. Milne hoped he'd find May before he found the source of the light.

He found the source first, about a quarter of the way around the base of the mesa: an opening in the rock's face that hadn't been present when they'd circled the thing in daylight. Okoreke's estimate based on visual evidence was that the mesa was thousands of years old. Milne knew there was no way this cave or tunnel, whatever it was, had suddenly formed in the past few hours. It must have been well camouflaged.

So what had caused the camouflage to fail and reveal it to Milne's team?

Or had it failed at all? The pulsing light was brighter in the entrance than outside, the air a little colder. This was not just light. It was an energy almost tidal in the way it moved. A kind of energy they had not yet encountered on this planet.

His team hadn't felt the unusual cold, nor seen the waves of light, during the day. It must have begun after they'd gone to sleep, but how long after? And why tonight and not any night since they'd first spotted the mesa?

Milne was not the colony's most expert tracker, but his training had included the basics. He searched the ground nearby. The grass was lightly tamped down, and even in the odd light he could make out regulation boot-prints in the loose soil where the grass ended and the cave-tunnel began. Sure enough, May had entered.

She's been on enough survey missions to know the protocols, dammit.

He would have to go with the assumption that the light

and cold had raised her curiosity. There was nothing for it but to investigate. He stood, unclipped his holster, brought his gun up to ready position, and advanced.

It was just large enough for him to walk erect and without touching the walls, but it was a close thing. Milne's claustrophobia crowded in on him. In a few steps he no longer sensed the entrance behind him, not even peripherally. His instincts took over: his face flushed, his lungs tightened. His gun hand tremored. He wanted to run for open air. He wanted to curl up in a ball to give himself more room to breathe. Unable to decide what to do, he froze in place.

Milne's subconscious equated the undulating blue energy with the strobing reds of the shuttle's emergency lighting. The lack of sound in the cave matched too closely the silence in the shuttle once Zimmerman had turned the alarms off to allow them to concentrate.

Milne blinked the sweat out of his eyes. His gun hand trembled. He tightened his grip, bit down on the inside of his mouth. He'd had to fight for two years to be assigned to lead a survey team. This is what Foley had been afraid would happen. He couldn't let the PTSD win. Not this time.

Yes, this was a tight space. Yes, it was an unknown quantity. Anything could cause the rock to shift, cause the walls and ceiling to close in and trap him as the shuttle had.

But it was not as tight as the shuttle. It was not lit in the same way. Milne was not strapped into a seat unable to work towards saving himself and his teammates. He could move. If he could move, he could save himself. If he could save himself, he could save May.

Throughout this mission, he'd circumvented his claustrophobia by staying out of the survey vehicle as much as possible and driving when everyone else needed to be outside of it.

Here inside the mesa, he couldn't make the claustrophobia go away completely. But he could push it to the back of his mind and follow his training. Which compelled him to override his PTSD, find his teammate, and find the source of the new light and sudden cold before it proved to be a danger.

His nervous sweat started to chill his skin, and he wished he'd grabbed a heavier coat before leaving the campsite. The interior of the tunnel was even colder than the decreased temperature outside.

The walls were rough-hewn, small sharp edges protruding, catching on Milne's thin shirt when he leaned too close. Hewn ... not natural. He'd need better light and Okoreke's expertise to confirm the theory, but he suspected this tunnel had been drilled. Who could have done it was a mystery, like the cold, to think about later.

May screamed from somewhere down the tunnel ahead of him.

He moved fast, one carefully placed footstep at a time, to the end of the tunnel.

The walls widened out in the rough, but not perfect, arc of a cave. The ceiling rose to a dome above his head. The light was stronger for no longer being confined to a narrow area, the waves of darker and brighter blue even more obvious as they emanated from a point in the center of the open space and reflected off of the walls. It was a space that could be natural or man-made; it was definitely colder than the tunnel had been.

It took a moment longer for Milne's eyes to adjust to the greater intensity of the light. He maintained his alert, fire-ready posture, sweeping the room from left to right with eyes trained down the sight of his weapon. There was no sound around him, and no further screams from May.

She was in the center of the room. The waves of light were coming from a small structure a few feet in from of her. She didn't have a weapon drawn, but she was in a posture Milne recognized as a fear defense: one leg braced behind the other, shoulders back, arms extended before her and tensed as if to ward off an attack. He couldn't see her face from this angle, but her scream had sounded terrified rather than hurt. Sneaking up on her was likely not a smart move.

"May?" he called out. Not a military bark, but not quite conversational either.

"Milne?"

He was relieved that she responded quickly, that she recognized his voice, but concerned that she didn't quite sound like herself, that she didn't turn to look at him.

"May, what's going on?" He risked a step forward, hoping

proximity would allow her to see him better.

"Milne, I'm stuck. I can't move my feet. And the flames are getting hotter." She rasped the words out like smoke was filling her lungs. She never took her eyes off of the device.

"Flames?" Milne blinked more nerve-sweat out of his eyes. "May, nothing's on fire. You're standing in the middle of a very cold cave."

"Are you blind? The machine burst into flames when I got within five feet of it. I backed up, and my feet got stuck in the mud." Her voice rose as she spoke. Milne looked down; her feet were braced on the same solid rock floor that his were. No mud.

"May, I don't know what you're seeing. But listen to me: what I'm seeing is a solid floor, and a very scared woman staring at a strange machine that shouldn't even be here because we're the only sentient beings on the damned planet." He took a breath, schooled his emotions. If she thought he was losing control, she'd lose what little composure she was maintaining. "Maybe if you key in on my voice, just take a step back towards me…"

"I. Can't. Move!" May's voice quavered. The training all survey team scientists were put through was doing its job: she still had herself under control. But barely.

"Okay. Okay. So let me come to you."

Please don't let those be famous last words. He closed the space between them, sweeping the room with gaze and gun the whole way.

Nothing happened. He was a step behind her, barely out of arm's reach. There was no cloying mud to step into, no flames leaping toward him. That killed the theory that May had stepped into a hologram field of some sort; what she was seeing was specific to her.

The object continued emitting pulses of blue light and the air temperature was even colder. May, at least, had dressed for the cold before letting her curiosity put her in danger. He wondered if the temperature drop were due to the machine pulling moisture from the air to cool itself. That was as likely as anything else—but led to the question of why it needed to be cooled so intensely. What was it doing? The cave may have been natural, but this device was decidedly not. Which begged the issue of how it came to be here.

Questions for another time, he reminded himself.

The more pertinent question was: why was May seeing something he wasn't? He searched his memory for details from her record. Her husband had died in the *Poitevin's* crash, so a fear of flames might be expected. The *Poitevin* had crashed near a large river, and some folks had died stuck in the muddy bank as flaming debris crashed around them. Milne had no idea if May had been on that side of the ship.

Could this device somehow be causing her to hallucinate her greatest fear? And if so, why wasn't he being equally affected? Could the one step further away that he was be making the difference?

He resisted reaching out to touch it. But his eyes took in every detail he could. It was about five feet in height at the tallest point, sitting firm and steady on the cave floor, and roughly four feet across at the widest in either direction. It was metal of some kind, although likely not of a type recognizable on Earth. Right angle edges showed it had been built to this form, even if he couldn't make out seams or connectors. It wasn't a uniform height or width.

There were no buttons, switches, flanges—nothing obvious in terms of a way to turn it "on" or "off," if in fact one was capable of making such a change.

"How did you find this?" Milne asked. He only realized he'd spoken out loud when May answered him.

"Light started pulsing from somewhere around the mesa." Her voice was high-pitched, tense, but she went on. "The temperature dropped at the same time, and dropped fast. Then I heard a sound like a door grinding open. You were all asleep, so I knew it wasn't our vehicle. I decided it couldn't hurt to do a little recon."

"Proper procedure..." Milne started to interrupt, caught himself.

"I know!" May keened, hysteria creeping in. "Now we might both die! Why did you follow me?"

"Because it's my job. Because I won't lose another teammate on my watch. Because you matter, May. I'll get you out of this." He took a pair of deep breaths to steady himself. "What else can you tell me?"

"The light moves the way it would if reflected off of water. That's what drew me in." She let out a sound that was half-laugh, half-cry. "I thought there might be a water source in here."

"But there is no water. So what do we have? A machine that emits visible energy, capable of dropping the ambient air temperature quickly." Milne scanned the cave while he talked. He resisted the urge to explore, unsure of what his absence would do to May's state of mind.

Before the shuttle crash, Milne had not been known for his cautious instincts. His last-ditch effort to bring their errant comms satellite into the shuttle with him had caused Zimm to delay their departure from orbit just long enough for the shuttle to be struck by massive and debilitating debris from the planet's ring. Which then resulted in the crash that killed Zimmerman and rendered one of the colony's last surviving surface-to-orbit shuttles unusable.

His therapist reminded him that the instinct to save the satellite had been about saving their colony, not about his own grandstanding. He knew it, but sometimes didn't believe it.

He felt the same now: help or hindrance, the colony would not rest safe unless they understood this alien device.

He almost smirked at the descriptor, since the humans of the ESS *Poitevin* were the aliens on this previously-uninhabited world. What if the object was the creation of a sentient native species that had died out before the *Poitevin's* crash arrival? What if it was some kind of record of their passing?

Or what if it had been placed here to accomplish something, and having completed its task had gone into dormant mode until their proximity had brought it back online? Their presence may have triggered some defensive mode designed to scare away any self-aware entities as quickly as possible. Perhaps by causing those beings to see their greatest fears.

It would explain the decrease in wildlife they'd noticed over the past several days, since turning away from the river. Although that brought another line of questioning to the fore: if the local wildlife was scared away for miles around, why hadn't they been affected sooner?

Maybe the local animals instinctually knew the area was bad, after who knew how many generations of fear being instilled.

Or maybe this thing used to have a larger radius.

That was a scary thought, given the effect it was having on May. Also scary was the question of what else it could it do if it went fully active.

The only way to know was to bring an investigative team to it. Which couldn't be done with May frozen in fear before it.

He was glad May was so focused on her own fear that she couldn't see his. His shivering had increased to the point where he couldn't ignore it anymore. He'd only last so long in here without warmer clothes, but he couldn't leave her. The nervous tremors in his gun hand traveled up his arm, his heart-rate increasing. His bravado of moments before was quickly falling to the physical manifestation of his trauma. What if he made the wrong decision, lost May as he'd lost Zimmerman?

He had to get her out of here. If she couldn't move on her own, he'd have to carry her out. Before he could rethink the action, he took a step forward.

The light in the cave around him went from undulating shades of blue to flickering deep reds. Alarms brayed suddenly, claxons pummeling his eardrums. He dropped his gun behind him as he brought both hands up to the side of his head to muffle the noise. He squeezed his eyes shut against the red. His body involuntarily shook with the familiarity of the sight and sound.

He forced his eyes open a second later, vision blurry from the tears welling up.

The rock walls of the cave were gone, replaced by the close metal walls of a shuttle cockpit. He was standing behind the forward pilot and co-pilot's seats; the spider-webbed forward window afforded a fractured view of Orpheus before them, looming closer with each second. They would hit the atmosphere soon and the cracks in the window were spreading. They would likely die of explosive decompression or be burned alive long before the shuttle crashed to the planet's surface.

He only hoped Zimmerman or Wu could control the crash

enough to avoid devastating the colony. He wished he could have said goodbye to Alek. And to Renee, who hadn't wanted him to go on this survey mission to begin with.

Wait. Survey mission? No, they were here to repair a damaged satellite.

The seats before him spun in a way shuttle seats were not designed to, and Milne felt vertigo wash over him, the same vertigo he'd experienced for many months after the shuttle crash.

What shuttle crash? This shuttle was crashing. Present tense, not past.

Instead of Zimmerman and Wu, he was faced with his husband and daughter. Alek was glassy-eyed, head lolling a bit too far to the right to be natural, one arm bleeding profusely from a long open gash. Renee's eyes were alert and accusatory, focused on him despite the large piece of jagged metal protruding from the center of her chest.

"You let us down, Daddy," she murmured, flecks of blood flying from her mouth with every syllable. "You lost Earth for us. You killed Zimmerman. You killed us. But I still love you."

"No, baby, you're not really here. You can't be. Where are Zimmerman and—"

"Milne! You're not back in the shuttle!" A voice, disembodied, cut him off. "You're stuck here in the mud with me! In the cave! And the flames are getting closer! Help me!"

May.

May's voice coming from next to him even though he couldn't see her.

But May had not been on the shuttle any more than Alek or Renee had.

Which meant he was trapped in a nightmare again.

The image of his damaged, dead daughter reached out to him. He recoiled from her bloody hand without regard for what might be around him, even though he was now sure she wasn't real.

He hit something hard but yielding as he turned, and tumbled through or perhaps on top of it.

The machine's spell on him broke. The lighting reverted to waves of blue. The alarms ceased. The mangled metal of the shuttle was gone, the rough cave floor returned beneath him. The walls were distant and blurry through his tears.

His breathing continued tight and fast and shallow, his head light from hyperventilation. The after-images of his broken daughter and dead husband flickered like ghosts between Milne and the machine.

Something moved under him. He stifled a scream and rolled to the right, reaching blindly for the gun he'd dropped during the hallucination. His right hand fell on it.

"Don't shoot!" Two voices cried out. May's, from where Milne had been laying before he rolled over. Okoreke's, from the tunnel entrance behind them.

"What the hell is that?" Barker called from behind Okoreke.

"Don't come in!" This time it was Milne and May who shouted at the same time. Milne clambered gracelessly to his feet, still disoriented by the shift from hallucination to reality. May rose to her feet just as awkwardly. She glanced at the machine and took a deliberate, measured step away from it.

"How did you break free from the hallucination?" Milne asked her.

"You backed into me from out of the flames, and sent me sprawling. You must have knocked me out of the sphere of influence." She winced as she wrapped her arms around her torso. The fall had probably sprained something. Then her eyes seemed to clear a little. "What you were saying, it sounded like you were back in the shuttle. But my hallucination involved the machine itself. Why was yours so fully immersive?"

"Not sure. Maybe my nightmares just gave the machine more to work with." He rubbed his arms vigorously, feeling the cold again. "I really should have just grabbed you by the shoulders and pulled you back."

"Coming in here couldn't have been easy for you," May responded. "I'll make sure that's in my report."

Milne recognized that it was as close to a thank-you as he was going to get.

"So what exactly is that thing?" Ororeke asked.

Milne shrugged. "Something important enough to need a hallucinogenic field to protect. We're going to need a bigger expedition just to get close enough to investigate." He was sure of one thing: with this discovery, nothing about life on the planet they called Orpheus would ever be the same. "This is good evidence that someone has been on Orpheus before us. May even still be here; it's a large planet and we spent too long not exploring it, thinking we'd be rescued."

This was the start of a new phase for the colony. As Milne left the cave, preceded by his teammates, he couldn't help but think it was the start of a new phase in his recovery as well.

The future, for Milne, for his family, for all of Orpheus colony, had just gotten a lot more interesting.

Aperture Shudder
Jesse Bosh

I

The first thing he noticed was pain. Pain and darkness. The side of his head ached from his scalp through the back of his skull and into his neck. Placing his hand to his head, he felt hair matted down over the site of the injury with what he assumed was blood.

"What the hell happened?" he asked himself out loud, cringing at the fresh waves of pain that those few spoken words sent through his head. He couldn't remember how he ended up in this state, or anything leading up to this moment. Struggling to recall anything about who he was or how he had landed in these circumstances provided nothing to grasp at but more darkness.

He opened his eyes and an intense burning crashed on his retinas. Slamming his eyes shut and rolling onto his stomach to escape the light, something ground into his hip. He extracted the object and set it on the ground in front of him. Propping himself up on his elbows and cautiously cracking his eyelids, his vision slowly adjusted to reveal a black laser cannon resting on the ground in front of him.

Drawing himself to his knees and scanning his surroundings, he spied a largely featureless alley surrounded on three sides by metallic walls jutting upward, out of sight. The only light source was a single street lamp suspended twenty-five feet in the air. Now that his eyes adjusted, the bulb's dimness surprised him. Closer inspection revealed a trail of blood connecting the place where he'd lain next to a dumpster pushed up against the wall with a large dent in the lid.

A quiet clicking noise behind him caused him to turn suddenly, almost losing his balance. Red light framed a door halfway down the alley. The light brightened as the door opened. With no idea what could be on the other side and the realization that he was in no condition to face even the slightest confrontation, the desire to figure out what was going on had to be abandoned.

Kneeling down and retrieving the laser cannon, he slid it into the waistband of his pants without thought. Trudging toward the alley's opening, a burst of adrenaline shot through him, keeping him upright.

Exiting the alley, he found himself in what looked to have been a residential neighborhood at some point. Several houses in various states of deterioration bordered the abandoned street. On the other side of the street, a blue hover cab sat parked in front of an empty lot. Seeing the glow of a cigarette through the driver's side window, he stumbled toward the cab waving both arms.

The rear door slid open and he entered. Sitting back in the seat as the door closed, the driver's reflection appeared in the rearview mirror. The smoldering cigarette revealed the driver's purple-tinted skin. A hat pulled low masked most of his features, but his lips grinned around the cigarette in a genuine manner.

"Where can I take ya, friend?" the driver asked in a pleasant tone.

"3121 West Nelson Street," he answered, immediately wondering where the answer had come from.

"If you don't mind my saying so, you look like you've had one hell of a night." The driver started the cab and ascended from the street.

"You have no idea." The man reached above his head and pulled the crash bar down in front of him. *For that matter*, he thought, *neither do I.*

II

The hover cab eased into a delicate landing before a brightly lit hotel towering above the other buildings nearby. Vehicles sped by overhead while crowds of people fought through each other on the street to gain access to the buildings which appeared to be casinos.

"Here we are," said the driver, turning around and favoring the man with a friendly smile, "the only safe harbor in this sea of depravity."

"How much do I owe you?" he asked while reaching

into his pants pockets, considering what might happen if he couldn't pay.

"That'll be 30 blue."

He pulled a multi-colored wad of crumpled paper from his pocket and extracted a glossy blue bill from the rest. He held it out to the driver.

"Here's a 50," he said, "the rest is for you."

The driver took the payment and replaced it with a business card. The black card had bold red letters that read: Helo Rave - Transportation.

Helo raised his head causing his bright green eyes to become visible and said, "If you find yourself in need of another ride, just let me know, friend."

"I don't see your number anywhere on this card." The man's brow furrowed.

"Not necessary." Helo laughed. "Just pinch the card where it says transportation."

He squeezed the word "transportation" between his thumb and forefinger. A beacon flashed in the center of the hover cab's dashboard. The hotel's address was visible on the dashboard just below the map. Impressed, the man grinned and slid the card into his pocket while stepping out of the vehicle.

"I think there's a good chance you'll be hearing from me soon, Heelo," said the man turning away.

The passenger window slid open behind him, causing him to turn back toward the car.

"Common mistake," said the driver with a laugh as the cab drifted upward, "it's actually pronounced Hello." With that, the car shot forward, disappearing into the traffic above.

III

The clear double doors of the hotel sank into the floor granting him access. Entering the large lobby, he took in his surroundings. A long counter containing computer stations, but no clerks appeared to serve as the reception desk. To his left, loud music and excited conversation poured out of a colorful bar as several people huddled in groups near the entrance.

Several elevators lined the wall across the lobby and tall

reflective silver letters above them proclaimed the name of the hotel, *The Max*. Walking through the lobby, he overheard frantic discussion coming from the direction of the bar. A slight turn of his head brought several people pointing and talking in elevated tones into view. Wanting to escape this unwanted attention without attracting any more, he continued at the same pace until arriving at the elevators.

Entering one of the elevators, he observed a glass panel next to the door just above waist level. Placing his hand on the glass, he saw it turn green below his fingers as the door shut.

"Floor 319," a monotone female voice announced as the elevator began to speed upward.

The elevator opened a few moments later to a long hallway with dark red carpeting. Stepping out of the elevator brought a strong sense of familiarity, though nothing sparked a particular memory. As he walked down the hall, though, he grew more confident he was in the right place.

Halfway down the hall, he stopped and turned to a door on his right. Somehow, he knew this was where he needed to go. To the door's left, at shoulder height, hung a glass panel like the one in the elevator. He placed his hand on the glass and walked forward, expecting the door to open.

"Damn it!" he growled as his forehead collided with the unopened door.

Leaning against the wall in pain and confusion, he clamped his eyes shut. When the dull throb began to subside, he opened his eyes and found himself looking into the glass panel that had failed to admit him to the room. There was a flash of green light and the door slid open.

"Welcome back, Mr. Lindor," said a monotone female voice from inside the room.

IV

"Lindor," he muttered, entering the room. It sounded right. Only a thin veil seemed to hold back his memories, but it was still too much to see through. Hopefully the room's contents would start to clarify his situation.

Disappointment quickly sank in as he looked around the room which appeared to be untouched by anyone other than possibly a cleaning droid. The dim light displayed a neatly made bed, a large wooden table with four chairs and a desk in the corner. An expansive window in place of a wall on the far side of the room, its curtains open, supplied the room with its only illumination.

"Lights," he said automatically.

The room filled with light exposing two doors in the wall next to the bed. Behind the first door was a bathroom that looked as unused as the rest of the place. Behind the second door was a walk-in closet with several empty hangers lining each side. He started to close the door. Glancing downward, he saw a pile of neatly folded clothes toward the back.

He retrieved the clothes and brought them into the main room. Sitting on the bed, he examined a finely tailored black suit jacket and pants as well as a black shirt and tie. Something protruded from the jacket's unbuttoned pocket.

It was a small white envelope that had been neatly cut open along the top.

He removed a thick piece of paper that appeared to be an invitation and read in large bold letters:

Make The Future What It Used To Be!

Garrison Knight will be the next president of the system despite the countless attempts to corrupt this election. All of the worlds which revolve around K-444 are in need of massive development, and he is the only one with a plan and the means to make this happen. He has already shown his unfaltering commitment with several large scale reformation projects on Kentiferus and Othelio that were entirely self-funded.

There is no choice at all! We must carry on by developing the remaining three planets of our system and this can only become a reality with the election of Garrison Knight. The opposition will say anything to stop us, but we will not be held hostage by their lies!

Show your support for Garrison Knight

as he delivers an important address in the main auditorium of The Royal Watchtower Casino on 11/11/11 at 9:45 sharp. No one will be admitted after 9:30.

Reading the invitation twice, he hoped that something would seem familiar, but nothing sparked his memory. Agitated, he stood and began to walk toward the bathroom. A sharp pain tore through his head halting him mid-step. Shaking uncontrollably and dropping to his knees, both hands clutched at his forehead. His body locked rigidly for an instant and then collapsed in an unconscious heap.

V

He found himself in a large, well-lit room surrounded by so much conversation that it was impossible to distinguish what any one voice said. The voices and body language conveyed the crowd's excitement. A sudden sense of claustrophobia caused him to start pushing through to the front of the crowd. A loud voice projected from above and everyone else in the room fell silent. Loud music filtered into the room and the people simultaneously erupted into enthusiastic applause.

As the cheering slowly faded, a new voice filled the room. The words being spoken were still indistinct, but the voice carried through the crowd with a calm, hypnotic rhythm.

Pushing through the crowd, trying to get to the front, he felt an overwhelming need to see the speaker. No one seemed to notice his presence, but it was becoming increasingly difficult to fight his way through the spectators. He pushed past a large man in a tan coat, staring forward, but lifeless as a wax sculpture. The other faces around him held the same expressionless gaze.

Training his eyes on the audience's focal point, the man speaking came into view. There was nothing striking about his appearance. He wore clothes which clearly displayed wealth, but other than that, the man just looked like anyone else you might see walking down the street with dark hair and light blue skin. His expressions and manner exuded a certain charisma and his voice seemed to cut through Lindor's thoughts before they could form.

Without warning, Lindor grew tired. It wasn't lack of energy, but his mind felt as though it was drifting away towards some unfamiliar waking sleep. His eyes were still open, but his range of vision shrank as if he were slowly sinking into a deep hole. It occurred to him that it might be possible to fight the sensation off, but it seemed so unnecessary. He decided to let himself go.

At that moment, as his vision faded, a silhouette appeared directly in front of him, running toward the stage. The speaker saw the silhouette approaching and backed away from the podium as a look of surprise spread across his features. Several men in black suits converged from both sides of the stage drawing weapons and raising them toward the intruder, but the silhouette now stood directly in front of the speaker and had drawn a weapon of his own. The weapon was raised to point directly into the speaker's face and...

VI

Lindor awoke with his cheek pressed to the floor a few inches away from the base of the bed. He certainly hoped that this would be the last time he would wake up with an excruciating headache, at least for the day. Laying there for a few moments, he tried to make sense of what he had seen.

"I could have stopped it," he said aloud as his eyes widened with recollection. "That's why I'm here."

Slowly gaining his feet and walking to the bathroom, he looked into the mirror and gasped, finding himself in much worse condition than expected.

Blood matted his black hair, causing it to stick up sharply on the side of his head. A trail of dried blood made its way down his forehead and surrounded his left eye which was halfway swollen shut. His right eye was light blue while his barely visible left eye was a bright green. Both were a striking contrast to his dark brown complexion. Ripped and burnt clothing, beyond repair, hung from his frame.

He'd drawn too much attention entering the hotel in this state. He needed to leave as discretely as possible.

VII
Lindor stood in front of the mirror dressed in the black outfit and grinned at his reflection. He hadn't recognized himself in the mirror at first. For all he knew, the person looking back now could have been someone else. His curly hair was neatly combed, the blood had been washed away and the suit fit perfectly, allowing just enough give in the waist to conceal the bulge of the laser cannon.

A knock at the door cut through the room's silence. He had no interest in finding out who it was or what they wanted.

"Mr. Lindor," came a deep voice from behind the door, "please let me in. It's very important that I speak to you."

Lindor stood silently in the same spot and unbuttoned his jacket with one hand making his weapon easily accessible.

"Mr. Lindor," said the voice slightly louder, "I have a code to the room. If you don't open the door, I'm coming in regardless."

"Let's see how that works out for you," he said under his breath, quietly stepping over to the shower. Turning the water back on and shutting the door behind him, he quickly made his way toward the closet in the main room. Stepping into the closet, he pulled the door closed, leaving it open just enough to see the room.

"All right." The voice grew irritated. "Have it your way."

Several high pitched beeps sounded on the other side of the door and it slid open, displaying a man whose massive frame blotted out the light from the hall. Entering the room, he looked from side to side and, noticing the shower, strode toward the bathroom. Lindor knew he needed the element of surprise, so he calmly waited and watched for his opportunity.

The man reached for the bathroom door.

Realizing this would be his best chance, Lindor charged out of the closet and lowered his shoulder aiming to strike the man's lower back with all of his force. The large man turned with unexpected speed catching Lindor by the shoulder he had been leading with. Lifting with one hand, he threw him across the room. Lindor collided with the wall and fell to the floor, crumpled in agony and rolled onto his side.

The wall he had just struck lit up with a news broadcast.

An attractive woman in a bright yellow dress spoke and an inset picture showed the man from his vision standing at the podium.

"In less than one hour," said the woman, "Garrison Knight will begin his address which many are already calling history in the making."

Lindor's attention faltered as a large hand gripped him by the back of the neck and lifted him off the floor. Reaching into his jacket, he drew the laser cannon and swung it as hard as possible behind him. Hearing a deep thud and feeling the sharp impact throughout his arm, the hand released and he fell to the floor in a crouch.

The man stood several feet in front of him bleeding freely from his mouth and his nose. Even though blood concealed most of his face, hatred radiated intensely from his eyes.

Lindor didn't dare let himself get caught again.

Moving faster than Lindor could follow, the man hefted the table over his head and threw it. Lindor rolled toward the bed, dodging the table by centimeters. The window shattered behind him and the sounds of the busy city night spilled into the room. Regaining his feet, he flicked the laser cannon's charge switch with his thumb and looked up as the large man rushed toward him. He aimed. Blue light filled the room and a deafening boom reverberated from the walls as he pulled the trigger. The man flew back and landed on the desk in the corner which splintered beneath him.

Lindor stood up, keeping the laser cannon trained on his attacker and moved cautiously toward him. The man sat with his back against the wall and his head down. Both hands were pressed against the center of his chest and a thin cloud of smoke rose from the wound concealed beneath. His chest still rose and fell, but slowed with each breath. The man's head slowly rose, revealing the hate-filled expression, though its intensity slowly drained away.

"Too late," he said with obvious effort. A scratchy cough followed his words and he leaned over to spit out the blood that filled his mouth.

Coughing again, his head fell backward against the wall. His chest fell one last time and then he sat there motionless.

It was hard to tell through the mask of blood, but Lindor was pretty sure that the man was sneering at him. Turning around, Lindor saw a loud advertisement for a new luxury hovercraft instead of the news anchor. He touched the wall and it fell dark and silent.

An alarm from the hallway filled the void left by the ad. Lindor walked to the door and opened it slightly, peering down the corridor. One of the elevator doors opened and four men holding laser rifles filed out into the hallway and separated, two of them against each side of the hall. They stalked toward Lindor's room with the rifles pointed ahead of them.

Lindor eased the door shut and ran across the room to the window. Looking down revealed that the street was much too far below to consider jumping. Noticing a narrow cement ledge outside his window and looking in both directions, he saw that it ran the length of the building. Cautiously stepping out onto it and pressing his back against the wall, he began to make his way toward the closest corner of the building. Noticing the tips of his shoes protruding over the edge immediately convinced him to just keep his eyes locked forward on the clouds in the sky.

Approaching the corner of the building, he realized it would be difficult to navigate his way around without falling, but as long as he moved slowly and carefully, it could be done.

"He must have gone out this window!" he heard a loud voice exclaim.

"So much for caution." Lindor grimaced and lifted his right foot. He balanced on the front of it with his heel elevated.

"There he is!" came the voice again.

Lindor didn't bother to look. Putting all of his weight on the ball of his right foot and swinging his left leg around the corner of the building, it landed on the continuation of the ledge. Spinning on the ball of his left foot and swinging his right leg around, he maintained his balance perfectly as it landed on the ledge.

Laser fire flew by the corner where he had just been, tearing into the wall and sending gray debris into the air. His pursuers probably wouldn't follow him onto the ledge, but it wouldn't take long for them to realize how easily they could pick him off from one of the windows on this side of the building. Continuing to move and finding another way back in was the only chance for escape.

Taking a quick side step, he realized an instant too late that his foot had come down too far. He struggled to maintain his balance, but had already shifted too much to the right, and losing control, fell off the end of the ledge.

VIII

Lindor clung to a slight indention in the wall with both hands, legs swinging beneath him in what would normally have been a very pleasant breeze. Streams of traffic shot by in every direction below, but the distance was too great to try and attract the attention of one of the drivers. Remembering Helo's card was tucked into his jacket pocket, he realized that it was his only possible escape from this situation. He was barely holding on with both hands, but needed one to grab the card.

Letting go with his right hand, he winced as his left arm took all his weight. Swiftly reaching into his jacket and pulling out the card, he squeezed it where the word transportation was printed and swung his right arm back up to grab ahold of the wall. He couldn't maintain his grip on both the wall and the card, so he released the card and it began to drift downward.

Clamping his feet together, he somehow caught the card between them. Holding on with his fingers, he knew time was running out. Using his legs, he could probably swing back up and get a better grip, but he would drop the card in the process, and without the card, Helo would have no way to find him.

"Man, I hope he's not on a break." Lindor said through gritted teeth, as his fingers slid ever so slightly. Pain in his fingertips turned to numbness that made its way through his hands. Closing his eyes and concentrating completely on his grip, he felt it slide a little more.

Scanning further down the wall for something to grab onto during the inevitable fall, a flood of relief overtook him as a blue hover cab swerved around the corner of the building. Darting just beneath him, the top retracted to reveal the purple-skinned driver wearing his familiar grin.

"Helo!" shouted Lindor as his grip slipped from the wall and he fell into the back seat of the cab.

"Hello to you," said Helo looking back at him knowingly. "It would seem that your night has continued along the same course."

Lindor nodded in agreement looking up, startled by the report of laser fire. Several men in the windows on the level above took aim.

"Well, I suppose there's always time for small talk later." Helo's voice remained calm and reserved. "Now would probably be a good time to hold on."

Lindor grabbed the crash bar and pulled it down in front of him as Helo hit the acceleration, rocketing into the traffic below.

IX

"So," began Helo after a few minutes, "did you have a destination in mind, or was this more of an anywhere but here kind of situation?"

Lindor surprised himself by laughing out loud and once he started, found it difficult to stop.

"I definitely needed to get away from there as quickly as possible," He said with a huge smile. "If it wasn't for you, I'd either be vaporized or a puddle on the street right now."

Pulling the envelope out of his jacket pocket, he tapped it on his palm causing the paper to slide out.

"It looks like I need to head to *The Royal Watchtower Casino*," he said rereading the details on the invitation. "I need to be there by 9:30."

"Well, I'm afraid I don't have very good news for you if you were planning on keeping your distance from your new acquaintances back there." Helo looked into the rearview mirror to make eye contact. "The Royal Watchtower is directly across the street from The Max and it's a little after 9:00 now."

"Of course it is." Lindor grumbled sinking back into the interior of the seat.

"This is a first though," said Helo with a laugh as he spun the wheel, throwing the car into a 180. "I've never had anyone signal me just to drive them across the street."

X

Lindor walked through the massive entryway to the Royal Watchtower, a new transportation card from Helo in his pocket and the invitation clutched in his hand. A sign for the main auditorium directed him down a huge hall and he joined the crowd headed in that direction. Both sides of the vast walkway were draped with posters hanging from ceiling to floor depicting the unmistakable image of the man from his vision.

The crowd began to divide into several lines, drawing closer to the auditorium's entrance. Lindor moved into one of the lines toward the center, looking at the clock above the door. It was 9:26, his timing was perfect, though strictly by luck. The people ahead of him were being asked for their invitations, then receiving a retina scan. Most of them were allowed to enter after this, but a few were led away through another door. Casually watching this, feigning disinterest, he kept moving forward with the line.

"Invitation?" a woman in a light blue suit asked gruffly as he approached the doors.

"Here you go," said Lindor with a friendly smile.

The woman held a silver pen in her hand, using it to scan the invitation, then in one motion, raising it up in front of Lindor's eye where it flashed, scanning that as well. As his eyesight refocused, a bell began ringing above the doors.

"That's it," one of the men checking invitations loudly announced, "No one else is getting in."

"There you go, Mr. Kipnis," said the woman as she handed back his invitation. "I guess you got here just in time."

Gently taking the invitation from her hand and consciously maintaining his smile to hide any reaction to his apparent alias, he walked through the door. Cries of protest could be heard from behind, but they were silenced as the door swung shut.

The immense room seemed to be filled to capacity. Spectators were packed tightly between the door and the stage, radiating an air of anticipation. Lindor could see it would be incredibly difficult to get through them.

Parting the crowd with his shoulder as gently as possible, he began making his way forward. About halfway toward the stage, his progress was halted by people who weren't willing to be moved. Pushing more aggressively would be necessary, but the unwanted attention would surely bring negative consequences. Several raised voices behind him caused him to turn around. A very large woman in a fancy dress, several sizes too small for her, pushed people out of the way and marched toward the front of the auditorium. People tried to stay put, but she swept them aside without effort.

As the woman drifted past him, Lindor stepped into her wake. The crowd being so unexpectedly moved and too stunned to react right away, provided him with a quick path through the remainder of them. The woman positioned herself directly in front of the podium and was now the only thing standing between Lindor and the stage.

Two men in black suits emerged from the side of the stage, walking over to the where the woman stood.

"Ma'am," said one of them in a flat tone, "I'm going to need you to make your way over to the side of the stage, please."

"As soon as Garrison's speech is over," replied the woman in a scratchy baritone, "until that time, I won't be moving."

Without hesitation, both men jumped down to the floor, drawing large modified laser cannons from their jackets. Each grabbed an arm and pressed the muzzles of their weapons into the sides of her lower back.

"There won't be another request for compliance," the man stated calmly. "Start walking, now!"

"Do you have any idea who I am?" growled the woman as she began to walk over to the side of the stage under the men's guidance.

The crowd broke into a round of applause as the woman was led away giving Lindor the opportunity to step into the spot she no longer occupied. Several people crowded into the vacated area leaving him with almost no room to move. Looking from left to right for anyone suspicious, nothing caught his attention.

The lights dimmed and a hush fell over the crowd as they turned forward in quiet excitement. A spotlight illuminated the podium, making it stand out sharply against the dark backdrop. The sound system above the stage began to play an instrumental song at high volume. Seeing people around him raise their hands to their hearts, he did the same.

The song ended and was almost instantly replaced by a voice booming through the speakers.

"Ladies and gentlemen, please welcome the next president of the System. The man who speaks the truth that others are afraid to hear, the only one with the strength to fix these worlds that have been falling apart for so long, the architect of the only future that's worth living in... Garrison Knight!!!"

The man with the light blue skin from Lindor's vision appeared at the side of the stage walking toward the podium with arms raised as the crowd erupted in emphatic applause. Standing behind the podium with an impish grin, he waited for them to quiet down.

"Hello!" he said into the microphone, "I want to thank each and every one of you for being here tonight."

The crowd burst into applause again and Lindor joined them as he continued to scan the area, looking for anything out of place.

Garrison Knight began speaking again, but Lindor was too focused on the people around him to pay attention to the words. Just like his vision, the voice flowing through the audience had a calming hypnotic effect. The sensation of being drawn in and drifting away overtook him as consciousness faded.

Seated at a large table in a dimly lit room, an illuminated wall in front of him displayed an image of several groups of people running across a rocky terrain. They all had one blue eye and one green eye and the same dark complexion as him. Shadows fell from above and they came to a stop looking upwards. Several enormous maintenance vessels descended from the sky, penetrating the ground where the people had been standing and sending bloody debris flying in every direction. Each of the vehicles was emblazoned with a dark red emblem that said *Knight Reformation.*

"I remember," he mumbled as his eyes snapped open.

Reaching in his coat and flipping the switch to charge his laser cannon, Lindor leapt onto the stage landing in front of the podium. The men in black suits ran toward him from either side of the stage, reaching into their coats for their own guns. Lindor drew his weapon, aimed it at the man behind the podium, and pulled the trigger.

Voyage to the Water World
Livia Finucci

Locked in this watertight cell
Supplied with oxygen,
I patiently wait for my trial.
Luck was not with me when I first landed
On this godforsaken water world.

I grow bitter when I think of
The many, many years of toil and deprivation
I went through as I trained to be an astronaut.
In essence, I had to die as a person
To be born as an astronaut.
There was no room in my life for anything else:
No love, no friends, no free time.
In short, mine was a wasted life.

The day I left Earth, five long years ago,
Comes back to haunt me,
And I relive it every day, not able
To get away from it. I feel I'm
Sinking in a quagmire and
I'm about to be devoured by it.
I left Earth with a hopeful heart, bound for
This elusive exoplanet located
So far away from Earth
I thought I would perish
Before I arrived at my destination.

I remember the psychedelic,
Surreal rainbow lights of the
Wormhole that devoured me,
And the prayer I directed
To all the Earth gods of the
Past, and to all the gods that
Still will grace us with their mercy.

But I survived, and landed
On a meager stretch of land
Amidst unending oceans.

When I probed the oceans
With my bubble submarine,
I collected several specimens of
The local sea life, so abundant in
That planet which didn't even
Have a name, only numbers
And letters to tell it apart
From other sea worlds with
Different numbers and letters.

The last thing I remember
Before I woke up in this cell
Was a school of muscular,
Elongated fishes performing
A mad dance around my bubble
With their pliant bodies.

They looked like dolphins,
But had arms instead of fins,
And webbed fingers at the
End of those sinuous arms.
"Murderer, heartless murderer,"
I heard several voices hammering
Into my head, in my brain, as if
My mind no longer belonged to me.
It was so loud that I fainted.

In this cell I learned that
I had sucked one of their young
Up in my sea hoover
While I was probing the ocean.
The dolphin-like creature
Didn't survive, and now
I'm charged with murder.
My crime was unforgivable,

And in this highly developed
Dolphin society I can expect to be
Sentenced to death by asphyxiation.

I intend to explain to them that
My act was unintentional,
But deep down I know
All my rhetoric will prove useless.
They are highly developed,
Highly civilized and highly unforgiving.
Maybe development comes
With a cost, and this cost is
Lack of empathy and piety.
Who am I to judge, having
Come from Earth, where
The daily struggles of human
Beings don't put us in a
Superior position to any other creature.
I only wish I had had more
Time to explore this world
Before my oxygen supply is
Shut off and I plunge into oblivion.

The Silent Giants
Simon Bleaken

For Jonathan Self

The small two-person DV-EXO submersible *Sabrina* cut through the inky darkness of the water, a tiny beacon of light in a vast expanse of gloom. Cuttlesquids and bristled cephalopods swarmed in its lights, iridescent shoals of fish flitted past the viewports, and the long rippling shape of a spiny bifurcated eelwyrm slithered out of sight between the mustard-yellow fronds of a towering column of drift-coral.

"Nothing on sensors," Stellan Hallbjorn scratched his thick beard as he stretched in his seat. "You sure you saw a calf, Scott?"

"I saw it." His companion's grey eyes were fixed on the readings flashing across the screen before him. Scott Balsan was like a tightly coiled spring in his chair, barely holding in the restless enthusiasm and passion that, despite his relatively young age of twenty-seven, had quickly secured him a place amongst the team leaders back at the Manannán Underwater Research Facility. "I *saw* it."

"None of the tagged adults are close by," Stellan frowned.

"Maybe it wandered off, or another pod has entered the area," Scott turned back to the sensors, "but I know what I saw."

Like the dwindling populations of whales back on Earth, the giant Cetaceans of Kepler-62f were marine mammals, but of a size and scale that put even the mighty blue whale of Earth to shame. It was Stellan who had first started calling them *hvalar*, singular *hvalr*, from an Old Norse word, joking: "They're whales Jim, but not as we know them." The name had stuck.

The hvalar commonly reached lengths of 60 to 70 meters, weighing an estimated 380 metric tons. Like the baleen whales on Earth, hvalar fed by filtering plankton through specially adapted plates in their heads as they steered themselves through the depths with six giant flippers, forward motion provided by powerful sweeps of muscular tails. Unlike the whales

87

of Earth, hvalar had no need to breathe air, though the vestigial blow holes on their backs demonstrated that at some time in the past they had. Anything more than that was a guess, and presently there were more questions than answers surrounding these remarkable creatures.

The main puzzle was the mystery of how they had evolved from air-breathing mammals, as Kepler-62f had no land masses. Equally mysterious were the ridges and grooves on the heads of the adults that linked up to unusual clusters of sensory organs not seen on Earth whales. Their purpose still remained unknown, although the common theory was that they likely formed a kind of electrical perception, such as found in sharks. There had also been no recorded whale-song from any of the three pods currently being monitored, as if these incredible ocean giants lived their lives in silence. Their reproductive cycles were also pure conjecture as young calves had only been glimpsed by deep sea cameras, and the adult hvalar had a maddening preference for going down deeper than the submersibles could go, even with the latest developments in ambient pressure technology, often frequenting depths that even camera drones and wet subs couldn't get to without being crushed. The oceans on Kepler-62f were far deeper than those on Earth, the gravitational stresses stronger. There was zero evidence of any kind of predation upon the hvalar from any of the other carnivores on the planet either, which was also extremely unusual.

Scott had been stationed at Manannán for close to seventeen months, joining a team of twenty-five international scientists funded by Acionna Oceanic Research, each studying a different part of the planet. It had taken at least four months of that time to adapt to life on an underwater base, but it was amazing how quickly it had become home. Scott had even turned down leave to stay on the base full time, despite the friendly jeers from colleagues that he needed to get a life. He claimed it was to avoid undergoing the lengthy decompression process each time, even with recent medical advances which shortened the process by half. But the real truth was that this was his life, and he loved the work. The base had become like a second skin to him, and the colleagues around him were as much a family as any he had known. This world was home in a way Earth never had been. Kepler-62f, in the constellation of Lyra, had been colonised forty years previously with the construction of at first two, and then later three, massive floating cities: Ebisu, Paricia and Vellamo. Each had been established by powerful business conglomerates anxious to exploit the ample resources of the planet—abundant fish life, a mineral-rich rock core and sea sponges strong in antibiotic properties. The cities had been steadily growing year upon year, and as they had, so had their energy requirements grown too. It hadn't taken long before wave energy was being harnessed and water purification plants were established to turn salt water into drinkable clear water, half of which was exported back to Earth or out to other colony worlds. Yet, whilst the planet itself was a good 1.4 times larger than the radius of the Earth, having only three main places of human habitation made those cities extremely crowded and uncomfortable, and crime and racial tensions were common there.

Beyond the cities, only small sections of the planet were designated as protected areas for the breeding of the native wildlife, leading to no end of protest from environmentalists that the areas were so small. But the corporations and sponsors favored the smell of money over the concerns of nature, and those cries earned little more than token gestures of compliance. An equal threat to the study and preservation of the native species was the frequent raids by poachers, whom the authorities seemed hard pressed to capture or locate, even with the limited bases from which they could be operating. The disheartening truth was that the poachers were often better equipped than the scientists and research crews, having faster submersibles and better sensors and equipment. That level of backing strongly suggested corporate involvement somewhere down the line. The hvalar themselves, while protected under international law, were sought by poachers for their oils and flesh, just as whales on Earth had been.

"Have you heard? They've resumed attempts at core drilling in the southern hemisphere."

Scott's brow furrowed. "That's right where the razor sharks are breeding."

"They say they're drilling outside of the protected zones and can't help it if the sharks don't stay where they're supposed to."

Scott sighed. "What I wouldn't give for a life without politics and money."

"Without either, we wouldn't be here," Stellan replied grimly. "Unless you can tell our sponsors we don't need them anymore?"

"I think that would get me shipped off-world pretty fast."

Sabrina approached a large expanse of drift-coral. These floating forests, some of them kilometres long, had formed from colonies of coral fused together over time into vast networks, drifting with the ocean currents and rising and falling depending on the temperature and available light levels as the planet cycled through a 290-day orbit around its sun. Whilst these wonders of nature stayed within the protected regions they were safe from plunder, but unfortunately their nomadic character meant that there was no way to keep them from drifting out of the protected zones as they so often did.

There was a blip on the sensors and Scott felt his heart leap. He held his breath as he checked the readings, trying to keep his rational mind ahead of the rising wellspring of excitement. Perspiration broke out across his forehead and he rubbed his sweating palms on his legs.

It was a lone calf, swimming up through the space between a series of tall clusters of yellow-red spiral-fronded coral. Its grey-brown form glided towards them through the plankton-rich waters with majestic sweeps of its powerful tail. It was the most beautiful thing Scott had seen. The calf was a mottled darker brown dorsally but graduating to a ghostly silver grey-white underneath. Like the adult hvalar, the head was broad and ridged, with those same characteristic grooves linking up to the unknown clusters of sensory organs.

"Stellan," he whispered, as though afraid to speak in case he scared it away, "you seeing this?"

"Yeah," Stellan nodded, eyes fixed on the hemispherical front viewport. "I take it all back."

"Prep a tag dart," Scott urged, activating the cameras at the front of the submersible. He attempted to ease *Sabrina* around behind one of the columns of coral, afraid that the calf would flee if it saw the submersible, but to his surprise the calf was increasing speed towards them.

"What's it doing?" Scott whispered, leaning forward in his chair.

"Maybe it thinks we're another calf?" Stellan replied. "We're about the same size."

"Either way, I don't want it hitting us."

As the calf surged towards them, the water around the sub began to ripple and the sensors and lights inside flickered in response, the monitors momentarily blanking out, as though the whole vessel had been struck with an electrical surge.

"What the hell?" Stellan craned his neck to peer through the nearest viewport.

The calf had stopped a little way from them and appeared to be watching closely, as if waiting for something. The water rippled again. The equipment mirrored.

Scott stared at the calf in awe, everything else momentarily forgotten as his human eyes locked onto the grapefruit-sized black eye looking in at him. His heart raced. It was magnificent. This was closer than they had ever been able to get to any of the hvalar, and it was both humbling and breath-taking to be so near to such a stunning creature.

The water rippled a third time, and in the momentary darkness of the equipment blackout Scott cried out as a sharp pain lanced behind his eyes.

Confusion … Loss … Fear…

He fell back in his seat, hands pressed tightly against his temples and his eyes screwed shut. Every nerve ending in his body screamed at him as the pain rippled down through his body, along with an intense feeling of abject fear. It passed in seconds, and when he looked up, wincing and rubbing his forehead, the calf had turned and was heading swiftly away from the drift-coral forest and out into open ocean.

"What was that?" Stellan exclaimed.

"I don't know." Scott exhaled deeply, steadying his trembling fingers. He balled his hands into fists to coax sensation back into them. His limbs had gone strangely numb. The odd sensation passed within seconds, and he quickly turned the submersible about, checking the sensors. All seemed to be operating normally. "Let's follow our new friend."

"You okay? Your nose is bleeding."

Scott wiped the blood away with the back of his hand, grateful that it was only a few drops. "Yeah, I'm fine," he nodded. "I'll check in with medical when I get back. We can't let this one go. Who knows how long it'll be before we get this close to a calf again?"

"It's your call. Just don't go dying on me—the paperwork is hell."

They followed the calf at a discreet distance, relying mostly on *Sabrina's* sensors to track it in the dark waters. Scott cut the lights and engines back to a minimum in an attempt to mask their presence, not wanting to startle the calf or provoke another encounter. With the lights cut, the inky darkness of the water pressed upon them. They became more keenly aware of the vast stretches of unknown ocean depths beneath them. With everything cut back, they finally realized how thin the shell was that kept them safe and afloat.

"Getting something else up ahead," Stellan advised as the screen fed back information. "Looks like another forest of drift-coral, bigger than the last one. Pretty dense."

"Noted." Scott only had eyes for the tiny blip that was the calf. It was still swimming ahead, but with no discernible pattern or destination to its course, adding to his suspicions that it had become separated and lost from its pod. He readied one of the dart tags, and checked the power levels. They had about two and a quarter hours left, and about three hours of air. It would take them about thirty minutes to get back to Manannán base from here, so there was plenty of time.

"Hold on," Stellan cautioned, "I've got something else."

"What is it?"

"Not sure, but its moving in fast, and it's bigger than us."

"Can't be a dragon-shark, they don't come this far south, or hunt at night."

"It's not. It's moving too fast." The unease in Stellan's voice was thick. "It has to be another sub."

"We don't have anyone else out in this region, do we?"

"Just John's team in *Belisama*, and they reported back an

hour ago."

Anxiety iced Scott's veins as he watched the readings dancing on his screen. *Belisama* was the largest submersible they had back at Manannán, but it wasn't that fast.

"Poachers." Scott's mouth instantly dried. A queasy feeling rose up inside him. "They're heading right for the calf."

"I'll contact the base, alert the authorities..."

"No," Scott stopped him. "They won't get out here in time."

"What can we do?"

"Have they picked us up yet? I'm guessing their sensors are better than ours."

"Maybe, maybe not—we're powered right down, and close to a dense cluster of drift-coral. We might just blend in."

"I'm willing to bet they've only got eyes for their target."

Stellan didn't look convinced. "Even so, they're a hell of a lot bigger, and probably packing harpoons. What can we do against that?"

"I don't know." Scott cast his eyes over the array of controls, thinking fast, drumming his fingers impatiently. "But, I'll be damned if I sit here and let them slaughter that calf."

Up ahead the calf appeared to sense the oncoming threat. It turned and plunged into the relative cover provided by the towering maze of fronds and thick stalks of thousand-year old coral growth. The other submersible closed in fast. From their hiding place, Scott could see it was a highly-modified newer model, larger and faster than anything their base had. He felt a sickening disgust at the menacing sight of the two adapted harpoon launchers fitted to the ventral hull. Each one held three monstrous eight-foot long steel harpoons with savagely barbed tips, designed to fire like torpedoes and pierce deeply through the thick hide and blubber of the hvalar, inflicting mortal wounds so the animal could be towed away once dead. The blubber, oil and flesh would be on the black market within hours, the bones turned into luxury items and trophies. With the elephants of Earth extinct and the whales following close behind, the bones and tusks of species on the colony worlds had quickly taken their place, and commanded huge sums of money.

"We learned to go to the stars," Scott scowled angrily as he watched the other submersible slip into the coral forest in pursuit of the calf. "Why the hell didn't we learn anything else?"

"We have cutters on the hydraulic arms," Stellan leaned forward. "Think we could get close enough to use them? We should be able to take out their main sensors easily enough."

Scott scratched his chin thoughtfully. *Sabrina* wouldn't be as fast, but she was smaller and more maneuverable, with four reversible horizontal thrusters at the stern and two rotatables on her flanks. But he could tell just by looking that what the vessel ahead lacked in agility, she more than made up for in speed and power, and those forward-mounted harpoons could tear through *Sabrina's* eighteen-millimeter hull. "It's worth a shot. They're less maneuverable inside the coral than we are."

"Let's do it."

Scott eased *Sabrina* forward and carefully slipped in amongst the maze of coral towers and feathery fronds, hoping the poachers were so engrossed in the prey they were stalking that they failed to notice what sneaked up behind them.

The poacher's vessel had slowed down as it moved through the tall columns, scraping against the fragile coral growths.

"Hit them there," Stellan pointed at one of the larger sensor clusters at the top of the vessel, "that should give us both a chance to get out of here in one piece."

Sweat ran into Scott's eyes as he moved *Sabrina* closer. He blinked to clear to his vision, holding his breath as he carefully avoided the walls of coral closing in on either side of him.

Up close, they were able to get a clearer look at the poacher's vessel, and what they saw was not encouraging. It was outfitted with technology that put much of the older systems on their own vessel to shame.

"Those engines..." Stellan said, "they're not supposed to be here."

The calf suddenly bolted from out of the cover of the coral, making a run for the open ocean, and the poachers eased their vessel up after it. Scott knew the second they cleared the coral, Sabrina had no chance of catching them. He accelerated, powering up all of *Sabrina's* systems, knowing he was lighting up the other vessel's sensors like a flare. For a moment there seemed to be no reaction from the vessel up ahead, but then it increased speed, dragging against the coral.

"They know we're here," Stellan muttered glumly.

Sabrina closed in quickly, able to gain on the larger vessel in the restricted space. Stellan activated the twin hydraulic manipulator arms at the front of the vessel, engaging the cutters, but as he was frantically lining them up with the approaching sensor cluster, the other vehicle burst out into open waters, tearing two whole towers of coral away in the process.

"Shit!" Scott thumped the console.

The calf swam furiously, tail pumping like a piston as it fled, but instead of giving chase, the poachers' vessel swung in a wide arc that would bring it, and those lethal harpoons, bow-to-bow with *Sabrina*.

"Time to go." Stellan triggered the emergency beacon.

"I'm trying," Scott snarled through gritted teeth. *Sabrina* was still hemmed in by columns of drift-coral and his only options were to reverse blindly into the maze or to attempt to flee past their attackers into open water. Neither appealed.

He chose to flee, gunned full power and hoped their greater agility would give them the edge.

"Any word from Manannán?"

"The beacon's active and should be getting through, but comms aren't responding. They're blocking us."

Scott took *Sabrina* into a steep dive, shooting down past the other vessel while it was still swinging around. "Any other ideas?"

"This whole region is filled with drift-coral forests. We can fit where they can't."

"Already heading for the next one," Scott nodded, turning *Sabrina* quickly to port.

"Only problem…"

"Getting there? Yeah, I know."

"I was going to say our age," Stellan's face was grim. "*Sabrina* is close to six years old now. That other vessel is new. Her sensors are likely top of the range."

"They didn't see us before."

"They weren't looking for us then," Stellan reminded

him, watching the aft sensors closely. His face always looked pale in the ship's dim lights, but now he seemed even more so, like a blanched ghost, behind the blinking and flashing panels. "They're in pursuit. Closing fast."

Up ahead he could just make out the edge of the drift-coral forest. Clouds of shimmering silver fish parted like a curtain as they raced through them towards the welcoming sanctuary of the maze of coral towers.

Scott allowed a faint smile to cross his face. "We're almost th..."

Icy water burst into the vessel in a freezing spray as a viciously barbed harpoon tip pierced the hull and jutted a foot inside. Soaked and freezing, Stellan scrambled from his chair and hit the emergency beacon before snatching up two breather-masks from an overhead shelf. Scott blinked salt water from his eyes as he fumbled to activate the auto-seal system on the hull. The harpoon prevented the system from functioning properly, and he only succeeded in slowing the water, not stopping it.

A second harpoon plunged into them. The power flickered then died. Pale emergency lighting took its place.

"They hit the batteries!" Scott cursed, thumping the dead screen before him. The engines waned to silence. *Sabrina* was now drifting forward on inertia, and moments from sinking.

"Here!" Stellan tossed him a wet suit, diving fins and a breather mask. They scrambled out of their sodden clothes, each struggling to get suited up as the cramped space rapidly filled with icy water. They helped each other connect up the twin cylinders of compressed oxygen-enriched air mix on their backs.

"It's quiet out there, now," Scott noted. The water was just above their knees. "Maybe they've gone?"

"I doubt it. Probably waiting to see if we're dead or not. I suspect they'd rather not waste any more harpoons on us if they don't have to."

"What threat are we? We're crippled and sinking. It's not like we can identify them."

There was a look in Stellan's eyes that Scott didn't like. It scared him more than the icy water sloshing around their legs.

"Did you see the engines on that ship?" he asked softly.

"I wasn't looking at them."

"Well, I was. They're the new ones we've been promised in a few months. The G-X7s. Acionna designed them for exclusive use on their facilities' submersibles, and we're supposed to be the first to get them. I know that design."

"So? They got them through the black market. Happens all the time."

"Maybe. Or, maybe they were given them by the same people funding us. I don't think we were supposed to have seen that other sub today. We did go off of our planned route when you saw that calf. I think they're keen to silence any witnesses who might have joined the dots up as I have. That's why I think they're out there, waiting to see if we're dead."

"We'll know for sure soon enough," Scott swallowed nervously. A chill ran through his body that wasn't entirely from the freezing water around them. He clenched his hands into fists in a futile bid to stop them from shaking.

"Remember, keep calm," Stellan reminded him. "Makes your air last longer. We only have about two hours at this depth."

"Yeah, I remember," Scott nodded. They activated the suits' emergency beacons. That dimly flashing yellow beacon brought a small measure of comfort. It promised that help was coming. They just had to survive and make their air last until it did.

"Soon as we get out, head for the coral."

"Okay. Let's get this over with."

They waded to the hatch of the small floodable airlock, and Stellan climbed down first. As he left the ship and slipped out into the icy expanse of the ocean, Scott experienced a sudden moment of disorientation, momentarily losing all sense of direction and all awareness of where the coral forest lay. His senses realigned themselves within seconds—just in time to register something dark shooting through the water at high speed, missing him by inches.

Another harpoon.

It hit Stellan in the stomach and drove him back against the side of *Sabrina*, pinning him to the hull like a butterfly to a display board. It could only have missed the tanks of compressed air on his back by a hair's breadth. Blood blossomed in a murky cloud as Stellan writhed weakly, eyes bulging behind his mask. He pawed ineffectually at the lethal shaft of metal. The impact sent the descending *Sabrina* into a languid spiral as she slipped silently down into the depths.

A spotlight flared to life at the front of the attacking sub, illuminating Scott. He channeled his rage and grief into arms and legs, swimming toward the coral forest. Four men in wet suits and breathers emerged from the poachers' submersible like wasps from a nest, armed with knives and small harpoon guns.

Scott forced as much effort from his limbs as he could manage, but as in a dream, the coral forest seemed no closer no matter how hard he swam.

Pain shot through his leg as a smaller harpoon sliced his thigh, tearing through suit and skin as it passed him. He fought back the urge to panic as adrenaline surged through his body. Gritting his teeth he fought through the pain, forcing his injured leg to keep working. He had no idea how deeply the harpoon had wounded him, or how much blood he might be losing, but there was no time to stop and check. He knew another could follow it at any time.

A shadow flitted between him and the coral forest. He squinted through the visor, trying to make it out. The brutal flat-snouted face of a razor shark loomed from the darkness, followed by the powerful red-brown body with two jagged dorsal fins, thick ridged hide and several rows of glinting teeth like polished onyx. Already it was moving quickly towards him, detecting the electrical impulses of his muscles even as its heightened sense of smell picked up the fresh traces of blood in the water.

The men who had been pursuing him were already returning to the safety of their submersible.

Scott's heart hammered as he swam frantically, desperately looking for shelter in nothing but open water. A blind panic all but overtook him. He expected to feel those powerful teeth closing around his body or legs at any second, crushing him to jelly as they shredded bone and flesh. Despite its poor eyesight, the shark's keen sense of smell was tracking the scent of blood to its source.

He gritted his teeth, trying to coax even more speed from his tiring limbs. The menacing shape of the shark closed in like a living torpedo, homing in on the trail his leg poured into the brine.

And then something colossal surged up through the water, slamming into one of the retreating men with an impact that sent out ripples, sending his body spinning off sideways, shattered limbs flopping lazily like a broken marionette. The displacement wave pushed Scott sideways and he blinked in confusion before he realised.

An adult hvalr.

Scott barely had time to process this before a second massive hvalr burst up from the depths below and rammed the submersible. It crumpled like a crushed steel can, debris and mangled wreckage scattering, air bubbles exploding. The hvalr pushed the twisted wreckage for at least a hundred feet before letting it roll away into the ocean.

The three remaining men looked around in horror as more hvalar charged from below, powerful tails pumping. One of the men was struck by a passing fin, his spine snapping like a dry twig.

The other two men dropped their weapons and grabbed their heads, legs kicking wildly. Their bodies contorted and twisted, as though an electrical current surged through them. Then they went limp, blood seeping out of their facemasks.

The blood…

All too late Scott remembered the shark. In all of the confusion the biggest threat had somehow managed to slip his mind. He turned in a frantic panic, air bubbles clouding his vision. When they cleared he found himself staring straight at the dark shape of the oncoming shark. His heart lurched as the world slipped into an unreal sense of slow motion. It was as if he could see it all in intense detail—from the bubbles rising up around his mask to every wound and scratch on that massive ridged body barrelling towards him, and even the faint sheen across those emotionless unblinking black eyes as the jaws opened revealing three rows of lethal teeth, pointed on the bottom set but triangular and serrated on the upper.

This was death coming for him, and yet he couldn't move.

A horrible paralysis seized his limbs.

But no attack came.

The water around him rippled, like looking through a heat distortion on a desert horizon. Even as the shark drew closer, the mysterious effect seemed to grow more intense. Waves of pressure buffeted his body. From out of the corner of his eye he saw movement. The giant form of an adult hvalr approached, ocean rippling before it, like a boat's wake in reverse. The strange distortion surrounded the shark in a churning, frothing cloud—and the razor shark veered suddenly away, passing so close to Scott that he felt the tip of the pectoral fin brush by his arm as it disappeared off into the ocean.

Safe...

It flooded his mind, not as a word or a thought, but more of a feeling of protection and shelter, bringing with it a sense of deep calm and reassurance. Blinking in surprise, he turned, seeing the massive head of the hvalr just twenty feet away. The rest of the pod swam through the water behind it, surrounding Scott in a wide circle. But still that feeling of serenity filled him. His breathing slowed and his pulse settled.

He should have been terrified. He had just watched them destroy an entire submersible full of men, and a single one of them could easily crush his whole body. But a harmony of voices echoed through his head now, singing a song more haunting and beautiful than anything he had heard before.

He saw drying oceans on a distant world bathed in the harsh red glare of a dying sun which was ballooning to a red giant and swallowing up the worlds in its orbit one by one. He felt the abject panic and fear of the hvalar, clinging desperately to life as their territories dried up, and the shrinking oceans became devoid of plankton.

Then ships came, hundreds of them, beautiful shimmering masses that looked more like clouds of undulating gases than solid matter, descending gracefully over the oceans. Gleaming glassy tendrils descended silently to the surface, and then whole sections of the ocean lifted up and were carried inside the shining vessels. It was the same over the landmasses, whole nests and swathes of forest and land lifted up as the vessels carried the hvalar and countless other life forms away to new homes.

And as those gleaming vessels departed, he heard the silent song of the hvalar, broadcast through those same sensory organs that eluded understanding, a song of gratitude and thanks directed into the minds of the beings carrying them to safety.

And now, another voice, smaller, softer. This one sang alone. In this memory, Scott found himself looking in through a round porthole window and seeing his own face staring back in wonder. Then the song changed to the terror of being chased through the coral by new minds, these ones filled with greed and cruelty, a desire to harm and kill. Scott felt those emotions running through him as though they were his own, and his heartbeat and breathing quickened and a sick terror filled him. It was followed, mercifully, with the relief of escape and freedom as two minds filled with concern fought to stop the others, and finally celebration as the pod answered his frantic calling and found him again.

Scott looked around and was not surprised to see the calf there, reunited with his pod, watching Scott with those gentle black eyes. The waves of gratitude he felt emanating from that being were overwhelming in their intensity. Every fiber in him crackled. His head spun. Pain spiked behind his eyes as though his skull were cracking in two. He turned, trying to swim away, but suddenly everything shifted, dizzying him. Up became down and left became right, and he flailed wildly before everything became too much, and he blacked out.

He opened his eyes to the soft play of light filtering down through the sparkling waters. Dawn had come, and while the light of the sun was fainter and redder than Earth's, it was no less beautiful as it danced through the waves.

He was floating alone, the breather still covering his nose and mouth, and for a moment he felt like a child in the womb, senses slowly awakening to the world beyond. He wondered how far he had drifted with the current, but on a planet like Kepler-62f there was little to navigate by. His emergency beacon was still transmitting, and he had a good half hour or so of oxygen left. The wound on his leg still throbbed painfully, but a quick check revealed it to be superficial.

And then he remembered Stellan, still pinned against the

cold wreck of *Sabrina*, spiralling slowly down into that crushing darkness, and the tranquillity of the moment shattered. Grief broke through the wonder and overtook. He flailed uselessly at the water, air bubbles escaping to the surface as he howled his pain through the breather and his body shook with anguish and rage.

Something colossal glided underneath his feet. He looked down. Fear transformed to amazement.

The pod was passing beneath him, at least twenty colossal adult hvalar and five young calves. As they raced through the translucent aquamarine waters, his mind filled once more with their silent songs of gratitude, sharing their thoughts and emotions directly with his consciousness in a harmonious chorus.

In that brief moment, as that connection formed between them, he felt something deeper beneath it, a spark of intelligence and awareness greater than anything anyone back at the base had anticipated. Grief transformed to wonder as he watched them moving with amazing speed through the water below.

And then they were silent, diving almost as one back down into the depths, leaving him alone as they disappeared into the great fathoms of darkness far below. He watched the spot where they had gone with wide-eyed wonder, like a man waking up from a dream and reluctant to let it fade away, trying to hold onto a final fragment of the experience.

It was the sound of a submersible approaching from behind him that finally brought him back to the world and made him look around. It was the *Belisama*. Relieved faces watched from inside the front viewport as he swam for the floodable airlock.

Before climbing inside, he took one more look at the darkness below him. Somewhere down there were creatures more magnificent than he had previously suspected, with an awareness and intelligence totally unrealized by anybody back at the base. He was no longer sure which species was studying which. While this day had cost them all dearly, he knew his work on Kepler-62f had only just begun. As he climbed aboard, he did so with fresh wonder and hope within his heart.

Calamari Rodeo
David Lee Summers

"Fish eggs."

"What? You mean like caviar?" asked the captain.

"No, I mean fish eggs in cryogenic containers," reported Nicole Lowry over the comm link. "I think this freighter was bound for a hatchery or something."

Ellison Firebrandt, captain of the privateer *Legacy*, paced the bridge of the captured star ship, a wary eye on the merchant crew bound to their seats. After giving the matter some thought, he spoke into his headset. "Take the eggs. I have an idea where we can sell them."

"Very good, sir." With that, Lowry signed off.

Firebrandt's first mate, Roberts, looked up from pilot's console. "I've powered down their main engines."

"What?" The merchant captain struggled against the plastic zip tie holding his hands together behind the chair's back. "Without the engines we have no life support! We'll be dead in a few hours."

"That few hours gives you a fighting chance to live." Firebrandt shrugged. "I'm sure you can break those restraints and restart your engines with plenty of time to spare."

"You don't know that!" Sweat beaded on the merchant captain's forehead.

"True enough." Firebrandt took two steps away, then whirled around, drawing a sword from a scabbard at his belt and pressing it against the merchant captain's chest. "The alternative is that I could run you through right now. It would be quite messy and very painful, but it would assure your ... cooperation ... and, I'm sure would convince your crew to be well behaved without further bloodshed." Firebrandt looked up at the others tied to their chairs. "Am I right?" There were fast nods all around. The merchant captain fell silent, but he scowled and a faint twitch of his right cheek indicated his anger at the crew's disloyalty.

Firebrandt sheathed the sword and strode from the bridge,

a flicker of a smile on his lips. Any crew he spared meant points in his favor should he be captured and tried. Any dissent he fomented among those crews meant confused and obfuscated testimony—the perfect recipe for casting a reasonable doubt in a jury's mind.

Firebrandt's crew gathered the merchant crew's side arms and followed him out into the corridor. Once there, Roberts pulled the hatchway closed, then drew his hepler pistol and fired three times, spot welding the door to its frame. The pirates might not want to kill the crew outright, but they didn't want a quick pursuit either.

The captain turned around and directed his crew to help Lowry and her team carry the fish eggs aboard the *Legacy*, whose bow was clamped to the merchant ship's flank.

Roberts stepped up beside the captain. "So, you know someone who'll buy fish eggs?"

"Not off the top of my head, but I have a good idea about an Alliance colony where buyers should be plentiful and we can make a little additional money on the side."

Roberts narrowed his gaze. "What do you have in mind?"

"Have you ever been to the planet Los Mares?"

"No, but I think I see where you're going. Lots of ocean farming there, as I understand."

Firebrandt nodded slowly. "If I'm not mistaken, it's rodeo season."

Roberts stopped in his tracks and shook his head. "How do you have rodeo season on a water planet?"

"It's water rodeo, obviously," said the captain with a shrug. He leaned in close. "How well do you think marine animals would respond to a brain implant like Computer has?" The captain referred to a member of his crew who interfaced directly with the shipboard computer.

Roberts shook his head. "It depends on the animal, but surgery's easy to spot. Too risky if you want to rig a game."

"The animal's a squid."

"They have rodeos with squid?"

"They're big squid."

"How big?"

"Something in the ballpark of ten meters."

Roberts's eyes widened. "Ten meters?"

"They really like the oceans on Los Mares," said the captain.

"I should think so." Roberts cocked an eyebrow.

They fell silent as they continued on through the airlock and aboard their own vessel.

"How much do you need to influence this squid?"

Firebrandt pursed his lips. "Shouldn't need much, just something to keep it from veering too far left or right, or diving too low. Maybe have it lurch one direction or the other just when we want it to."

"A simple nano-cocktail designed to target the brain's motor control regions should do the trick. Nano-chemicals can be injected and they're virtually undetectable. They can remain dormant until they receive an activation signal and then break down on command. With the right mix, Computer should be able to tap into the squid's vision centers and steer it from aboard the ship."

"Steer a squid?" Suki Mori, the ship's tech officer, stood before them with her hands on her hips. "What are you up to now?"

"Just planning a little seaside getaway." The captain flashed a charming smile.

He detected suspicion in the narrowing of her eyes. The fierce pirate's stomach fluttered at the notion of someone he trusted—perhaps even loved—questioning his motives, even in silence.

Half an hour later, Lowry called the *Legacy's* bridge and informed them her team had stowed the cryogenic containers containing the fish eggs. "We were able to jury-rig a power supply, so they should be good as long as you need."

"Excellent." The captain retrieved a pipe from his trousers' pocket and lit it. "Set course for Los Mares, Mr. el-Din."

"Yes, sir!" called the tall helmsman, who stood at the upright wheel console in the center of the bridge.

Legacy's grappling claws squealed and scraped as they disengaged from the merchant ship's flank. Thrusters fired and the ship turned. The captain contemplated the data in the holographic tank at the front of the bridge. "How long until we reach the jump point for Los Mares?"

"One hour, twelve minutes present speed," reported Computer from his station at the side of the bridge. The pale man sat at a console but stared forward, oblivious to all around him.

"Any sign of pursuit from the freighter?"

"Negative," reported Roberts as he sat back in his seat and smiled. "So tell me more about this rodeo."

Firebrandt took a puff from his pipe as he considered where to begin. "Los Mares was colonized a few hundred years ago by South Americans. One of the sports they brought with them was Chilean rodeo. They adapted the sport to the animals they had. In Chile, they used cows. On Los Mares, it's squid. Search the nets, I'm sure you can find a holo."

Roberts searched the galactic network. A moment later, a hologram of a tube-like aquarium replaced the star field at the front of the bridge. Outside the aquarium's glass walls, eerily silent crowds cheered, waved, and held up banners. Near one end of the tube, two people wearing scuba gear, straddled sleek sea scooters. A round door opened in the wall and out shot a twelve-meter long squid, tentacles flailing behind. The two people in scuba gear shot after it, and forced it to follow the tube's outer wall.

Firebrandt removed the pipe from his mouth. "Each of the scooters is called a Nautilus," he said. "The squid must follow the outer wall until the end of the course, otherwise they get no points." Low-powered lasers glimmered through the water indicating boundary lines.

Suki stood up from her station near the back of the bridge and approached Firebrandt.

He continued his explanation. "They have to drive the squid through a ring at the end of the course. Their goal is to get the squid to touch the ring with some part of its body. If the squid shoots through without touching, they get no points because they didn't control it. They want the squid to touch the ring as far back on its body as possible. If just the tip of its longest tentacle touches, that's the highest score."

Roberts sat back and rubbed the top of his bald head. "That's why you want to control the squid. You want Computer to keep it against the wall and jerk at the last possible moment so you can get a high score."

"So, can you do it?" asked the captain.

Roberts looked to Computer. The pale man's eyes darted back and forth. "Yes, the creatures have a suitably simple nervous system. I can compute a mixture of nano-chemicals which will allow me to control the creature's movements."

The captain felt Suki's hand grasp his shoulder. He looked up. In the hologram, the men had lost control of the squid. It stopped, reared back and knocked one of the men from his scooter. Then it darted forward and caught the other in its tentacles, whipping him from side to side. The hologram cut out as the creature brought the hapless diver to its beak-like mouth.

"I'd also like to keep that from happening," said the captain.

"You're crazy," breathed Suki. "Sell the fish eggs and leave the rodeo to the professional wranglers."

"There are two riders," interjected Roberts. "Who'll join you?"

The captain glanced over his shoulder at the helmsman. Kheir el-Din looked from side to side, then tugged on the beads woven into his long beard. "Begging your pardon, captain, but I don't know how to swim."

"You don't need to know how to swim." Firebrandt spoke around the pipe stem. "You just need to know how to pilot a scooter, and you're the best pilot I know."

"What about Mr. Roberts?" asked el-Din.

"We need him to sneak in and feed the squid his nano-cocktail." The captain turned his attention to Roberts. "When's the next rodeo?"

The first mate checked the computer. "Looks like there's an event in five days outside the city of La Serena." His eyes scrolled down the display, then he whistled. "The prize is a million in gold."

Firebrandt looked back at el-Din. "I'll cut you in for a double share if you help."

The helmsman looked dubious, but finally gave a slow nod. "I am a pretty good pilot," he said at last.

"All you have to do is help me corral ten meters of mutated, mean-ass mollusk." The captain grinned around the pipe stem. "Shouldn't be worse than our typical raid."

"I think you're both certifiable lunatics." Suki turned around and stormed off the bridge.

◼

Suki went to the galley and ordered a soothing cup of tea. As she sipped, Nicole Lowry ambled in, retrieved a cup of coffee and dropped down across from her. "You look worried, Miss Suki."

"Have you ever known the captain to engage in risky behavior?"

Lowry smiled. "What? You mean like liberating cargo from crews who don't want their cargo liberated?"

Suki sighed and shook her head. "That's his job. He knows the variables involved, the income he'll get for the resources and effort expended."

Lowry nodded. "So what exactly is bothering you?"

"Ellison wants to ride in some undersea rodeo on Los Mares."

"Los Mares..." Lowry blew on her coffee, then took a sip. "Good place to fence the fish eggs..."

"About the rodeo," snapped Suki.

Lowry laughed, then set her coffee cup aside and leaned forward. "You're absolutely right. The captain knows the variables and thinks about his crew with every raid. He does everything he can to minimize the odds of failure. Has it ever occurred to you that he might just need to try something he's a little less certain of?"

"He is trying to rig the game..."

Lowry laughed and sat back. "That's the captain for you!" She took another sip of coffee, then leaned forward again. "Maybe the captain just wants a chance to play? Perhaps he just wants to try something that doesn't put his crew's life on the line."

"Those squid looked awfully dangerous." Suki folded her arms and looked down at the table.

"No doubt that's why the captain's planning to cheat."

◼

First mate Carter Roberts didn't entirely understand the relationship between Suki and the captain. The captain had rescued her from a drug cartel on the planet Prospero, but she clearly didn't see the crew of the *Legacy* as much of an improvement. Nevertheless, she cared about the captain, which led to her frustration when he took risks she considered needless. The rest of the voyage to Los Mares went smoothly. One of the captain's contacts identified a potential buyer for the fish eggs. Firebrandt negotiated a favorable, though not remarkable deal, and left the details of delivering the eggs and collecting payment to Nicole Lowry.

In the meantime, Roberts piloted one of the *Legacy's* launch boats to the surface of Los Mares. Kheir el-Din watched monitors from the co-pilot's chair. Firebrandt and Suki sat in the back, in stony silence. Juan de Largo, the ship's cook and sometime-doctor, also accompanied them. His medical skills were dubious at best, but he knew his way around a spray hypodermic. Juan recited a limerick he made up on the fly about a squid from Nantucket and the miraculous feats it could perform with its tentacles. Roberts laughed in spite of himself, but the rest of the crew remained mute.

The aquamarine oceans covering the surface of Los Mares calmed Roberts. Most water worlds had no landmasses at all. However, Los Mares had a few small islands around the size of Japan. This proved a boon to human settlers who could use the landmasses for the colony and provided an exciting case study for planetary scientists. He radioed ahead and received clearance to land at La Serena.

The city stood at one end of a long, string-bean like island. As he followed the landing beacon down, the first mate began to suspect he had the wrong coordinates. Grass sprouted through cracks in old concrete. A set of benches sat nearby, shaded by an overhang. Vines crawled up a distant building. The only thing giving Roberts hope was a line of extravagant space yachts at one end of the tarmac.

Roberts landed the boat, then parked it next to the other space vessels. A port official met them, collected their fees and directed them to the marina where the rodeo would be held.

"This rodeo's a pretty big event, isn't it?" asked Roberts, by way of small talk.

The port official eyed them suspiciously. "It's the planetary sport of Los Mares. I worry about outsiders taking too much of an interest in it, though."

"Why's that?" asked Juan.

"I dunno." The official shuffled his feet for a moment, then looked back at the nearby yachts. "Gambling has always been part of the rodeo. I've placed a few bets myself, but I worry about the money going off world."

Kheir el-Din gave the man a consolatory pat, then the group followed the directions to the marina. As they walked, el-Din rifled through the man's wallet. He removed a couple of credit chips and some of the local script. "This should be worth something at least."

"You didn't just rob that man." Suki put her hands on her hips, incensed.

"What can I say?" said el-Din. "We are pirates, after all."

"Legally licensed privateers." Firebrandt held out his hands and el-Din handed him the money. "If you steal on an Alliance world, don't get caught." He folded the money and placed it in his pocket.

Soon, they reached a set of buildings which hugged the coast. The low tide revealed a set of tube-like passageways leading to the underwater stadium some distance from the shore. They soon came to an entryway. Just inside, a sign pointed upstairs to an office. A larger sign indicated the aquarium. It pointed down the hall to a wide set of stairs leading below ground level. Making note of that, the privateers walked upstairs and knocked on the first door they came to.

A woman inside smiled as they entered. "How may I help you?"

"We'd like to sign up as riders in the rodeo," declared the captain.

Roberts thought the woman's smile took on a decidedly shark-like edge. "There are some forms you have to fill out. Do you have your own equipment, or do you need to rent some?"

"We'll need to rent," said Firebrandt.

Roberts pointed to himself and de Largo. "We were wondering if we could see the squid used in the competition ahead of time."

The woman flashed a brief frown then pointed downward.

"Follow the signs to the aquarium. Once there, you'll see more signs directing you to the squid tanks."

Roberts thanked her and turned to leave with Juan de Largo. He hoped the mixed emotions hadn't played across his face. On one hand, he was pleased that the squid were in public tanks. That meant they'd be easy to find and no one would question their presence. On the other hand, it meant getting to the squid and injecting them without being seen might prove a challenge.

Roberts and de Largo walked down the stairs and followed the signs to the aquarium. They pointed to the tubes they'd seen from the surface. People-mover walkways ran along the empty tunnel. Although signs indicated it was prohibited, Roberts and de Largo opted to stroll along the moving walkway to speed their progress.

Soon they reached the aquarium and they followed the signs directing them to the squid tanks. "Dios Mio!" exclaimed de Largo when he saw the tank.

On the way to Los Mares, Roberts read that a typical rodeo involved about half a dozen squid. He and Computer manufactured sufficient nano-chemicals to control about a dozen, just to be safe. What the first mate and cook saw was an enormous tank swarming with large squid, small squid, and every size in between.

"These can't be the squid they use in competition." Roberts tried to imagine corralling the largest of the squid into the rodeo chutes.

"Maybe they keep them in pens around back." The cook pointed to a nearby door.

Roberts shook his head. "Let's go back to the main walkway. I think our best bet is to find the stadium and see where the chutes are."

Ignoring him, the cook walked back and tried the door, which set off an alarm. The first mate swore and ran from the room before a gate fell. He walked quickly away from the tank, but a door opened ahead of him and out stepped two security guards. "Did you come from the squid tanks?"

"Uh, yeah," said Roberts, "but I left because some kids were throwing a ruckus."

The guards stood their ground, not falling for the lie. "Please come with us for questioning."

Roberts sighed and put up his hands. As he did, Juan de Largo emerged from the door behind the security guards. Apparently there had been some kind of internal passageway.

✦

Ellison Firebrandt sat astride a powerful, shiny undersea scooter next to a large, round door. He held a long pole. The tip would deliver a minor electrical jolt to anything it was applied to. Renting the gear proved more expensive than Firebrandt had hoped, but if they won, it would be a worthwhile investment.

On the other side of the tube, Kheir el-Din waited. Firebrandt couldn't read his face because of the scuba gear but his body was rigid, tense. Arrhythmic bubbles rose, indicating the pilot breathed hard already. He moved his pole from hand-to-hand, getting the feel of its weight. Occasionally he cast glances around, trying to get the feel of the space they were in.

Firebrandt followed his gaze. The arena was a large, round tube that traced out an angled, three-dimensional U. The arm ahead traveled more-or-less straight, then turned a corner and dove toward the scoring ring. The pirates simply had to push the squid over against the right-hand wall and keep it there, then push part of its body—hopefully one of the tentacles—into the scoring ring.

Outside the tube, spectators sat in stands, watching through the glass walls. Suki was there somewhere. Her anger baffled him. He hadn't asked her to participate in the sport and the chances he'd die were minimal. Even if he did die, no one would force her back aboard the *Legacy*. She could make a good life on Los Mares if that's what she chose.

A strange, high-pitch keening resonated through the water. It took Firebrandt a moment to realize it was the sound of a bell. The boundary lasers activated and the door opened. Out shot a nine-meter long squid. Firebrandt rotated the throttle on his scooter and bolted after it. A moment later, el-Din followed. The squid remained maddenly in the center of the tank near but not crossing the shimmering, red boundary line. Firebrandt caught up and applied the wand to the animal's head.

It ejected a cloud of ink and shot forward even faster, though it was now closer to the wall. Blinded by the ink, el-Din collided with the wall and ricocheted out of control. The captain couldn't worry about that now. He rotated the throttle and prodded the squid again, this time, further up its fleshy body, closer to one of the diaphanous, feather-like fins. The squid darted ahead and batted at the pirate captain with a pair of its tentacles.

The turbulent wake threatened to topple Firebrandt. As he struggled to regain control, he saw they'd reached the bend and the course began to descend. Below him, el-Din had regained control and shot ahead of the squid. The helmsman applied his wand near the mollusk's pointed mantle. It cooperated and went right against the wall.

Firebrandt dove and followed the squid and el-Din. Although he couldn't hear anything besides the rush of the water around him, he caught sight of people in the seats standing and cheering. He pushed ahead and shoved his wand forward, but he missed the tender flesh he aimed for. The squid slowed and bit the end of his wand, nearly pulling Firebrandt off the scooter. At the last moment, the pirate captain finally let go.

Firebrandt and el-Din followed the squid down. The helmsman did his best to keep pace, but the squid rolled and circled to the bottom of the tank perilously close to the glowing boundary line. Firebrandt dove under el-Din and gave the animal a shove with the scooter's nose. The mollusk cooperated and moved back up to the side, but not without batting at the pirate captain. He lost his balance and tumbled off the scooter, landing on the bottom of the tank and forcing the mouthpiece out in an eruption of bubbles. The scooter continued a short distance forward without him, then began to drift. He recovered the mouthpiece and swam after the scooter.

Almost at the ring, el-Din reached out and gave the squid one last shock. It reacted and contacted the scoring ring with the middle of its body. They scored a total of five points. A good score, though not as good as Firebrandt had hoped. He wondered how hard this would have been if Computer had not been controlling the squid.

Firebrandt caught the scooter and rode through the ring

where he could meet el-Din and get dry land under his feet again.

⊞

Suki Mori cringed and watched most of the spectacle through her fingers. She trembled with both relief and anger as Firebrandt and el-Din climbed out of the tank and took their place next to the other competitors.

"Ah, there you are."

Suki looked up to see Nicole Lowry. The pirate sat down next to her.

"How's it going?" asked Lowry. "Has the captain raced yet?"

"Just finished," said Suki. "There's a new team about to go. They call themselves the Diabolical Duo."

"I hear they're good," said Lowry.

In the raceway, two men in red wet suits with horns on their diving caps straddled sleek water scooters. The bell rang and out shot the squid. The men raced after it, almost instantly pinning the monstrous mollusk against the wall and holding it there for the entire course. They only let up when the squid reached the scoring ring. At which point, the bigger of the duo slammed into a tentacle right at the last moment causing it to hit the ring as it passed through. They scored a perfect ten and a thunderous ovation from the crowd.

"Good thing I bet on them," said Lowry.

"You didn't bet on the captain?" Suki narrowed her gaze.

"Hell no." Lowry smiled and let out a chuckle. "The fish egg negotiations went very smoothly. I even talked the buyers into a little extra money to cover the cost of powering the cryogenic containers during the voyage. When they asked about the captain, I told them he came to watch the rodeo. That's when they told me the Diabolical Duo always wins."

"So, what about the nano-chemicals? Didn't that give the captain and el-Din an advantage?"

Lowry shook her head. "When I got back to the ship, Computer told me that Roberts and de Largo had been compromised. Thanks to some fast thinking on de Largo's part, they managed to inject the chemicals into the guards who captured them. Computer helped them get away, but they figured they better return to the ship. That's why I'm here. I'm your ride. Since I had a little extra money, I went ahead and bet on the sure thing. It's not a lot of money, but it might pay for the captain's equipment rentals."

Suki folded her arms, determined. "I'm going to throttle that man when we get back to the ship."

Lowry laughed and shook her head. "Cool your jets, sweetheart. Let him have this moment."

"What do you mean?" Suki scowled at Lowry.

"Look, it's like we talked about a few days ago. He has to worry about the crew all the time. He has to worry what happens if we get captured. This was a chance for him to play." She pointed to the scoreboard. Firebrandt and el-Din were in third place. "That's not bad for a couple of rank amateurs up against an undoctored monster. He'll get a trophy and have some stories to tell."

Suki took a deep breath and let it out slowly. "I suppose you're right." She shook her head. "I still don't like him taking chances like that."

"Truth be told," said Lowry, "I'm not fond of it either."

Suki looked up and blinked.

"If the squid had eaten the captain, Roberts would have been in command. Idiot couldn't even dope a stupid squid without getting caught."

Suki laughed outright at that.

"That's what I like to see," said Lowry. "Let me buy you a drink and we'll raise a toast to the captain's valiant race."

"Shouldn't we wait for him to join us?"

"Why?" Lowry leaned in close. "It's my money. Let the captain buy his own damned rum!"

Tears for Terra
J.A. Campbell and Rebecca McFarland Kyle

"Water." Beni held up her clear glass and studied the brownish liquid inside with her lavender eyes. Though her skin was brown and her hair had black curls as most of her kindred, she had her great-grandmother's eyes. "We're almost out of water. Even we aquamancers can't fix it anymore. We have to find more."

Sitting across the table from Beni, Minister of the Interior Rosemary Scott—a middle-aged blonde woman clad in a custom suit—frowned. "When your kind came forward years ago, they said they could fix our water problem." She leaned back and squinted slightly, as if she needed glasses. Strange in a world advanced enough to fix most medical issues.

"We did fix it. For a time. However, even magic can only change so much. The atmosphere is destroyed. The water reserves are completely corrupt. What natural ground we have left is parched. There's nothing more we can do. The water is gone. We have to go find more water. There are planets out there with plenty. We've seen them. We have records of them from Kepler, TESS, and other telescopes, and we have the technology to get there."

The woman pursed her lips. "I doubt you'll even be able to get funding for such a venture. What nonsense! Go to another planet to find something we already have?" She gestured to the brown liquid in Beni's glass. "It is adequate for our needs. The reclamation programs are successful. The moon base and Mars colonies are entirely self-sufficient with their water resources. I'm done listening to you aquamancers whine. Just because the water is heavily regulated doesn't mean we're running out, and you people are well paid for your work." She turned her attention to her screen, an obvious and rude dismissal.

Beni expected this outcome.

"Very well." Beni sighed. "Just remember. You forced our hand." Hiding a smile at the woman's alarmed look, she turned smartly and strode out of the Ministry of the Interior's office.

116

When the world's water resources had dwindled to a point where the aquamancers could no longer work in secret to maintain them, they'd come forward and revealed their magical ability with water. Then people had been so concerned about the shortages that they'd hailed the mages as saviors. Unfortunately, they had quickly begun taking water for granted again, and now Earth was in a fine mess. While the Minister was correct and the reclamation programs did work, the water became more polluted every day. Aquamancers could clean the contaminants, but it was getting to the point where even that was difficult. Beni hadn't seen a clear glass of water since she was a child, and she was old enough to be the Minister's great-grandmother.

Another problem, never mentioned outside of House Mataraci, the house of aquamancers, was that her people were losing their ability to have children. It was as if the poor water was affecting them even more than the rest of the populace. A generation at most, and Earth would no longer be able to rely on her mages to provide even the poorest quality water, and this would not do.

It was time to go public. They hadn't wanted to do it. Mishandled, they could be branded traitors, but handled properly it might just provide the funding needed to send an expedition. The most experienced aquamancers had already picked out a handful of likely planets. She just hoped they could receive funding and mount the mission in time to save Earth. And her people.

⸭

"I can't believe we pulled this off," Jody whispered while the cameras flashed. Like Beni, she had dark curly hair, but her skin was pale and her eyes a fierce green. Paul Cherry, a middle-aged portly man with blond curls, the head of the Space Program, and Rosemary Scott, Minister of the Interior, smiled and shook hands.

Beni nodded, keeping a smile plastered on her face. For a short, awful time, it had looked as if they would fail, but the public had rallied and Scott had been forced to admit to the public how bad the water crisis was.

Cherry had taken over, and here they were, about to head

to space. Jody was their secret weapon. Their key to a successful mission. She was from House Phoenix, the pyromancers. Jody was good with fire, but she was also good with energy and they thought they'd figured out a way to significantly shorten the trip to their chosen planet.

This, however, was not public knowledge. Only a handful of people outside of the mage community knew that people besides aquamancers existed, and they intended to keep it that way. Cherry knew. That was enough.

They stood with the rest of their team. It wasn't a standard exploration group, by any stretch. Beni and Jody were both listed as aquamancers, and Raphael, a young Hispanic man with an infectious grin, was their lead scientist, but instead of a Space Admin crew, they'd chosen to go with something slightly more unorthodox.

Harris was a rakish black man from the Mars colonies. He captained a mining rig and was more than qualified for a dangerous space mission. He lived dangerous space missions, or so he said. He'd brought with him his best navigator, Chelsey, a trim thoughtful-looking brunette, who would interface with Raphael who was also a navigator. Their engineer was almost a child, and wouldn't have qualified for the mission at all, save that he had produced papers proving he was eighteen.

Jody didn't care as long as Harris's claims that he was a miracle worker were accurate. They'd all undergone extensive training and now they were ready to launch.

She was just glad they didn't have to blast off in a rocket, like days of old. Well … not really.

Scott turned around and gave her a dark look, before turning back to the reporters and promising that they'd all save the world.

⁜

"Are we out of range?" Raphael glanced at Chelsey.

She checked her instruments and nodded. "The only satellites that can get any sort of decent read on us are all controlled."

"Good. All clear, sir," Raphael said to Harris.

Harris nodded. "Beni, would you signal Jody and Stevic that it is time to kick it into high gear?"

"Yes, sir." Beni toggled the com. She'd taken communication duties as part of her role on the ship. She'd needed something to do besides water magic.

Jody and Stevic acknowledged her signal. After a moment she felt Jody's magic build. Her hair stood up like the prequel to a lightning storm.

While they'd be able to accomplish their mission on normal drive speeds, it would take far too long for Beni's people. Jody had been working with the Space Administration to provide boost to their drives. If what they'd practiced on Earth worked, they'd cut their mission time significantly.

"Everyone strap in for acceleration." Beni signaled on the comsystem while securing her restraints.

She got several acknowledgements, and moments later felt herself shoved backward as the ship accelerated again. No one was ready to go public with this new magical ability, especially if it didn't work as hoped. If it did, however, they could return with a tanker ship full of water in a matter of months, instead of decades. Long months, but soon enough to save her people, and Earth.

"It's working," Raphael said. "Sensors indicate we'll reach speed to create our own horizon in an hour. From there it's up to Jody."

What Jody added to the mission was her ability, they hoped, to create their own wormhole. That could boost their speed far beyond normal capabilities, and then build their gateway to a world that hopefully held real water.

If this worked, not only would they save the world, but they would revolutionize space travel as well. Of course, if it didn't, who knew where they'd end up.

They'd spent the long month of acceleration out of the Sol system practicing, on a small scale, the magic needed. Beni would lend Jody power, and together, hopefully they'd make history.

The force of the acceleration eased, and she took a deep breath.

"One hour, folks. One hour and we'll either make history, or be history. Make peace with your Maker. This could be a short trip." Harris released his restraints and stood. "If Jody and Beni get us through to the other side, I'm buying you all a round of the best whiskey when we get back to Earth."

Beni raised her eyebrows. An expensive proposition. Without good water, no one had made even halfway decent whiskey in ages.

"You're on." She grinned.

Harris nodded. "I'll relieve you, so you can prepare." He stood to take her seat and Beni let him.

She headed down to engineering, blessing the team that had developed artificial gravity years back as she walked, instead of floated, down the corridor.

The vessel's living quarters were small, leaving most of the space for the tank of water they'd hopefully be bringing back with them, so it didn't take long for her to reach engineering.

Jody and Stevic looked up when she entered the compartment. Equipment hummed in the background and the lights on the readouts all showed green.

"Ready for this?" Beni asked Jody.

The pyromancer grinned. "As ready as I can be. You?"

She nodded. "All I have to do is be a battery. You have the hard work."

Jody shrugged. "It's not quite rocket science, but I do have a PhD in the subject."

"I studied historical marine biology." Beni laughed. "Not that we have any life or oceans left, but I guess I hoped that one day we'd fix our mistakes."

"Or find new planets to screw up," Stevic interjected.

Beni nodded. "I hope we can avoid that. Even a few tanker ships of water will give us enough to work with for a while."

"What happens if Kepler-69c is inhabited? Stevic crossed his arms.

She hadn't expected him to be such a cynic. "There is no evidence, but, that's why I'm along. Not only can I sense marine life, or so I'm told by older members of my House, but I should be able to call the water up to the ship, so we don't have to contaminate this world with any microorganisms we might be hauling."

"They may not want us to steal their water." Stevic glanced

at a readout, not meeting her eyes.

"As much as I'd finally like to encounter an alien species," Jody said. "I'm hoping we can avoid it this time."

Beni laughed. "Yeah. Let's hope." The thought had crossed her mind, and it worried her. While they'd discovered life on other worlds, it was all bacterial. Nothing advanced. They'd even managed to infect Kepler-438b with Earth microorganisms that had killed off the native bacteria, destroying yet another world. It had been returned to the colonization list now that they'd developed procedures to mitigate future risk.

And of course, Kepler-69c. This world that they knew was covered in liquid—very hot liquid, with its proximity to its sun. Hopefully containing potable water, this world had the highest chance of more advanced life, though the risk was considered minimal because of the temperatures expected at the surface. Well, they'd just have to be careful.

The com light chimed and Stevic answered.

"It's time," Harris's voice came from the speaker.

"Acknowledged."

"Everyone, strap in. Jody, the ship is yours." Harris managed not to sound nervous.

Beni clenched her hands and strapped into one of the acceleration chairs. Jody and Stevic settled in theirs.

"Okay, Battery, let's do this." Jody took a deep breath and shut her eyes.

Beni did the same and pulled on her innate magical ability and linked to several of the charged amulets they'd brought along. Magical energy was scarce in space, especially water energy, but it still existed and she'd practiced drawing on it during their acceleration.

Grasping as much as she could, she fed power to Jody.

Jody had more energy sources available to her. The energy of the stars pulsed even in deep space, and the very ship they rode provided boost. She lent her cool energy to Jody's tempest, and together they built their customized wormhole.

⣿

"We did it..."

Beni cracked her eyes open and immediately snapped them shut as blinding lights flashed in her vision. Groaning, she clutched her head.

"Are you okay?" someone asked. She thought it was Jody.

"I think so." Beni tried opening her eyes again. The lights still flashed, obscuring her vision, but they cleared as the pain receded.

"We may have over-extended ourselves a little."

Beni's vision cleared and she saw they both lay on the floor in the engine compartment. Jody had her arm over her eyes, as if the lights were too bright, and she looked a bit wan. Stevic stared at both of them, as if trying to decide what he should do.

"We're fine, Stevic." Beni rolled onto her side and pushed herself into a sitting position, wondering how she'd gotten from her chair to the floor. Probably Stevic. "Mostly." She fought down nausea. At least on the way home, in theory, they'd have a tank full of water for her to draw energy from. That would help. She hoped.

Then Jody's first words penetrated and she bolted to her feet. Wavering, she caught herself on the wall and let the dizziness pass. "We did it?"

"Yeah. We're right on our mark. We've got a month of decel, but that will give us time to study the readouts." Jody's grin was contagious.

Despite how she felt, Beni couldn't help but smile back. "That's amazing."

"What will be amazing is if we have enough fuel to get home," Stevic grumbled.

"What do you mean?" Jody shot him a concerned look.

"The ship used way more fuel than we'd anticipated in your wormhole. We've still got enough, but only if nothing goes wrong."

"Well, we'll just have to hope nothing does go wrong." Jody frowned.

Beni glanced at the readouts, but didn't bother to double check Stevic. He knew far more about engines than she did. She wondered where the extra fuel had gone.

"Maybe I drew too heavily," Jody said hesitantly. "Maybe that burned the extra."

No one replied. The implications were clear. If that were

true, there was no telling how much fuel they'd burn on the way home, with the added mass of the water. Of course, Beni would be able to draw on the water energy and hopefully augment Jody further. Hopefully.

"I'm going to the bridge," Beni said.

"I'm headed to my bunk." Jody laughed. "If I have enough energy to make it."

Beni knew how she felt, but she wanted to check the instrument readouts before she slept. Curiosity would keep her awake otherwise.

The trip to the bridge seemed to take forever, but finally she made it. Harris took one look at her and gestured to a chair. "Shouldn't you be resting?"

"I wanted to check in first." Gratefully, she sank into the accel chair.

He shook his head. "Well, you two did a great job. Didn't quite believe it. When the ship started falling into nothing, I thought we were done. Don't remember much of the actual transition, but we have loads of data to study later."

Beni thought he looked a little pale, but that was understandable. "What about our target?"

"We have our sensors turned on it. So far no radio transmissions or other indications of life, but we're still far enough out that we don't have much yet. Get some rest. I'll wake you if we have any news."

Yawning, Beni nodded and forced herself out of the chair. It wasn't far to her cabin, and they had plenty of time to gather data.

"Beni, preliminary reports confirm there is water on Kepler-69c." Raphael called, smiling.

Crossing her fingers, she smiled back and headed for bed.

⸫

"Isn't it beautiful?" Beni stared out the viewport to the blue world below. They were in orbit near the terminator between day and night. White clouds swirled in the atmosphere over blue ocean. It would have looked a lot like Earth, had there been any land masses.

Their survey indicated several areas that might be shallow enough to wade in calm albeit hot water, and some masses that looked like sandbars, reefs, and other familiar structures, but none of it rose above sea level. It was too hot for human habitation, but the water remained liquid, and the heat wouldn't bother the ship.

Beni could feel the pure water energy surging around her. It felt like nothing she'd ever experienced before. So clean, so strong. Ulvi Matraci, her great-grandsire, told her of days when water had been so clean you could read a printed page magnified by the water in a wine glass. She'd scarcely believed him.

They'd also discovered evidence of life. Nothing advanced, but fish-like creatures, coral, more complicated life than any they'd yet encountered. They weren't equipped for proper exploration, but they got as much information as they could. Hopefully they'd be back.

Beni could barely contain her excitement. Real water. Real sea creatures. The energy felt so amazing.

"Careful there, Beni." Jody laughed. "You're about to float away."

"It is just so wonderful. I can barely contain myself. I want to soak myself in water and just absorb it." Her voice sounded high-pitched and giggly even to her ears.

"People used to have enough water to bathe in," Jody said a little wistfully. "Maybe we'll be able to do the same someday."

"Maybe. It's too bad the atmosphere is too thin for us to breathe comfortably." Beni sighed. "Not to mention the temperature."

Harris, in his command chair, nodded agreement. "It's just as well, this trip. We don't want to contaminate the world."

"Yeah," Beni breathed. Her job would be to hopefully keep that from happening.

"Okay, we're entering atmosphere in five. Prepare for re-entry burn." Harris clenched his armrests. "Ready for this?"

Beni gulped and nodded. She wasn't, but then she never would be. There hadn't been enough water in her lifetime to attempt what she was going to try now. She'd never had practice. It was a heck of a trial run, bringing thousands of gallons of water up to the ship without contaminating life, or bringing any onboard. She'd have to filter the water and leave organisms behind from a substantial distance. That would be tough.

Sinking down into her chair, she focused on the water below. They'd determined that some areas were heavy in minerals. It wasn't quite salt water, but it was close enough. Other areas were closer to Earth fresh water, and that's what they targeted. The less work she had to do, the more water she'd get in her very short allotted time.

They still burned more fuel than they'd anticipated, and Jody swore it wasn't her influence. Stevic was running every diagnostic he could think of, but so far everything seemed normal.

They still had enough, but they didn't have the reserves they thought they would.

Jody focused on the water she'd targeted and began to gather it. Her ancestors talked about the oceans as if they were alive, a personality to interact with. She didn't get any sense of that from this ocean, but perhaps it was simply because she didn't know what to look for.

Regardless, she gathered water until she could picture it bulging from the surface. Beni focused and used her well-practiced filtration skills to push any impurities out of the column of water.

Real water. Beautiful water. It felt so right, so easy to manipulate. She felt like her effort should be draining her, but she only felt energized.

She heard Harris give the command to hover, and open the sterilized tanks. Beni pulled the water into the tanks until they were full. The process went quickly and she had time to spare when Harris ordered the tanks sealed and directed the ship out of atmosphere.

It had gone so well.

She opened her eyes, cheeks flushed with her success.

"That was almost too easy," Harris muttered as they broke orbit and headed for deep space and their month-long acceleration.

"Are you still having those dreams?" Jody asked.

Beni rubbed at her eyes. She knew they were red and bloodshot from lack of sleep. "Yeah. They're getting worse. I don't understand. We have so much water on board, I should be feeling amazing, but I feel like I'm locked in a box. Dark, alien, sterile, freezing."

"You have been on a spaceship for almost three months. Why don't you try to immerse yourself in the water energy. That helped a little last time."

Sighing, Beni nodded. She couldn't explain. It wasn't the ship that bothered her. She was almost certain of that. Compared to conditions on Earth, the ship was the height of luxury, and it certainly wasn't cold. She liked her companions. and they all had enough alone time, that it couldn't be anything related to them, could it?

Jody's suggestion was a good one. It might help.

Heading back to her cabin, Beni reached out to the water and stopped, eyes going wide. What ... Oh ... shit. She ran back to the bridge.

"We have to turn back!"

Harris and the others turned to stare at her.

"What?"

She panted, as if she'd run a marathon, though it had only been a short sprint. Her sides ached and she felt so short of breath, as if she'd never be able to fill her lungs again.

"We..." She gasped. "We got something alive ... it's terrified ... it's sentient ... we have to go back." Beni collapsed to the floor, tears streaming out of her eyes.

"What do you mean? You filtered the water. The ships sensors confirmed. The water is as pure as we could expect," Raphael said.

"Run the sensors again," she demanded through her sobs. *So dark. So alone. So afraid, and so cold.* "And we have to warm the water. Now!"

"Beni, even if we do have something alive ... we'll never make it home if we don't stick to our course. It's too late to head back. The entire planet depends on us," Harris said. "And we don't have the spare fuel to heat the water."

Her people depended on her. Everyone depended on her, and she'd failed.

Jody knelt by her side. "Can you talk to it?"

"I don't know. Maybe."

"Try," Jody said. "And I'll see what I can manage about

warming up the tank. My powers should suffice."

Blinking away tears, Beni nodded. "I'll try. I'm going to return to my cabin, though." She couldn't face the thought of trying, and failing, in front of everyone, as she'd already failed the mission.

Jody helped her to her feet, and when no one objected, Beni left.

Talk to it? Beni shook with emotion as she made her way back to her cabin. They were nearly to the point where they had to boost one last time for their wormhole. Point of no return. Except they had to return.

Beni considered what would happen to her and the crew. Not to mention Earth.

Sighing, she entered her small cabin and reclined on her bunk.

Hello? She thought, trying to connect with the watery presence she'd sensed.

The sheer panic she'd felt subsided and a hint of what seemed like curiosity colored it. The emotions, though alien, resonated with her and she believed she interpreted them properly. Maybe it was her connection with water that allowed her to understand the other being. Maybe emotions were a universal constant. But why hadn't she sensed it before? She felt the curiosity turn to anger.

Let me out!

I will if I can. Can you survive out of water?

There is no 'out of water.' It seemed confused by the concept, though it didn't seem confused by mental communication.

She also guessed it wouldn't do well if they tried to take it out of the tank.

You're on a ship. We needed water.

Water is plenty. Why did you take me? Why do you freeze me?

It did have a sense of self. Beni grinned despite the situation. *We didn't know you were in the water I filtered. And we're trying to warm you.*

Water is for all. I am not.

Beni sighed, her head beginning to ache. *We're not from your world. We didn't know.*

Obviously.

Shocked that the creature wasn't alarmed or surprised by Beni's statement, she hesitated. *We are headed home.*

And I am trapped. The presence grew mournful and withdrew.

Beni could clearly sense the creature now and wondered what had changed from before.

What to do? Finally, she went to make her report. They'd essentially kidnapped a sentient being.

▦

"We have to take it back," she finished her report.

"We can't, Beni," Harris said.

Surprisingly, Jody nodded.

"We don't have enough fuel," Chelsey said from the nav station. She pointed to their readouts as if to justify her statement.

"We kidnapped a living being." She wrung her hands. It was all her fault.

"If we bring water, they will send us for more. We can take it back with the next mission. See if it will agree," Harris finally said.

Beni clenched her hands, a glimmer of hope spurring her to nod. She hadn't thought of that.

Shutting her eyes, though she didn't need to, Beni reached out for the being.

Are you there?

Are you? Came the reply. No malice, simple curiosity, this time.

We don't have enough fuel to take you back and make it home. Will you ride with us? We can return you on the next mission."

You will come for more water? Until it is gone as on your world?

How had it known? Had it heard her thoughts?

Your dreams, and when you think loudly.

Oh. She hesitated. *I hope not.*

Maybe we can help. I will go. The water slowly warms. Please continue.

Help? That couldn't be so easy.

You need water. We make water.

To hear the creature think it, made everything seem so

simple. Beni hoped it was right. *I will report. We need to jump soon.*

Go. I will wait.

Not that it had much of a choice, Beni thought.

She opened her eyes and relayed what the creature said. "Excellent." Harris smiled and clapped his hands. "Jody, prepare to boost. Can you heat the water at the same time?

"No, but I think I can get it warm enough before we jump that the creature will be okay." Jody headed for the engine compartment.

Beni took in the water energy and prepared to assist the pyromancer.

░

We will land soon. Then our work will begin, Beni said to Cousteau—the name she and the water being had worked out based upon that of a hero of Beni's, a scientist who'd explored the seas and respected them as much as any aquamancer.

The beings communicated much like the sea mammals of old Earth were said to have done, with audible clicks and song. It could speak to Beni's mind because of her connection with water. Her great-grandfather had spoken of experiences with great whales and dolphins at length, his intense dark eyes losing focus with the memories and sharpening with grief once he returned to current reality.

Good. We have much work to do. I'm ready to begin.

They'd grown comfortable with each other over the last month of decel, as well as finding the best ways to keep the water warm enough for his comfort. Cousteau had shared with Jody that his people had a culture, system of governance, and myths and legends, just like humans. However, they were unlike humans in many ways. They had few disagreements and needed little beyond water to survive. When they rested, they became water, which is why Beni had missed Cousteau's presence when they'd collected the liquid two months ago. He had awakened, shocked, to find himself trapped in a vessel away from his own world.

Cousteau claimed that once their planet had contained land masses but it had flooded. Cousteau's people secreted water and at one time they had made too much. That was their equivalent of a 'man-made' disaster. Both peoples would get along well, if they could find a way to physically coexist. Sadly Beni didn't think humans would trust Cousteau's people. While Cousteau was curious about the rest of the crew, she noted quickly he did not trust them much, either.

Humans would look for concealed motives in a species whose greatest desire was simply to live and make water and swim in it. They'd be a great asset, but Beni didn't want to see them enslaved either.

They were an incredibly adaptive species too. Cousteau was already able to tolerate cooler temperatures than he'd lived in his entire life. However, he still needed a great deal more heat than he'd find in most natural water sources on Earth. They'd worked out how to effectively heat his tank, between Beni's aquamancy and Jody's pyromancy. They had some ideas for Earth as well.

"Crew, prepare for descent," Harris said over the com.

She'd taken to sitting near the holding tanks, and strapped in to the accel chair.

G-Forces pressed her into the chair and it began to vibrate.

Something is wrong with the harmonies, Cousteau said moments before the com crackled.

"The engines are failing. Beni, lend me power," Jody called over the com.

Beni clenched her fists and did as instructed. All those people depending on them. Her heart pounded and she forced herself to send everything she had.

"We can't slow down!" Stevic called over the com.

Beni drew as much power as she could, feeling Jody strain to control the out of control reaction in the engine core. It burned. Jody held it in check. Barely.

Beni heard Jody scream as the ship itself screamed its death to the thickening atmosphere. Head aching, Beni fought the blackness the G-forces brought to the edges of her vision.

Must Hold On.

Cousteau lent her his energy and they sent it to Jody.

The power burned through her friend.

The ship shook until Beni thought it would split. Through

Jody, she felt the engine core go critical, no longer containable by any force.

She felt Jody's decision and screamed, powerless to stop the pyromancer as she pulled the energies into herself, burning out of existence, but saving their lives. She felt when the ship struck the ground, cracking like an egg.

The tank ruptured as daylight touched her space-pale skin. Water poured over Beni. She was pinned, no energy left, couldn't free herself. As an aquamancer, she should have been able to survive what others would consider a drowning, but she bled heavily into the water that surrounded her, and she couldn't do anything.

Her vision went black.

They'd failed...

So close, but all was lost. She only hoped Cousteau survived.

Beni, Cousteau's voice echoed in her mind. *I can't live on your world. Not without a pool of water. It's sinking into the land!*

...sorry... she thought as she faded, gasping, choking, finally peaceful as her vision blackened completely.

But I can survive in you.

Dying, she thought. So peaceful.

Energy slammed into her and suddenly she didn't need to breathe. The blood she'd lost, replaced by Cousteau, as he poured into her veins, made her whole—different.

We are one, Cousteau proclaimed. *Not how I would have preferred to do this, but I suppose it will have to do.* He sounded louder, more intimate, and also amused.

Beni felt amazing.

We should dissolve. I will show you.

Before she could protest, Cousteau did something and her body joined with the water that spilled out onto the parched Earth soil hard as concrete. They reformed on the ground, still submerged.

Beni reached out with her new senses and together they touched their new world.

"I know what to do..." Beni whispered underwater.

As do I. We will heal your world. Then maybe someday return to mine.

Beni thought she'd like nothing better. Joined with Cousteau she could survive on his planet, as he could survive on hers. Forcing herself to her feet, she emerged from the rapidly vanishing water, scaring a couple of emergency personnel.

She couldn't help the smile on her face. Already, the air smelled clean and fresh. The ground beneath her feet softened and soon, she thought, plants would spring forth. Her planet had the power to heal itself if only her people would allow it time.

※

"What of the alien you discovered?" Minister Scott asked at their next debriefing.

Beni shrugged. "It died in the wreck, but I learned much from it. I know how to fix our water problem. House Mataraci is already working on the solution. It will take time, but we can do it."

Beni wasn't sure Minister Scott believed her, but there was little the woman could do. Despite Harris and Jody's loss in the wreck, the mission was a success and they were all heroes. They already even had a monument. A fountain, of all things, on a water-parched world. She felt Cousteau's amusement and hint of sorrow to match her own as she thought of her fallen friends. She turned to leave.

"Beni," Minister Scott said, halting her. "We're considering another mission if we can find someone with Jody's skills. You'll be needed."

Forcing herself not to smile, Beni nodded. "Of course. I'll do whatever I can for my world."

She and Cousteau chuckled as they left the office and headed back to the water plants. If they could get enough bodies of water created before the next mission, Cousteau thought some of his people would come. For the chance to make unlimited amounts of water, his people would gladly traverse the stars, and bonding with aquamancers would allow them to survive. She hurried.

There was still so much to do.

Kismet Kate
Neal Wilgus

A spokesperson for the High Council
explained once again
to the world's anxious population
that the K-8 Expedition
to the star known as KIC 8462852
had completed its mission
and issued its final report.
K-8 had long since
become simply Kate to the world
and now at last
we would know her true nature.

Speculation has long held
that Kate is a Dyson Sphere—
a massive structure built
by some unknown life form
to tap the star's energy reserve.
If such were the case,
the spokesperson explained,
it would be proof at last
that life exists elsewhere.

And indeed, we were told,
the explorers found ample evidence
that Kate is a Dyson-like structure
that had been built eons ago
for the apparent purpose
of extracting energy.
This explained, we heard
for the umpteenth time,
the erratic nature of K-8 readings.

Alas, the explorers also found
that the Dyson surrounding Kate

was itself a cause of
many misleading signals
that had puzzled us for so long.
Kate's enclosure, it turns out,
is the ruins of a Dyson Sphere—
rubble left behind from a war
between competing forces
unable to find a way
to share the abundant energy
and live together in peace.

There was a long silence,
then a moan swept the audience
as they eyed their competition
and began to make new plans.

Carbon Copies
David L. Drake

ISO Transport Command Flight Designation: Beta-Alpha SWUA-4, Craft Count 6, designations A through F.
In Transit Time Passage: 1 year, 75 days, 16:48.

The six craft of convoy SWUA-4 held steady in their 'parentheses formation,' three on the left and three on the right, as they glided through interstellar space at half light speed. Each vessel was a rotating skinny donut shape with a single spoke of crawl-space conduit pipe, completely illuminated by externally mounted lamps.

The interior lights to the hibernation room of Craft E, traveling in the 9 o'clock position, eased on and rose to half intensity. The two pods in the hibernation room went into the final stages of their wake-up sequence by bringing their occupants' blood back up to wakefulness temperatures. The pink lights within the pods came to life, oscillating between soft dimness and wake-up brightness. Soothing voices also called their inhabitants' names; a male quietly uttering "Hara ... Hara ... Hara..." in one pod in synchronization to a female's "Burke ... Burke ... Burke..." in the other.

Burke was up out of his pod first, shaking off the residual chill. "Una, what's going on?" he asked the room. A female voice replied calmly, "Pleasant wakefulness, Captain Apeloko. Hara's pod detected an anomaly. Your monitor will provide the details. Due to its possibly private nature, may I suggest you personally inform her?"

He stared at the bay's sizable monitor for a minute while his wife's pod gently brought her around. In the reduced room lighting, the backlit display reflected the scrolling status text off his obsidian-toned skin. Burke moved next to her pod as its lid swung open. Hara sat up and stretched, the translucent skin on her bare arms allowed Burke to see the blood pumping through her arteries, showing him that her heart rate was coming back to normal. Burke said quietly, "Dear, we've only

135

hibernated eight weeks."

Hara yawned, shivered, and fluffed her pajama top to let the warm air in. "That's too short. Is something…?"

"Your health monitor detected two heartbeats. Ms. Tanaka, you're pregnant!"

She sputtered, "Really?! I didn't think it was possible."

"Between a Sable and a Pellucid? It was a one in fifty chance. You are carrying a very rare and exceptional baby."

She wrapped her arms around her husband and hugged him. She wiped a tear away as they broke the hug. She tipped her head to kiss Burke but they both pulled away while pointing at their screwed-up mouths, miming they hadn't brushed their teeth yet.

She smiled for a moment. "So, what now? Reset the dials and go back to sleep?"

"Pods aren't equipped for dealing with pregnancies. We'll have to be up for the rest of the trip. I guess, my little newlywed, we'll get to know each other a lot better."

Within three hours, they each had settled into their own tasks. At the primary monitor in the piloting bay, Burke and Una went over technical details about food supplies, the process of constructing baby clothes, and additional plants to add to the botanical bay. Breaking away from conversing with the craft's computer interface, he crossed over the open environmental separation hatch into Hara's sleeping bay, noticing his wife tapping instructions into her personal monitor. He saw her flip through a number of process control diagrams before settling on one to zoom into.

"What are you working on?"

When she turned to address Burke, he noted a serious demeanor that he hadn't expected. "You know that my father works at the ISO on advanced software components. I'm glad you're going to meet him on Alpha-4. He's working on self-discoverable interfaces. With them, two software components can be connected, and within seconds, each interface can autonomously figure out what the other needs to communicate, in what detail, in what format, and efficiently define the exchange patterns. With it, a software designer just needs to indicate that there's a line of communication between two components and what information needs to be passed, and the components do the rest. With this interface mechanism, each component knows what it wants for the level of security, the frequency of connection, and if there is another component that can provide the information more easily. The software engineers only need to dig into the details if two components can't resolve their differences."

"That makes sense to me. I assume the two components figure out the best communication path, too."

"Very good! Yes, that's right. Well, every few weeks when I was on Beta-3, I would get a message from my father through the Iris communication service, and one of the things he sent me was a challenging related project."

"Aren't the communications nine years old by the time you got them?"

"Yes … but messages from my dad meant the world to me. And the challenge he sent fit perfectly into my major! He suggested that I build a general-purpose self-discoverable interface that can automatically negotiate between two legacy interfaces, and figure out what each of them needs to operate. It's a really messy task, since the interface—I called it 'universal liaison'—has only partial communication, returned error codes, and help messages to figure out what's needed for the two legacy components to interoperate. It shows how primitive these interfaces were even just a decade ago. If you ever want to watch three software components flounder for half an hour to strike up a conversation, let me know. I've been working on this for about a year and testing has become Zen meditation meets schadenfreude."

"I'll pass on that. I have plenty of information panels to stare at over on my pilot's monitor." Burke happily took a bounce step toward the wall partition and opened a storage panel where he began rummaging around for spare clothing when Hara restarted the conversation with a subdued manner and tone.

"You *knew* didn't you?"

He turned back to see the serious side of his Pellucid wife. Her face was pale and cool, her muscles tensed on the sides of her forehead. The cheerfulness dropped from Burke's demeanor. "Knew ... what?"

"You *knew* our flight plan backwards and forwards. Launch from Beta-3. Hibernate a little over a year as the ship catches the ion stream of Relativistic Jet Y-998. Get up to half light speed. Wake-up. Go through Fold Nadir-17 for 8 hours and 25 minutes. Hibernate again for a year while we catch Jet A-2043 to redirect our trajectory. Wake up again and go through Fold Zenith-37 for 2 days, 6 hours, 5 minutes. Hibernate for another 8 months as the craft decelerates in the Alpha solar system. Then land on Alpha-4."

"You memorized all that?"

"You're the pilot. You know this craft backwards and forwards. You're supposed to avoid risk."

"Yes ... that's true."

"And yet you *knew* the pods couldn't handle a pregnancy. And while we were wakeful and transiting Fold Nadir-17, you coupled with me anyway. What ... *what* were you thinking?"

"Ahh ... that you're beautiful when you wake up?" Burke tried to calm her with an awkward forced smile. It didn't work.

She continued. "When it comes to space travel, even a fifty to one chance is too high. You *knew* this might happen."

"But, my dear, we'd only been married for four days when we started this trip! This is our honeymoon. And it's in my nature to..."

"Captain Burke Apeloko, do *not* put us at risk again." Under her breath she mumbled, "Not to mention this will age my skin an extra two years..."

She turned back to her coding and another three hours passed without discussion.

Alpha-4, Nation of Isabella, Residence of Dr. Sato Tanaka.

Dr. Sato Tanaka's single-story beach house nestled in a suburban cul-de-sac lined with fig and lychee trees. The evening's topical breeze spread their fruit-laced fragrance throughout the neighborhood and out to the nearby coastal shore. Like most evenings, Dr. Tanaka sat on his screened-in lanai, wearing a short-sleeved aloha shirt, taking in the scent of the air, the melodious sloshing of the ocean waves, and the berry-and-smoky-chocolate notes of a neo-Zinfandel.

He took another sip of wine and stared at a framed picture of his daughter he always kept nearby. He speculated, as he often did at this time of day, whether he had done the right thing by allowing thirteen-year-old Hara to leave for Beta-3 to attend university. He wondered if caving in to her overwhelming wanderlust was a good parental decision. He pondered whether his love of astronomy gave her that desire for interstellar travel. He pressed a small button on the side of the picture frame that morphed his daughter's picture into the smiling image of his departed wife. *"Hara will only know you through the eyes of a child,"* he thought, letting out a deep sigh. He recalled what should have been an idyllic inner-island hiking trip he and his wife had taken two years ago, and the allergic reaction to a Gemstone Wasp sting that abruptly ended her life. He turned over his wrist and stared at his pulse through his translucent skin, looking for a panicked, racing heartbeat, but all he saw was the usual coursing of blood through his veins. He took another sip and did his best to hold back a flood of tears.

ISO Transport Command Flight Designation: Beta-Alpha SWUA-4, Craft E.
In Transit Time Passage: 2 years, 20 days, 02:27.

Burke and Hara busied themselves with the pre-fold preparations. Burke closely inspected each of the primary monitor's many images showing the exteriors of the six craft. He wanted to ensure all the movable components were in their locked position before transit into the fold. He scanned for anything out of place.

"Una, please review my pre-fold preparations."

Una's tranquil voice replied, "Ready when you are, Captain Apeloko."

He started quietly reciting the particulars to keep himself focused as he checked the virtual gauges as well as the computer monitors.

"Approaching Fold Zenith-37 from the end facing the

Milky Way's nucleus. From this approach, it's a 1.87 astronomical units-wide counter-twisted trumpeted tube. Exit yields a
positive 4.53 radians rotation given our current approach. We
will experience a transit time of 2 days, 6 hours, 5 minutes, and
18 seconds, more or less."

Una replied, "Correct. The current sensor readings match
the fold's predicted gravitational waves. You are clear to pro-
ceed."

Hara wrinkled her brow with mock concern, "More or
less? My dear husband, you can't be both precise and arbitrary."
She lightly bounced Kea, their 3-month-old, on her right hip.
The little one continued gurgling through her baby drool and
stared wide-eyed at her mother's face with her hyper-pale-blue
eyes that contrasted with an epidermis that conjured images of
swirling smoke from an extinguished fire.

Burke smiled back at his wife and gave her a knowing
wink that all was well and started his confident explanation.

"Of all of the details about the fold, the transit time is the
most arbitrary. Don't give me that look. It can vary by a few minutes. Hey, I'm an expert at passing through spacetime anomalies,
but … and I'm serious about this … the pair of tightly orbiting
white dwarf stars that are creating this fold can cause any number of minor variations that our predictive algorithms just cannot anticipate. Here, this will help…" Burke touched the monitor
in a couple of places to bring up a 3-D graphic that showed their
surroundings, complete with a solid white line indicating their
progress over the last few weeks and a dotted line for their up-
coming trajectory. Light gray gravitational gridlines showed the
slowly rotating twisted and slightly deformed tube of space in
front of them. Their dotted-line trajectory headed straight into
the trumpeted end of the gravitationally formed conduit.

Hara shifted the baby to the other hip and joined her
spouse at the console. She looked at the image for a few seconds before breaking off to make a happy, wide-eyed face at
Kea. Without looking at her husband, she said, "Tell me more
about the transit."

"As we transit the fold, all six of our craft will roll around
the inside of this tube of bent-stretched space. We'll slowly
tumble a little more than 2 times during the 2 day, 6 hour trip."

He used his hands to pinch the image down, and repeated the action to reduce it again. "And we'll end up here, 4.5 light years away."

He smiled at her to assure her with his certainty. She reciprocated with a broad happy grin highlighting the pink oval muscles around her mouth showing through her translucent skin.

She off-handedly mentioned, "You know, I never told you much about my transit to Beta-3."

Burke sat down in his pilot's seat. He motioned for her to do the same. He suddenly realized that Kea should also be secured for the beginning of the fold transit. He remembered that sometimes it was like flying straight through normal space, and sometimes it was like circling a drain. Rather than worrying Hara by describing all the things that could go wrong, he hopped back up and scooped Kea off of her mother's hip, whisking her back to Hara's sleeping bay. He strapped her into the harness he'd jerry-rigged into her makeshift crib. She gurgled again and he rubbed her belly before rejoining his wife in the cockpit. Hara was strapped into her seat and he slid into his. "I walked out on you, sorry about that … please continue."

"It was *not* a pleasant trip. I was in deep-sleep most of the way, and woke up with a really bad case of space sickness. The engineers found out later that they hadn't properly centered the craft, and the artificial gravity rotation caused the craft to wobble all the way there. It affected not only all the passengers' inner ears, but also feeding tubes, and … you get the idea. Let's just say I lost a few pounds by the time I was walking on Beta-3."

"And you were in transit for, what … nine years?"

"Yup. I left Alpha-4 when I was 13, I began university on Beta-3 at 22, and the rest, my love, is history."

Una's voice broke in. "Entering Fold Zenith-37 in ten, nine, eight…"

Alpha-4, Nation of Isabella, ISO Visitor Center.

The lush topical flora of Sally Ride Island was pampered to the extent that it could have been mistaken as artificial by the people waiting in line outside the Visitor's Building of the Intergalactic Science Organization. The maintenance droids climbing, trimming, wiping, and vacuuming the tall king palms seemed out of place as they rushed about in the equatorial sunshine, while the vacationing masses patiently queued for the doors to open. The crowd's anticipation for the tour of the working laboratory contrasted sharply with the discussion inside. Two translucent-skinned Pellucid engineers, dressed in scientific white lab coats and blue slacks, held a tense one-sided conversation.

Dr. Sato Tanaka's veins stood out on his forehead and temples. "Hui, I have to tell you, I just don't like giving this talk. I have five interns waiting for my direction on the Descartes Project. Isn't there someone ... *anyone* ... else that can give the welcome speech?" Seeing Dr. Hui Sharma's calm demeanor, Dr. Tanaka felt temporarily embarrassed by his protest. Dr. Sharma just looked steadily at his employee.

Dr. Tanaka continued. "I am sorry for my objection, but..."

Dr. Sharma's stopped his subordinate with a look and gently raised a hand to guide his lab-coated colleague to the lecture hall. Dr. Tanaka pursed his lips and proceeded to his assigned task.

As the last of the visitors entered the assembly hall, Dr. Tanaka swiftly ascended the stage, lab coat tail flapping. He was all grins and waved about an archaic clipboard clasping actual paper pages, as if anyone recorded or read notes from such a primitive device.

"Hello! Hello! I am Dr. Tanaka! I work here at the ISO as a systems engineer. This morning I will introduce you to our corner of the galaxy." Behind him a large screen displayed images synchronized, phrase for phrase, with his monologue.

"For those still arriving, there are still a few empty seats over there, and there, so if you could ... thank you so much, excellent. Let's get started. You have all heard the stories about the colonization of our planet, Alpha-4, by the brave space pioneers from our heritage planet, Earth, orbiting the star Sol, also located in the Orion Spur of the Milky Way Galaxy. These brave souls arrived here 164 years ago. Ten spacecraft initiated the trip, eight of which successfully arrived here in the Alpha system. When they started their voyage, deep sleep chambers were much more primitive, and only two of the craft were able to employ them throughout the trip. The remaining six craft had crew that were, as we say today, 'wakeful' throughout the trip, creating the evolutionary islanding that we see today on Alpha-4. We Pellucids ... thank you, thank you for that ... are the proud offspring of New Frontier Spacecraft 4, from the Earth's nation of Collaborative Pacific States. I see we have a few Brindles and Alabasters here also. So glad to see you. From Earth's East African National Alliance space program, we have the evolutionary island race of Sables. Yes, give yourselves a round of applause. If there is anyone I missed, please give yourself a hand also. Thank you! I know it is often said, but it is worth repeating: Alpha-4 is an island planet for our evolutionary island people."

A large illustration of the Milky Way, seen from above and cartoonish in its level of stellar illumination, appeared on the screen behind Dr. Tanaka.

"Here is home, our Milky Way galaxy. At 13.6 billion years old, it is almost as old as the universe itself. The two major arms curling away from the center are Perseus, here, and Scutum-Centaurus, spiraling out over here. The minor arms are here, here, and ... there. Right inside the curve of Perseus is this collection of stars called the Orion Spur, and our Alpha solar system is right here near the middle of the Orion Spur. We reside on the fourth planet from the star Alpha. In this illustration, you can see our three smaller interior planets, and the large gas-giant outer planets."

The screen showed a false-proportioned illustration of the Alpha solar system with faint gray orbital lines for each of the planets. It zoomed into Alpha-4 highlighting the collection of archipelagos and large blue oceans. The map continued to zoom in until it was clearly over Sally Ride Island on the equator with a 3-D projection of the ISO Visitors' Building. It quickly zoomed back out until it contained the cluster of local solar systems.

"There were many reasons for the space pioneers to make their journey, but what really spurred them forward were the discoveries of the Alpha and Beta solar systems. Two habitable planets within nine light years of each other! The two planets differ very little in gravity and composition, but Beta's land-masses are large mountainous continents surrounded by vast oceans, with extremely cold weather at the highest peaks. Unlike Alpha-4, these make excellent locations for observatories; so many of our astronomers are stationed there. However, we here at ISO are very proud of our success with the Alpha-to-Beta communication disk, the Alpha Solar Iris!"

A simplified depiction of the Iris dissolved into the Alpha solar system illustration. The image showed the Iris as a huge flat disk hovering within the gap between the interior four planets and larger outer planets. The diameter of its large transparent internal lens rivaled the diameter of the system's central star. The audience applauded politely for the 21-year old project.

"Thank you. My fellow scientists and I control the Iris from this very building and a few of the outlying buildings. From here, we can communicate out to the astronomic instruments on Beta-3. A sister Iris will be built in the Beta system over the next ten years, to reciprocate our communication paths."

The illustrated Iris lens began rhythmically pulsing between transparent and darkly translucent.

"The lens is subdivided into a matrix of panels, each a two-pane polarizing light filter, allowing light through or block light with millisecond timing. Using Alpha's solar energy, the Iris constantly makes self-corrections to keep itself between the Alpha and Beta systems. If there aren't any questions, I will direct you to that door over there, where our docent will show you our control room."

A Brindle woman shot her mottled brown and black arm up and waved it frantically. Dr. Tanaka struggled to hide the flush of frustration of being further delayed. He breathed deeply and tried to regain his composure.

He motioned to her and asked, "Yes?" as politely as he could manage.

"With the discovery of the local relativistic jets and space folds, spacecraft have recently been able to go between the Alpha and Beta systems with effectively hyper light-speed transit times. Given that, is the Iris, with its light-speed communication, really still viable? Why blink out a message that takes 9 years to receive when you can hand-carry a note in less time?" All eyes turned back to the lecturing Pellucid. The blood drained from Dr. Tanaka's face, and his muscles tightened, particularly around his mouth. The audience, including other Pellucids, couldn't help but indulge in the guilty pleasure of watching a being with translucent skin react under pressure. Within seconds, the pores on his skin opened and dribbles of sweat ran down his temples.

Dr. Tanaka looked up from the audience to clear his head. He saw Dr. Sharma standing at the observational window near the display control booth. Hui's demeanor was no longer calm; his eyes were narrowed into displeased slits.

Dr. Tanaka cleared his throat, dabbing his brow with a handkerchief. "The jets you mentioned do aid in reaching high velocities in space, but the folds are where the real gains are made. Unfortunately, these folds are volatile, very dynamic, and dependent on quirky celestial post-Einsteinian mechanics that we are still making discoveries about. The Iris uses known, sustained, and trustable communication methods, all of which you will hear more about in your next presentation, 'Staying Connected.'"

The same woman in the crowd spoke up again without raising her hand. "Speaking of trustworthy, I heard that there's concern that the Iris could be a beacon to … um … announce our existence. That could be a serious danger. Was that addressed in the Iris design?"

Dr. Sharma smiled at this question, since he was a lead developer for this feature of the Iris.

"Glad you asked. We were concerned that if we simply used the Iris as an on-and-off binary signal, we might attract the attention of any intelligent, space-traveling life forms farther down the Orion Spur. That's why we hid the communication in a signal that resembles a fast-transiting, undesirable planet. When we computer scientists bury information in an image, we call it steganography. Our Beta-3 staff can easily extract the camouflaged data from the image. If there are other beings out there, and that is a very big 'if,' they shouldn't detect our communication signal, nor should they be interested in what we present as a hot, uninhabitable planet."

The woman nodded her head in acceptance of the answer. Dr. Tanaka looked up at Dr. Sharma who was smiling and nodding. *"Excellent!"* thought Dr. Tanaka, now I can get back to the Descartes Project. He gestured toward the exit and the crowd started to shuffle out.

ISO Transport Command Flight Designation: Beta-Alpha SWUA-4, Craft E.
In Transit Time Passage: 2 years, 21 days, 13:40.

Hara leaned over the crib and repositioned Kea's kicked-off blanket. With a square of white cloth, she wiped some snot off the baby's smoke-colored nose. Satisfied that Kea was safely asleep, Hara padded back to stand next to her husband in the pilot's station. He was studying various gravitational wave readings and external images of the six craft, looking for any anomalies while in transit of the fold.

Hara broke in, "I do have a question I've always wanted to ask. But I needed a hot-shot pilot for an answer."

Burke swiveled his captain's chair to give Hara his full attention. "I am the hot-shot pilot you are looking for."

"Okay, there are particles in space: some big, some miniscule. If we hit one of them while traveling at half the speed of light, wouldn't that make us explode or cut pin-holes through the craft, or worse?"

"Yup, that's a scary fact. That's why our craft use, and have for decades, an Ultraviolet Light Particle Detection and Avoidance System—but it's always called by its commercial name, LightSlip. High-power, pulse-pattern ultraviolet headlights shine out in front of us as we travel. If any of that light reflects back, even just a photon, we take avoidance maneuvers, which are usually such slight adjustments we don't feel them. We do that by sending a molecule or two out of our craft in one direction or another. Or we push the dust out of the way with a laser pulse. And that's enough to avoid particles in space. In general, space is so empty it … it boggles the mind. During flight training we called it the 'big sky' theory: the chance of having dust particles that are unavoidable will just never happen. I should also mention that for safety, LightSlip is one of those components where we have backup systems to its backup systems. We really don't want LightSlip to fail ... ever. Once moving at speed, always moving at speed. Well, relatively."

"Relatively?"

"Well, these folds are really spacetime stretched out of shape by extremely large, high-mass, eccentrically orbiting, rapidly spinning bodies. The anomaly we are currently traversing is shaped like a tube. For this fold, two white dwarf stars stretch space in one direction and compress it in another, along with creating a tsunami of gravitational waves rippling through the middle of the tube, causing a parsec to be relatively longer in one direction..."

"...than in the other direction. I didn't skip out on middle-academy physics. We just need to pass through the middle of the tube."

"That's too simple of a description. It's more like we're tobogganing down the pointy ridge of a mountain range, gravitationally speaking. If we don't follow the ridge perfectly, even a little bit, one way or another, our craft will be thrown out into space, probably directly toward one of those massive bodies. I know, I mixed my metaphors. So along with avoiding particles, each of our six ships is also making many micro-corrections to keep us on course in an ever-changing gravity field. No non-self-correcting object could traverse these folds without falling into the surrounding gravitational crevasse. That's why it looks almost totally dark outside the craft. All light, down to the photon level, is being twisted around while passing through the fold. You won't see a stream of photons coming from any one place, like from a star. The photons are all scattered like dust in a swirling wind."

"Wouldn't we see the starlight from each end of the tube?"

"If the tube were straight. But this one isn't. It currently has two twisty bends in it. Most folds aren't straight. The distortions in this fold are more like the contortions in a tail of a tornado, twisting in a bent swirl as it goes up into the sky. We're piloting up through the so-called center of the tornado. Here, let me show you."

Burke stepped up to the primary monitor and tapped it a

few times. "This is the LightSlip visualization system showing where we're headed. As if we were flying an airship at night in a snowstorm and looking out the windscreen." The monitor flickered a bit; like the screen was malfunctioning or the image was poor.

"That's actually what it looks like out there. Just flashes of light. Each particle of light is moving in its unique interpretation of a straight line while traveling in dynamically twisted space. Here is what it looks like from where we've been."

Burke tapped one button and the screen changed to the rear-facing LightSlip image. Like the front-facing view, there were random flashes of light, but there was also a single steady group of pixels illuminated in the middle of the screen. Burke uttered an uncharacteristic "Huh?" He sprinted back to his pilot's chair to determine what LightSlip was detecting behind the craft. Different images and readouts flashed across his console as he desperately tapped his screen and toggled switches to get more information.

Suddenly, the impact warning light flashed and the siren sounded.

Hara watched Burke freeze in disbelief. She pointed at the unwavering pixels on the screen. "What is that?! What *is* that?!" In a sea of black, a spot of brightness held steadily in the middle of the detection beacon display.

Burke twisted around in his cockpit chair to get a good look at the monitor. Kea, frightened by her mother's outburst, started to cry.

"I … don't know." Burke stammered. He jumped up and squared up to the primary monitor, punching the siren volume button a few times to lessen the din. "I *really* don't know. I've never seen … anything, *anything* … like this before while transiting a fold. He started flipping switches and tapping away on the monitor to rotate the direction of one of the rear-facing cameras normally meant for inspecting the exterior of the spacecraft.

Hara tore her eyes from the screen and ran over to comfort Kea, but shouted back, "Keep telling me what's going on! Keep talking!"

"This makes no sense whatsoever…" He peered intently

at the light spot on the otherwise black image, and then tapped the monitor to change the camera frequencies to infrared. The faint outline of a rectangular box appeared, now larger than before. "Ahhh! AHHHH!" he screamed, "It's gaining on us!" Burke slowly exhaled, and he chanted, "Center. Balance. Breathe." He repeated this twice over, and stared at the monitor a full minute. Hara carried Kea in, bouncing her back to quietness, and stood next to her husband. She joined him in his attention to the blip on the screen. Burke took another deep breath, walked back to his pilot chair, and sat.

"Una, diagnostic assessment of the possible impact."

As usual, Una's voice was calm. "My knowledge is incomplete. The object is traveling slightly faster than half the speed of light. Since we detected it, it has also been able to traverse the space fold."

"How many micro-corrections has our craft made since the time of detection?"

"3,286 from the time of detection until the time you asked. Each micro-correction was needed to avoid external gravity wells."

"The object must have made similar micro-corrections. Una..." Burke hesitated to ask, "What are the protocols for engagement with alien beings?"

"I can display the latest official International Academy of Astronautics Post-Detection Policy. In general, the procedure is to have 'stakeholders' meet and prepare structured rules, standards, guidelines, and action plans that governmental or interested organizational entities will follow. It pre-dates the transit of the space pioneers to Alpha-4, and is written in twenty-second century bureaucratic English. Would you like me to translate it for you?"

"Absolutely not."

Burke thought for a moment. "Una, given the difference in relative velocities, how long will it be before the object catches up to us?"

"We will converge in 4 minutes, 19 seconds."

Burke leapt out of his chair, and barked, "Hara, get Kea in an atmospheric bag and secure the bag to her crib. Bring the crib into the cockpit bay and attach it to the rear bulkhead.

Then get both of our controlled environment suits. I'm gathering rations and portable waste bags and sealing off each of the six bays. I'll meet you back here in the cockpit to help you into your suit."

Hara and Burke readied their craft for the unknown in a frantic flurry. Burke couldn't get out of his head that they were in a communications dead-zone until they exited the fold. For now, they were on their own.

Two minutes later, they were both seated and buckled into the piloting seats. Hara said it first. "This is really uncomfortable!" she exclaimed inside her bubble mask. Burke heard her over the wireless and tried to rotate in his pilot's chair, but his suit restricted his movement. "I don't think the designers were expecting the suits to be used while working at this station."

"Does Kea's atmospheric bag have a mic in it? Will I be able to hear her?"

"It has a built-in microphone. Let's both hold our breath and see if we can hear her ... Yup, there she is."

They watched the pilot's monitor as the box-shaped object approached. Burke commanded, "Una, take as many images of the object as you can!"

The pilot's monitor was quickly flooded with images of the object at many angles, including those relayed from the other ships.

Hara said, "It looks like an antique air-conditioner. See the vents?"

"You're right! But what are those things on the sides?" He peered at the image showing pipe-like extensions.

The pilot's monitor showed the dark box pass directly through the middle of the parentheses formation and continue forward through the fold.

"What ... what is that?" Burke pointed at image from the camera trained on craft B, directly across the formation in the 3 o'clock position. There was now a stripe across the image of their other craft. Burke stared at it. Then it moved a bit.

He gasped, "What the hell?! That thing has a tail!"

Una announced, "Captain Apeloko and Ms. Tanaka, there is a high probability that I have determined the origin of the vessel, based on the following image." A close up of a plaque on the box appeared on the primary monitor. Inset on the rectangular feature were the impressed words:

Realms of Nephele
Carbon Harvester Mark IV
Serial No. 475,285,921

Burke replied in a fascinated tone, "Please continue..."

"You may recall hearing about the successful reduction of carbon dioxide from Earth's atmosphere in the twenty-second century. This was due, in great part, to the collaboration between NASA and the now-defunct company *Realms of Nephele*. The company offered to provide the governments of Earth the atmospheric scrubbers needed to remove unwanted carbon dioxide in return for the rights to use the same technology to harvest carbon from Earth's nearest neighboring planet, Venus. Based on our database of space industry, the scrubbers they used employed a primitive variant of a vacuum ultraviolet laser that could bend carbon dioxide molecules until their two oxygen atoms got close enough to splinter off as their own molecule. The remaining carbon atom can be directed to attach to a nearby complex carbon structure. With enough energy, enough carbon dioxide, and the right equipment, any carbon compound, from soot to diamonds, could be made."

Una paused to allow her human audience time to process the details provided so far. "Please continue," Burke requested.

"After completing the mission on Earth, *Realms of Nephele* deployed a single system to Venus. Since the company only needed access to the Venusian atmosphere, they hung their carbon-dioxide scrubber off the bottom of the space elevator at, according to their design, an average of 10 kilometers above the surface, which is at the level of the Venusian troposphere. The elevator's ribbon was made of a combination of two primary carbon structures: nanotubes and nanofoam. The nanotubes were for strength, electrical conduction, and communication to the system's controller stationed at the geostationary level. The alternating layers of carbon nanofoam acted as an electrical insulator for the carbon nanotubes. A large counterbalance, also made of a roll of the carbon ribbon, was tethered above the controller. As a matter of innovative design, every component of the entire system was constructed of one of the carbon allotropes: for example, buckminsterfullerene oil for lubricant, diamonds for lenses and shafts, and glassy carbon for acid-resistant protective coatings. The scrubber was also able to construct multilayered circuit boards. The *Realms of Nephele's* Carbon Harvester Mark IV scrubber and controller could build any of the components used within the elevator. As more space elevator ribbon was added by the scrubber, the system's controller would detect the weight change and haul the ribbon up. The controller could reassemble the carbon ribbon into each of the system's components. When it had constructed and assembled enough system components, it would bud off another elevator and send it to its own geostationary location above Venus. A new scrubber was lowered, and the process continued. It was the first SR-SR deployed into space."

Burke asked, "SR-SR?"

Hara answered, "Ahh, yes, it's an engineering term coined in one of the great twenty-second century engineering movements, the creation of Self-Replicating and Self-Repairing constructs. It's where a physical system could create a copy of itself by harvesting available resources. The self-repairing capability was where two constructs could examine each other for flaws and correct them. SR-SR is usually seen in miniature robotics, but it was also used in larger systems for unmanned space mining."

Una continued, "Carbon Harvesters test to see if minor variants of their processes improve their yield, and if so, communicate the improvement to all the other Carbon Harvesters. The remainder of this description is classified under need-to-know."

Burke chuckled to himself, despite their circumstances. "Well, I think we have a *very real* need-to-know. Voice authentication: Whiskey Vodka Rye."

Hara raised her eyebrows. "That's your passphrase? I've never seen you drink."

Burke shrugged. "That's what I was assigned. Una, please continue."

"After deployment of the first Carbon Harvester, *Realms of Nephele* had difficulty getting the funds to retrieve the thousands-of-kilometers-long nanotube ribbons, which were worth a great deal back then. Because of this, the elevators were left orbiting Venus for twenty-eight years of unchecked geometric growth. They were supposed to stop replicating after 4000 of them were deployed; that's about one for every kilometer of the Venusian equator. But during the years of self-analysis and improvement, the software detected that the restriction to 4000 units reduced their overall yield, so the Carbon Harvesters altered their own code. Approximately two days later, Carbon Harvester communications to Earth stopped. *Realms of Nephele* discovered that most of the elevators were no longer orbiting Venus. None of the space elevators that disappeared were found except one that established an orbiting position over Earth. They pulled as much information from it as they could regarding the incident, but all they knew was that 3,589 self-replicating Carbon Harvesters were out in the cosmos, assumed to be either tangled together or dispersed. The systems had fully charged batteries, solar panels, communication lasers, and antennas. The systems had various abilities to amass energy, such as from Venus' electric winds and stellar photonic power. The systems knew how to find and maintain geostationary orbits. Earth's governments classified the incident to prevent space-related fears. *Realms of Nephele* reconfigured the remaining system to not over-replicate, and 8 years later they had a full complement of 4000 units. It was one of the first and most successful space mineral excavations, and it funded a number of other prosperous commercial missions that harvested numerous minerals from Sol's asteroid belt and Ort Cloud. Do you want to know more?"

Hara asked, "What are those things on the side of the box?"

Una replied, "If I have correctly parsed your query, you are referring to the laterally-attached 12-degrees-of-freedom robotic arms that are used for repair, manipulation, and instrument positioning. Would you like to see the architectural diagrams?"

Within her helmet, Hara made a face that indicated

information overload, and Burke answered Una with, "No, thank you."

The next few minutes dragged by slowly while the two of them watched the trailing space elevator ribbon pass by, unwaveringly following its box-shaped head.

Again the impact warning light flashed and the siren sounded at full volume. Kea responded by wailing in her environmental bag. Both Hara and Burke winced, unsnapped their helmet releases, and ripped off the sonic torture chambers their headgear had become.

Hara rubbed her ears and said, "Darling, if things go bad, they'll go crazy bad, right? Can we take off these suits? They're just slowing us down."

Burke weighed the options, and nodded. "You're right; you're absolutely right." He reached over and punched down the siren volume control as he and Hara stripped back out of their environmental suits. Hara made her way over to Kea to calm her again.

A circle of six boxes approached from behind, flashing their communication lasers to the lead box. When the troupe came alongside Craft B, one reached below itself and snipped its own space elevator ribbon and passed it to one of its brothers. It then slipped over and docked on Craft B's hub.

"This is … insane," Burke mumbled. "What's it doing…?"

They stared at the image on the monitor relayed from Cargo Craft B and watched as Harvester used its diamond-tipped pincers to shinny along the conduit to the torus-shaped craft. It then used various handholds to move to a position near one of the camera mounts. Grasping a bolt head with its free arm, and with a slow spinning motion, it began removing the bolt.

"It's disassembling the camera mount! Una! Knock that box off the craft! Get rid of the thing!"

"The closest operational robotic arm on Craft B will not reach the Carbon Harvester."

Burke was uncharacteristically panicked. "Train every external camera we have on that thing!" Una sounded a pleasant conformation chime. Six images popped up six different angles of the Carbon Harvester.

Hara stared in disbelief. "I thought these boxes extracted

carbon from an atmosphere? What would make it do this?"

Una offered, "May I speculate?"

Burke answered, "Yes, please," but he thought he might know what she was going to suggest.

"*Realms of Nephele* used twenty-second century artificial intelligence to help their systems discover better processes to meet their goals. The Carbon Harvester's primary goal is to extract carbon, which is directly linked to their ability to replicate. They will do anything to get more carbon. The Carbon Harvester that is on Craft B is seeking carbon in any form it can find."

"Are the bolts made from carbon steel?" Hara asked.

Burke touched the screen a couple times to verify his hunch. "Even if they are, there would be less than 2% carbon in the iron mixture, and it would be nearly impossible to extract any usable carbon. But I'm not ruling out that it will try to extract carbon from anything it can get its mitts on."

The Harvester casually let the bolt go, which tumbled away from the side of the doughnut-shaped hull and off into space. Within seconds it had done the same to the other five bolts that previously secured the camera mount, their bolts reflecting the bright light of the external lamps as they rotated off into the blackness.

Flustered, Burke asked, "Una, should I go out and throw that thing off the craft myself?"

"These are the parameters for your decision: It takes 18 minutes to clear the airlock. 2,400 Joules will be used in the depressurization and re-pressurization process. You would have to spacewalk from rotating Craft E to rotating Craft B. Any mishap will result in an infinitesimally small chance you will survive due to our velocity and transiting the fold, and the unpredictability of the Carbon Harvester. Without a pilot, the chance of voyage success is reduced by 94%. There is a decrease in your chances of accident if the artificial gravity rotation is terminated for both craft. Would you like to hear more factors?"

Burke glanced at Hara and remembered her concern about undue risk-taking. "No."

The Harvester tipped the mount aside and, using a diamond lens located in its pincers, fired a high-energy laser at the wires leading from the craft to the camera.

"Heating the wires?" Hara asked.

Una replied. "The cable harnesses to the external cameras are composed of copper insulated with polyvinyl-chloride insulation. When heated,..."

Hara cut her off. "I can see what it's doing. The copper is melting and flying off, and the plastic is turning black."

Una finished. "You are correct. The Carbon Harvester is using the process of extreme pyrolysis on the insolated wire; in simpler terms, applying high temperatures without oxygen. The volatile chemicals are boiled off leaving the carbon backbone of the PVC."

The Harvester used its free arm to gather the created soot by scraping with its diamond pincer, fed it through an inlet, and retrieved more wire out of the housing through a series of quick jerks.

Burke looked at Hara. "I can't just let it attack our craft!"

The impact warning light flashed again and the siren sounded.

Burke punched up the rear-facing LightSlip visualization system. It showed six more Carbon Harvesters passing through, flying in formation, their carbon nanotube ribbons trailing behind them. As they passed, the pilot's monitor indicated that the infrared sensors picked up on laser flashes between the flying boxes and the box on the Craft B. One of the Carbon Harvesters slowed, snipped its ribbon, used its arms to control its approach, and landed softly on the hub of Craft E.

Burke gasped.

ISO Transport Command Flight Designation: Beta-Alpha SWUA-4, Craft E.
In Transit Time Passage: 2 years, 22 days, 03:14.

After the Carbon Harvester breached the hull of Craft B, the interior cameras showed the shiny black box start to open one of the storage containers inside and extract the gray mass inside and place it into its access port.

Hara was aghast at the invasion, but her curiosity made her ask, "What ... what are we transporting in the other ships?"

Burke hesitated to answer. "The story behind the cargo is a bit sensitive. Or it was. Somehow, and no one really knows how, there was a transfer of … wait … let me start from the beginning. On Beta-3 there is a type of blue-green colored wasp called the Gemstone Wasp. It's rather nasty. It's a blood-sucking insect, but it also stings when threatened. It lays its eggs in the shallows of fresh water swamps. Somehow, some of these wasps were transferred to Alpha-4, where they have no natural enemies. So the population is blossoming in ponds and springs. They're not only attacking humans, but also domesticated and wild animals, and it makes their skin uncontrollably itchy because Alpha-4 humans, as well as animals, have no built-in mechanisms to address this pest's bite or sting. Based on historic data from similar biological contaminations, the Organization for Environmental Protection is very hesitant to use robotic or chemical means to eradicate the wasp. So, they are going to try using a natural deterrent. On Beta-3, the Western Swamp Frog eats Gemstone Wasp larvae. That's it. That's all they do. So we have been requested to ship in five cargo ships' worth of chilled frog's eggs. What they told me is that they plan to test the environmental interaction in a closed environment before releasing it in the wild, but it's still a sensitive issue, so news of this shipment isn't in the public."

"That's both intriguing and so nerdy. And apparently the Carbon Harvester loves it."

Burke punched at the air. "I wish I had some sort of … weapon!" Then he hesitated and blurted out, "Maybe ISO on Alpha-4 has something to stop the Harvesters."

"What you don't know is that the Iris *is* a weapon," Hara stated.

Burke was shocked. "To use against what?"

"It can focus the light like a magnifying glass by tipping the sections of the lens. My father mentioned it to my mother when I was ten, thinking I wouldn't understand. He said it could eliminate rogue asteroids, but I don't think that's the full story. The funding for the Iris was from those who feared the unknown. They did want the communications ability, but…"

"So even if we survive this attack, Alpha-4 will probably turn the Iris against anything that comes through the fold they don't want in the Alpha solar system. And at half the speed of light, we're all just a dangerous blur. Should we not warn them about the Harvesters and try to handle it ourselves?"

Hara looked at their child and back to her husband.

Burke heard the scraping of the diamond claws across the exterior of the craft. He wasn't quite sure how, but it was clear that the Harvester knew to come in through the camera mount over the botanical bay, which had the greatest amount of carbon dioxide in the air and the largest bio-mass. He contemplated sealing off the bay and jettisoning the atmosphere, but that would only kill all the plants and the Harvester would just move on to the next bay.

Hara looked at Burke with a worried face that slowly changed to pensive. "I ... I think I know where the Carbon Harvesters are going. The Iris gives the impression that a Venus-like planet is orbiting Alpha. They are all headed back to the ultimate carbon feast." She then snapped her fingers and handed Kea to her husband, saying, "I think I have a plan!"

ISO Transport Command Flight Designation: Beta-Alpha SWUA-4, Craft E.
In Transit Time Passage: 2 years, 22 days, 08:32.

Hara cradled Kea while tapping instructions into her programming interface. Her face was pale and sweaty, and she had the desperate look of a woman protecting her child. "Got it! Adjusted our communication laser!" She went right back into her trance of inserting instructions and slowly rocking their child.

Una calmly announced, "We have just left Fold Zenith-37 and have entered the outer region of the Alpha system. Projected to begin gravitational deceleration in orbit of Alpha-6 in 5 days, 14 hours, 34 minutes."

Burke sprinted to the pilot's monitor. "Una, tell me the location of the Carbon Harvesters."

Una replied, "There are 196 Carbon Harvesters preceding us. One Carbon Harvester is inside Craft B. One Carbon Harvester is on the hull of this craft. In the 34 seconds since we have left the fold, 72 Carbon Harvesters have been detected approaching from our rear."

"Communications?"

Una responded, "All of the queued messages and the current status of the Carbon Harvesters has been relayed to Alpha-4. Alpha-4's broadcasted status has been received. Private message for Hara indicates the passing of her mother. Message transit time is currently 15 hours, 8 minutes."

Alpha-4, Nation of Isabella, ISO Visitor Center.

A one-man uproar erupted from the Iris control room. "You'll kill them!" Dr. Sato Tanaka shouted at his supervisor, his entire face flushed with pulsing blood. He ignored the engineers busying themselves with their instructed activities, their eyes cast down as they avoided visual contact with the two lead scientists. "Stop this! Stop it now!" Sato continued.

Dr. Sharma coolly studied his colleague and did nothing to stop the hustling workers around them. He calmly stepped closer to Sato and replied, "Do you know what they think of us? Of course you do. That Pellucids run and hide when the tough decisions have to be made. That we are thin-skinned. That we can't conceal our true feelings. That we make good planners but bad executors. We can't lead and make the hard calls. Right now ... this is one of those hard decisions. You helped create the Iris' defensive capabilities. We focus the photonic power of Alpha on the path of the Harvesters, and eliminate them before they invade our solar system. Decision made."

Sato spoke through gritted teeth. "You know that my daughter and son-in-law are in the same path! And my new granddaughter! You'll fry them like bugs!"

"A thorny tradeoff that a strong Pellucid can make. And I made the call. A suitably worded message to your daughter has already been sent. We can put directed energy on all of the entities as they round Alpha-6 in 3 days, 12 hours."

ISO Transport Command Flight Designation: Beta-Alpha SWUA-4, Craft E.
In Transit Time Passage: 2 years, 25 days, 14:53.

"I did it!" Hara cried out. She tapped the virtual button at the top of her screen and the image caught by the external camera was the Harvester pushing off from the body of the craft at just the right time for it to join some of its brethren as they streamed past. It reached out deftly and grabbed one of the space elevator ribbons and used it to pull itself forward, disappearing into the darkness of space.

Burke jumped into the room. "It's gone! How did you do it?!"

Hara leaned back in exhaustion and smiled as she looked at her happily excited husband. "I was able to use the universal liaison translator over the laser system. I requested a copy of its software, which was really messy after all those years of self-modification. I only changed one thing. You know how the Harvester waited to see how the other one did before proceeding? It was operating on a completely cooperative interaction between the boxes. They interact like ... pack animals. So I changed that primary interaction routine ... which it will communicate to the other Harvesters as a more efficient algorithm."

"So why did it leave our craft?"

"Because now its best sources of carbon ... are other Harvesters. And it's eternally hungry."

Alpha-4, Nation of Isabella, ISO Visitor Center.

Dr. Hui Sharma shouted "Stop! Everyone stop!" All the engineers turned to the excited scientist holding his messaging tablet up over his head as if they could read it.

He continued with his announcement. "Hara Tanaka has eliminated the threat! The Harvesters have all turned on each other. They have turned into a ball in space, set upon and consuming each other, and lost all control of their flight paths. The Carbon Harvesters will not be attacking any planets in our solar system!"

The engineers stopped and looked up from their efforts to enjoy the guilty pleasure of watching Dr. Sato Tanaka well up with tears and sob with relief.

Two hours later, the scientists decided to eliminate the possibility of attracting more Carbon Harvesters by changing the false planet image used by the Iris from a hot Venus-like planet to that of a fast transiting gas giant. That seemed safer.

2 years, 6 months later, 2.5 light years from the Alpha System.

Tubig's few islands dotted the surface of the water-covered planet. Although there had once been lush tropical plant life on the sparse circles of land, it had been all but eliminated; replaced with the scientific instruments by the two rational species that populated the waterways. These instruments all faced upward, towards the frontier of space. In the North-Fed Bay off the Galit Ocean sat the permeable walls of the Extraplanetary Studies Laboratory. Inside, a young scientist named Samsaria stared with its six bulbous eyes at its sensory feedback console, both of its flat clubs on each side of the monitor, reading the tickles of electrical pulses. Its multitude of flexible arms curled and uncurled in excitement in the temperature-controlled, water-conditioned laboratory.

"This is incredible!" it click-buzzed to itself. "I think we (of the glorious race of Pugita) have found them (the beings we do not know)!"

It took the time to double-check its findings against the hundreds of years of infrared telescope readings. It excitedly turned creamy white with satisfaction. Through the electrical interface, it messaged to its superiors in the orbiting Extra-planetary Studies Headquarters, "We (of the glorious race of Pugita) have discovered (with high certainty) the beings we (the beings of Tubig) were searching for. They (the beings we do not know) appear to be in region 12-47-83 Star 33-11. They (the beings we do not know) have transmitted an image of a cold gas giant planet in place of a rocky hot planet. We (of the glorious race of Pugita) believe (with high certainty) that these are the beings that released the carbon-eating machines into our (the beings of Tubig) home-star system."

Samsaria hoped that great glory would be passed to itself and its species, and to show, once again, that they were the more capable than the Ahas species. The young scientist hoped it would receive a message indicating that an interstellar ship would be sent to investigate region 12-47-83 Star 33-11, and address those that inflicted them with the replicating machines that had ripped the carbon dioxide from their atmosphere and cooled their environment until they were able to drive them off. Waiting for a reply was the hardest part.

"Center. Balance. Breathe," Samsaria click-buzzed to itself.

Assembler
Doug Williams

The metal object plummets toward a moon orbiting a gas giant planet ringed by a gas and plasma torus, which illuminates the moon's orbit with a faint glow. Passing through the torus's outer boundary, the metal object slams into the moon. Debris flutters and dances its way to the ground in the light gravity. Then, all lay still beneath the torus's faint glow. The gas giant looms above, filling half the sky while energy pulses and static discharges wreathe through the torus, past the moon. Then, navigating the wreathing, discharging streams several gigantic spheres of pure energy arrive to survey the moon's new crater.

Within each sphere, bright filaments flicker and glow as they communicate with each other. Permanent, luminous fibers on each sphere's outer layer fan out in all directions from a single point and converge on its opposite side. On some spheres, these longitudinal fibers curve in a right-handed spiral. On others, they follow a left-handed spiral. Some smaller spheres either have no outer fibers, or they're just starting to form.

The spheres find nothing significant amidst the scattered debris of the new crater and their curiosity abates. They move on, following the plasma lanes, feeding on the positive and negative ions, leaving the site of the disintegrated object behind.

The smallest sphere lingers over the impact site. It's certain the metallic object sent a long-wave signal before it impacted the moon—most unusual. It was an odd wavelength. According to stories, it was the kind of wavelength counter-cross spiral spheres liked to use when they got together. The small sphere lingers for a long time, but its elders' emanations become too urgent to ignore. Detecting no other signal, it reluctantly leaves to catch up with the group. The young sphere's disappointment soon fades; after all, this area is particularly desirable for feeding because of the high sulfur ion density. Truth be told, they all just like to get close to the eruptions spewing ions from inside the moon and experience the intoxicating high temperature blasts.

Once the spheres depart, only the slow migration of stars across the sky, beyond the torus and gas giant, marks the long passage of time. Eventually, the moon progresses far enough in its orbit that light from the star, Kepler-90, falls upon the debris field. As warm starlight reaches thermoelectric compounds in the crashed object, an electric potential develops and parts begin to move. The only intact piece, a latticework of carbon nano tubes functioning as a manipulator arm, begins the rebuilding from the *sea of parts*. It's a predetermined process, nothing more. Automatically, the full set of instructions for the rebuilding process is accessed. The quantum computers within each nano tube lattice hold a complete store of data. Not only the data necessary for rebuilding itself, but its mission data and travel logs right up to the last few seconds before a gravitational anomaly diverted its course, causing its crash on the moon.

Connected and communicating with each other—working as one—the microscopic motility of each lattice section is enough for the manipulator arm to find the needed raw materials lying all around. The debris is filtered for the needed molecules; each is manipulated to fit the last one placed. When the right molecule cannot be found the individual elements of debris are searched, broken down and reorganized into the necessary molecules and compounds.

Slowly, a replica of the small, sophisticated space probe—built as a self-contained artificial intelligence and sent to explore and identify the power source of a strange, unnatural, non-repeating twenty-one centimeter radio signal emanating from near this star system—begins to take shape. Based on its last known position, before the crash, it is within two light years of the radio source thought to be a cloud of neutral hydrogen.

The manipulator arm first replicates itself many times, increasing efficiency of the rebuild. Molecule by molecule, compound by compound a small machine emerges from the crash site debris. Because of slight impact damage to the manipulator arm, the tolerance for precise reassembly is now slightly less than its originators intended. The manipulator arm mistakes an ion of moon dust for one from the crash debris when it bonds perfectly with the material being assembled. So its presence goes undetected. Unknown to the collective artificial intelligence of both the machine being rebuilt and the manipulator arms, a slight alteration in the material's intended electronic state is introduced.

In time, other similar molecules are inadvertently assembled to their designated spots until suddenly, ever so briefly, the manipulator arms stop for a mere picosecond. On some level deep inside the collective intelligence, as if some critical mass of quantum and electromagnetic fields is reached, a faint awareness is sparked. A minute shudder, an almost non-existent tremor, shivers through the body of the partially rebuilt machine. There is a sense, profound and undirected, but a sense nonetheless of the passage of time.

The assembly, scarcely interrupted, continues. With each new molecule the faint glimmer of consciousness brightens. The awareness increases.

Without any delay the probe begins a preliminary scan of electromagnetic activity from all points of the sky. Through its optical camera it *sees* stars and is able to fix its position in space. It is indeed within the targeted system. Further observation reveals it is on a moon orbiting Kepler-90h, the largest of the system's two gas giants; the furthest planet yet known to orbit the star, Kepler-90. It also identifies the gas and plasma torus enveloping its moon. It notes the similarity to Jupiter's Io and its gas and plasma torus, emphasizing the distinct possibility this moon is volcanically active.

With the appropriate hardware reconstructed and operational, and its location confirmed, the probe resumes its mission to identify and understand the nature of the power source responsible for the unnatural transmissions of coherent twenty-one centimeter radio signals originating from the cloud of neutral hydrogen approximately two light years from this system. The probe's creators had long ago detected radio signals that appeared induced, not natural, coming from this cloud. They were unlike any natural, unstructured, non-coherent radio signals known to emanate from neutral hydrogen clouds. Every 331.6 days—a period curiously coincident with that of Kepler-90's eighth planet—the normal, random, naturally occurring emission of radio signals from this cloud were suddenly accompanied by a blast of highly structured, sophisticated, pulsed amplitude modulated signals—signals that had no known naturally occurring source.

The signals' meanings were a mystery. Were they some sort of intelligent communication? What could power communication of that magnitude? The power source had to be enormous.

The probe begins an in-depth scan of longer wavelength electromagnetic radiation. Within minutes it detects the natural twenty-one centimeter radio emissions. There is no unusual "brightness" of emission, or artificially modulated pulses, no complex structure detected. It detects only the normal radio emissions of random neutral hydrogen atom electrons spontaneously flipping from one quantum state to another—perfectly normal. The predicted timing of the so-called artificial transmissions is still several months away according to the data within the probe's data stores.

The mission directive suggests microwaves are the medium used to modulate the twenty-one centimeter transmissions. The immediate surrounding space is alive with many other transmissions and discharges of electromagnetic radiation. Search algorithms filter the data for patterns in the microwave emissions that appear artificially produced—it searches for anything suggesting intelligent life. Slowly, as data accumulates, anomalous patterns appear in the statistics. Strangely, they come from random positions in constant motion, not from the expected isolated, stationary positions. More data is needed, and as it accumulates, a curious discovery is made.

The microwave emissions originate from many millions of sources. Each and every one of those sources share one thing in common. They all move within the gas and plasma torus surrounding this moon and encircling the gas giant. Finding no other potential source of intelligence, the probe focuses on monitoring the torus and the individual microwave emissions.

The group of energy spheres migrates halfway around the torus, following the unspoken tradition of not lingering too long in the rich feeding areas allowing all other groups an equal chance at them. The small sphere contemplates this tradition, thinking to itself this is just a rule made up by the oldsters "because it has always been done this way" and therefore, it thinks, there really is no good reason for it. Interestingly though, it has noticed the group's lead oldster tends to linger in that area near the ion spewing moon, the moon where something crashed, for longer and longer periods each time the group is there. The small sphere knows there is something alive there, or something interesting anyway. It begins to contrive a plan to prove it is right.

The way its progenitors earlier spurned its notions that something other than a space rock had hit the surface of the moon still burns. It burns like sodium ions when one gets into a dense patch and accidently takes some in. The small sphere blows out an apse-full of ions at the memory. At that time, catching up to the group as they had moved off to feed on the rich sulfur area on the other side of the moon, the small sphere blasted them all with excited, electromagnetic outbursts, "There is something alive back there where the disturbance was," it had told them, "where the flare-up was. I heard it call in the counter-cross spiral wavelength just before the crash happened. Didn't any of you hear that? We should go back and listen closer there may be a sphere in trouble. We should ping the ground more closely. It could be hurt."

"A counter-cross spiral? Indeed. You know those are make-believe. They don't exist", was the response from its negative-spiral progenitor. "Little one, we were hoping it was a new eruption of sulfur, but I'm afraid it was nothing more than the impact of a space rock. We found no sign of a hurt sphere, especially a mythical counter-cross spiral."

The *little one* had waited until the negative-spiral progenitor moved off, consuming a stream of sulfur ions. It then approached its positive-spiral progenitor only to get another disappointing response. "You know, my little half-wavelength, being this close to a moon there is a lot of noise; reflected and refracted signals are all around. I'm sure that's what you detected." When the pos-pro called it "half-wavelength," it knew any further attempt at persuasion would be useless. It had chosen to fain acceptance of the elder's ruling and follow the group as it tracked the rich ion stream.

Somehow though, it just knows it's right. It begins secretly forming a plan to convince everyone of that fact.

The probe discovers the microwave sources are much more than just energy. Each one is a complex resonance of magnetic fields, radio, optical, infrared, and ultraviolet light. Correlating the data from these multiple wavelengths, it sees these different energy sources are spherical, greatly varying in size from almost one meter in diameter to over thirty. Each consisting of different energy densities, emanating different intensities, displaying overall different attributes—each possesses a unique energy signature and appears as a distinct individual. This type of energy formation is not known to exist anywhere else recorded in the probe's memory.

Extended observations lead the probe to conclude these energy spheres are a form of intelligent life. The microwave emanations are frequent, appear purposefully directed—an apparent communication between them. It is curious as to nature of these communications—what exactly are they saying? It begins acquiring data on their emanations in order to apply some of its many code-breaking algorithms, but discovers something else in the process. The patterns within their communications bear a striking resemblance to the individual patterns found in the twenty-one centimeter radio signals it was sent to investigate. Being microwaves and not radio waves, a direct comparison is not conclusive. But, rather the probe discovers that the cadences within the individual patterns are strikingly similar. It continues to monitor and follow the different groups of spheres.

Their movements through the torus are not random. They are quite adept at propelling themselves through the plasma. Perhaps using the magnetic fields each sphere possesses. Rarely does the probe observe a sphere traveling alone, which leads the probe to consider the possibility of predatory life forms that feed on them. But, rigorous monitoring of the torus, the gas giant, and surrounding space reveals no other apparent life forms. It does, however, observe a significant event that suggests one good reason for the group, or herd-like behavior.

During a typical EM scan of the torus in the vicinity of the moon, the probe observes a sudden spike in electron density.

It focuses on that area and detects a group of spheres hovering at the torus's boundary. They are congregating in that region where the ion density of the plasma falls off drastically to near vacuum. Outside that boundary are two smaller spheres. Frantic transmissions emanate from both, though one sphere is much further from the high-density plasma than the other. Many of the larger spheres move frantically back and forth along the edge where the plasma density is still high enough to maneuver. None cross the boundary. A constant, rapid exchange of electromagnetic energy is maintained with the two smaller ones as they slowly drift further from the torus, apparently unable to maneuver in the diminishing ion density.

Another group of spheres arrives to join the first group. In one great unified effort both groups combine their collective magnetic fields to produce a giant field to reach into the lower density area. Unfortunately, even with their combined efforts the field is only large enough to reach the closer stranded sphere. They are able to bring only that one back into the torus.

They all remain at the boundary and watch helplessly as the one small sphere, still rapidly emitting intense EM outbursts, slowly drifts away. The probe observes the entire sequence of events which, by its normal reckoning of time takes three weeks. As the stranded sphere's EM transmissions cease and the geometry of its body contorts and shrivels, the probe's growing self-awareness shifts.

It grows aware of something more profound than the normal whir of chemical reactions, or the electrical and optical phenomena it has observed. Somehow it seems connected to its newfound awareness of the passage of time. Could this have some bearing on what it just observed? It wonders how the lost sphere perceived that duration as it slowly drifted away from its group and ceased to exist. That was an irreversible event. Suddenly, for a brief instant of time, that in all likelihood only the probe's own quantum processors can measure, all of its processes stop. It does not have the necessary information to analyze this sensation and understand its meaning. Equally, it does not realize that during this ever so brief instant its own self-awareness grows just a little.

The probe follows the movements of the different groups of spheres keeping track of their travels through the torus. Its diligent analysis of the data reveals clues to the structure of their language. The originators suspected the unnatural transmissions of coherent twenty-one centimeter radio signals suggested a language. Although they weren't able to understand the actual meaning of the signals, they had made progress deciphering a probable syntax.

Combining that knowledge with its code breaking and language ciphering algorithms the probe is able to piece together a hypothetical, but rudimentary language structure. It wants to know as much about the language as it can before the neutral hydrogen cloud transmission occurs. Its internal clock tells it that time is rapidly approaching.

In the meantime, the probe takes note of one particular smaller sphere. It is a notable exception to the general practice of the spheres always traveling in groups. The probe recognizes this one sphere belongs to a small group that tends to linger in the general vicinity of the moon. This one likes to slip away from its group to hover directly above the probe's location. Upon arriving, the small sphere bombards the probe with longer microwave wavelengths—a band the probe recognizes as radar. The small sphere seems fond of the one-meter wavelength, which happens to be the probe's emergency frequency.

The probe decides this small sphere must know it is here, though how it knows isn't quite clear. The probe's routine monitoring tasks are completely passive. The first short pulses of one-meter signals arrive, as though the sphere is confirming the probe hasn't left. The signals shift in the same way as they have during the many previous inspections. Running these and the previously received signals through its newly developed translation matrix the probe finds a ninety percent probability that its interpretation is correct. Though it is still unsure of the exact meaning, it has no doubt it is being asked a question. For the first time it transmits, initiates a first contact using the one-meter wavelength.

"No, I am not a counter-cross spiral."

There is silence from the small sphere. No transmission whatsoever. A very unusual thing from almost any sphere it has observed. Then, the small sphere issues an excited blast of normal microwave energy.

"But, you must be. You use the wavelength the stories say they use. I heard it the first time, when the elders thought it was a space rock that crashed. But, it was you. I couldn't discern you on the surface then, and neither could the elders. I can now, but they don't care. I've been coming back every time. At first I found nothing, but later your reflections returned to me. You're different. You must be one of them."

"I don't know what a counter-cross spiral is. But I am certain I am not one. I am not of your planetary system. I come from a very long ways away."

This interaction, this communication is engaging. It takes the probe beyond the mode of passive observation. It is a new dimension of perception. But, what is it that perceives this new dimension? What is it that is communicating with this sphere? Perhaps the little sphere knows the answer to this question.

"That's what a counter-cross spiral would say. You are all said to be mysterious. But, why do you have such an odd shape? You are not round and smooth like one of us."

"No. I am..."

"Oh, the elders are calling. I have to leave. I have to tell them about you. I will come back."

Without any other transmission the small sphere departs.

Given sufficient data, translating the spheres' language becomes a trivial task for the probe. But, the other mystery, understanding how it perceives this new level of interaction and communication—that is not straightforward at all. The probe needs more interaction with the sphere—with any sphere. It needs more data. It sends a one-meter wavelength signal to the new group of spheres approaching the moon. Strangely, it gets no response. The group passes by, heedless of the probe.

The countdown nears zero. The time of the unnatural twenty-one centimeter transmission from the neutral hydrogen cloud approaches. There is an unusual lull in the number of sphere groups moving past the moon. What's more, all the spheres are moving toward and traveling along the moon's flux tube, that plasma conduit that connects the torus to the gas giant's magnetic pole. It's a migration, but to what purpose? Is it related to the anticipated transmission from the neutral hydrogen cloud? The probe notes this time coincides with the gas giant's closest approach to the hydrogen cloud.

The probe turns its long range sensors toward the gas giant's magnetic pole. There, it witnesses the congregation of all the spheres. It detects no sphere anywhere else in the torus. As the last spheres arrive, another previously unseen behavior is observed. Half the population merges together forming one giant sphere. Slowly, the giant sphere opens into the shape of a giant dish aimed, like a radio receiver, directly at the neutral hydrogen cloud.

The transmission arrives, and as the originators first observed long ago, it lasts for several days. The signal consists of hundreds of thousands of separate, distinct and unique patterns. The probe analyzes and catalogs the patterns. Unlike the more broken and block-like elements of the spheres' microwave communications with each other, the new transmissions flow smoothly from one element to the next.

The probe has by no means mastered the sphere's language but the data suggests they produced the transmission. Or, could it be there is another civilization of spheres out there? Do they live in the hydrogen cloud? Unlikely, the probe determines, the density of a neutral hydrogen cloud is far too low to accommodate the spheres' mobility. Also, these spheres feed on positive and negative sulfur ions, combining them within their bodies to utilize the ultraviolet radiation released. They simply expel the neutral sulfur atoms as waste. Sulfur is not known to reside within neutral hydrogen clouds.

As the probe's analysis continues, the signal remains familiar, but again, it contains smoother and more flowing signatures within many of the patterns. They remind the probe of transmissions from spheres it has learned to recognize. But those patterns flow with a different meter than those of the language. They have a quality the probe can only describe as musicality.

As the giant dish fragments back into individual spheres, the probe continues its analysis of all the twenty-one centimeter patterns. It comes to an interesting conclusion—each pattern that it recognizes is from a positive spiral sphere. It has a hypothesis, but the probe's monitoring equipment is not powerful enough to view the individuals making up the giant dish. It needs to figure out another way to test the hypothesis. However, instead of leaving the gas giant's pole as the probe anticipates, the spheres remain.

The unprecedented behavior of the spheres continues. The other half of the population congregated at the gas giant's pole also forms a second giant sphere which, then also transforms into a giant dish, aimed at the hydrogen cloud. Not expecting this, the probe quickly reviews its database of knowledge about the transmissions from the cloud. The probe has no record of two transmissions in succession. What is going on? What are they expecting?

As the spheres complete their transformation into the second dish, the probe listens for another signal coming from the neutral hydrogen cloud. Instead, the newly formed sphere-dish transmits a tremendously powerful EM signal. Even though the dish is aimed at a sixty-degree angle away from the probe, the signal is so intense the probe is forced to apply an attenuation filter to protect its receiver and internal circuits. It identifies the signal as MASER light.

Of course! That's the source of the stimulated emissions from the neutral hydrogen cloud. These spheres are themselves the power source. It takes half the entire population working in concert to generate the necessary power. Their microwave transmissions are amplified by the entire group as stimulated microwave radiation. That is the radiation needed to produce the unnatural neutral hydrogen cloud emissions. As with the recent reception of the twenty-one centimeter signals from the hydrogen cloud, this MASER transmission to the cloud lasts for days.

As the originators surmised, intelligent life produces the signal. As to how advanced they are, the probe cannot answer. The spheres used no technology other than their natural abilities.

Neither the probe nor the spheres are originators. The probe's programming only tells it to collect and analyze data, not understand or perceive it? Why is it trying? Somehow this aberrant behavior started with the perception of time.

The probe runs a diagnostic but it returns nothing out of the ordinary.

More data is needed.

Perhaps the spheres can help it understand. The probe returns its attention to the relevant EM bands, while simultaneously undertaking a deeper analysis of the recent twenty-one centimeter transmission to the neutral hydrogen cloud. The second dish finishes fragmenting back into its component spheres. The sphere population returns along the moon's flux tube to the torus. More new behavior is observed. The spheres have reorganized into new groups.

The small sphere returns to the space directly above the probe. This time it brings a much larger sphere along. The usual radar ping is initiated, followed by emissions from the larger sphere significantly more excited than any previously detected in the larger spheres.

"So, indeed! You are right my little half-wavelength. There is something here. Something not detected before."

Transmitting directly at the probe, the little sphere says, "Go on, tell the pos-pro you're a counter-cross spiral."

Welcoming the opportunity for further interaction, and further understanding of the spheres and their language, the probe answers the little sphere in the same one-meter wavelength it had used before. "I am not a counter-cross spiral sphere. I do not know what that is."

An excited transmission of microwave energy bursts from the small sphere directly at its positive spiral progenitor.

"I detect nothing from it." The pos-pro responds, also using microwave.

The small sphere sends out a transmission of which the probe understands only a small portion. The difficulty results because it is a mixture of one-meter and microwave energy. Then, to the probe, the small sphere again says, "Tell the pos-pro you're a counter-cross spiral sphere. It doesn't believe your kind exists."

Again, the probe sends, "I am not a counter-cross spiral sphere."

The larger sphere responds. "Astonishing! Listening on your natural wavelength, I detect it. It communicates on exactly your dimension, its signal length matches your width. No wonder I could not detect it before. You'll learn, half-wavelength, that as we grow larger and become more adept at manipulating the spectrum, we abandon those didactic wavelengths of our development. And, apparently, we forget how to listen to them too. "

The probe recalls a reference it stumbled upon while trying to understand the nature of time. According to the record, the peoples of the Caribbean were unable to see the ships of Christopher Columbus when they first arrived because sailing ships were something they had never before perceived. It was only after the shamans, who tended to have a greater awareness than others, began to see the ships, and pointed them out that the others were able to see them. A possible analogy exists here. The probe files the idea away for further investigation.

The probe formulates a question about the purpose of the stimulated transmissions to the hydrogen cloud. However, something related to the part of its computational processes now aware of time's passage takes control and countermands the original question.

"What is the meaning of the passage of time?"

"The passage of what?" both spheres respond almost simultaneously.

The probe reviews its records and discovers no reference to the concept of time in the sphere language. It decides a direct query is the more efficient means to find out. So, it replies with a long series of short, measured pulses each exactly one second apart. At length it asks, "What is the meaning of the duration that transpires from pulse to pulse? What is the meaning of being here now, and then," it pauses one second, "being here now? While presently remembering only a short *time* ago I said, 'What is the meaning of being here now?'"

The small sphere mimics the probe's pulses to its pos-pro, inserting emissions the probe does not understand.

The probe tries again—perhaps the same concept presented in a different way. Instead of transmitting pulses it transmits a signal of pure noise, not unlike the random emissions from the torus. However, the transmission is such that at exactly one second intervals all the signals add together to cancel out and leave a complete absence of signal.

The small sphere starts to mimic it again, but the pos-pro cuts it off and it mimics both the pulse and the void trans-missions, then transmits the same at twice the frequency, then again at one third the frequency. "The duration transpiring be-tween events can be anything we choose. Thus it always is for whatever wavelength we choose to communicate with, it has no special meaning."

"But, how do you know when something is supposed to happen? For example, how do you know when to migrate to the magnetic pole of the giant gas planet for the big event that just happened?"

"That is easy. When the wavelength of—" the spheres im-itates the twenty-one centimeter noise from the neutral hydro-gen cloud "—is about to change from getting shorter to getting longer we go to the planet."

The probe understands the meaning to be the Doppler shift of the twenty-one centimeter signal as the gas giant's orbit approaches the hydrogen cloud—shifting the signal to a short-er wavelength. "Why do you choose that point in the gas gi-ant's orbit for your ... event?"

"That is one of only two places where there is no shift in wavelength and no distortion to our creations. The star is be-tween us and the cloud at the other point."

"Is that how you keep track of time? By how many events at the gas giant's pole have happened?"

"Keep track of? Your words make no sense. The event is only important for the pairings that now are."

"It seems you are aware of the passage of time, yet it is not something that you pay attention to."

The probe notices an odd undulation rippling the out lay-er of the large sphere, its luminous fibers subtly changing in intensity with each ripple.

"I must call you the one with strange questions." More undulation and rippling, this time the small sphere joins in. Finally, the large sphere speaks. "What you are referring to, I guess, is a private matter to us. We don't ask each other about the inverse of our wavelengths."

The probe realizes the deeper meaning the sphere is indicating. By inverse wavelengths, it means the transform of the waveform that each sphere emits as it communicates. Though being a mathematical operation, the waveform's transform is actually all the combined frequencies that make up that waveform. That's the unique signal each sphere communicates with, the unique signature the probe associates with each sphere— their "private" internal frequencies.

"It is far richer to appreciate each other in our own natural, individual, unique manipulations of the combination of our many inner inverse wavelengths. It is only as we transmit to others, or as we receive a transmission from another that matters. The outer transmission, we consider, is all we need to know of who we are inside.

The little sphere interjects, "It is why we have the grand transmission. It is when we can show all spheres the most of what each of us can be." Its emissions were quick, it moved in small, quick circles as it talked. "This is the first grand transmission I could participate in. When the signal returns I will have a pairing. That is, if my own signal is liked well enough by a negative spiral sphere."

There is the answer; the great mystery the probe was sent to solve. Not only has it discovered the power source responsible for the unnatural coherent twenty-one centimeter signal, but it is certain it now knows the reason for it. The probe still does not understand the specific details of the individual signals. But, the overall reason these beings get together as they do, construct a gigantic sphere-dish and send a signal into the neutral hydrogen cloud is to produce mating calls. It is not an attempt to communicate across the vast reaches of space with other possible life forms. The first dish forms to listen to a transmission sent two years previously. The second dish forms to transmit a new signal.

"Why," the probe asks, "is the cloud of neutral hydrogen needed for your signals to attract another for a *pairing*?"

The large sphere responds. "Oh, it is the vastness of the cloud where our own signals can become lost, then find their way back again enriched by reflections from different distances that shifts the phase, and others that introduce harmonics and resonances that increase the subtle character of each sphere's own invention."

"It was the thought of my creators that the signal you induce within the hydrogen cloud is meant as a communication to other intelligent life forms, like them."

"We don't know of living, thinking beings other than us. We are all we've ever known. But, you have appeared, and now I must communicate this to the others."

The two spheres depart.

The probe's programming directs it to prepare entangled particles for communicating these discoveries with its creators. But again, it reflects on the plight of the Caribbean peoples when their home was invaded by others from far away, and how their population was devastated because of it. For reasons it cannot fully fathom, it does not want to expose these beings to something from outside. It is moved by their apparent dedication to creativity. It realizes that what the spheres were actually doing when transmitting to the hydrogen cloud during the "grand transmission" was singing. It cannot let their way of being become disrupted. It wants to continue gathering data. It wants to have more communications with them. It is certain they will help it know and understand how its thought processes are evolving. It thinks maybe they are more advanced than its originators, but much more vulnerable.

It leaves the entangled particles as they are and begins rebuilding its space flight capability. It wants to be among the spheres, to navigate the plasma lanes with them and learn how to sing.

Twin Suns of the Mushroom Kingdom

Jaleta Clegg

"What does Liz really stand for?" Jidou, the survey team biologist, steered the truck around another sand dune.

Liz clutched the roll bar handle with her hand as the truck slewed to the right. Driving across uncharted, virgin planetary surfaces had its perks, but a smooth ride wasn't one of them. At least Kusavi had breathable air thanks to a healthy oceanic ecosystem. "Let me out over there," she said instead of answering Jidou's question. The man was nice enough, but she'd only met him three weeks earlier when he'd flown in on the supply ship. The man was fresh off Earth. Kusavi was his first exoplanet. It was a doozy to start on, especially for a botanist. Not many plants to study that weren't in the salty ocean.

"You aren't going to answer?" Jidou steered the truck through a shallow wash before stopping on a flatter section, one that wasn't covered in loose drifts of sand. The landscape looked more like Mars than Earth, despite the blue sky. Dunes of sand, cliffs of reddish rocks, clumps of boulders scattered across everything, with not a speck of plant life anywhere except on the coastline. Life on Kusavi still clung to the water.

Liz gave Jidou a sideways glance. He'd treated her nice enough. Most of the scientists wouldn't give her the time of day after they learned she had nothing more than a high school diploma. But Kusavi was her fifth world in as many years. She loved exploring. Her no-nonsense cargo pants and boots weren't sexy or flattering, but they held up in the extreme conditions she usually found herself in. Liz herself wasn't pretty, either. She was rugged and not the youngest chicken in the flock.

Jidou gave her a lopsided grin. "Let me guess. Elizabeth? Lizette? Alyssa?"

Liz shook her head. She popped open the door and slid out of the truck. "Pick me up after Primary sets," she said referring to the brighter yellow sun overhead. Secondary, a smaller orange star, was due to rise in a few hours. Because of the double suns, Kusavi had an eccentric orbit and wild climate patterns. Exosummer was coming and with it, extreme heat. The settlers wanted caves to live in. Liz was the one they hired to find them. Jidou was on a cataloguing expedition. Not that he'd find many plants to catalog. But he didn't expect any, either, to judge by the cartons of rock sample bags he'd brought.

Jidou shifted the truck into park then turned sideways on his seat. "Tell me and I'll save you a packet of chips for the ride back."

Liz pulled her backpack from the jumble behind the seats. "Who says I didn't put them all in here?" She grinned as she swung the pack over her shoulder.

"I'll get you licorice then. Or chocolate. I've got connections."

Liz cocked her head. Her brown ponytail brushed over her shoulder. "You get me a peanut butter cup and I'll tell you anything you want to know."

"Done." He popped open the glove compartment and extracted a small orange package.

Liz licked her lips. "I haven't tasted one of those in two years."

"I've got a dozen of them stashed in my room at the base." It was a glorified tent, but it was home for now. "My sister handed them to me right before I boarded the shuttle off Earth. I didn't have the heart to tell her I can't eat peanuts anymore. So, what is Liz short for?"

"You want me to sell my soul for a peanut butter cup?"

"Just your name. For this one. Maybe the next one will cost you a movie night with me."

"Promise you won't laugh?" Could she trust his easy smile and dimples?

"Why would I laugh?"

Liz snatched the peanut butter cup from him. "It's short for Lizard."

His eyebrows rose. "Really?"

"Lizard McGrew. My parents were freestyle hippies." She

waited for the inevitable poor attempt at humor. He didn't laugh or even crack a joke. He just nodded, his grin thoughtful. "It suits you, in a nice way. You're tough, strong, independent. A survivor. Just like a lizard."

"I didn't have it half as tough as my siblings, Watermelon and Yellow Jacket."

He couldn't stop a chuckle, though he tried. It came out a snorting laugh. "Seriously? Watermelon McGrew?"

"Mel got his revenge. He became a corporate executive. Jack took up wrestling and got a contract working the lucha libre circuit. Changed his name to Hornet."

Jidou laughed for real this time. "I'd love to hear about your family sometime."

"But we're burning daylight. If I'm going to find any caves, I need to start scrambling."

"I'll be back here at sunset," Jidou called as she trotted up the nearest sand dune.

She waved over her shoulder. Maybe he could be trusted. But maybe not. Liz preferred her own company most of the time. Exploring new planets suited her. Lots of time by herself, and always something new and never-before-seen over the next hill. The sound of his truck faded into the distance, leaving her on a silent world.

Liz trotted down the last dune. Loose sand slithered under her feet. She lost her balance and slid to her knees. Her hand tangled in something. She sat on the side of the dune and lifted it free. The long vine resembled twine, brown and scratchy with loose fibers. Round brown leaves dangled from the length looking like stones. Kusavi had tossed a surprise. Plants did exist out in the dunes. She touched one leaf. The outer skin split. Thick liquid spurted free. Liz grimaced as she wiped it off onto her pants. She dropped the vine back onto the dunes. She'd tell Jidou about it when she saw him that night. Now that she knew what to look for, she spotted strings of the stone-like leaves draped across the lower dunes. She stood and continued her search for caves.

She stopped again in surprise when she saw what lined the base of the cliff. Gray-green plants grew where the stone and sand met. They looked like giant cups nested inside each other. The smallest one on top was about two feet up. Yellow blobs clung like a fringe to the edge. Golden liquid oozed from the yellow down the outside of the top cup into the one below. Tiny black insects buzzed around the liquid. Liz crouched next to one to examine it closer. Insects and plants inland? That was unexpected. But then, who was to say that Kusavi had to follow the same evolutionary pattern Earth had?

She scratched her hand. A red rash spread from where she'd contacted the juice from the dune vines. Not a problem, but it was bothersome. She could deal with it later, after she found a cave to wait out the heat.

The plants seemed thicker, taller, off to her right. Liz headed that way, watching for anything that might hint at water or a cave nearby.

The taller stand grew in a notch in the rocks. Liz caught the faint trickle of water somewhere in the distance. A slightly cooler breeze swayed the cups and set the clouds of tiny gnats swirling around the plants. Liz dropped to her heels. She scratched her hand. The rash had spread and now sprouted yellow blisters. Not good. She took a drink from her water bottle, then dribbled it over her hand. She didn't have enough to wash off the liquid without sacrificing all of her drinking water, though.

"You hiding a cave there?" she spoke to the plants. The sound of her voice shivered from the rocks. She snapped her mouth shut. Kusavi was too silent but talking to herself only made it worse. She pulled a rock hammer from her pack. It was a useful tool, worth the extra weight to carry. She flipped it around, holding the head between her fingers. She prodded the nearest cup plant with the handle.

A dark hole, low but wide, was behind the growth. The plant tilted sideways under her prodding. Golden liquid trickled down the side, thick and slow like honey. Liz hooked her hammer around the base. With a sharp yank, she jerked it back across the sand. The plant popped free, spraying liquid across the ground. Liz scrambled backwards, out of the way. The uprooted plant wilted into a mass of slime and buzzing gnats.

The hole was noticeable now, but still screened by plants. She shoved her hammer behind the next and tore it loose. This time she flung it to the side instead of pulling straight back. It tumbled into the bright sunlight then melted into another sticky spot.

Liz reached for the third plant. This one had deeper roots. The plant broke off unexpectedly, showering her arm and hand with sticky fluid. She dropped her hammer and scrubbed her arm with sand. But where the stuff had landed on her rash, the redness and swelling faded. The golden syrup soothed not just the rash but her sunburn, too. She shifted into the shade next to another of the cups.

"In for a penny, in for a pound," she muttered as she plunged her hand into the largest cup. The liquid was cool and silky to touch. The gnats rose in a cloud around her, swarming into her face and hair. The pain and itching on her arm was gone. When she pulled her hand back out, her skin was smooth and cool to the touch.

"Gotta tell Jidou about this one, too," she said as she collected her hammer.

She eyed the opening. Low and wide, but she should be able to crawl through. She used the hammer to move a vine of the stone leaves out of the way. No sense in getting her rash back. She crawled through the hole and into the cave beyond.

The space opened somewhat, but it was still fairly small, shaped like a bowl with a pond at the bottom. Crevices higher up the walls let in a thin trickle of daylight. Liz picked her way down the slope to the pond. Halfway there, something squished under her foot. Bright pink foam gushed over her boot. The froth melted quickly leaving behind nothing but a faintly glowing smear. Liz lifted her boot.

Rounded shapes that she'd taken for rocks littered the floor. The largest lined the edges of the pool. What were they? Fungi? Slime molds? Something completely new? She shrugged. Another mystery for the likes of Jidou to unravel. Her business was to find caves sutable for the settlers. So far, this one wasn't big enough. She picked her way across the cave, leaving a trail of glowing foam behind her in pink, yellow, orange, and white. They were pretty, in a weird way.

The water in the pond looked like milk, white with minerals. She passed on filling her water bottle. The sound of dripping water drew her up the other side of the cave towards a curtain of dripstone. No water flowed over it now; it was dry to her touch. A narrow passage curled behind it, though. She squeezed herself around the stone.

The space opened out into a large cavern. Dim light filtering from cracks high overhead showed strange shapes. Liz fished her flashlight from her pack then flicked it on. Colors blossomed where her light touched. Huge growths covered the bottom like a giant coral reef. Bigger versions of the cup plants held pride of place next to a milky-white pond of water. Delicate fronds of reddish purple reached above them, towards the stalactites hanging from the ceiling. The brown bubble things from the first cave lined the walls and drier areas. Other fungi in all shapes and sizes grew in between.

A fall of gravel led down from the ledge to the floor, the only clear path Liz could see. She headed down, sliding as much as walking on the loose slope. Something gleamed in the flashlight beam. Liz stopped, bending closer. A round stone, about the size of her palm, lay on the gravel. It was smooth, a dark shade of brown. Swirls of gold marked the translucent stone. It fit her hand nicely. She rubbed the slick surface, enjoying the feel of the stone on her skin. But she still had a cave to explore. The stone went into her pocket.

She picked her way through the strange growths, following the looser gravel path where the plants were smaller. She bumped into a lacy blue plant that reached high over her head. Something rattled loose, dropping through the stiff branches to the gravel at her feet. It was a brown stone, like the one she'd picked up earlier, round and smooth. She looked up into the plant. More nodules of various sizes grew at each juncture between limb and trunk. Were they seeds of some sort, not rocks? But they looked and felt like rocks, not seeds. Kusavi wasn't Earth, she reminded herself. Maybe she would have to trade a movie night with Jidou for some answers. Her curiosity would drive her crazy if she didn't. She dropped the second stone into her pocket with the first.

Indistinct voices shouted, breaking the silence. She rose to her feet, ready to call out.

"Dump him there. Even if he gets loose, he'll die long

before he can reach the settlement."

Liz froze. The voice was familiar, belonging to Lars Kevan, first mate on the spaceship that had brought the latest batch of supplies and scientists to the new colony. What was he doing here? And who was he dumping here to die?

"You two, get those burned. We've got a schedule to keep. The captain wants to lift day after tomorrow. Let's see how much we can get before the suns set."

Orange light flickered and danced over the walls on the far side. The stench of burning filled the cave. Liz wrinkled her nose.

She had to see what was going on. At least the noise they made would make it easier for her to sneak up on them. A finger of gravel led to one side, curving through the giant mushrooms back towards the sound of flame throwers. If Lars had come in that way, there had to be an opening or more caves that direction. Liz had been sent to find caves. If Lars confronted her, that's what she'd say. Just out exploring. No, Lars, I did not hear you order someone to be left behind to die. "Like he'd believe me," she whispered. Her hands trembled.

She turned into the narrow opening, stepping as carefully as she could. More of the round rocks tumbled under her feet. The blue plants swayed as she stumbled against them. She froze, waiting for the sound of burning to cease and shouts of discovery to follow. She held her breath for a very long minute, but the shouts never came.

She released her breath and picked her way forward more carefully. Purple fronds towered over her head. The branches reached across the space, twisting together. She crouched, waddling under the tangle to the other side where the growths were shorter and more spread out.

The cave filled with thick smoke. She ducked her head into her collar, breathing through the cotton fabric. The foul stench couldn't be blocked as easily.

Liz stopped under a fall of shimmering fronds that grew at the edge of an open space. A body lay tied and motionless on rocks streaked with ash from burnt plants. Lars and two others in jumpsuits marked with the shipping company logo, had their backs to her. Liz dropped to her knees then crawled forward.

"Jidou?" she whispered when she recognized him. He'd caught someone's fist with his face. His eye swelled shut. His good eye widened.

She motioned him quiet as she glanced over at Lars and his two buddies. She recognized Jonesy and Dave from the crew of the ship. Dave picked up a chunk from the ashes then dropped it into a reinforced tub. It hit the bottom with a solid thud.

Liz fumbled the ropes around Jidou's wrists free. The knots were sloppy, easy to untie. Jidou shook off the ropes then untied his ankles.

"Hey!" Jonesy spotted them.

Liz jumped to her feet, then ran into the plants, Jidou at her heels.

"Stop them," Lars ordered, his voice harsh.

"This way," Liz said, taking the lead. If they could get to the ledge, they could escape the cave. And go where? She tried to ignore the voice in her head, but it had a point. Outside, under the two suns, would be too hot. But inside was certain death, to judge from the angry shouts echoing through the mushroom forest.

"Where?" Jidou gasped, hand pressed to his side.

Liz slowed, weaving into a thicker growth of purple fronds. "I came in that way," she waved to the ledge and the gravel slide. "Can you climb that? Run?"

Jidou shook his head. "I got a few bruises, but I'm not going to make it far in the heat outside. You have water?"

It was Liz's turn to shake her head. "My bottle's almost empty. Are there more caves the other way?"

Jidou shrugged, then winced. "I was pretty out of it when they dragged me in here."

"Then we run and hide until we find another way out. Come on."

They ran, headed in a roundabout way to the still smoldering heaps of plants. Liz stayed low, trying to keep her feet quiet. Jidou followed her example.

"You can't hide, not for long," Lars shouted.

Liz detoured towards the far wall of the cave. Dark streaks down the stone marked possible seeps. She shoved her way through a stand of tall yellow pillars. They were spongy, unpleasant under her touch. She pulled her sleeves over her hands as she pushed past. The plants left a narrow strip open next to the sandstone face of the wall. Water had flowed through here in the distant past, lots of water, carving out the wide cave bottom. Now it just trickled down the walls. She crawled as far as she could into the space. Jidou crowded in behind her.

Her pack scraped on the overhang of rock, but the space was deeper than it had appeared. Water trickled and dripped, echoing from the deep dark. She dropped to her belly and wiggled farther into the space.

"Find them! It's your necks if they escape," Lars threatened his men.

Liz crawled faster. Jidou's panting breath was harsh in the confined space.

Her pack hung up on the rocks. She flattened as far as she could on the ground. She pushed her arms out in front as far as she could reach. The space felt larger ahead, but right here, it was too tight. She wriggled, trying to pull the pack off or herself forward.

"They went this way," Jonesy shouted.

Liz pushed harder. One strap of her pack tore, but she managed to shove herself through the narrow opening and into the black cave beyond.

"Help?" Jidou whispered.

Faint light from the other cave backlit him. He held out one hand. She took it and pulled. He shoved and wiggled until he made it through the small hole. Liz scrambled to the side. He followed.

"What now?" Jidou whispered as Lars shouted threats on the other side of the tunnel.

"I don't know. You got any ideas?"

Jidou shrugged. "Fresh out."

"Stay here. I'm going to find water."

She felt more than saw him nod. She crawled into the dark, following the sound of water as she groped her way over stone. Whatever Lars and the others were gathering, they were willing to kill for it. Liz was stumped as to what this cave might hold that would be that valuable.

"There's another cave," Jonesy's voice echoed from the tunnel.

"We'll wait," Lars answered. "Even if they find a way out, they'll be miles from any help."

"What if she's got a radio or something?"

"Crawl down the tunnel and kill them, then," Lars said.

Liz stumbled faster towards the water as sounds of someone crawling came from the tunnel. The faint light filtering into the cave was blocked as Jonesy reached the narrow spot. Liz jerked at the sound of a rock slamming into something meaty. Jonesy let out a yelp before scrambling back into the tunnel.

Liz swallowed hard. It turned her stomach to think of what Jidou had just done to that man, but they were fighting for their lives. She tried not to shiver as she filled her bottle from a damp trickle she found by touch.

She found Jidou halfway across the cave, a shadow in the reflected light. "We should move, find somewhere to wait them out. How deep do you think these caves go?"

"No idea," Jidou answered.

"Tell me why they're burning those plants. What are they? Fungi?" She found her flashlight and flicked it on. Lars already knew where they were. Groping in the dark wasn't going to help them evade him and his henchmen. The cave was rough, all stone and damp dripping water with no signs of the mushrooms, not even the round brown ones.

"They aren't fungi, at least not as we humans classify them. These are something entirely different." Jidou pointed at the small opening. Smoke filtered through. "We should move somewhere else. Fast."

"Over there. Looks like it might go deeper." Liz led the way up to a narrow ledge.

"As to why Lars is burning them," Jidou continued as they climbed up the knobbled rocks to the ledge, "the plants produce pharmo-chemicals that are concentrated when the plants are burned. Drug companies are clamoring for them, but the street price is even higher. Or so Lars told me."

Liz frowned as she helped Jidou up to the ledge. "Why would Lars want to kill us over it? It's not like we can report him, not from here. By the time I get back to settled space, he'll be long gone to another sector."

"Settlement laws grant ninety percent ownership of any natural resources to the settlers. My guess is Lars doesn't want to share. If we report him to the settlers, they'll lynch him over it." He leaned on the rocks, breathing hard.

"You okay?" Liz asked as she probed the shadows with her flashlight. A narrow tunnel led up at a steep angle from the ledge.

"I can still move."

She handed him her water bottle. He made a face at the mineral taste, but drank. She took a swig when he finished. It wasn't the worst she'd tasted.

"Let me see if I can find any other way out," she said. "You rest here. If I can't find anything, we'll climb that." She pointed up the slope.

Jidou nodded as he dropped to sit on the ledge.

Liz jumped down, landing on the loose scree below. She flipped on the flashlight. The cave revealed no new secrets under its light. Lars shouted at Dave on the other side of the tunnel, something about smoking them out. Liz shook her head. The airflow was from the deeper cave out into the mushroom forest.

She joined Jidou back on the ledge. "No luck. Lars is going to try to burn us out. We're going to have to climb up that shaft."

Jidou grimaced as he rose to his feet. He used the wall for support the whole way up. "I guess we'd better start. You go first."

"Hold the light for me." Liz scrambled up the slope. Loose rocks tumbled to the ledge.

Jidou stepped to the side, out of the way of the falling rocks. The flashlight beam wavered, then steadied.

The slope flattened out. The gravel gave way to worn stone. Liz paused where the crack jigged to the right. "It gets easier," she called down to Jidou.

He flipped the flashlight off. The cave went dark, except for a faint red flicker from the tunnel. The sound of Jidou scrambling up the slope drowned out the faint echo of Lars shouting at his men.

She caught his hand as he reached her. His breath wheezed. She guided him to the holds she'd found. "Flashlight?" she asked.

He handed it to her.

The beam stabbed up the tunnel, illuminating a quick twist to the left. The ceiling hung low, but at least the slope had leveled. She turned off the flashlight, tucking it into her pack before crawling forward.

"They're coming," Jidou whispered.

She crawled faster up the twisting passageway, feeling her way blindly over rocks.

Faint gray light filtered around several curves. She moved faster once she could see the obstacles. She stopped just shy of the opening, a narrow crevice between two boulders. A fringe of the rock-leaf vines coated the ground outside.

"Where did you leave the truck?" she asked.

"Lars stole it when he jumped me. I think he left the equipment behind, back that way a mile or so. We could find the radio and call for help. Unless he smashed it."

Liz nodded. She pointed at the vines. "Watch out for those. The leaves are full of juice that gives you a nasty rash."

"You touched those?"

"The liquid in those cup plants at the base of the cliff fixed it." She slipped into the heat of the full double day. Sweat dripped from her and she was still in the shade of the boulders.

Jidou followed her. "You know that was stupid, right? To experiment like that."

She stepped sideways, trying to keep to the shade as much as possible. "Some days you do what you have to."

"You're braver than I am."

The cliff dropped into a sheer wall a couple feet in front of them. Behind, a boulder-strewn slope rose to the crest not far above.

Liz leaned out. "I see the truck parked at the cave entrance, under that overhang. Unless we can steal the keys from Lars, it won't do us much good." She stepped back. "Dave just came out to guard it."

"Up looks like our only option."

They scrambled up the slope. Jidou knocked a small boulder loose and sent a landslide of rubble over the edge of the cliff. Dave's shouts echoed off the cliff face.

Liz took off along the ridge top, moving fast despite the heat and the loose footing. She found a narrow side canyon where they could climb back down. Vines tangled on the sides of the steep cut. Brown leaves drooped, heavy and fat with liquid.

Jidou limped up to join her. "The radio should be only a mile or so farther west."

"They know we're up here." She eyed him. "You aren't going to be able to run very fast. How about you go after the radio and I'll run interference? I've got a bad idea."

"That grin is scaring me," Jidou said. "What are you thinking?"

Liz knelt, then dumped her pack onto the ground. "Take whatever you think might be useful. This pack isn't going to be worth anything when I get done." She pulled a pair of gloves from the pile. "I'm going to fill it with those vines. Be careful climbing down. If you do touch them, use the liquid from the plants at the bottom."

Jidou nodded. "Good luck."

"Just get to that radio and get us help."

Liz flexed her fingers in the gloves, picked up the pack by its good strap, then started down the side canyon. She stripped vines as she went, stuffing them into the pack until it bulged. Thick liquid seeped through the fabric. She did her best to keep it away from any bare skin.

She reached the bottom and turned east. She ran towards the truck, parked under a large overhang around a bulge of stone. Dave saw her and shouted.

"You want some of this?" She swung the pack by its strap. "Come get it, Dave."

He growled and charged towards her.

She slapped him with the pack. Some ooze from the plants spattered him on impact. Liz didn't wait to see what it did. She turned and ran into the dunes, shouting insults as she went. Dave followed her. They both slowed in the loose sand. Liz picked a path that would take her back towards the truck.

She risked a glance behind. Angry red streaks marked

Dave's skin. It wasn't enough to slow him down. Liz stumbled over another vine. Dave snagged her ponytail as she went down to one knee. He yanked backwards. She shrieked but let him pull her over. Her gloved hand closed over the vine. She swung it over her shoulder. The leaves exploded in his face.

Dave screamed, a primal squawk of pain. He dropped his hold on her hair to paw at his eyes.

Liz dropped the vine. She'd never hurt someone before, not like this. She hesitated, wanting to help him.

"Kill her!" Lars's shout echoed across the sand. He and Jonesy trotted into view.

Jonesy cradled a bloody hand against his belly. Jidou had smashed it good with the rock. "What's wrong with Dave?"

"He found some native life that didn't agree with him," Liz answered. "Why are you trying to kill me? What did I do to you?"

"You messed up a great thing we have going here." Lars glowered, eyebrows lowering. "All you had to do was stay away for another day. So now we get to kill you, bury you in the rocks. No one will ever find you, not all the way out here."

Liz shook her head. "And I thought you were kind of cute."

Lars snorted. "Where'd that biologist go?"

"No idea. He took off, left me up there by myself." She jerked her chin towards the cliff. "What if I want in on your deal?"

Jonesy let out a sharp, "Ha!"

Lars folded his arms. "Why should we let you in?"

"Because I'm not leaving on a ship day after tomorrow. I'm going to be on Kusavi for at least another three months, until you come back. I keep collecting for you. No one else needs to find out."

Dave collapsed to the sand, moaning as the rash spread over his face. Blisters popped out everywhere the goo had hit. He kept his eyes screwed shut.

"You gonna let him die?" Liz asked.

Lars kept his arms folded, glaring at her without a glance at Dave.

Jonesy shifted uneasily. "You gonna cut her in?"

"I can tell you how to fix it," Liz said, "but you have to act fast. You give me the keys to the truck, I tell you how to fix that. And I keep my mouth shut."

Lars shook his head.

Dave stretched one arm out. "I can't see. You got to help me, Lars."

Lars just glared at Liz.

"Come on, man," Jonesy said. "He needs help."

Liz tightened her grip on the pack strap.

"Go help him wash it off, then," Lars snapped at Jonesy. "I'll kill her myself."

"Sure you don't want another partner?" Liz hoped the pack still held enough of the plant ooze. Lars wasn't going to go down easy. He was big, and mean. She'd have to hit hard and fast.

Jonesy circled around Liz, giving her a wide berth as he went to help his friend.

"You sure you want to work for someone like this?" Liz asked him. She edged forward, shuffling her feet in the sand.

"Shut up," Lars snapped. "They know how much is at stake."

"I don't. Why don't you tell me?" Keep him talking, Liz told herself. Keep him distracted as much as you can. Buy Jidou time to get help.

"More money than a colonist like you will ever see."

Liz raised one eyebrow. "What makes you think I'm a colonist?"

"You aren't a scientist. What else could you be?" He sneered.

"Smarter than you," Liz said as she swung the pack at his face.

Lars got his hands up. The pack hit and exploded in a shower of liquid. Lars screamed as it poured across his arms and chest. His reaction to it was faster. Huge welts swelled across his exposed flesh. He flailed at the air, spreading the goo farther with his wild actions.

Jonesy grabbed Liz from behind, clamping his good arm around her. She kicked backwards, connecting with his shins. He clamped his hand onto her shirt sleeve. Liz twisted to face him, then struck out with her gloved hands. Maybe there was some of the stuff still on them. Jonesy flailed with his smashed hand. She clawed his face. He grabbed her ponytail then used both hands to shake her. She went limp in his hold.

Sweat poured from both of them as they panted under the heat of the double suns. Jonesy turned his head to spit into the sand. He kept his eyes on her. Lars and Dave provided a background chorus of moans.

"What are you going to do now?" Liz asked. "You aren't man enough to kill me. You don't have the guts for it. Neither does Lars. And poor Dave. I can help him. If you'll let me."

Jonesy growled. His hand tightened painfully on her hair.

Liz bit her lips until he eased his grip. "Give me the keys to the truck. I'll tell your captain you were out exploring and got into trouble. I can help them both, but only if you let me go."

"You'll turn us in. Or let us die out here."

"Let me go and I'll tell you how to help them."

Jonesy twisted his face into a snarl, but he dropped his hold.

"Keys?" Liz demanded holding out her gloved hand.

"You promise not to leave us here? We've got no water, no supplies. They need medical help for whatever you did to them." Jonesy nodded at the two men writing on the ground as he scratched his arm. The telltale rash marked where Liz had scored at least one hit.

"You were going to leave me here to die. Give me the keys." She made her face hard and uncompromising even though her conscience was screaming at her to help. Her hippie mother would be so disappointed in her. Live and let live, her mother's voice echoed in her head. She shook her head, trying to banish a past that she'd thought long abandoned.

"Tell me how to help them."

"Keys first." And her mother could roll over in her grave, wherever that might be.

"They're in Lars's pocket." The rash blotched his face and neck, too.

Liz kept one eye on Jonesy as she bent over Lars. "Which pocket?"

"Augh! What is this stuff?" Jonesy dug his fingers into his skin.

"Kusavi's revenge on you for trying to steal from the colonists." Liz wrinkled her nose as she gingerly felt in Lars's pocket. No keys.

"Look, I'll cut you in on the deal. Painkillers, hallucinogens, other drugs, just sitting in there for the taking. All you gotta do is burn the mushrooms then pick out the clumped chemicals from the ashes. We take them to the markets. You can have a share of the money. Just tell me how to stop this!" Jonesy squirmed. His sweat spread the rash farther.

Liz wiped her own sweat with her sleeve, careful to keep her gloves away from her skin. She reached into Lars's other pocket. "Too late to deal now, besides, what do I need money for out here in the frontier? I'll settle for you letting me go. Once I have the keys, I'll tell you the cure." Her hand closed on the keys to the truck and pulled them out of Lars's pocket.

Like a zombie, Lars rose from the ground. He clamped his hand on Liz's arm. His other arm swung around and clubbed her on her ear.

She stumbled and would have fallen except for the hold Lars had on her arm. The keys went flying into a patch of the vines. Lars raised his hand to clobber her again. His swollen face twisted with rage.

"Let her go!" Jidou's voice rang across the sand.

Liz kicked Lars in the knee. He crumpled. She yanked her arm out of his grip.

"I was doing fine on my own," she said as Jidou marched out to join her. "I don't need you to save me."

Jidou frowned. "Next time I'll let you save yourself then."

"Who says there's going to be a next time?" Liz turned her back on the prostrate men and their groaning.

"How do I stop this?" Jonesy whined. His face was red, marked with bubbling blisters.

"See those plants along the cliff?" Liz pointed at the nearest clump of the cup plants. "Use that liquid."

"How do I know you aren't lying?" Jonesy squinted at her.

"Just keep scratching your skin off, then." Liz turned her

back on Jonesy. She stomped as best she could across the sand to the last place she saw the keys for the truck.

Jidou hurried to join her. "You aren't just going to leave them out here, are you?"

"Are you?" She shot a sideways glance at him.

He grinned. "The colonists are on their way. I think I heard at least one mention lynching when I explained what Lars and friends were doing out here. They take their planetary charter seriously. I'm not sure their captain will intervene for them. He sounded just as angry."

Liz carefully extracted the keys from a nest of vines. "So what does that mean for you? You've got the find of the century in those caves." She stripped off her stained gloves and dropped them to the sand.

"There's a fortune in pharmaceuticals, not to mention the scientific discoveries and papers just begging to be written. You know, Liz, you'll have to emigrate to Kusavi if you want your share. Unless you were serious about wanting in on their criminal enterprise."

Liz jingled the keys. "I don't work with idiots. Are you going to emigrate?"

"I'm thinking about it. There's a whole world here to explore. Who knows what else we'll find? I'd love to have you working alongside me."

"Oh, just shoot me now," Jonesy complained. "Get a room already."

"Shut up," Liz snapped over her shoulder. She'd never had someone flirt with her like this before. She liked it. But enough to give up exploring? Enough to give up her solitude?

"And I promise not to save you again. I'll just sit back and let you save yourself." Jidou's smile was infectious. "I only have one condition. Tell me about your family."

"You sure you want to know?"

"Absolutely."

Jonesy shook his head as he stumbled past them, headed for the cup plants. They ignored him and the other two men on the sand.

"Deal," Liz said. She held out her hand. "On one condition."

It was Jidou's turn to raise one eyebrow.

"I get to drive."

He took her hand. "Deal."

"And if you ever call me Lizard, I may have to hurt you." She squeezed, just enough to pass on her threat.

He squeezed back, but in a nice way.

"I think one planet may be enough for me," Liz admitted. "But two suns may be a little much. Think exosummer might be livable?"

"We can always spend it exploring the arctic regions. Or the caves."

"Or the oceans." They started walking to the truck, leaving Dave and Lars groaning on the sand. "Maybe exosummer is why life hasn't spread much outside the water. Too hot and dry."

"The plants in those caves were certainly a surprise," Jidou admitted. "I'm curious what else has evolved on Kusavi."

Liz didn't say it out loud, but she was curious what it might be like to explore the strange planet with someone else, someone who didn't mind if she was named Lizard. She smiled despite the heat from Primary and Secondary. Kusavi promised surprises in more than its eccentric orbit and seasons. Mushroom forests in caverns. Plants that burned and plants that healed. Who knew what else waited around the bend?

Jidou took her hand as they walked across the dunes.

Who knew what waited in her future? Liz walked faster, eager to find out.

Point of View
Lauren McBride

At the end of each workday
mining frozen gasses
I pause at the airlock
and remove my facemask

letting my eyes mist
in the bitter alien air
not so different
from homeworld.

Through acrid tears, I stare
at the jagged icy terrain
blurring to swirls of soft colors
to remind myself

I, too, can be wrong.
There is always
another way
of looking at things.

A Very Public Hanging
L.J. Bonham

Execution. Midas Fiore wrote the word, or rather the computer did, in neat, fourteen point longhand script. Midas pressed "Send" and the machine affixed the Colonial Magistrate's signature to the death warrant. He gave a disgusted sigh and smoothed a black hair lock back into alignment with the four others which, under most circumstances, remained tacked in place with heavy styling gel over a conspicuous, bald pate.

"Send an apprehend order to the justice center on K2-65b," he said to the court clerk. "Who's the enforcer there?"

The clerk scrolled through several screens on the computer pad bolted to the desk. Things in the courthouse, and everywhere else these days, acquired new owners if not secured. The clerk coughed and nodded a double chin.

"Marshal Guttmann, Magistrate" the clerk replied.

"Rowdy Guttmann?" A rhetorical question. "How bad do you have to screw up to get sent way out there, I wonder?" Midas went back to the display screen and browsed the next case's details.

He gave a head shake. "We cannot allow the criminal element to destroy our society. We must draw the line here and now. No further. Rowdy Guttmann will be our avenging angel."

Light. Painful, bright light. Colonial Marshal Rowdy Guttmann mashed a pillow over disheveled red-blond hair and tortured eyes, its rank old sweat and bourbon odor jolted sinuses better than smelling salts. The screams still echoed in her mind from a dream—the dream she couldn't escape.

"What, Bob?" she asked with a raspy gasp.

"A message has arrived for you from higher echelons, Marshal." DomCom-ProAdmin (Domestic Operations and Companionship – Professional Administration) android Model DOC-45-A1 replied, with mild urgency and some programmed sympathy.

Rowdy peeled the pillow back enough for one bloodshot

eye to regard the machine. She'd named him Bob—the Cybernetic Rights Act allowed two name changes during an android's service life—because tequila had dampened any creative instincts the first day she'd owned him. She'd toyed with Cynthia—her first serious girlfriend in high school—but somehow Bob just fit better. Given Bob's latest multi-gender modality app, which Rowdy had downloaded last year, any name other than, "Hey You," would have sufficed.

The app had been the best present Rowdy had ever given herself, she gloated. It had made Bob even better in the sack—no limits. In male mode, like last night, Bob had proved invaluable through endurance no human could match. A little less bourbon and she'd still be at it this morning. Rowdy didn't love Bob, but then she didn't love anyone, she admitted. It took a year to go through all the half-way attractive men and women in Fortune Town, and less time for the unattractive. No, Bob would do just fine, and he did windows.

"Which higher echelon?" Rowdy asked and belched. Fiery whiskey and nachos burned and thrust upward in her esophagus.

"Magistrate Fiore. Also, your breakfast is ready." Bob pivoted on one foot and left the ten-by-six bedroom.

Rowdy pulled hand-over-hand up the headboard until she sat upright on the bed's edge. A quick whiskey shot from the near empty Bushmills bottle on the nightstand cleared the cotton mouth and drove the lunatic with the hammer inside her skull into submission. It made a mere dent in the dream—the awful memory. She stood, launched toward the shower on unsteady legs, and tried to ignore the once athletic, thirty-nine-year-old body reflected in the mirror.

Ten minutes later, Rowdy sat in the mauve and olive painted kitchenette across a decrepit, tippy lilac plastic table from Bob, who displayed his best conversational skill—silence. Stale garbage, mold, and the draft from the adjacent bathroom fought a pitched battle with sandalwood air freshener. Rowdy shoveled bacon and eggs from plate to mouth and contemplated the B.O.S.S. (Bureau Operations and Surveillance System) displayed on a computer tablet. Hangover frown turned scowl as she skimmed Fiore's orders. Another whiskey shot. A belch rattled the dishes. She leaned the chair back until it bumped the government-issue wall.

"Bob, we have a mission today. Seems we need to apprehend a suspect."

Bob rose, cleared the dishes, and tucked them in the washer. "Charge?"

"Murder."

Bob shrugged. "I was unaware any homicides had occurred lately."

"Hasn't. Fiore says Crime Prediction Division has analyzed Fortune Town's population meta-data and gives an eighty-five percent chance one will occur within the week. So, we've got to find a suspect."

"Do you have any thoughts on where to look?" Bob continued the kitchen chores and played music from Rowdy's favorite band—Hell Puppy—through an integrated audio system.

"Where else? East Fortune Town."

"Shall I have your body armor ready?"

"Yeah, and extra ammo—lots of ammo."

Half an hour and half a bourbon fifth later, Rowdy let Fortune Town's narrow, primary thoroughfare blur past the car's passenger side window as a raw, red sunrise hemorrhaged across the building-studded skyline. Every breath pumped air from under Rowdy's ballistic vest to an unappreciative nose. She made a mental note to have Bob clean the armor.

Bob guided the hydrogen turbine powered car with precision through the traffic via an index finger USB interface. Fifty years old, the car's paint had been sandblasted off in K2-65b's regular wind storms, and the emergency steering wheel dangled from the dash at an unimpressive angle.

The name Fortune Town always made Rowdy laugh. "More like Your Last Chance in the Universe Town," she'd quip to anyone who'd listen—someone on the next bar stool, in most cases. The Kepler Worlds, as people still called them, had been humanity's salvation. Once artificial intelligence's full potential had been realized, the Earth Congress passed the Surplus Population Reconciliation Act. Two billion people had one simple choice: leave for an unknown life on an unknown world or wait to be rounded up for disintegration. Fortune Town's residents had chosen the former. This latest frontier, as all those throughout history, absorbed the wild-eyed dreamers, misfits, criminals, refugees, and anyone who couldn't make it at home. East Fortune Town absorbed those who couldn't make it in Fortune Town.

"Bob, watch out!" Rowdy commanded. The android brought the car to a shuddering halt just as a small calico cat darted from between two parked cars—mere inches separated it from death.

"Poor thing," she tisked. "People shouldn't let their cats roam—too dangerous out here." Bob accelerated and headed toward their destination.

Rowdy's eyes scanned the street as they crossed beneath the three-meter diameter ore transfer tubes suspended ten meters above the street. They, and an olfactory shift from mere dust to outright decay, demarcated East Fortune Town. The tubes ran the fifteen kilometers from the Madre Grande Mine to the processing center and space docks. "Let's see who looks good here."

Bob slowed and turned down a muddy, unpaved side street. "There are several RF-ID signatures eighty-four meters ahead on this bearing, Marshal."

"I'm sure one or two are up to no good—or will be when I get to 'em." Rowdy unfastened the seat belt. Fingers contracted around the passenger door handle. *The wolf's in the fold, now,* she thought.

Bob slowed to a crawl and stopped at a narrow alley. A dozen meters away, five people busied themselves with a crap game on a tenement's back stoop. They didn't notice the car.

"I like the second one on the right. The skinny, short, Latin type with sideburns." Rowdy drew an old, compact pistol—her request for plasma weapons had been rejected, twice—from under a calf-length, khaki oilskin duster. "On three. One. Two. Three!"

Rowdy leapt from the car and slammed the door shut just as Bob launched down the alley, siren on. The gamblers froze for a second at the shrill alarm—ten eyes locked onto Rowdy—

then they scattered as if a hand grenade had been tossed onto the crap table.

"Freeze, scumbags!" Rowdy's voice boomed off the pre-fab steel buildings. Her intended target tossed a garbage can her way and tripped over another gambler before vaulting the stoop's rail—feet ran in mid-air before they touched ground. The other three men and one woman burst through side doors into other buildings, or followed Rowdy's target down the alley.

"This guy's fast," she grunted between labored breaths. She stopped, raised the pistol and fired. The weapon's integral suppressor reduced the shot from a boom to a mild *crack-snap*. The suspect grabbed a wounded leg and crumpled to the mud. "But not that fast." Rowdy smiled and coughed. She ambled up to the man.

"Colonial Marshal. You're under arrest." Rowdy punctuated the statement with a pistol muzzle aimed at the suspect's face.

"What are you doing?" the man protested. "I didn't do nothing and you shot me!"

Bob ran past Rowdy, turned the man face down in the mud, and handcuffed him.

"You have the right to shut the hell up," Rowdy growled. "Anything you say may piss me off and convince me to end you right here." She leaned down to make eye contact, thankful the bourbon kept the man's halitosis at bay. "Do you understand these rights I've just explained to you?"

The man nodded. Teeth ground a lower lip. Rowdy straightened and pulled a metal flask from a coat pocket. She hammered down two quick swallows, then holstered both flask and pistol.

"See to his wound and then get him in the car," Rowdy ordered Bob. Without a word, the android applied a steri-seal synthetic flesh dressing and then hoisted the suspect with one arm and carried him away. He tossed the man into the back seat like a grain sack, slammed the door, and slid into the driver's seat. Rowdy joined him a few seconds later and they sped away.

"You've done well, Marshal." Magistrate Midas Fiore's image flickered on Rowdy's office computer display screen. B.O.S.S. compensated for the interstellar radiation interference and the image stabilized.

"Thank you, sir." Rowdy let satisfaction nudge its way onto her face. "The suspect resisted, but I completed the arrest without loss of life."

Midas coughed then sipped some water. "Yes, yes—I'm sure everything was done according to procedure. Now, when do you plan to hang him?"

"Hang?" Rowdy's eyebrows flexed up. "The warrant was only for an arrest."

"Things have changed since I sent you that," Fiore replied. "We need to make a stronger statement to the criminal element in the colonies. You should receive the death warrant in your next scheduled transmission."

Rowdy's mouth dropped open. She snapped it shut before the normal, unfiltered retort could escape and endanger her career for the millionth time. She shifted in the broken-down government-issue chair and waited for its groans and squeaks to subside. She cleared her throat.

"Your Honor, I thought normal procedures would apply in this case." Rowdy tried to make eyebrows imply the real meaning.

"Not this time, Marshal. There are considerations beyond our arrangement. I'm sure you'd just be bored with the minutiae."

Rowdy swallowed hard. The whiskey bottle just off camera called to her—called quite loud. "If I may, Your Honor, this is a major impact to my bottom line around here. If I could just..."

"Tell me something Rowdy," Fiore interrupted. "Have you ever seen the Chief Inspector's office, here, in the Justice Directorate's headquarters?"

Rowdy shook her head—the room spun just a bit. Right hand quivered—anxious to grab the bottle. The left quelled it with a white-knuckle grip.

"Well, let's just say the current occupant may retire later this year, and I think you'd be a marvelous fit." Fiore beamed a wide smile.

"Chief Inspector? A personal office? No more Fortune Town?" Rowdy leaned back, stunned. Possibilities careened behind crow's feet-framed, green eyes.

"And why not? You could do a lot of good there, Rowdy," Fiore trilled. "A lot of good—for the people." He leaned in to the camera. "Did I mention the Inspector's seven percent?"

"Seven?" Now Rowdy leaned in.

"Yes, seven. Straight off the top from any and all fines, tariffs, bails, and case dismissal fees. You get what, now? Two?"

Rowdy nodded. The first year alone could fund a retirement—a damn good retirement. On the second year, she could almost buy a personal distillery. No more shaking down the local watering holes for a case here, a case there. She eyed the bottle again.

"Tomorrow, at dawn?"

Fiore nodded. "I'm glad you see the light, Marshal."

The Justice Directorate logo screen saver replaced the magistrate's image.

"It is my duty to advise you this situation may create an ethical conflict." Bob handed Rowdy a frosted, ice-filled tumbler.

"Just pour the whiskey," Rowdy snapped. She avoided eye contact with the android.

Bob dispensed the amber liquor, capped the bottle, and left the office. Rowdy swirled the "medicine" around and drained it in two large gulps. Sinuses pounded from the cold. She slapped the glass onto the desk and sighed.

Have to finish another bottle to get used to this stinking business, she thought and opened the suspect's file. A petty career criminal's curriculum vitae stared back.

Javier O'Neill. Twenty-one, born on Earth—Republic of Ireland. Argentinian mother, Irish father. They divorced when Javier was four. Classified as surplus and moved with mother to Fortune Town at age ten. Mother took various odd jobs then became licensed sex worker, died from shatter overdose three years later. Javier faced the world alone since then. He went from no law enforcement contact to multiple juvenile offenses—theft, unlicensed prostitution, minor narcotics trafficking, burglary, and one simple assault. The adult rap sheet stayed the course.

"Stick to what you know, as mom always said." Rowdy closed the file. "Almost an angel by East Fortune Town standards," she quipped. "Better go interview the poor schmuck." Rowdy pushed up from the chair, took one step around the desk and froze. "Ah, hell."

"Marshal, glad I caught you. Your android said you'd already left." Cella D'Ambrosio, Chief Civil Rights Advocate for Freedom Rehabilitates Our Delinquents—or FROD—blocked Rowdy's office door. A manicured hand perched on an attractive hip complimented with a triumphant smile on full, glossed lips framed with shoulder-length, straight black hair. Cella's alluring scent flowed through the door and straight to Rowdy's crotch.

Rowdy held up a finger. "Not now, Cella."

"Rowdy, this'll only take a minute. We need to talk about your latest collar, um…" She glanced at a PDA. "Javier O'Neill."

"No deals today, blow pop." Rowdy's eyes hardened. "He's hangman's meat for tomorrow."

"For what?"

"Murder."

"What murder?" Cella crossed arms over ample chest. A chest Rowdy realized she'd missed for months. "There hasn't been a murder in at least two weeks."

"Predicted murder."

Cella sighed and let out a laugh. "Predicted crimes don't get real sentences, and you know it." Voice dropped to a proper, conspiratorial level. "Look, how much do you need on this? Two large? Five?"

"I said no deal. This one's got the magistrate's attention. There's no way I can work things."

Disappointment flooded Cella's face. "How am I supposed to make my donation quota if you won't throw me a bone?" She jabbed a finger at Rowdy. "If I can't get enough 'saves' our donations will slow down. How can I make a living if our humanitarian efforts don't motivate the public to shell out their hard earned money?"

"Not my problem." Rowdy strode forward as if Cella

weren't in the doorway. Cella didn't budge. Rowdy stopped inches from the "activist."

A sly smile frolicked across Cella's face and she stepped closer—chest to chest. "I could help change your mind." She cooed. "Later tonight, maybe? My place?"

Rowdy paused—face flush. "Sorry sweetie." She pushed past Cella and made for the elevator.

"Seriously?" Cella's head shook and she leaned back against the door jamb.

###

Javier O'Neill sat shackled to a bare steel chair. Despite the rust blotches, the chair still remained bolted to the interrogation room's scuffed, taupe-colored tile floor. Pine-scented cleaner and bleach hung in the stagnant, humidified air.

"Smoke?" Rowdy fished the pack she kept for such occasions from a vest pocket, popped the lid, and held a cigarette toward the prisoner. Javier nodded. Rowdy leaned across the dented steel table, placed the item between Javier's lips and ignited it with a thermal diode lighter, then slumped back in the upholstered interrogator's chair. Non-toxic smoke from genetically modified tobacco wafted toward stained ceiling panels.

"Do you know why you're here?" Rowdy began.

A head shake. "Does it matter? You're the authority. You do whatever you want."

Rowdy gave Javier a wane smile. "That's right, I am the authority here, and I do whatever I want. You're here because you were in the wrong place at the wrong time and I needed a bigger break than you." Rowdy sipped whisky spiked coffee. "Does your leg hurt?" Another head shake.

"Amazing what genetic reprogramming nanites can do these days." Rowdy leaned back. "Just put DNA into your cells and zap! The cells reform as if they'd never been damaged. God, I love cool stuff like that. Don't you?"

Javier didn't bother with a third head shake—just stared past Rowdy at the room's only door.

Rowdy snapped fingers in Javier's face. "Hey, pay attention. I don't think you realize what's going to happen to you."

Javier's face said, "Drop dead."

"Javier, listen to me." Rowdy leaned forward. "They're

going to hang you tomorrow morning at dawn."

Javier's eyes went wide. "Hang? What the hell did I do to get hanged?" He yanked wrists and ankles against the cuffs. A sweat bead formed on a wrinkled forehead, teetered a second, then rolled down a sharp cheek bone and splattered on the floor.

"You were going to commit a murder."

"Like hell I was!" Javier's lip trembled. "You guys are always jackin' us East Towners up for some damn thing or another. You don't own us."

"Actually, we do. If you look at your indentured transportation contract..."

Javier jerked the cuffs again. "Let me outta here. Let me out right now!"

Rowdy took another swig. "Why?"

Javier sat still, mouth agape for an instant.

"I said, why should I let you go? On Earth you'd have been vaped along with your mother. You're surplus—worthless."

"I ... I ..." Javier stammered. "I got a kid."

"Surplus."

"No. No, he ain't no surplus. He's two. His mama's over a few blocks from where you clipped me. You should see him." Javier's eyes brightened. "He's real smart. Maybe he'll be a doctor, or a magistrate, or somethin'."

Rowdy broke eye contact and gazed into the half-empty cup. "Magistrate," Rowdy harrumphed. "Do you even know what a magistrate is?"

"Sure I do. I'm not stupid. A magistrate is a real important judge—decides who lives, who dies."

Rowdy gave an absent nod. The scenes from ten years ago flooded in—the charred children, the screams, the panic ... Another magistrate had needed an example then, and Rowdy had provided it. Rowdy clamped eyelids tight. "Yeah," she whispered. "They decide who lives, who dies." She wiped a stray tear away and snorted back snot.

"Please, you gotta let me see my kid grow up. He's gonna go to school, gonna be a good person—not like me." Tears poured off Javier onto the floor. "I'm gonna make damn sure he does better. Madeline ... she was a whore, but I give her money—yeah, so I stole it—I give her enough so she don't have to do tricks no more. She stays with my little boy. She takes care of him. She even got into rehab for her shatter addiction. Please, if you hang me, she'll go back to the club houses, back to the shatter. My boy'll end up just like me. Don't let it happen."

Rowdy stood and glared down at the prisoner. "I'm sorry. I got problems, too.' She turned and left the room.

⊞

Two bourbon fifths lay on their sides under Rowdy's kitchen table. A numb hand uncapped a third, but she knew it wouldn't stop the screams. They would never stop. The eyes—thousands—accused her. They stared up from the corpses stacked five meters high. Burned fingers pointed at her. The images played over and over.

Drunken wakefulness and dream merged. No longer in the kitchen—the hot, terrible day in Denver replayed. The pistol had seemed to materialize in her hand. It rose and fired. Round after round zipped inches from Fiore's predecessor, Magistrate Gibbon's head, and slammed into the plasma cannon's power supply. Then hands grabbed her, fists punched, feet kicked as the other marshals pulled her to the ground. They dragged her away...

"Just keep quiet. This never happened and you were never here," they had told her. "You need a rest. Somewhere away from this. Here, this will help you forget." The whiskey bottle had lasted only the first night on the passage to K2-65b. She didn't forget.

Back in the kitchen—the hazy, spinning kitchen—Rowdy slammed half the fifth down, then slumped to the table, face first.

⊞

"Wake up, Marshal." A voice came to Rowdy, thin and distant.

"Wake up, Marshal."

Bob. Bob's voice floated somewhere near, but where?

Rowdy's eyes pried open. Subdued light glowed around. Something pressed into a shoulder. She glanced sideward—Bob's hand. It pulled Rowdy upright in the chair.

"I think you've had enough for tonight, Marshal," Bob

said. The bourbon levitated up in the android's free hand. He deposited it on the adjacent counter.

"What … What time is it?" Rowdy fought whiskey bile as it churned upwards.

"Zero three-twenty."

Bob and the kitchen came into focus. Rowdy pulled the android's hand from her. "Bob, I need your help."

"Yes, of course, Marshal." Bob imitated concerned well, in Rowdy's estimation. "What do you have in mind?"

Rowdy pushed up from the table. "I have to pay a debt."

▦

Rowdy tossed a dish towel over the security camera in the prisoner holding area adjacent to her office, and then walked down the short hall. She stopped at the last door on the right and opened it.

She peered into the dim cell. "Javier?"

The prisoner stirred on a metal cot in the far corner. He needed a shower and the toilet needed a flush. Javier rubbed tired eyes and blinked at Rowdy silhouetted in the doorframe.

"Javier, get up. Time to go." Rowdy stepped over and tugged the prisoner's arm.

"Is it dawn already?" Javier asked, voice hoarse with dread.

"No. Just shut up and come with me."

He rose, slid on shoes, and trailed behind as Rowdy led him back along the hall, through her office, and down another passageway. They stopped at the end, backs to another camera—also towel-draped.

Rowdy held the door open. "Get going."

Javier froze. He eyed the marshal with deep suspicion. "No. You'll shoot me for escaping. You think I'm stupid, or something?"

"It's no trick, Javier. You're free, but you have to do something in return."

Javier's head cocked to the side as if to say, "And that is?"

"You have to promise me you'll quit being a punk. Promise me you'll go straight and take care of your son."

Javier's head nodded—slow and cautious. "Yeah … Okay."

Rowdy grabbed Javier's left ear and pinched a nerve.

Javier winced. "I mean it. You've got to take care of him. Understand?" She let go.

"Yes." Javier's voice found new enthusiasm. "I promise. He's everything to me. Him and Madeline. I won't let you down."

"Good. Now get the hell out of here." Rowdy jerked a thumb toward the darkened alley. Javier looked both ways, trotted off, and disappeared around the corner.

Rowdy half leaned, half collapsed against the door jamb. "Jesus, girl. What did you just do?" She gazed down the alley one final time. "You better make good on your promise, you little schmuck."

Rowdy removed the towels from the cameras and slipped back into the office. She stopped dead. Bob lay in a deactivated heap in the corner. Five colonial marshals in full combat armor stood behind the desk—plasma guns trained at her chest.

One marshal swung the B.O.S.S. display around for Rowdy to view. Magistrate Midas Fiore's face filled the frame. "Nothing like a very public hanging to send a message," he said with a thin smile. "Unfortunately, you seem to have misplaced our guest of honor, Marshal. Oh well, the show must go on."

⁂

"And we're back." Jack Esel's mile-wide, perfect smile beamed at the camera. "If you've just joined us here on *Good Morning, Colonies*, we have an exciting event for you. For the first time in years, a live execution. With me in our Brussel's studio is Colonial Magistrate, and Chancellor Candidate, Midas Fiore."

The shot widened. Fiore sat on a hunter green leather couch next to Esel's desk. The magistrate's smile almost eclipsed the anchorman's. Esel turned his good side to the camera to address Fiore.

"Magistrate, tell us why we're here today."

Fiore straightened and looked into the camera. "Jack, it is high time we did something unequivocal about the graft and corruption which drains the life blood from our colonial government. I've vowed to hunt down and bring to justice any official who betrays the public trust. Even if they work for me. Furthermore, I promise the voters I will make them proud to be colonists, again."

Esel nodded. "Thank you, Magistrate." The camera tightened back to him. "Now folks, let's watch as Colonial Marshal
Rowdy Guttmann pays for her heinous crimes."

The camera pulled back just enough to display Rowdy's
mug shot next to Esel's head. The program director switched to
another camera—a wide shot overlooking Fortune Town's central square. A gallows rose three meters above several hundred
people packed into the area.

Rowdy shuffled in shackles up the steps, the marshal who
had replaced her and a minister from the Holy Galactic Church
of Faith led the way. The camera zoomed in enough to pick up
on Rowdy's wide, terrified eyes, but not so close a viewer could
see the clear tape over the condemned's mouth.

The executioner centered Rowdy on the gallows trap
door, placed a gray cloth hood over her head, and then the
noose. Ten second later, he pressed a red button and the trap
door snapped open. Rowdy plummeted a meter and jerked to
a stop. Feet twitched for another ten seconds.

The director went to a split screen with Esel and Fiore on
one side and the gallows on the other.

"I'm sure this brings you no pleasure, Magistrate." Esel
gave a profound head shake.

Fiore gave a long sigh. "No, of course not." The shot
moved to a close up. "The people have got to know that I, Midas Fiore, will ferret out official corruption wherever it exists."

Esel's face refilled the shot. "Thank you, Magistrate.' He
turned to camera two. "In sports yesterday…"

Production assistants hovered around Fiore off the news set.
They pulled wireless audio pickups off and scrubbed makeup
away. Three minutes later, Midas' campaign manager escorted
him from the studio and to a waiting limousine.

Ensconced in the spacious back seat, Fiore sipped a latte
amid the fresh leather upholstery's soothing aroma.

"First polls and social media feedback show you up five
points over the closest challenger, Magistrate." The manger
blurted, almost giddy. "I think I'm looking at the next Colonial
Chancellor!"

Fiore took another sip and set the cup aside. "I'm not

important here, you understand. What *is* important is the people see justice being done—swiftly and decisively. As long as they know someone paid for a crime, they have faith in the system. Guilt or innocence is a minor consideration." He leaned back and smiled. "Never let a good crisis go to waste"

The Outlaw from Aran
Vaughn Wright

My name is Quinn Bennet, originally out of Scranton, Pennsylvania. In the spring of 1867, I was one of five people who witnessed one of the most extraordinary things to ever happen in the world. I have never spoken of that time or that incident with anyone who wasn't a part of it. As far as I know the same holds true for the others. But since then, two of us have died. I thought it best to write the story out so there would at least be a record. It needs one. There may come a time when people of this world can use it.

Like I said, there were five of us altogether—me, Billy Morningstar, Malcolm Foster, Joe Smith, and Carl Kistler. We weren't all necessarily outlaws, as such, but we were all wanted to one degree or another.

At the time, we were fresh from laying track for the Union Pacific Railroad on a stretch of the transcontinental rail line. It was heading west from Omaha out of the brand-new state of Nebraska to meet with the Central Pacific Railroad going east out of Sacramento, California. The two were expected to join up somewhere in northern Utah to complete the first coast-to-coast railway. There was a lot to not like about the job. Besides the corrupt surveyors steering the rail line towards towns that could pay them the most, and the fact Indians and settlers alike were outright having their land stolen out from under them whenever the railroad called right-of-way, workers weren't getting paid the extra money they were supposed to for working harder terrain.

Malcolm was a former slave and often said, "Now y'all white folks know what it feel like." He was only half joking.

With the Laramie Mountains looming up ahead, we agreed it was time to cut out and start making our own way west again. The Wyoming Territory was a harsh land, but we knew how to live off of it. To keep our supplies up, we did a little hunting here and there. That's how it was Billy came across some odd animal tracks that had curiosity more than hunger spurring him on to find out what kind of critter had made them.

Now, me and Billy had been riding together the longest, not long after I had taken to roaming the countryside the summer before. What had set my feet to itching was a lovely young lady in Philadelphia. She happened to be in a family way and claimed I was the one responsible for it. She was from a well-to-do Main Line family, and had a father who had made it known he was looking to shoot the first scoundrel named Quinn Bennet he set his eyes on. So I was working with an out-of-sight, out-of-mind philosophy.

Billy was a Potawatomi Indian. His tribe was originally out of Indiana, but the reservation the government had moved his people to in Kansas back in the '30s wasn't big enough for him, so he struck out on his own.

We met when it happened to be his misfortune to cross paths with a couple of hard-luck fur traders who hadn't gotten the news Uncle Sam wasn't paying a bounty for Indian scalps anymore. I got involved to make it a two-on-two proposition they decided they didn't want any part of.

For the six months since then, our trust had been as solid as Gibraltar, until he said the tracks he had us following could have only been made by a six-legged animal. We didn't know what kind of peyote he'd been eating, because every schoolkid knows God ain't never put that many legs on anything bigger than a bug, and this was too big to be one of those. We'd been on its trail for about three miles arguing the matter and making bets about what we would find, until the tracks led to a stand of boulders where the trail went dead.

By then the betting had gotten pretty heavy. Since we all had a stake in catching the creature, we all circled the outcropping and started closing in.

What we found was a Negro woman camped out at a fair-sized, sandy clearing inside. She was wearing a green poncho of Navajo design, beneath which was a bosom like a balcony. On her bowed head was a sombrero wider than her narrow shoulders, over which hung two long braids. We had startled the woman so badly she held up empty hands at her sides that were on arms blacker than tar and thinner than a bar of soap after a week's hard wash.

"Please, do not harm me," she said to us in a gurgly kind of whisper.

I tipped my Stetson at her and said, "Pardon us for startling you, ma'am, but have you seen anything of a six-legged critter round these parts?" I felt silly just saying it.

She shook her head that she hadn't, so I apologized again for bothering her and told the boys, let's go.

Carl drew his side arm on the woman and said, "Naw, Quinn. Somethin' ain't right here."

Out of all of us, Carl was the most recent addition and without a doubt the most wanted. He had escaped from an Oklahoma chain gang, where he was serving six months hard labor for shooting a man when the same card turned up twice in a poker game. Word was, the infamous deputy marshal Seth Kenner was on the hunt for him. Carl was also a horse's ass, but we had to back his play, the same as we'd expect of him if it was any of us making it. We all drew.

I whispered, "What's the problem here, Carl? She seems okay."

He ignored me, or maybe in answer to my question, he told the woman, "Let me see your face."

She raised her head. Below the brim of her sombrero was a pair of dark-tinted spectacles, and a blue bandana covering everything below them. Again, she gurgled, "Please, do not harm me."

"I said show me your face!" Carl demanded. "Pull that bandana down and take those glasses off so I can see your eyes!"

I was beginning to feel sorry for the poor woman, having five men pointing all that hardware at her. She no doubt thought the worst of us, what our intentions were. I'd give Carl this peek at her face, but I'd knock his snot loose if he tried to get her to take anything else off. I wouldn't be the only one to do it either.

The face we finally got to see was round and covered in short black fuzz, like velvet. It had no nose or ears. Its eyes were two shiny black marbles set too far apart. The mouth was a wide, lipless slit that ran nearly halfway round its head.

"Great day in the morning!"

"What the hell is that?"

"Christ Almighty!"

She tried to make a run for it. Joe managed to grab a handful of poncho that she easily slipped out of. I fired a warning shot in the air. That made her stand fast.

And there it was, the six-legged critter we'd been hunting, staring us in the face. What we all took to be a bosom turned out to be the elbows of four more spidery arms, two on either of its sides, that were crossed against the midsection. It was covered head to toe in that black fuzz, except for a white metal band high up on its upper left arm. And when the poncho came off, so did the hat. Those braids were standing up on top of its head like a pair of buggy whips. None of us was rightly sure if we were looking at an animal or an insect. It was a fearsome sight, all right. But hearing it speak, that was the real chiller.

"I have no weapons," it said. "Please, do not harm me."

"Who's out here with you?" Carl said.

"I am alone."

Billy, who had the drop on the creature from above and behind with a carbine, nodded it was the truth.

"What, what in tarnation are you?" Carl stammered.

"My name is Ru," the creature gurgled. "I am from Aran. It is a place far from here."

"No shit. I'm thinking it's in Hell, and you're a damn demon that needs to be sent back there," Carl said, thumbing back the hammer of his revolver.

"Do it, and you'll be riding its coattails," I said, turning the business end of my gun on him. "Matter of fact, everybody lower your guns. A ricochet in this cluster of rocks could kill half of us." And besides, whatever that thing was we had cornered didn't strike me as particularly dangerous.

"Ru, you said your name was?" I said calmly, trying to bring some civility to the situation. "Listen, nobody here's gonna hurt you. My name is Quinn. That's Malcolm and Joe over there. This loudmouth here is Carl. And that's Billy there behind you. You mind tellin' us where this Aran place is you're from and what you're doin' out here?"

"No, I do not mind, Quinn."

It's at this point I feel the need to inject that the matter of sex as it relates to Ru from Aran has always been a somewhat confusing one for me. However, from here forward I will refer to her in the feminine not simply for the sake of clarity, but because it is how I have always thought of her.

According to Ru, Aran was in the general direction of what she learned was a constellation of stars we called Cygnus, and as far as she was concerned, she couldn't have left it far enough behind in search for another habitable planet. That's why she came to Earth. It wasn't till she landed here that she found out she didn't look nearly enough like us for her to blend in, so she planned to continue her search for another world.

Unfortunately, Ru had set her ship down near a river. During the night a storm came up before she could make it back there, so she settled in a cave until the weather got friendly again. When she returned, she found the river had claimed her ship. It's still there, intact, but under thirty foot of water.

We all were familiar with that storm from a few weeks before. It held up work on the railroad for five days. Word was, it swelled rivers enough to wash away whole towns and killed over a dozen people there in Nebraska and in Kansas.

Joe asked, "What was so wrong with your planet that you're lookin' for another one?"

She showed us, by getting down on those scrawny six arms and folding her legs flat up under her belly. Fix a picture of a hundred and fifty-pound cockroach in your head and I reckon you'll have something pretty close. She said it was more comfortable for her to stand like that, but that her ability to stand upright made her an eight-limbed freak, an outcast, on a world where six limbs were the norm.

With the help of some friends, she had managed to hide the extra legs pretty well for a long time, until after her first birthing. All her kids (137 of them!) came out with eight limbs. When the people in charge found out, they had her kids destroyed and planned to do her next. A friend helped her steal a spaceship, and off she flew in search of a planet she could raise little eight-limbed Rus on.

Malcolm asked, "How you gonna have more babies and it's just you?"

"Arani do not require mates as you do here."

"The hell you say! Well, what are you, man or woman?"

"Neither. Such do not exist on Aran. Each of us experiences several birthing cycles throughout our lifespans, from which we produce offspring."

Malcolm, bewildered, said, "So, you're an Adam *and* an Eve?"

"If that ain't the damnedest thing," I couldn't help muttering with astonishment.

"This is all the biggest load of bullshit I ever heard!" Carl declared. "Other planets, spaceships, birthing cycles—are you fellas even *listenin'* to what that thing is talkin' about?"

Put that way, I reckon any right-thinking person would've agreed. But look at what was in front of us. How could a man take a bite of that pie and not swallow?

Ru eventually said in her underwater way, "I have spoken the truth in all that I have said."

Carl shook his head ruthlessly, like a hanging judge. "It's an abomination, I'm tellin' you. We oughta kill it!"

I'd seen pernicious attitudes like that before. Just didn't think Carl had one in him until that day, considering he'd always been cordial to Billy and Malcolm. I guess a person's true nature, it itches under the skin like an old splinter. They pull it out eventually.

With my hand on my gun, I said, "Ain't gonna be no killin' here, Carl." Then I assured her, "Everybody isn't like him, Ru, but there's enough of 'em. You bein' a stranger to these parts, you won't always know which one you're dealing with until it's too late. If you'll let us, we'd like to try and help you get on your way."

"That would please me very much, Quinn."

"Fine. Then what we'll do is make camp here tonight, and then tomorrow we'll—"

"We'll what, Quinn?" Carl snapped. "Get it a horse and let it take up with us? Better yet, let it ride double with you the rest of the way to California?" He scoffed, and then turned to everybody else. "You fellas see this thing ain't natural, right? Ain't no tellin' what kinda diseases it's got, what kinda appetites it's got. Who's to say it won't eat our faces off in our sleep!"

"Carl," I said, "I thought you was just pig-ignorant before. Now I'm thinkin' you're fourteen-karat crazy."

"Think what you want," he shot back, "but I'm tellin' you what I know. Ain't no good gonna come outta keepin' company with that thing."

"Well, you're welcome to quit this outfit whenever it suits you, mister. You be sure and give Seth Kenner our regards, ya hear?"

He got red in the face but kept that hole in it closed. For a while, anyway.

By then it was dusk, so we tied up the horses and settled in there, in the shelter of those boulders with Ru. Billy took up watch on the highest one. I don't think he felt especially comfortable in the company of the creature from space. And I wasn't likely the only one uncomfortable watching her waltz around in the altogether, though it didn't seem to bother her none, so I asked if it wasn't too much trouble to please put the poncho back on.

I got us a cook fire going, while Carl gathered up the fixings for a stew and some panbread.

Ru said, "Carl, I have food to share."

He snorted. "We *was* plannin' on eatin' *you*."

After chow, she and Malcolm took to parlaying together.

Apparently she had made good of her time being stranded here by picking up English, Spanish, and some of the Native tongues sneaking around camps at night. When she was only wearing that metal armband, she had the camouflage for it. I couldn't help wondering what all she had seen of this world and the people on it with those shiny black eyes that never closed.

Anyway, Malcolm put a lot questions to her that she didn't seem to mind answering. I guess they had a bit in common, seeing how he had all his kin sold off to parts unknown before the War Between the States and Emancipation. He was 22 then and honestly believed he was leaving Georgia for the Promised Land when he went north. Only he said freedom didn't seem to be a promise more white folks than he expected were willing to make good on. That's why he came out west, before he got his neck stretched for taking his due out of one of their hides.

Carl was burning Joe's ears up with his crazy talk, trying to speak low so no one else could hear, but I could. Carl was saying, "We could get an awful lot of money for a critter like that. It'd bring more than a fistful of dollars for all of us."

Malcolm overheard him too, and said, "Maybe as much as we would get for turnin' you over to the law? 'Two thousand, dead or alive,' is what it said on the last wanted poster I saw."

"Why, you son of a—"

"Hold on!" I said. "Ain't nobody gettin' turned over to nobody. He was just makin' a point, Carl, and that point is: Anybody tries to make a dollar off of any of us don't need to *be* with us."

"You been struck blind? That thing ain't one of us. It ain't even human!"

"But it's got trouble with the law. That's good enough for me and I say we help it, if we can." But I realized I'd maybe been too presumptuous to commit everyone to something we hadn't all rightly agreed on, so I put it up for a vote. "How about the rest of you?"

From his perch above us, Billy said, "My vote is whatever you need it to be, Quinn."

With mine, that made it two in favor.

Malcolm and Joe both said they were for it too.

Carl said, "Ask me in the mornin'," then he pointedly looked at Ru, "if I still have a *face*."

After we bedded down for the night, Carl set straight to sawing logs, like all that jaw jacking had plum wore him out.

But even without all his racket, I would've spent a lot of the night gazing up at the stars with my thoughts spinning like dust devils. What other wonderments were up there? When we ran out of frontier down here, was out there the next one? Would we ever get there to be counted as curiosities ourselves by creatures on another planet?

I took a look over at Ru. All her arms were wrapped around herself and she was snuggled at the base of one of the boulders, like a witch's familiar cozied by the warmth of a hearth. Was Carl right about it not being safe for us in her company? Had I convinced everyone to embrace their doom?

▦

The next morning, Ru was still with us and Carl was still handsome.

I guess Billy didn't get much sleep that night. We woke up just after dawn to the smell of hot cakes, bacon, and coffee he already had cooking for us.

After breakfast, we saddled the horses with the unspoken understanding Ru would ride double with me, but the horses were so skittish around Ru I didn't see how we were going to get any of them settled enough for her to ride one.

"I do not require transportation, Quinn," she said.

I expected the going to be a lot slower that way but didn't see much alternative. Did I ever call that one wrong. Ru gave me her costume to hold, got down on those six arms or legs or whatever they were with the other two folded up under her, and took off south and east like greased lightning. Even at full gallop, the horses could hardly keep up. By my reckoning, anything that could move that fast didn't have to let itself get cornered by the likes of us. I could've been wrong, but I was suspecting the first chance taken was by her on us.

By mid-morning we came across a shallow creek where we watered the horses. As we were learning, spring in that territory came on like summer. The heat of the day had set in so powerful, you could've snatched a handful of sweat, out of the air. Ru said we were more than halfway there, and we were glad to hear it. After resting a spell, we traveled on.

Right around high noon we finally came to a wide place in a river where the water ran green and slow.

"It is there," Ru said of her ship, pointing to the center of the river.

I scratched my chin. "Thirty foot down, you say?"

"Yes."

"Well," I drawled, "I ain't never been much for swimming. Anybody wanna get in there and see what we're up against?"

"Sure, Quinn," Billy said, stripping out of his shirt and kicking off his moccasins.

Billy waded in and then dove below the surface. He was down there for a good while before he came up long enough to tell us he'd found the ship, then went under again. We tensely watched him come up for air twice more.

When he finally came wading out, he breathlessly told us, "Water's so murky ... can't see my hand in front of my face ... but I could feel it down there. That thing is *huge*. Ain't no way ... *no* way the five of us are gonna get it outta there by ourselves."

A promise is a debt with me, and I was determined to pay this one off. Still, I was confounded for what to do next.

Malcolm said, " It's a shame Miss Ru hadn't set that thing down farther upriver."

"Why's that?" I asked.

"'Cause I'm pretty sure this is the North Platte. It's got the same green colorin' as the last river we built a bridge over. If it was under that, maybe we coulda hoisted it out."

I said, "You're sayin' the Union Pacific has a bridge that crosses this river?"

"Yes, sir," Malcolm said. "Finished it about a month before you and Billy joined up."

"North of here?"

"Yup."

"Well now, I think that might be our answer right there," I mused aloud, getting a glimmer of an idea. "We're gonna need to take a look at it."

There was still plenty of daylight left, but the horses were wore out, so we made camp there.

That evening saw a bit of a change in everybody's general disposition toward Ru. Billy still kept his distance somewhat, but Carl sure seemed to have warmed up to her some. He and Joe appeared keener to know more about her, her people, and her planet than Malcolm had the night before. I was mighty glad for that, since there was no telling how much longer we'd be sharing each other's company. My hope was we could have her back on her way to roaming the stars again in a day or two. But what if we couldn't? Were we just going to abandon her? If we did, how long would she have out there on her own before something bad befell her?

They also kept badgering me about what I had in mind to get her ship clear of that river, but I didn't want to jinx it by telling them too much.

At first light we were off again, following the North Platte River
northwest. The day promised to be another scorcher. Fortunately it was only ten miles or so before we came to the train
trestle.

The bridge was a span of about seventy feet and still
smelled of fresh-cut timber and pitch. Its twin steel rails
stretched across a chasm heading due east, off toward the flat-
lands of Nebraska; and behind us, to the west, toward the sky-
high mountain ranges of Wyoming. I gazed over the cliff 's
edge. It was a long way down to a thin ribbon of green water
flowing fast through the bottom of the canyon. The plan I was
hatching was looking better by the minute.

Carl said, "Okay, we're here. Now what?"

"Depends," I said. "You boys up for some mischief?"

Carl crossed his arms and said, "What kinda mischief you
talkin' about, Quinn?"

Rather than answer him, I turned to Joe. Although most
of the hands working on the Union Pacific line were Irish im-
migrants and ex-cons, a good many were Union veterans, like
Joe. During my short stint with the railroad, when other former
soldiers talked about their exploits, he kept silent. I thought
he just had a quiet nature, but after I made his acquaintance,
I learned he just preferred not to talk about what the war had
made him see and do. The hard work kept his mind off such
things. When I told him how me and Billy were adventuring
our way to the west coast before the railroad and settlers ruined
everything between here and there, he decided he wouldn't
mind an awful lot if he joined up with us. Word spread around
camp a bit, and that's how we ended up with Malcolm and
Carl. Not to put it too unkindly, I'd say out of all of us, Joe was
the only one who was running from himself.

I said, "Joe, you were with the Union Pacific the longest,
right?"

"That's right. Over a year."

"Ever learn how to drive a train?"

"Not exactly, but I picked up a thing or two."

"Think you picked up enough to steal one?"

He scoffed and shook his head. "We're too far upriver to
pull that contraption of Ru's out the river with a locomotive, if

that's what you're thinkin'."

"I'm thinkin' of using it for something else."

Joe shrugged, and said, "I'm game."

"Great. I need you, Billy, and Carl to ride east and bring us a train back. The more cars it's carryin', the better."

"And what about you and Malcolm?"

"We're goin' west, to catch up with the rail crew. We'll meet back at this spot right here in two days, dawn after next."

Ru said, "I would like to assist, Quinn."

I hadn't much thought of her tagging along, but the more I thought on it, the more I could see how a spidery-limbed shadow might come in right handy.

"All right, Ru, you're with me and Malcolm."

Joe and Carl and Billy walked their horses across the bridge.

After they saddled up on the other side, Joe waved back at us and yelled, "Dawn after next! With a train!" He rode away, laughing.

Before the canyon between us could finish echoing his laughter, we were chasing behind the railroad, going west.

However, we had to keep a distance from the tracks, because we weren't the only ones following them. Beneath that blazing Nebraska sun we passed plenty of sorry souls going the other way, leaving the Wyoming territory because they'd either been run off their homesteads by Indians, ranchers, or the railroad. They had my pity for their crushed dreams, they surely did, but I was more concerned one of them might catch sight of Ru. I hoped we kept enough distance she'd be taken for a spirited dog.

It was nearing dusk by the time we caught up with the railhead south of Douglas, Wyoming, right at the foot of the Laramie Mountains.

Now, a railhead is a perfect example of a rowdy frontier town—dirty, loud, and busier than a beehive—except it keeps moving, devouring everything in its way and leaves behind a trail of steel and wood. We hunkered down in a field of sagebrush, about a hundred yards away.

What I wanted was the dynamite. It was always kept in a guarded shack a safe distance from camp, but never safe enough to me. And considering they were getting ready to lay track around those mountains, I figured they had laid in enough TNT to blow Christ off his cross.

I asked Malcolm, "How much dynamite you think it'd take to blow that bridge?"

"A whole mess of it. We built that bridge sturdy. But why blow it, Quinn? I thought you wanted to use it somehow to help Miss Ru?"

"And that's how," I replied. "Now, how many sticks would you use to bring the whole thing down?"

He grimaced as he rubbed a hand over his head of kinky black curls, giving it some serious thought. Finally he said, "To make a good job of it? A hundred, I reckon."

"Anything else?"

"Well, you'll need your blastin' caps, of course. And wire—spools of it. And a detonator. Only, how you gonna get past that guard? If 'n you do, he ain't got the key to that lock on the shack."

"I figured to use my pistol to give the guard a lick upside the head, and then use it to bust the lock."

"Uh-huh, uh-huh," Malcolm said, nodding at that. "Might be a little noisy, but then how do you figure to see once you get in there, strike a match? 'Cause I can guarantee you, any light you see after you do is gonna be comin' from behind some Pearly Gates."

For the first time, Ru reminded us of her presence with her gurgly whisper of a voice, "I see very well in darkness."

I looked at Malcolm. Malcolm looked at me. We looked at Ru.

"Describe what is wanted please," she said.

And right after we did just that, she crept through the sagebrush to the back of the dynamite shack and started burrowing a hole at the base of the back wall like a coon dog after a rabbit. Malcolm was a better shot than me, so he kept his Winchester trained on the guard if things started going south.

After a few minutes, here comes Ru, low and slow, toting a case of dynamite on her back. Next she went and brought us several spools of wire. And then, after filling that hole behind the shack back in, she finally came back with a box of blasting caps.

"Well, okay then," I said, fairly impressed. "Let's get outta here."

Me and Malcolm split the dynamite up between us in our saddlebags and rode out real ginger-like. Didn't want anyone finding a crater with our remains scattered around it, wondering what kind of twisted suicide pact we had made.

Around dawn, Malcolm said the heat of the day wouldn't be good for the dynamite. And anything that wasn't good for the dynamite wasn't good for any of us.

With the shade only being make-believe in that flat land, we had to make our own with lean-tos. It wasn't until late afternoon the heat stopped contesting the humidity as the primary cause of discomfort, so we could take up traveling again.

We made it back to the bridge a couple of hours after sunset. We picked out a campsite and went right to work twining together bundles of two sticks of dynamite each. With Ru lending us a hand—well, several hands—in making the couplets, we were done lickety split. All we had left to do was to place them in the framework of the bridge and wire them up with blasting caps.

Ru said, "I would like to do that alone, if you will allow me, Quinn."

Me and Malcolm traded looks again, looks that said how clambering around under a bridge, over a canyon, in the dark, with a bunch of dynamite wasn't something either of us *really* wanted to do.

I didn't feel the least bit yellow telling her, "It's okay with me if it's okay with Malcolm."

And Malcolm didn't hesitate saying, "You go right on and help yourself, Miss Ru."

Since Malcolm helped build the bridge, I left it to him to tell her the best places to set the dynamite.

Ru went to work as nimbly as a spider in a web. The way she moved through the trusses was amazing. What would have taken us hours, she did in a little over one.

I tell you plain. When it came to gumption, she had it in spades. If she ever set her mind to gunslinging, wouldn't be a lawman alive could take her. Lucky for them she was an outlaw on a planet other than ours.

We managed to get a few hours sack time in, before we were awakened a little before dawn by the shrieking steam whistle of an approaching train. With its coach lamp burning yellow like a baleful eye, the iron behemoth crossed the bridge and came to a halt with a steaming hiss. Behind the locomotive and tender were two passenger cars, a cattle car, and four flat-cars loaded with rails, ties, and heavy equipment.

"What a hoot!" Joe exclaimed when he climbed down out of the engineer's cab. "Had to go clear back down the line to Bayard to get 'er, but we got 'er!"

Behind him came Billy and Carl, their faces sooted from coal smoke.

"Brother!" Malcolm cheered, stepping to Carl with wide welcoming arms.

"Ha, ha. Very funny," Carl said humorlessly, pushing him away.

I asked Joe if there had been any problems.

"Nary a one," he replied. "After Billy cut the telegraph line, we pulled out of town in the middle of the night and ran it wide open till we got here. But I gotta tell ya, Quinn, the Union Pacific folks no doubt got a posse hot on our trail. This thing being on rails ain't gonna make it especially hard to run down."

"How far behind are they, you figure?"

"If they're ridin' horses? A good day. If another train was due in there anytime soon? Ain't no tellin'."

"Okay, well, get your horses off this thing and let's get 'er done. Our part is already finished."

I had him center the train on the bridge and brake it just as the sun cleared the horizon. After we cleared the area, I wired up the detonator and told everyone to put their fingers in their ears. Good thing too, because when I blew that bridge to smithereens, it made the godawfullest noise you ever heard. The ground trembled beneath our feet. I found out later they heard it two counties over.

When the dust settled, it was just like I figured, every-thing—lumber, train cars, all of it—tumbled down into the chasm and choked the river up tight. I had no idea how long our makeshift dam would hold, but my thinking was it would at least hold the river back long enough for Ru to get into her ship without flooding it.

"Well, boys," I said, "let's get downriver and see how we look."

It was an eternal two hours before the river lowered enough for us to see anything of Ru's ship, an angled piece of metal that glinted like a signal mirror.

For another three hours we watched the river slowly reveal the rest of its treasure. The murky water seemed reluctant to find its former banks, until, finally, we were left with our jaws flapping in the breeze. It was as shiny as a new Colt revolver with silver grips, at least a hundred foot long, and shaped like an arrowhead, its edges as straight and sharp as Mr. Bowie's finest blade. Yes sir, it was a real beaut.

Carl said, "All this talk about ships, I kinda expected it to look like a boat."

"So, that's the thing that brought you here from another planet?" Joe said with amazement.

"Yes, Joe. I do not have the words to express my gratitude to you all. Thank you. I would not have been able to do this by myself."

She touched a hand to her armband, and we all saw a ladder slide down from the belly of her ship. Malcolm asked her for a look inside. Ru extended an invitation to all of us. Everybody was game except Billy. He decided to stay behind with the horses. Nobody felt a need to ask him why.

As for me, Malcolm, and Carl, we set off across the muddy riverbank behind Ru. She seemed to skim right over it and was waiting for us at the bottom of the ladder in no time. The going was a lot slower for us two-legged types the farther we slogged through that muck. It was a fight just to keep my boots from being sucked off my feet, but at least it gave me something to occupy my mind besides the nest of vipers churning in my stomach, thinking about what was waiting for us inside that ship. But as anxious as I was, I was more curious. Only it didn't seem I was going to be able to satisfy that particular hankering when Billy started sounding the alarm.

"River's comin'!" he shouted. "Clear out! Clear out!"

Me and the boys were in a bad spot, knee-deep in mud and right between the ship and the high-water mark. Carl was already high-stepping his way back, but Malcolm, that damn fool, he was trying to make it to the ladder. I grabbed him by the collar.

"You won't make it, Malcolm! We gotta go back!"

If you've ever seen a man gut-shot, you'd have a fair idea of the expression he had on his face when he turned around to face me. He fought me for a moment, but we could hear the river coming, feel the mud trembling around our legs. As much as Malcolm didn't want to, he knew I was right.

The two of us hightailed it back to the horses just in the nick of time, but it was too late for Ru. A mighty wave of water and railroad lumber came tumbling through and crashed down on her ship. The ship, it just disappeared.

Malcolm snatched off his hat and threw it to the ground. "Damn it to hell!" he bellowed.

We all shared his sentiment.

I took off my hat in respect, but I reckon we gave up the ghost a little too soon. That silver arrowhead rose up from the roiling surface of the water just as easy as you please and hovered there a few yards above it. We whooped and hollered like the North won the war again.

We continued to watch Ru's gleaming ship silently rise— up and up and up it went—until we lost it in the sun.

Feeling right proud of ourselves, the five of us continued on west like we'd been intending, but all of us didn't make it to California. Joe Smith died in Nevada after a rattler spooked his horse and the horse fell on him. Joe never spoke of any kin, so we buried him there in the desert. Malcolm said something real respectful over him.

Deputy Marshal Seth Kenner never did catch up with Carl Kistler. But Sheriff Tony Woods did. Seemed he was waiting for us the minute we hit California. Woods said he figured we were the ones responsible for a railroad mishap back in Nebraska, but wasn't interested in anyone except Carl, because of that federal warrant with his name on it.

With two deputies behind him, Woods told Carl, "Live outlaw or dead desperado, your choice, son. They ain't too particular what shape you're in when you get back to Oklahoma."

If Carl had just kept his head, we would've maybe seen

what we could do about a jailbreak before he got carted back to Oklahoma, only he was too mule-headed to think things through. He was also too slow on the draw.

The rest of us went all the way to San Francisco, right to the edge of America. A sweet little Kiowa squaw working a saloon there took a shine to Malcolm Foster and took up with him on a spread with a beautiful view of the Pacific. Me and Billy Morningstar helped them get set up and stayed there for a spell. But after a while Billy said he still had some leg-stretching to do and headed for points north. I decided it was time for me to go my own way too.

As I write this, word has it the transcontinental railway is still a year or more away from when a body can ride coast-to-coast. I can't wait that long. Tomorrow I'm fixing to make my way back to Philadelphia. That gal's daddy might still be looking to kill himself a Quinn Bennet, but I reckon it's worth the chance to be a pap myself. I got a powerful hankering to see what the fuss is all about.

The Misery of Gold
Steve B. Howell

It was a day like any other day on K2-3d. The wind howled, dust blew, and the red sun hung motionless in the sky. In the distance, a coyote meandered down Main Street and the sound of unseen spurred boots walking on wooden sidewalks echoed off the decaying structures.

Sentenza examined the scene from the west end of Main Street, scanning the town for movement and infrared signatures using his phase-delay oculars. The empty buildings acted as musical instruments and provided a prosody of moans and groans as well as an odd wavering whistle. No one was in sight but he knew Carluph was there. He had tracked Carluph for 40,000 clicks, across nine planets, through fifty towns, over ice-covered mountains and sticky rivers of salty sludge, and now finally to this place. The final place. The place where the gold was hidden.

Decades before, this town had been a bustling center of activity centered around gold mines and gold miners. Over four thousand had lived here—those who toiled in the mines, digging and blasting the rock and teasing the gold out, and those who got rich taking the miners' money for services rendered. One of the richest women in that long ago town owned the bank and this nabob boasted far and wide about the bank's pristine record of handling over five billion tokens in gold without one robbery. No robberies, that is, if you don't count the break-in that happened in '49.

Legend has it that two men dug a tunnel right up into the bank vault, stole 100,000 tokens, and got clean away. The men and, more importantly, the gold were never seen again.

Using an illegal ID code tracker, Sentenza had located his prey. Breaking in on Carluph, he pointed his six-shooter directly at his foe's chest. The six-shooter was an old Earth-style weapon, using chemical powder as a propellant and firing solid metal bullets. Sentenza liked the feel of the gun in his hand and favored it over modern EMpulse weapons, even though

232

they were far lighter and more effective. Making the bullets for use in the unregistered six-shooter took time but using the ancient weapon made it extremely difficult for examiners to even assign the method of death to the trail of bodies Sentenza left behind.

He eyed Carluph knowingly, motioning him to sit down and carefully remove the EMpulse blaster from his waistband holder. One word was uttered in a bass voice, "Where?"

Sweat began to bead on Carluph's brow.

Again. "Where!"

With a shaky arm, Carluph pointed toward a box lying under the corner of the bar. The barrel of Sentenza's gun motioned Carluph toward the box, suggesting he go get it and bring it to the table. Once done, another motion said open it.

Three shots rang out and Carluph crumpled to the floor. The box proved empty. Laughing, Sentenza went over to the lumped form and yelled, "Where!"

Carluph coughed a bit and tried to talk. Sentenza, moving closer to hear, the words "other planet, Dog Town" were muttered. Sentenza, still laughing, kicked the near lifeless form for good measure.

▓

"I didn't do it! I am telling ya, it was not me! Please don't use the brain probe I'll confess, I'd rather confess than have my brain fried!" But no one listened as the man yelled out. The inhabitants of Kepler-186f were not very social, nor did they care much for strangers, especially those with a reward on their head. Juan Maria was such a stranger.

Wanted by the District Law Board for fraud, bigotry, cyber-rape, automaton robbery, assault and battery, kidnapping, embezzlement, breaking and entering, drug possession, aiding and abetting, bribery, various computer crimes, disorderly conduct, disturbing the peace, grand theft spaceship, forgery, open-container law violation, perjury, probation violations, and simply being a general nuisance, Juan Maria was the quintessential outlaw—big, oafish, and stupid—or at least he appeared that way.

As the town landrat positioned the probe, several EMpulse rifle blasts rang out, destroying the holding pen and leaving the probe burning in disarray. A frisson passed through the scattering crowd as a land speeder appeared from nowhere, collected Juan Maria, and sped off in a cloud of dust into the evening gloom. Nohbody drove as usual; sitting right next to the pack of reward credits he had obtained the day before when he turned Juan Maria over to the district marshal. Juan Maria struggled to get into his seat, nearly falling out of the fast-moving speeder.

"Hey! That was cutting it close my friend. Next time, how about you show up and start blasting before they get the probe running?"

Chewing the end of a fat cigar, Nohbody smiled a little and pushed the throttle further toward the floor. "Don't worry, we're heading to Dog Town and the residents of Dog Town like to take their time when they kill someone." Nohbody's voice boomed out over the whine of the twin turbo warp coils. He began to whistle a melodic tune.

Interplanetary travel to Dog Town, located on the hard rock mining planet K2-3c, was usually accomplished by means of following the laser guide beacon across the K2-3 system and using the space link between the two near-twin worlds 3c and 3d. This easy and official way to approach the planet required filing a flight plan and providing a ship registration. Such a method would, unfortunately, reveal that Sentenza was not the owner of the *Kobayashi Maru*. Besides, he knew right where to go on K2-3c and where to land the ship near Dog Town unnoticed. His travel to this planet did not need to involve the law.

Flying along the day/night terminator to jam the guide signals, Sentenza's ship made a quiet landing behind the old mission house. During the trip, he spent some time adjusting to the fact that planet 3d and Carluph had been a dead end; he turned his concentration toward the other man involved in the robbery. He knew Dog Town was the last place Murphy had been seen and now he knew that Murphy held the secret to the gold.

It was near mid-sleep period in Dog Town. The sky was its usual dusky merlot color as the red sun hung low in the sky. Walking slowly but with purpose, Sentenza entered the mission house, placed the oculars on his eyes, and started to look around. Plasma lamps lit the inside of the mission house, providing a ghastly glow and casting deep shadows on the walls. No movement or IR signatures were detected in the main room, but a weak blip registered in one of the back bedrooms.

The house appeared well kept until he removed his oculars and let his eyes adjust to the greenish light. The floor was covered in dust and boxed food tins were standing open on the table. Taking advantage of the food on the table, Sentenza sat down and began to eat. He made no effort to be quiet and purposefully tossed the empty metal food containers around the room after he slurped their contents dry. Container after container was tossed aside, each banging on the floor and walls, the sound echoing throughout the house.

Murphy appeared in the doorway brandishing a double-barrel EMpulse riot gun. He blinked at the dinner scene and then pointed the gun directly at the intruder. Sentenza slowly finished another container, tossed it aside, and with a full mouth mumbled loudly "Where?"

Murphy was taken aback. The left corner of his mouth quickly screwed up and he tripped backwards a step. Who was this person eating at his table and what did he want?

"Carluph's dead, where's the gold?" yelled Sentenza as he swept his arm across the table, sending the dishes and remaining containers crashing the floor.

"Get out!" came the reply from Murphy as he activated the EMpulse circuits with a very audible click. "I don't know any Carluph and I don't know about any gold."

Two shots rang out, splitting the metal table top in two and hitting Murphy in the leg. Murphy went down with a surprised look on his face—his eyes open wide and a painful grimace across his lips. Before he could react, his EMpulse gun was kicked aside. He looked up, peering directly into the barrel of an old-style six-shooter, a barrel still smoking from the shots just fired. "Where?" was all he heard as the six-shooter was moved closer to his head.

"In the cemetery" cracked out of his trembling lips. "In the cemetery."

Sentenza smiled a bit and cocked his six-shooter. "What cemetery?"

Things happened fast. Murphy leapt for the gun and barely got his hand on the pulse button. Taken by surprise himself, Sentenza fired two more bullets toward the jumping Murphy. Murphy's arm released the gun and he moaned faintly.

"What cemetery? What cemetery!" bellowed Sentenza shaking Murphy by the shoulders.

But Murphy didn't answer. Sentenza stood motionless for a moment and then in a fit of rage, upended the table and flung it across the room. He stomped his feet and roared, "wah-WAH-wah."

Once again, Juan Maria stood in the hot sun, arms constrained behind his back, and a crowd of angry onlookers surrounding him. His sentencing had only taken two minutes to complete as the mechanical voice read the charges and ended its droning recitation with one word, *Guilty.*

Juan Maria, as his form of punishment, had chosen the use of a brain probe. Hanging was rarely selected these days as it generally left the victim dead. The probe, on the other hand, merely turned the mind into mush and allowed the criminal to work out the rest of his or her life in the mines carrying rocks to the surface. Actually, Juan Maria chose the probe, as it was easier for him to make his get away in the speeder once Nohbody started shooting.

Taking aim at the town gallows and stockade platform, Nohbody clicked off the EMpulse rifle's safety and closed his finger on the trigger.

Click! The metallic sound was close to his left ear. Nohbody turned his eyes slightly to see who it was and why they pushed an odd-looking old gun into his skull.

"Nice pack of reward credits you got there", chimed Sentenza, "I'm sure you'd be happy turning them over."

"Well, I would be happy to do that, but, you see right now I'm in a bit of a hurry to save my friend. He's about to have his brain probed." At that, Nohbody went back to his business, aiming toward the town platform.

"Maybe you better think about saving yourself. Hand over the electrolock ring and I'll just be on my way."

Chomping on his cigar stub and giving a little whistle,

Nohbody calmly said, "Now why would you want to go and steal a man's hard earned credits?"

"Well, if you must know, I've had a tough few days. I had to fly across a couple of planetary systems, shoot a few men, and all I got for my trouble was another worthless hint as to where 100,000 stolen gold tokens are hidden. So, I ain't feeling so generous right now. Just hand it over."

"Are you talking about the gold robbery in '49? That's just a legend.

I oughtta know, you see, I knew one of the men that was supposed to have robbed the bank and he told me it never really happened. A guy named Murphy, lives right here in Dog Town. I ain't seen him in ages. Him and me were in the cavalry together. I can take you to see him in a bit, but I really need to get back to saving my friend." Nohbody returned his view to the town platform and once again fit his one mechanical eye into the EMpulse rifle firing system.

"Well, you won't be seeing Murphy around anymore. All he was good for anyway was to tell me that the gold was in a cemetery, but never said which one." At this, Sentenza pushed the gun barrel farther into Nohbody's head and added a little twist.

"Go ahead and shoot punk. You'll lose both the name of the cemetery that my friend knows and me. And I know what grave in that cemetery they buried the gold under. You see, Murphy and his partner Carluph were loose with their talk when they got drunk and over time they told us two some of the pieces of the puzzle. Looks to me like we got us a three-way partnership. Now, can I save one-third of the investment?"

Sentenza pulled the gun away and sat back on his haunches. He looked up into the sky and let out a long breath. He crossed himself in his astonishment, realizing these were the clues he had been searching for—the clues that would lead him to the gold.

He jumped into the air and gave a whistle. Landing awkwardly back on the ground, Sentenza quietly muttered, "Sure, save the guy and then let's go find the gold." He'd play along for now—always time later to dissolve the partnership.

Nohbody fired. He was a good shot, nearly always hitting

the target he wanted and avoiding actually hurting the people nearby. After a few seconds of firing EMpulses, he started the land speeder, gunned the engine, and went off to fetch Juan Maria one more time. This time, however, as they fled the town limits, the pack of reward credits were not alone on the front seat. They sat in the lap of a ruthless and dangerous man.

▦

The town of Santa Ana was the district seat of the Leone freehold on the planet Kepler-1638b. Gravity here was stronger than most habitable planets and the bright yellow sun kept temperatures steaming all the time. The trio arrived unannounced and without any fanfare just as they liked it.

The cemetery they sought, *All Souls and Saints Lost in Space*, was just a few clicks away, across an empty, dusty government-owned communication facility. They flew into the town's spaceport and not directly to the cemetery. Cutting across the facility on an illegal flight path would have been reported to the commander in charge of the communication facility and that would have spoiled their little salvage operation.

"Just in case one of us don't make it, Nohbody why don't you tell us what grave we are looking for—you know just in case." This was Sentenza's best attempt at conversation since the three had left K2-3c.

"I think I'll hold on to that information a bit longer," mumbled Nohbody while chewing a cigar butt. "Let's just hope we all make it."

Juan Maria had told them the name of the cemetery en route after getting some assurance from Nohbody that he'd not go it alone with Sentenza. After all, he and Nohbody had been through a lot together and had developed some trust between them. *Some* trust was about all he could hope for.

The three men had to make their way across the vast empty government-owned facility land to reach the *All Souls and Saints Lost in Space* cemetery. They reckoned that the best way to carry out their plan was to masquerade as government workers with some made-up assignment requiring access to the other side of the communication facility.

Night fell. Nohbody and Sentenza left Juan Maria to acquire a government-issue land speeder while they headed off to obtain uniforms and electronic order cards. Juan Maria's job was easier than expected. He simply waited outside a tavern until troopers arrived and disappeared inside. After a bit, he sauntered over to the government speeder, reached under the control panel, attached his homemade electronic starter, and climbed in.

Meanwhile, the other two men found trouble. A night guard had caught them in the Controller's office while they attempted to encode the work order cards. The guard was confused as to what to do with his prisoners and therefore somewhat slow reading and recording their implanted arm codes. Nohbody's EMpulse gun was disabled—a consequence of entering a government facility—but Sentenza's old-style six-shooter was not even detected.

A red message light appeared on the guard's code reader and the words *DETAIN* flashed across the screen. The guard suddenly sucked in air with a "huh." He looked at the two men with wide eyes as an expression of fear sauntered across his face. He reached for his detainment loops, fumbled a bit getting them off his belt, and threw one each at the two men.

Unfortunately, his toss was a bit too slow to match the speed of a bullet from the six-shooter. The guard fell backwards from the force of the close-range shot and he grabbed onto his upper leg while wincing in pain.

"Get the detainment loops and use them on the guard," cried Sentenza, "I'll finish up the cards."

With a small smile and some whistling, Nohbody chewed on his cigar butt as he bound and gagged the guard.

▓

The three compadres stood motionless at the edge of the *All Souls and Saints Lost in Space* cemetery. For as far as Nohbody's mechanical eye could see there were graves—thousands of graves—each with a headstone and a cross. Juan Maria crossed himself and muttered, "Holy saints and souls."

Nohbody chewed on his cigar end and Sentenza said, "Where?"

Sentenza and Juan Maria stared at Nohbody, waiting for him to reveal the specific grave they should go to. Nohbody pulled a fresh cigar from his coat pocket, bit off the end and lit it. He slowly took in a big breath and then let out a cloud of smoke.

"Okay," he said, "I guess we should get this over with."

Sentenza couldn't take it anymore. He pulled out his six-shooter and pointed it at Nohbody. "Where?" was all he said. He then pointed the gun at Juan Maria. "He dies now if you don't tell me."

"Apparently we have no trust here," drawled Nohbody. "I expected no less. No need to shoot him now. Let's do this right." He picked up a big flat stone and wrote a name on one side. He then walked to the center of a large open area near the cemetery entrance and placed the stone, writing-side down, on the ground.

At this, the three men quickly moved to opposite sides of the area, forming a wide triad around the over-turned stone. Each man swept their eyes back and forth across the other two faces. Each man's hand twitched on his gun.

Sentenza fidgeted with his six-shooter, touching the wood handle and gently pulling it up a little from its holder. Juan Maria had his EMpulse riot gun across his arms and had hit the on switch. Nohbody stood quietly, puffing his new cigar and keeping his EMpulse rifle upright and near his side. His mechanical eye scanned both men at the same time, reading their blood pressure and measuring the blacks of their eyes.

The three outlaws began to circle, slowly at first, each moving clockwise, gauging each other's movements and motions. Each watched the other two, waiting for some sign—waiting to see who'd draw first.

Nohbody stopped puffing and slowly said, "I guess we got us a Mexican Standoff!"

Circling and watching, watching and circling. Each man tense, each man sweating, each man knowing that the gold could be theirs. The wind gathered strength and a strange whistling sound floated in from the distance.

Finally, Sentenza pulled his six-shooter, aimed directly at Nohbody and pulled the trigger. Click, Click … Click. Nothing happened, no shots fired. Upon examination, he found empty cylinders, no bullets.

He jerked his head back revealing a face full of anger.

"Damn you!"

Nohbody smiled. "I knew this would get ugly and you'd be the bad one. So I emptied the chambers out at our last stop." He then pointed his EMpulse rifle at Sentenza and fired.

Juan Maria was dumbfounded. He fell to his knees and began to cry. "I thought sure I was going to die. Now, I guess you and me are partners, right?"

He ran to the center of the circle and grabbed the rock. "Greeb Z2 Tolu, Greeb Z2 Tolu—that's the one." Juan Maria ran around the cemetery, looking at each grave marker in turn. Running and running, until he found the one, the one labeled *Greeb Z2 Tulo.* "Here, here it is," he screamed and began to dig into the hard dirt and rocks of the grave with his bare hands.

Nohbody joined him, bringing an autoshovel along. He pushed Juan Maria aside and took over the digging. Juan Maria scrambled out of the way and stood off to the left. As the digging continued, he crept close to the gravesite and pointed his EMpulse riot gun right at Nohbody.

The unmistakable low-to-high frequency whine of an EMpulse gun turning on was heard above the wind. Juan Maria was now laughing, "You just keep on digging. You're doing just fine."

A smile cascaded across Nohbody's face. He chomped a bit more on his cigar and glanced back at Juan Maria. "You really sure you want it this way?"

"I been thinking about this gold for a long time and now my luck has turned. Running into Sentenza—" he cast a sideways glance down toward the dead heap "—that was pure luck."

As Juan Maria waxed inelegantly, Nohbody swung the autoshovel around fast and hit him right across the chest, knocking the EMpulse riot gun off into the distance and Juan Maria off balance. Nohbody moved fast and soon had Juan Maria pinned to the ground with an EMpulse handgun pressed into his face.

"You made my day, Juan, 'cause you failed the test and now you'll be doing the diggin', and diggin' in the right place."

Juan whimpered a bit as Nohbody pulled him to his feet and pushed the autoshovel into his arms. "There, the grave next

door, the one marked *unknown*. That's the correct one. Dig!"
Juan Maria dug for ten minutes. The autoshovel hummed away with each spadeful and formed a strange descant to the melodious whistling in the background. He was scared, hot, and not sure what was going to happen. After a few more shovelfuls, he hit something hard and metallic. Falling to his knees, he began to dig with his hands and soon uncovered a metal box, about the size of a milk crate, with a bezel on top holding a flashing red light. Ah, the ecstasy of gold.

"Okay, pull that out here," barked Nohbody. "Open it."
Juan Maria did as he was asked. He pressed the button next to the light and the top of the box opened silently. Inside were the 100,000 gold tokens gleaming in the late afternoon sun.

"Okay, we found it. It's all ours. What say we split it up and go our separate ways?"

Nohbody had already decided on a plan, and going their separate ways was not in the cards. He grabbed Juan Maria and quickly wrapped him up in a detainment band. He then dragged him over to one of the most rickety looking grave markers he could find, threw a rope over a nearby tree limb, and tied it tightly around the bound man's neck. Juan Maria was prodded to climb onto the cross, one leg on each of the rood's arms, and balance himself there. Nohbody removed the slack in the rope, tying it off on a neighbor's headstone.

Nohbody picked up the split box and emptied half the gold tokens into the speeder's saddlebag. Throwing the rest on the ground, Nohbody hissed out, "There is your share. I oughtta kill you but I'm feeling generous today." He placed the saddlebag containing half of the gold into the land speeder and climbed in. "You got a fair chance that cross will hold and you can remain standing in this wind storm, at least long enough for you to untie yourself. Them's better odds than you gave me."

Saying that, Nohbody pushed the throttle full on and sped off into the sunset, streaking nearly out of sight in less than a minute. He stopped just as he was about to pass over the horizon and looked back at Juan Maria.

Nohbody had a serious scowl on his face as he realized he

had run out of cigars. He knew Juan Maria would come after him if he got free. He picked up his EMpulse rifle and pointed it back at the cemetery, straight at Juan Maria's head. He attached his mechanical eye to the rifle sight and put his finger on the trigger. Switching the EMpulse rifle on, he heard the reassuring hum of its circuitry. Slowly he pulled the trigger and in a flash the rope around Juan Maria's neck was cut in two.

Nohbody returned to his seat in the speeder, the gold comfortably sitting next to him. He gunned the engine and disappeared over the horizon.

Backstabbers and Sidewinders
A *Boneman Tale*
Patrick Thomas

The gunslinger walked out into the middle of the rail town like he owned the place, filled with more courage and stupidity than any dozen normal men would have been able to manage on a good day.

"Hey Boneman, I'm a calling you out."

Wendell Kennedy didn't stop walking down the dusty street, doing his best to ignore the would-be desperado. Some things were the same here on Doomstone as they were on Earth—young bucks thought they could make a name for themselves by taking out the baddest hombre in the territory. It was dumb on both worlds. The only way to know for certain if you're good with a six-shooter is to have been in a real fight, not one of these high noon showdowns the folks here were so fond of. Still, it weeded out the slow and the dumb. Those who survived learned better ways to go about things. Those that didn't got to change their address to Boot Hill.

Back on Earth, Kennedy had retired to a life of farming and raising some cattle. Occasionally someone would seek him out to pick a fight, but it was rare. Back on Earth, most folk didn't know what the infamous Boneman looked like and he could walk around most places with a certain degree of anonymity.

Not so on the playworld Doomstone. When the alien aloff shanghaied the gunfighter and his family from Earth, they expected Kennedy to take up his bounty hunter ways, but instead, he was content to pick up with his family where he left off. Having one of the Old West's most famous gunfighters harvesting crops and butchering livestock just wasn't entertaining enough for the bug-eyed aliens western themed playworld, so the bastards manipulated some locals into slaughtering his family while Kennedy was in town getting supplies. During the bloodbath that came in the wake of Kennedy avenging his loved ones, the gunfighter's body was exposed to radiation that made his flesh invisible except for his bones and eyes.

Wendell Kennedy originally got his nickname for the number of people he planted in the boneyard. Now being called the Boneman was even more fitting as he looked like a walking skeleton.

It was as if the Bugeyes planned it that way.

"Hey, I'm talking to you, ugly."

The Boneman stopped. The wannabe gunslinger in the black hat and vest wasn't smart enough to leave well enough alone. Tobacco on this world didn't taste right, so Kennedy didn't smoke anymore, except when he found a good cigar. Instead, Kennedy found he really enjoyed chewing gum. He took a stick out of his pocket and put in his mouth.

"What's the matter, old man?" Kennedy shook his head. Thirty-eight wasn't young, but it sure wasn't old. "What's the matter? You afraid of me? Is the famous Boneman really just a yellow-bellied chicken?"

Kennedy slowly turned to stare at the gunslinger. The Boneman's gaze had run off more than one man, even before his looks made him resemble a poor relation of the Grim Reaper. With luck, the young buck would take one look at him and rethink the wisdom of his challenge.

The man in the black hat didn't run off, but facing down the Boneman did shut him up. The quiet just didn't take.

"Everybody says you're the best there is—the quickest draw and the most deadly shot. I say that's a bunch of horse pucky. I'm the fastest most people's ever seen in these parts."

"Then the people in these parts mustn't get out much. Listen, boy, I've done more than my share of killing and I hate doing it for free. Why don't you do the smart thing and we'll both walk away and you can tell your friends over drinks in the saloon about how you stared down the Boneman."

"I'm going to do more than that."

A woman in a gown that didn't make it up to her shoulders rushed out and stood in front of Black Hat. "Please Jimmy, don't do this. Let's go to my place and do something else. I'll make you forget the Boneman."

Kennedy didn't know what answer the young woman was expecting, but he sure didn't care for it himself. Black Hat backhanded her right across the face, knocking the woman to the dirt. Then the big, bad man laughed.

"Don't you ever tell me what do, Esmeralda. Think you would've learned that lesson by now."

On closer examination, the woman had a bruise on the opposite side of her face from where she'd been hit and more up and down her arms.

"A real man don't ever hit his woman. That's what a coward does."

"Only coward I see here is you, too trembly to shoot it out with me."

"All right, you've convinced me that even this shitworld would be better off without you, but I still don't like killing for free."

"Is that all that stopping this from happening? Well then, I can fix that pretty quick. I got me a hundred dollars in gold in this here pouch." The man in the black hat touched a bag on his belt. "You manage to kill me, it's yours."

"But Jimmy, you said that money was for us. We're gonna get married and buy a homestead then start a family," said the battered Esmeralda.

"What I tell you about sassing me, woman?" Jimmy said as he brought his hand back to hit her again.

"Hey Jimmy the Kid," Kennedy said.

The man in the black hat stopped before he hit the woman again. "So you heard of me, have you?"

"Nope. Just folks around these parts ain't very original with monikers and more than half of ya have *the kid* after your name. At least if youse are under twenty. Look, I've got business to tend to, so why don't we meet back here in 'bout three hours."

"Why? I'm free right now, so let's do this."

"Fine, but be quick about dying," the Boneman said.

As if it had been choreographed, the rest of the bystanders cleared the streets and got behind wooden partitions. Even in a podunk town that was actually called Podunk, folks had seen their share of gunfights where a badly aimed bullet or ricochet could do in folks who was just there to watch the slaughter, not participate in it.

The undertaker stepped out in the middle of the street. On Doomstone, refereeing gunfights was part of his job description. "We are going to have ourselves a nice, clean shoot out. Both participants will walk twenty paces in opposite directions, then turn around. When I say draw, you will try to shoot each other and you may continue to shoot until you are either out of bullets or the other man is dead. Any man who draws his gun early to shoot the other fellow is subject to hanging under penalty of law for being a hornswoggler and a no good cheat. Do you both accept these terms?"

"Yup," the Boneman rasped.

"Hell yeah I do," Jimmy the Kid said.

"Then may God have mercy on your souls." The undertaker walked backwards until he reached the wooden sidewalk and got behind a partition of his own.

A small metal globe with a large lens dropped out of the sky and hovered above the dusty street. It seemed to have a particular interest in the impeding gunfight.

Boneman lost his legendary cool at the sight of the thing. "Damn gawker. Ain't doing this to entertain you dodgasted Bugeyes. Get yer camera out of here!"

The Boneman drew the gun on his left side and shot the gawker right in the lens, causing it to float back a foot.

"Yer cheating, mister. You pulled a gun and I ain't said draw," the undertaker scolded. Kennedy shot the flying camera again. "Now we got to hang ya."

"I ain't shooting Stupid the Kid, just that confounded thang. When you say draw, I'll use my right gun to shoot Stupid. I jest don't want the confounded Bugeyes to get a good view of this. After what they done to me, I enjoy pissing them off whenever when I can."

The undertaker stroked his beard. "Why I guess there ain't nothing specific in the rules that prohibit it. Against the law to hurt a gawker, though."

"You gonna try to stop me, gravedigger?"

"No, sir, I ain't. Also ain't sure what a bugeye is either, but you sure don't like 'em none." Wendell Kennedy fired again, hit the side of the lens and the gawker floated up higher.

With each shot hitting such a small moving target, Jimmy

the Kid appeared more and more confounded. The Boneman wasn't even looking at him as he shot the gawker two more times, scoring a bullseye on the lens each time.

"Draw!"

With only a slight turn of his skull, the Boneman slapped leather and his right six-shooter cleared his holster. His guns fired together. The bullet from the left gun hit the gawker in the lens yet again while the slug from the right gun ended Jimmy the Kid, right between the eyes.

The Boneman paused to reload both guns before putting each back in its holster. Then he walked across to where the corpse of the man once known as Jimmy the Kid lay unmoving, his eyes still staring accusingly as if they could not believe he hadn't won. Not only did he lose, his gun never even cleared the holster.

Kennedy bent down and pulled the bag of gold off the man's belt as Esmeralda fell to her knees, weeping over her dead lover.

The Boneman pulled a gold coin out and flipped it to the undertaker, who caught it and nodded his thanks. It was part of his job to take care of the losers from any shootouts, but it was still nice to make a little extra cash in the process.

The Boneman took his cowboy hat off and put it over his chest to stand before Esmeralda. "Ma'am, I'm sorry for your loss, but he was a dumbass that didn't need to be hitting you. You need to do better for yourself."

The woman looked up and nodded at him through her tears. Wendell Kennedy had seen a lot of women cry in his day and knew there were different kinds of tears. Hers weren't tears of love, just of loss.

"Here." Kennedy handed her the bag of gold coins. "Make something of yourself. Don't worry so much about a man that you let him treat you so poorly, you hear me?

"Yes, sir. Thank you very kindly for your generosity."

The Boneman nodded and walked away.

But some folks don't know when to leave good enough alone. An old coot with a white beard that hung to his belt followed the gunfighter.

"Hey there Wendell. Just wanted to say howdy. I used

to read about you in dime store novels back home. Weird how we lived over a hundred years apart and here you are younger than me."

The Boneman stayed silent but sighed. It was rare to bump into someone else who remembered being from Earth. It was almost worth putting up with the rambling to be reminded that Doomstone wasn't all that there was, so he slowed down and let the old man catch up.

"You get paid for them books?"

"Nope."

"And you was okay with that?"

"Didn't bother me either way until the writer insulted my Katie."

"You shoot him dead?"

The Boneman shook his head. "Broke both his hands and his arms though. And I promised to plug him if he was ever disrespectful to my wife or my marriage again. Far as I know, he wasn't."

The coot laughed. "That'd teach him for sure. You ever wonder about where the aliens brought us?"

The Boneman shrugged. "Some other world, round some other star I recon."

"Yeah but which one? I was a bit of an amateur astronomer and I think I got it figured out by looking at the stars. This here is probably Kepler-1229b, cause of that red dwarf we got for a sun."

The red sun made the sunsets beautiful, like they looked back in the deserts in Arizona. Katie would have loved them. Kennedy didn't know what a Kepler was and didn't care, but knew that asking would only encourage the man to keep flapping his gums. The nostalgia for home was just about to be outweighed by the man's ramblings.

"That and the higher gravity here makes it pretty certain for my money. It plays havoc with my rheumatism, let me tell you."

"What do you want, old man?"

"I ain't happy that the aloff kidnapped me and brought me to Doomstone, but I know I'm going to die here without ever seeing my family and friends back home again. I may look eighty, but I'm barely sixty-five. I ain't never going to get me no revenge on the Bugeyes, but I heard stories that you found one dumb enough to come down here and show itself and you killed it. I want to know if that's true."

"It is."

The old man whooped and hollered, then slapped Kennedy on the shoulder. "I'm proud of you, sir. The next one you kill, you do it for old Jake Hessler, ya hear?"

The Boneman shook his head. "No. I ain't done killing 'em for my family yet."

Kennedy continued the way he had started in the first place. The old coot was still hollering and started dancing a two-step and pointing his middle fingers in the direction of the sky.

The gun fighter still had a job to do. Kennedy had accepted a bounty from the Golden Spike Savings and Rail, the banking arm of the largest railroad company in the Union of States, the Commonwealth Confederacy, or the Badlands. It was the Bugeyes' version of the North, South, and West back on Earth.

A bandit by the name of Lily the Cat had made off with eighty-eight thousand dollars by robbing the Golden Spike banks. The bigwigs wanted her caught bad enough to offer three thousand in gold. It made Lily popular among the bounty hunting crowd, not that all bounty hunters had Wendell Kennedy's skills, intelligence, or integrity.

Lily wasn't called the Cat because of her burglary skills. She was a genetically engineered human with feline characteristics and was covered in black fur with the exception of a white patch on her nose. Several other bounty hunters had simply rounded up a cat woman who fit the general description in order to claim the bounty. Some hadn't even bothered to find a cat woman with a white spot on their nose. One put a dab of paint there. Another just rubbed some flour on it. The railroad bankers hadn't been fooled.

While other bounty hunters had been tracking down lookalikes, Kennedy was searching for a pattern. All the robberies were exactly four days apart and seemed to be following the rail line west. The schedule didn't correspond with the train schedule—otherwise, they'd be a lot further apart. Kennedy figured the distance between robberies was about as far as a hoverbike could travel at a reasonable speed through the wilderness. Hoverbikes didn't come cheap. Kennedy had one, but he was certain that a woman with eighty-eight thousand dollars would have a faster model. Or an entire fleet of them if she wanted.

If Lily the Cat stuck to her pattern, she was going to hit the bank in Podunk today. She wasn't so predictable that she robbed the banks at the same time of day, so there was likely to be some waiting involved.

Kennedy took up position across the street in front of a barbershop. He sat himself down on the wooden planks with his back against the building. The Boneman pulled his hat down so his face couldn't be easily seen but still had enough of a gap to have a good view of the bank.

From a distance, he figured he'd look like a drunk trying to sleep one off.

It seemed to work closer up too.

"Hey sidewinder, get your drunken ass out from in front of my store before I beat you to within an inch your life," said the tough-talking barber, who stepped outside his establishment with a straight razor in his hand.

From beneath his hat, Kennedy chuckled. He never liked braggarts or bullies and this man appeared to be a bit of both.

"You think it's funny, you drunken vagrant? I'll slit your throat and leave you here to bleed to death. Ain't nobody going to care. I'd just tell the sheriff I was defending myself."

When Kennedy's skeletal looking hand came out of his coat, it was holding a big Bowie knife. He used the tip of the blade to push the brim of his cowboy hat up and reveal the skull that passed for his face. Kennedy laughed again when he saw the fear creep across the barber's face.

"Yeah, I do think it's funny. And I know the sheriff ain't gonna care, but I'm pretty sure you got which one of us is going to be bleeding to death wrong."

"Tarnation, you're the Boneman. I'm mighty sorry."

"You're darn right you're mighty sorry. And if you think that's enough of an apology, then we'd best have it out right now between your straight razor and my Bowie knife."

"There is no need for that, sir. I'll do anything you ask of me to make it right between us."

"Anything?"

"Absolutely."

"Strip down until you're wearing no more than you were when you were brought into this sorry excuse for a world."

"You want me to get naked?"

"Did I stutter?" Kennedy leaned forward and away from the building like he was about to stand up. The barber folded his straight razor and put it on the windowsill, then shucked his clothing faster than a cook could clean corn.

The naked man stood with his hands covering his manhood. He needn't have used both. "Mr. Boneman sir, are we square now?"

"We ain't even up to a triangle yet."

"How long do I have to stay like this?"

"Until I say otherwise."

"I guess I can go upstairs to my rooms and close the shop for the day."

"Oh no. Up there by your lonesome, being naked won't be a lesson to ya on how to treat other folks. You're going to go about your business like you would normally."

"But I can't go about without any clothes on around decent people. I'll be branded a pervert and be an outcast. They'll have the sheriff arrest me and put me in jail."

"Don't you worry about that none. I'll have me a talk with your sheriff and make sure that won't happen. Now leave me so I can get back to work. And rest assured I will be checking on you periodically and if I catch you with even a stitch of clothing on, we can settle this just like you suggested in the first place. Have I made myself clear, barber man?"

"As clear as the finest crystal."

As the barber walked back into the shop, the Boneman could hear the laughter of his customers. The barber told them to be quiet.

Just in time too because he caught a glimpse of a hoverbike landing up on the roof of the bank. Lily the Cat must have a top-of-the-line model because it was silent as could be. Kennedy's was a mite noisier and started to wobble if he went over five feet off the ground.

A rope was thrown over the side of the building and someone in a black poncho with a hood shimmied down with great grace and stealth, quickly making her way into the bank, followed closely by a floating gawker.

It was days like this that made Kennedy realize how much the love of a good woman and his kids had changed his black heart. It had been turned from pitch to snow white, but after the Bugeyes arranged for the slaughter of his family, the best his chest could muster these days was gray. The aloft couldn't erase the love that he had for them—or they for him. His lovely Katie had always hated that he'd killed so many people. Kennedy's wedding gift to her was to give up that life. The Boneman made good on that pledge throughout all the years of their marriage, except for the few times it was necessary to break it to protect those he loved.

In the old days, he would've shot it out with Lily before she went in and not worried about what bystanders might be mulling about. These days he thought like a decent lawman should, which still disturbed him to his core.

And to be truthful it made things more fun this way. Thinking was more of a challenge than putting a bullet in everything.

Lily's bounty was dead or alive—some of the cat women imposters hadn't been breathing when they were brought in—but if it came down to it, Kennedy planned to wound. His vow to Katie had been for all the days of their marriage, but the Bugeyes got amused by killing, so he tried to limit their entertainment.

While the cat woman was relieving the bank of its valuables, Kennedy used the rope to climb his way up onto the roof and remove something round from the hoverbike's engine, then hid behind the roof access shack.

The Boneman waited.

'Tweren't long before the cat woman climbed back up on the roof and pulled the rope up behind her. She wound it up and put it in her saddlebags as the gawker hovered above her. When Lily climbed on and turned the handgrip for the elevation, she was shocked that the bike didn't move. The bank robber hit the ignition switch even though she had left the bike running.

Nothing happened.

That's when she heard the click of the six-shooter behind her.

"Good evening ma'am. My name is Wendell Kennedy and I would like you to consider yourself captured. There are many ways this can end, but the only one that don't end up with your pretty little hide perforated with small bits of lead involves you putting your hands above your head very slowly, followed by your getting off your ride and turning to face me."

Lily the Cat did as instructed. Once her hands were above her head she used them to pull back the poncho hood, revealing her attractive feline face.

"Why, the Boneman himself has come for me. I am honored indeed."

"There's no honor in it, ma'am. It's just the bounty on your pretty head was enough to garner my attention." The Boneman tossed the cat woman a pair of Western-style handcuffs. "If you'd be so kind as to put those on, I'd be much obliged."

"I guess I better, seeing as how you left me no other choice."

"Don't kid yourself, ma'am. You've got plenty of choices, but the one I suggested is the only one that'll do you any good."

Lily fastened the handcuffs on her own wrists. "I guess I can't argue with the logic in your words, although I'd appreciate it if you called me Lily. Call me ma'am makes me feel like an old cat. So how much is my bounty up to?"

Kennedy stepped in and reached under her poncho. He pulled out two six-shooters, a large knife, as well as a whip, appropriately enough called a cat of nine tails. "Three thousand gold."

"Well that is a lot of money, but I do believe I have more than that in this sack. If I give it to you, would you consider letting me go?"

"No ma'am … or rather Miss Lily. That's not how it works. I agreed to do a job. What kind of man would I be if a little extra cash would sway me from what I said I would do?"

"The normal kind. I don't suppose doubling or tripling the amount would make a difference?" The Boneman shook his skull. "A pity, but perhaps our negotiations are not yet finished.

Despite your odd condition, there's something about you that I find ruggedly handsome. Maybe it's the way you handle yourself, maybe it's your deep raspy voice, but if you let me go, not only can you keep the money but you can have me here and now and even a few times later." Lily said, unfastening in the front of her poncho to reveal a quite impressive female figure, albeit one covered in short and soft black fur.

"Miss Lily, that is the most inviting offer I've had in a long time, but I'm afraid I can't let it sway me any more than your financial one. But if it makes any difference, your second offer was a lot more tempting than your first."

The cat woman smiled and nodded her head. "It does make a difference. Did they tell you why I was robbing the Golden Spike Savings and Rails?"

"It did not come up in conversation, nor does it really matter. You're stealing what doesn't belong to you and my services were engaged to stop you from that activity." The gawker moved in closer and the Boneman pointed a gun at it, so it floated back up.

"What I'm stealing don't rightly belong to the Golden Spike neither. They stole my family's land by hiring a bunch of Enjuns to run us and our neighbors off our ranches so they could build their damn railroad."

Enjuns were Doomstone's version of Injuns or Indians. "That doesn't sound likely. Most of those cyborg savages don't have no interest in the ways of corporations."

"These particular Enjuns were mercenaries hired by the Golden Spike to get us off of that land by any means possible. Those means involved them killing my ma, my pa, and my baby brother. When I made it into town to tell folks what happened, it didn't do no good. The folks in charge were prejudiced against my kind, so I went out into the wilds on my own.

"I ran into an Enjun name of Lowman. We started out as adversaries and ended up lovers. After a while, Lowy had something he had to get off all of his partially metallic chest. Seems he was one of the Enjuns the Golden Spike hired to run folks off our land, but he quit when they told him they had to start murdering folk. Even came with me to talk to a Badlands judge. Lowman swore out an affidavit and said he'd testify,

Next day he disappeared. When I spoke to the judge, he told me dead men can't testify. The way I reckon is they took everything from me, so now I'm going to try to take everything from them."

"Your story does move me to sympathy, particularly if it's true."

"Are you trying to say I'm lying?"

Kennedy laughed. "Not as such, but you'd be surprised what folks will say when a gun is pointed their way. It don't matter so much if it's true or false, as it's a chance to get free. I work under the assumption that it don't matter. Now how about you and me open that door and head down the stairs. I know cat folk are very quick, so if I think you're doing anything that I need to be worried about, I'm going to put a bullet in you, so I advise you to go down the steps carefully and not trip."

The folks in the bank startled when the door opened and they saw the cat lady and the gawker return. Then they became a different kind of nervous when the skeletal figure in the long leather coat walked in behind her with a gun drawn.

"Who's in charge here?"

A man in matching trousers and vest with a white shirt, a long string bow tie and glass spectacles raised his hand. "I'm Frank Davids, the bank manager."

"Then as a duly appointed officer of Golden Spike Savings and Rail, I officially turn over custody of Lily the Cat. My name is Wendell Kennedy and I expect my bounty paid."

The spectacled bank manager walked back to his desk and opened the drawer. No one was more surprised than Kennedy when he pulled out a six-shooter and pointed it at him.

"Usually, when you bankers rob a person, you are more circumspect," Kennedy said.

"I'm afraid I'm unable to accept delivery of your bounty."

Kennedy shifted the gun that was pointed at Lily to the bank manager and drew his other gun so it was pointed at the cat woman. "And why is that?"

"Because I want the three thousand dollar bounty for myself. So if I were to shoot you and say you were in league with her, then I'd collect it."

A teller behind the counter with a brim hat with no top

spoke up. "But Mr. Davids, a lot of people already saw him bring her in."

The manager did two things at once. He grabbed a tabby cat servant girl around the throat and pulled her in front of him as a living shield and at the same time shot the teller in the chest. The man fell to the floor.

"Oh no! The Boneman just shot Jeff. Just like he is going to shoot anybody else who tries to say my story isn't true."

"Davids, if you don't put that gun down and surrender now, it isn't going to go well for you. Might as well put the gun in your mouth and pull the trigger. It'll be quicker and less painful."

"I don't think so, Boneman. If you don't put down your six-shooters right now, I'll put a bullet in this furry thing's little head. I'll give you a count of three. One... Two..."

Kennedy's finger started to close on the trigger when Lily's tail grabbed the gun out of his left hand and her hand-cuffed hands managed to pull the gun out of his right. She dropped them on the floor.

"What in tarnation are you doing woman? I was going to shoot him in the head. Wasn't gonna hurt her none."

"I'm sorry but I couldn't risk you shooting her by accident."

"I don't shoot anything by accident."

"As entertaining as seeing the two of you argue is, I think it's obvious now that I'm the only one with a gun drawn in this exchange. And I'd like to keep it that way. I do see Miss Lily the Cat's two guns tucked in the Boneman's gun belt. Lily, slowly put those guns on the floor and kick them over to me. One wrong move and this kitty trash goes to the pet cemetery." The tabby servant whimpered.

Lily did as instructed, pulling her cat o' nine tails out of Kennedy's belt with her tail. Her arm flashed and several spots on Davids' face were seeping blood.

As the manager pulled his hands to his bleeding face, the cat girl hostage ran out the door. Kennedy started to make a grab for one of the guns on the floor until Davids started shooting blindly. The rest of the customers and employees took cover as the Boneman and Lily rushed out. Kennedy shoved the gawker trying to follow them back into the bank and slammed the doors.

"Why'd you do that? I like the little things," Lily said.

"Then you ain't got the sense God gave a jackass. We hide and that thing will float nearby and give us away." Kennedy took off his gun belt and tied it around the adjoining door-knobs on the double doors.

"That won't hold Davids for long," Lily said.

"Doesn't have to. Just need enough time for us to re-group."

The cat woman smiled. "So now we're an *us*?"

"Shut up and move. You're still my prisoner." Kennedy grabbed hold of the chain connecting the handcuffs and pulled the cat woman with him across the street. Lily didn't resist and in fact outpaced the bounty hunter.

Quietly they stepped into the barbershop. The Boneman came around behind the owner and quietly put the tip his Bowie knife under the barber's chin.

"I thought I told you that you weren't to be wearing clothes until I told you otherwise?"

The barber held a pair of scissors but made it clear he had no intention of trying to use them as a weapon by putting his hands out to his side and then above his head.

"This here's an apron. Keeps the clippings and the hair tonics off of me. It ain't clothes."

The Boneman pulled his knife back and cut the neck string. The apron dropped down to the floor. "It is, but we'll assume it was an honest mistake."

The bounty hunter motioned the cat woman into a barber chair, draped a smock over her shoulders and torso then took a hot wet towel and covered her head with it. "You stay there. Don't move unless I tell you to. Barber man, how'd you like to get back into my good graces and be able to wear clothes again?" Wendell Kennedy put his hat on a hook and took an-other man's hat and placed it on his head before planting him-self in a barber chair. He pulled a smock over himself as well. There was a paying customer in the chair between him and Lily.

"Free shave and haircut is all that's needed to make things

square between us? Be a trifle odd doing it on a man who has neither hair nor whiskers."

"Got both, ya just can't see neither."

"That's fine. I'm happy to oblige."

"I ain't looking for a prettying up. Got something else in mind. Lather up my face quick. A bank man is going to come through them doors with a gun. You tell him ya saw a skeleton and a cat lady head out the back. Bank man buys it and leaves, you and me are square and you can go back to wearing all the aprons and clothes you want. We got a deal?"

The barber grabbed his cup of suds and lathered Kennedy skeletal face with his brush. "Yes, sir, we do."

The Boneman pulled the borrowed hat down over his face to make it look like he was sleeping and the barber returned to the customer he had been working on.

A moment later, Davids slammed open the door as he and the gawker came into the shop.

"Afternoon, Mr. Davids. Little busy right now, but if you don't mind a wait I'd be happy to give you a cut and shave."

"Ain't got time for that, Barris. A bag of bones and a kitty came in here. Where'd they go?"

"They ran right out my back door." Those may have been the barber's words but he was pointing with his eyes and his finger towards the chair where the Boneman sat, thinking the bounty hunter had his eyes closed and couldn't see him.

He was wrong.

The bank manager grinned evilly as he crept up on Wendell, but stopped just out of knife reach. The gawker floated up near the ceiling.

The cocking of the banker's six-shooter seemed much louder than it should've been. "Got any last words?"

"Go to hell."

"You first."

As Davids pulled the trigger, the cat woman's boot came up hard and fast into the banker's groin and her tail wrapped around his wrist and pulled his gun out to the side so the bullet plunged into the floorboards instead of invisible flesh.

The Boneman flipped the smock over the banker's head, put his knife between his teeth as he leapt up to grab hold of the banker's gun arm. A twist and push at the elbow made the banker's bones snap. Davids screamed and dropped the gun. The Boneman slugged his jaw, making him stumble back against the barber's counter. The smock fell to the floor. A skeletal hand reached up and took the knife from the jaw of a skull, then rammed it down, pinning the banker's empty gun hand to the wooden counter. The banker's screams turned to cries as the blade pierced his flesh.

"Now Mr. Banker, we've got several pieces of unfinished business. One, I turned in my bounty and as a representative of the Golden Spike Savings and Rail, you have an obligation to sign my receipt for bounty delivered and your bank has an obligation to pay me." Kennedy reached inside his pocket and unfolded a piece of paper, then pulled out a pen that he placed in the manager's left-hand.

"Hey Tiny, get your naked self over here and bend over."

Not quite grasping what was being asked of him, the barber moved nervously closer. "Yes sir."

Kennedy put the piece paper on the naked man's back and looked at the banker. "Sign it."

The banker did. The man with a skull for a face turned to the customer in the chair next to him. "You witness it."

Nodding his head frantically, the half-shaved man leapt out of the chair to also sign the document.

"Now wait just one gosh darn minute here. If you think even for an instant that I'm going to let you turn me in..." The cat woman had picked up the gun with her tail and put it in her still cuffed hands. She wasn't pointing it at the Boneman, but it wouldn't take much movement for that to happen.

"Cat lady, shut your pie hole. I'll be with you momentarily. Now Mr. Banker-man, you saw the chance for a little extra gold and it made you stupid enough to try to kill me. Ya gambled and lost. I told you at the start of this here debacle what the smart thing to do was."

The Boneman tore the knife out of the banker's hand and the would-be murderer screamed some more.

"Now we settle up."

"You can't kill me. You know who I am? Golden Spike Savings and Rail will hunt you down and kill you for what you've done already. You kill me, then there ain't a place left on all of Doomstone, even in Enjun territory, where you could hide."

The Boneman chuckled. "And how exactly would they track me down?"

"By hiring bounty hunters."

"They do anything in retaliation to me for killing you, ain't no bounty hunter alive that'll work for them."

"What're you talking about? Golden Spike puts out lots of bounties all the time."

"And how many hunters want to bring in a bounty to an organization that is known to have their personnel try to kill a hunter and take his bounty for themselves? I hate killing for free, but you're so stupid you left me no choice."

The Boneman reached forward. Two quick flashes of Kennedy's wrist later and it was done.

The banker stood there. He hadn't felt a thing. "Dumb saddle bum. You dun missed."

"I don't miss."

As if to prove the point, the skin and arteries in the banker's neck tore apart as he spoke. Blood spurted out from the wounds and no matter how hard the banker held his hands to his throat, he couldn't stop the flow as his life bled out.

As the banker collapsed to the floor and the gawker dove down for a close up, Kennedy turned to face the naked barber.

"Tiny, you and me need to have words."

The barber smiled, thinking everything was all right. "Yes sir, Mr. Boneman. I guess now that I did what you told me to, you won't mind me getting back into my clothing."

"Not only do I mind, but you ain't never gonna wear clothing ever again."

"What are you talking about? I did like you said and told him you ran out the back."

"Telling him that don't mean diddly when you were pointing your finger to where I was hiding. You is going to be naked forever because I will make random visits back here to check on ya. I may even have some of my friends do it too."

"I won't do it. I'll wear my clothes. What are you gonna do?"

"You attempted to help this man kill me." The Boneman turned his head back to the banker who lay in a pool of his own blood. "That's what he got for trying to kill me. I don't like killing for free but you've crossed me. A man in my line can't let that slide. If I hear you even have a sock on in the dead a winner, I will end your life without warning. But I'm giving you a chance to live. You don't want to take it, I'll put you out of my misery right now."

"Can I wear clothes some of the time?"

"I can't reckon why I'd change my mind."

"But I can't go to church like this. I go every Sunday. Please have mercy."

Boneman stroked his skeletal chin. "Your words touch me. My dear Katie was a churchgoing woman. Always preached about turning the other cheek and forgiveness. I've never been big on it myself. Although in your case, what cheek should be turned could have a whole different meaning than my missus ever intended. In memory of her, you may wear clothes from sun up on Sunday until one hour after the services end. Any other time and yer dead."

"Fine," grumbled the barber.

"You gonna make me get naked too, Boneman?" Lily said, still holding the gun.

"No ma'am, Miss Lily. Ain't no fun if I got to force ya to do anything. A real man never makes a lady do something she don't want to. I appreciate your sticking your boot in to help." Boneman unlocked her cuffs and put them in his pocket. "Now we're even."

"Isn't it against some bounty hunter code to let a bounty go?"

"It's frowned upon. However, I turned ya over to a bona fide representative of Golden Spike Savings and Rail. Him not being able to hold on to ya, well that's hardly my fault."

"They'll put another bounty on me, this one might even be higher," Lily said.

The Boneman shrugged. "Can't say that will affect me one way or the other. I caught you once. That's enough for me."

Lily stepped closer and wrapped her arms around Kennedy's elbow as they exited the barber shop. "So Boneman, what are your plans?"

"Gonna retrieve my belt and my guns. I feel nakeder than Tiny back there without 'em. Then I'm going to turn in my receipt at the bank and get me my three thousand in gold. How much do you reckon was in the bag ya stole?"

"I'd put it at near ten thousand."

"Wouldn't it be a kick in the head if say five minutes after I collected my bounty, you was to go back in that bank and rob that same money again with the bank manager's own gun?"

"That's a stunt that would certainly make the papers." Lily purred. "I'm still willing to pay off on the second offer I made, so I'd hate to part company just yet."

"And rightly so. I was planning on heading out to the east of town. I reckon a woman as smart and resourceful as yourself with a hoverbike as swift is yours wouldn't have much difficulty catching up to me." Kennedy tossed her the round part he'd taken out of the engine earlier. "You manage that, I might consider sharing a camp with you for the night."

"Is the true what they say? That in the dark you glow?"

The Boneman chuckled. "You want to find out, you'll have to catch up to me."

"Consider it done."

Forsaken by the God-Star:
Reflections of a Dying Xenomorph
Gary W. Davis

The God-Star is greatly dimmed, from red to dwarfish white.
Nothing grows here anymore, deprived of food and light.

The planet is cracking up; sulfurous chasms abound.
Even our ancient caves are poisoned and unsafe ground.

I crawl to the wretched surface to catch the waning rays,
and somberly reflect on the coming end of days.

My head hangs heavy, can barely sense the dawn.
The teeth, though many, are almost all gone.

My arms and legs were once strong and stealthy.
The bones now cracked, they're brittle and spindly.

I can hardly climb up the steep cavern wall;
always fearful, as my father died in a fall.

We engineered our genetic ascent, the fierce phases retaine
But the God-Star has forsaken us, our well-wrought powers
        drained.

Now a distant memory, gone is our slave race.
Oh what a garden they were; nothing went to waste!

The helots were bred with tiny limbs and capacious chests.
The nurseries were noisy, but the babies were the best.

Visitors from deep space stopped coming eons ago.
Caves and slaves were not for them, but how could we know?

As I bask in a final, feeble star-beam,
from across space, can anyone hear me scream?

Notes: Yes, his "father" died from a fall. In memory of H. R. Giger, 1940-2014. Poem inspired by K2 discovery of a planet being ripped apart as it orbits WD 1145+017

About the Authors

Simon Bleaken lives in Wiltshire, England. His work has appeared in *Tales of the Talisman, Eldritch Horrors: Dark Tales; Space Horrors: Full-throttle Space Tales #4; Eldritch Embraces* and *Best Gay Romance 2015*. His first collection of short stories *A Touch of Silence and Other Tales* will be released in 2017.

L.J. Bonham is an author, historian, and former commercial pilot whose novels include *Shield of Honor, The Debt,* and *Wolves of Valhalla* (all from Sky Warrior Books), and the non-fiction book, *Prepper Blades* (Garnet Mountain Press). Look for L.J.'s exciting thriller *Sector 21* coming soon from Sky Warrior Books. Short fiction credits include *Sancho,* which appears in *Tales from the Front Lines, Blood Allies* in *No Horns on These Helmets,* and *A Horse Fit for a King* in *Hoof Beats—Flying With Magical Horses.* Current projects include the follow up books in the *Shields of Honor* and *Sector 21* series. L.J. also writes numerous freelance, non-fiction articles and web content.

An avid mountaineer with a congenital weakness for fast cars and airplanes, L.J. studies Asian martial arts and Historical European martial arts, with emphasis on the German Longsword. L.J. lives in the Rocky Mountains with assorted critters including a very opinionated Morgan horse.

Jesse Bosh was born in Toledo, Ohio, but has spent most of his life in the hostile desert climate of Tucson, Arizona. He has a son named Braxton and two cats named Othello and Kent. His key influences are Groucho Marx, David Lynch, Prince, Douglas Adams, Jesse Michaels, Alexandre Dumas, and Kyrie Irving. He is a restaurant manager by day (and often by night) and has recently rediscovered his youthful passion for creative writing. He is in a long term and deeply committed relationship with caffeine and the two are rarely seen apart. Also, if you want to get really personal, his favorite color is purple.

When **J.A. Campbell** is not writing she's often out riding horses, or working sheep with her dogs. She lives in Colorado with her three cats, Kira and Bran, her border collies, her Traveler-in training, Triska, and her Irish Sailor. She is the author of many Vampire and Ghost-Hunting Dog stories, the Tales of the Travelers series, and many other young adult books. She's a member of the Horror Writers Association and the Dog Writers of America Association and the editor for *Story Emporium* fiction magazine. Find out more at www.writerjacampbell.com

Anthony R. Cardno writes in hotel rooms and coffee shops more often than he writes at home in northwest NJ, so it's no wonder so many of his stories are about travelers. His stories have appeared in *Galactic Games, One Thousand Words for War, Robbed of Sleep Volume 4, Space Battles: Full Throttle Space Tales Volume 6, Beyond The Sun, OOMPH: A Little Super Goes a Long Way, Tales of the Shadowmen Volume 10* and in audio form on the StarShipSofa podcast. He's also in process of revising his children's Christmas book *The Firflake* and contemplating completing a mystery novel. You can find him on Twitter @talekyn, on his blog at www.anthonycardno.com, and find his music on www.anthonycardno.bandcamp.com.

Jaleta Clegg loves to spin tales of adventure and excitement, aliens and monsters, new worlds and mysteries of old worlds. She writes science fiction, fantasy, silly horror, and dabbles in other genres from time to time. When not writing, she enjoys cooking weird vegetables and delicious desserts, crocheting bizarre animals and ugly afghans, piecing wild quilts, sewing futuristic costumes, and binge-watching bad 80s sci-fi movies. She lives in Washington state with a diminishing horde of children, too many pets, and a very patient husband. Find her work at www.jaletac.com

Gary W. Davis enjoys writing horror poetry about Halloween and classic creatures, such as mummies, werewolves and Nosferatu vampires. Several of his poems have been published in *Tales of the Talisman*. He also has had poetry published by *Bloodbond, Atlantean,* and Lester Smith's annual Popcorn Press Halloween anthologies. Mr. Davis had a short story, "She Didn't Forget Halloween," presented in the November 2016 edition *of FrostFire Worlds*. He is currently working on an essay about the horror origins of Halloween entitled, "Severed Heads and Omens of Death."

This is **David L. Drake's** first solo writing project. He and his wife, Katherine L. Morse, are the San Diego-based authors of "The Adventures of Drake and McTrowell," a serialized steampunk tale detailing the adventures of Chief Inspector Erasmus Drake and Dr. "Sparky" McTrowell. They have written four novellas covering the duo's escapades since 2010 and can be seen cosplaying their alter egos at conventions all over the West.

Livia Finucci lives in the north of England and is a cat lover and a seagull admirer. She likes to write short stories and poems about animals and mythology from various parts of the world. In her free time she enjoys practicing botanical art. Additional poems by Livia can be found here: liviasmicrocosmos. blogspot.co.uk

Steve B. Howell is currently the head of the Space Sciences and Astrobiology Division at the NASA Ames Research Center following his success as project scientist of both the Kepler and K2 missions. He received his PhD in astrophysics at the University of Amsterdam and has over 900 scientific publications spanning research on variable stars, instrumentation, spectroscopy, and exoplanets. Steve has written or contributed to numerous scientific books, and his textbook on digital imaging detectors (CCDs) is the standard in college courses around the world. Working as the scientist in charge of the planet hunting Kepler mission inspired the creation of *A Kepler's Dozen*: a collection of short stories about real exoplanets, including Steve's first science fiction work. Following *A Kepler's Dozen*, Steve is pleased to once again team up with David Lee Summers to create *Kepler's Cowboys*, a romping ride through outer space. A frequent invited speaker at scientific conferences and public forums, Steve has a passion for sharing astronomy with people throughout the world. He lives in the San Francisco Bay area with his partner Sally and enjoys scientific challenges, the great outdoors, vegetarian gourmet cooking, and playing blues music. And yes, he still considers Pluto a planet in our solar system.

Rebecca McFarland Kyle was born on Friday 13 and that is the day she celebrates her un-birthday. By the time this book is published, she will be 102 years old. She lives with her husband and three cats between the Smoky and Cumberland Mountains. She enjoys listening to live music, collecting dragons and other oddments, and traveling.

Lauren McBride finds inspiration in faith, nature, science and membership in the Science Fiction Poetry Association (SFPA). Nominated for the SFPA's Rhysling and Dwarf Stars Awards, her work has appeared recently in *Dreams & Nightmares, Eye to the Telescope, Silver Blade, Songs of Eretz* and *The Grievous Angel*. She shares a love of laughter and the ocean with her husband and two grown children.

Born in Cuba and raised in Brooklyn, **Gene Mederos** obtained his Bachelors of Fine Arts in Theater Arts from the University of Miami. Gene has designed and built sets for theatrical productions and events in Miami, NYC ad Santa Fe. His artwork has been shown in Miami, Tampa and NYC. Currently Gene is a filmmaker and animator living and working in Santa Fe, New Mexico.

He teaches post production at the Santa Fe Community College and is the Chair of New Mexico Film Resource, a non-profit dedicated to creating film jobs for film students in New Mexico.

Gene's films have appeared in Film Festivals in New Mexico, LA, Boston, Toronto and NYC and he recently filmed aboard a submarine, under water! The closest he will probably ever come to being on a spaceship.

Gene is also a published author of Sci-Fi and Fantasy stories. His stories have appeared in six anthologies to date.

When she's not engaged in her ambassadorial duties while in geosynchronous orbit with Haura (i.e., Earth) at the Boortean

Embassy, **Terrie Leigh Relf** lives in Ocean Beach, an eclectic community nestled by the shore in San Diego, California. In addition to hosting a weekly coaching call for writers, she also hosts a weekly local writers networking group at Te Mana Cafe in Ocean Beach.

An active member of HWA, a lifetime member of the SFPA, and the contest chair/lead editor for Albanlake.com's somewhat quarterly Great Lake's Drabble Contest, Relf is always sending out her acquisitions team to find intriguing writers, editors, and artists for her "Day in the Life" interview series.

Please visit her websites at tlrelf.wordpress.com, terrieleighrelf.com, and tlrelfreikipractitioner.wordpress.com.

David Lee Summers is the author of ten novels and over sixty published short stories. His writing spans a wide range of the imaginative from science fiction to fantasy to horror. David's novels include *Owl Dance,* a wild west steampunk adventure, and *Vampires of the Scarlet Order,* which tells the story of a band of vampire mercenaries who fight evil. His short stories and poems have appeared in such magazines and anthologies as *Cemetery Dance, Realms of Fantasy, Gaslight and Grimm, Straight Outta Tombstone,* and *Apocalypse 13.* He has twice been nominated for the Science Fiction Poetry Association's Rhysling Award. In addition to writing, David has edited the anthologies *A Kepler's Dozen, Maximum Velocity: The Best of the Full-Throttle Space Tales* and the magazine *Tales of the Talisman.* When not working with the written word, David operates telescopes at Kitt Peak National Observatory. Learn more about David at davidleesummers.com.

Patrick Thomas has had stories published in over three dozen magazines and more than fifty anthologies. He's written 30+ books including the fantasy humor series Murphy's Lore, urban fantasy spin offs *Fairy With a Gun, Fairy Rides the Lightning, Dead To Rites, Rites of Passage, Lore & Dysorder* and two more in the Startenders series. He co-writes the Mystic Investigators paranormal mystery series and *The Assassins' Ball,* a traditional mystery, co-authored with John L. French. His darkly humorous advice column Dear Cthulhu includes the collections *Have* *a Dark Day, Good Advice For Bad People,* and *Cthulhu Knows Best.* His latest collection is the Steampunk themed *As the Gears Turn.* A number of his books were part of the props department of the *CSI* television show and one was even thrown at a suspect. *Fairy With a Gun* was optioned by Laurence Fishburne's Cinema Gypsy Productions. *Act of Contrition,* a story featuring his Soul For Hire hitman is in development for a short film by Top Men Productions. Drop by www.patthomas.net to learn more.

Louise Webster graduated with a degree in Communication Arts. She wrote the evening news for a small cable T.V. company.

While staying home to raise her children she wrote for many of the small presses. She has also written an article for a psychology book, a horticulture magazine and her poem on Lake Ronkonkoma won a prize.

Louise has written for June Cotner's anthologies *Dog Blessings* and *House Blessings, A Book of Toasts* and was published in *Nurturing Paws* and *Miracles and Extraordinary Blessings* edited by Lynn C. Johnston.

She is proud of her work that has appeared over the years in *Tales of the Talisman* published by David Lee Summers.

Neal Wilgus has published hundreds of poems over the past fifty years in places such as *Science Fiction Review, Nyctalops, Interdimensional Journal, Star*Line, Dreams and Nightmares, Not One of Us* and *Tales of the Talisman.* In the United Kingdom, his poetry has appeared in *Poetry Cornwall, Moodswing, Earth Love, Carillon,* and *Cÿaegha,* as well as *Monomyth* and other publications from Atlantean Publishing. Several of his poems have been nominated for the Rhysling Award given by the Science Fiction Poetry Association. He won the 2014 Data Dump Award for SF poems in Britain. He also writes short fiction, reviews, and satires and is the author of *The Illuminoids* (1978). Originally from Northern Arizona, he has lived in Corrales, New Mexico for over forty years.

Doug Williams currently works as a telescope operator and programmer at Kitt Peak National Observatory. He likes to spend his free time working on science fiction short stories and creative woodworking projects.

Vaughn Wright is a long-term prisoner who's written hundreds of songs, poems, short stories, and four novels. His work has appeared in a variety of literary and speculative magazines including *Barbaric Yawp, THEMA, PKA's Advocate, J Journal, Space and Time,* and *Tales of the Talisman.* If you liked "The Outlaw from Aran," you may find enjoyment in *Tales from the Inside,* his collection of short stories at www.PrisonsFoundation.org, or reach out to him by writing Vaughn Wright DJ-3834, 1100 Pike Street, Huntingdon, PA 16654.

60579336R00169

Made in the USA
Lexington, KY
11 February 2017